ALEXAH KEYES

In Her Honor

First edition

ISBN: 9798325189012

Proofreading by Ivey Zimmerman
Cover art by Stefano Buro
Editing by Salima Alikhan

This book was professionally typeset on Reedsy.
Find out more at reedsy.com

Here's to the stories that inspired and guided me along the way. May history remember you as fondly as I do.

Contents

I

Part One

1

Chapter 1

Sweat stings my eyes and I taste blood on my tongue. I circle my opponent, dragging my spear in the sand behind me. Her own spear was turned to splinters before the end of the first match. Her eyes keep darting to the deadly point carving through the sand. She's trembling. Exhausted. Rightfully so, since she's been getting her ass kicked for the last half an hour. It doesn't help that the air is hot and muggy, the sun beats down on us, baking the sand beneath our bare feet.

She's watching the point of my spear like a hawk, so when I lunge in for another blow I let the shaft of my spear slide through my loosely held hand. I'm just seeing her confused look as she sees the point next to my rib cage... when the butt of my spear catches her in the jaw.

She collapses, red hair fanning out like blood in the sand; her breathing ragged and hitching as she coughs up actual blood. I turn my head this way and that, working out the kinks, popping joints as I watch her.

Desma is her name, only a level 9 Initiative, despite being six months older than me. I stand over her, my spear held loosely by my side, and check the clock out of the corner of my eye, willing my Instructors to end this beating. Dozens of girls gather around us, the youngest of them no older than seven. The oldest of the inductees fall closer to my age, early to mid twenties. Desma is my age, at twenty-three, but she doesn't look it, skinny and pale as she is. She looks more like a picture of an emaciated Victorian child than a chosen Initiate. The cheers and screams of the others encircle me, I can't even hear my own thoughts so loud are they.

Desma spits out another mouth full of blood and pushes herself to her feet. I let my head drop back and roll my eyes as annoyance pulses through me. Who does she think she's kidding? This isn't some fairy tale movie where the underdog impresses everyone by their refusal to give up; then she'll land a miracle hit on me that puts me down and keeps me down and they'll all cheer her name and carry her on their shoulders throughout the arena room. I admire her tenacity but some common sense needs to be utilized here; who knows how many of her brain cells I've annihilated in these beatings. I tip my head up and look to our Instructors, motioning with my one hand in exasperation to the girl. They shrug back at me and motion that she's standing. And that's the only real rule: if you can stand, you can fight. I shake my head and move in.

Again.

I've been avoiding causing serious harm to this girl but now she's just pissing me off.

"Desma." I call to her, aggravated and condescending. "Enough. Let this be done." Desma spits a mouthful of blood at my feet and lunges at me with a clumsy right hook. I sidestep her easily, openly rolling my eyes, and grab her wrist,

4

pulling her roughly to the floor. She hits it hard— too tired to brace herself as she normally would— and groans as another coughing fit starts up. The sand that covers the floor of the arena plasters to the side of her face."Desma, please. I don't want to hurt you."

"I don't need your pity, Aris!" She grinds out through gritted teeth. She struggles to her feet again. By this point I'm so done with all of this, as soon as I see one of the Instructors signal that she's up and able to fight I throw my spear to the ground and close the short distance between us with quick, short steps. I dodge a pitiful attempt of a side hook from her and then land a perfect uppercut to the bottom of her jaw.

All I see is white as her eyes roll back into her head and she crumples to the floor.

I shake out my hand, we're not allowed to wrap them, as I walk out of the fighting ring. I don't bother watching as Desma is placed onto a stretcher and taken to the medical wing. She'll be fine. Our healers are well versed in healing magic, she'll be right as rain by morning.

"Why does she insist on fighting me every time?" I gripe to my main Instructor: Tessa, who, as usual, pushes her way next to me to clean me up and debrief me on what I did right and wrong. A no-nonsense legend with striking steel gray hair and flat blue eyes, she too rolls her eyes as she grabs the back of my neck with one of her rough and calloused hands. My attempts to pull from her grip do not impress her, as she barely seems to register them. "She's never going to beat me. She shouldn't even be here. If it weren't for her mother, she never would have been allowed in."

Tessa sucks her teeth as she scrubs my face off with a washcloth. "Truer words have never been spoken, Aristomache." She smirks as I reflexively scrunch my nose at my full name— she and my mother are the only ones who call me by it. "Hopefully one day, she'll get sick of you kicking her ass but it doesn't seem like that will be anytime soon. So I suggest you use her to practice your weaker moves."

Another scrunch crosses my face."It feels wrong, Tessa," I confess. "I mean I'm the best of us. You all elect me a leader and then let her continue to choose me for Match days? She has no defenses against me, she's just a punching bag with a pulse to me." Tessa shrugs as she finishes cleaning me up. She shoves her fists on her hips, the bloody washrag dangles from her one, swinging back and forth.

"I know her Instructor has told her several times to quit picking you for match-ups. She refuses the advice. So as far as I see it, she's volunteering to be your punching bag." I roll my eyes at the helpfulness of my Instructor but rest my forehead on her shoulder for a moment in thanks, as is our tradition, and make my way back to my friend group.

The crowd of thirteen-year-old's that are surrounding me and Tessa jump out of my way.

"Her whole family has been Initiates!" One whispers to her friend, who must be new if she doesn't already know.

"From the very beginning they've been here! They're practically royalty," another chimes in, awed.

"Aris has been top of her class since she was like *seven*."

Tessa gives me a significant look before leaning in to whisper in my ear.

"Remember. They're always watching you, aspiring to be like you. Act like it."

I force a smile for her but gently pull my arm out of her grasp and push through the crowds. As if I could ever forget the microscope I'm under. I go through my daily training's with the weight of a hundred eyes pushing down on me. It's exhausting, always having to be "on".

My friends stand at the very back, all early to mid twenties, all level 11 initiatives, and all deadly down to their fingernails.

How I love them. But even around them, they look to me for answers and leadership. I'm so tired of being the one to make the decisions all the time.

I receive nods from everyone as I settle in between a couple of girls: legs shoulder-length apart, arms crossed, spear strapped to my back, just as we're taught to stand, and pretend to watch the next match. Two fourteen year olds, eager to prove they're ready for the next step of their training. My knuckles sting but I resist the urge to rub them or acknowledge the pain in any way.

"Good match, Ris."

"Yeah, well done, form looked great."

"Don't know why she keeps asking to fight you."

I shake my head in exasperation. "Gods only know." Mutters of agreement go up.

"I can't believe that," one girl jerks her chin towards the medical wing, "came from the legendary Melenthe." Several of us, myself included, shake our heads in wonder.

"It's only because of her mothers' great feats that she was allowed entry in the first damn place." I mutter under my breath. One girl, who came from no direct line and had to fight her way in—literally, my own roundhouse kick to her jaw was the hit that earned her entry— spits on the floor. "I thought we left that type of posing for the men."

"Unfortunately, politics are unisex." Someone from the back of the group quips, which gets a laugh from all of us. The fourteen-year olds are vicious in their beatings of each other. Blood and spit flies around the ring but neither of the girls loses her footing or stumbles. To stumble outside is to die, and we don't die. I remember being that young. So desperate to prove that I belonged here. Some members, who have since phased out, called the ring barbaric and refused to fight.

We don't need to shed blood to be closer to the gods. That's what one of the women said. It was Tessa who shoved her face in the woman's, the two of them stood nose to nose. I still remember the gravity of Tess's voice: *blood was shed to bring you into this world and you're a fool to think blood won't be shed when you leave it.*

My gaze wanders as I lose interest in the match.

I find my younger sister, Alena, in the crowd. Her face is alight with energy as her eyes greedily drink in the match in front of her. I smirk at nothing in particular as my gaze continues to wander.

The towering trees of the Mark Twain National Forest that surround us provide cover from the scorching July sun but do nothing to protect us from the suffocating humidity. I swear I could swallow the air, it's thick. Squinting into the sun, my gaze follows the path that leads to the dormitories. Our dorms are made of long log-cabins, connected by wooden paths, that are raised several feet above the ground for when the snow fall hits. Girls are cordoned off by age, each sleeping wing holds about 20 girls each. We actually used to be separated by whatever level Initiative you were, but Desma put an end to that when she seemed incapable of getting pass level 6. There are actually only eleven girls in my age group; eight of us stand together now, another is Desma and the other two are still only level tens and prefer to associate themselves with other

8

level tens.

The entire camp is connected by the wooden paths, with various cabins and buildings for whatever we need. Down to the southern path that Desma was just carried down is where the infirmary lies. As I survey around my I hear the chopping beats of a helicopter nearby. Maybe a search and rescue looking for a hiker lost in the National Park we call home. Maybe some random rich dude with too much free time. Anyone's guess really. Some of the younger girls look up in fear, though the girls in the Match do not lose focus for a second.

"Easy," I tell a group of young girls next to us. Their eyes dart over to me, awed and startled. "The Mist will protect us." And it does. The helicopter bounces around the edges of our camp. Unable to come any closer to us as the magic of the Mist blinds the mortals and protects us from their probing eyes. The all give a huff of relief before turning back to the match.

I force my attention back as the match ends and our head Instructor, Antiope, steps forward into the ring. Behind her, one of the girls is being carted off to the Infirmary, her opponent steps off the sand and is congratulated by her own Instructor.

Antiope need only raise a single hand for silence to fall over the entire room. I'm told she used to be a great beauty when she was younger, with rich brown hair and striking green eyes. Now, as she enters her 70's, all that is left is remnants of that beauty, but her strength remains always.

"Another great day of training. Nothing gives me as much joy as seeing you all progress and succeed in the name of our goddess and the Wronged One we have sworn our lives to." A roar goes up around the room at these words, I let myself feel the pride and join them, raising a fist with the rest of the girls. Smiling, Antiope raises her hand again. "In Her Honor!"

"IN HER HONOR!" Our roar comes out as one, I feel it fill my chest.

"Come forward as I call out your names." All around the room girls shush their friends and hold their breaths as they wait to hear if they will be allowed to move up to the next level of training. There are thirteen levels in total, and once you surpass level 13 you are considered fully trained and sent out into the world on various missions.

The last girl who left, was chosen as a strategist of the goddess Eris. The girl before that became a Hunter of the beasts who roam this world. The one before her became a strategist for the conclave, honing our training methods for the generations to come. And so on and so forth.

Young girls lay awake at night, whispering about what they will become when they leave here; and once a month we gather this way to challenge and fight and prove our worth. It's not guaranteed that someone will move up in training every month, there have been plenty of Match Days where no one has advanced. Just last month that happened. Then there are other months where it seems every single girl advances. Those days are always so long.

Of course so few get chosen for the job that everyone wants. The one we all daydream about being good enough for— myself included. The job that is the reason we exist. The great goddess Athena created this conclave of women, who knows how many millennium ago, with one purpose: to protect her most beloved Priestess, Medusa.

Everyone knows the story of Medusa: she had a relationship with Poseidon in Athena's temple and Athena, in her righteous

10

rage, turned Medusa into the gorgon she is now. As punishment. To remind her of her place in the world. If she wants to desecrate a goddess's temple with a man so bad she would never again know a man's company.

Or that's what the men say.

The women know the truth. The know how Poseidon, hearing of Medusa's great beauty had taken advantage of her naïveté, forcing himself on her. Medusa had escaped his grip once and ran to the safety of her Goddess's temple, praying for protection. But what is wisdom against the might of the sea? Poseidon had his way with Medusa and left her, used and bloody and broken on the floor of Athena's temple.

Athena had come herself, wiping the blood off her most devoted Priestess and ignored her murmured apologies and begging for death. We are told Athena's rage was a mighty thing, though she had to be careful. She could not punish Poseidon, for he was a god whose powers greatly outweighed her own and the rest of the gods would expect a punishment. Not against Poseidon of course, but against Medusa. For violating a gods temple. Athena had to think quickly, how could she avenge her most devoted Priestess without invoking the rage of another god? But Athena was not named the goddess of wisdom for nothing. She gave Medusa the greatest protection she could: the gift to kill any man who dare even look at her, let alone try to violate her. Of course the gods saw this as the ultimate punishment. A woman of great beauty being turned into a monster? What worse punishment could there be? But women all over the Earth saw it for what it was: the greatest gift Athena could have given her most beloved Priestess.

Male heroes all over the world still seek her out. To kill

her for what they call glory. Our job is to stop them— no matter what. Only the best of the best are chosen for this job and even if the conclave chooses a girl as a Protector, Athena herself must also approve them. My own mother, Atalanta, is currently one of the three Protectors who guards Medusa, as is Desma's mother, Melenthe. Being selected for this job is an honor in more ways than one. Obviously to be hand selected by the goddess we serve is the ultimate goal, but it's more than that. Lady Medusa's existence provides a fail safe of sort, similar to Persephone and Demeter. As long as Lady Medusa remains safe and protected, Lady Athena remains level headed and analytical. If Medusa's life were to be threatened, or worse, taken, the wrath of Athena would be world shattering. For the sake of both the mortal world and our world, Medusa must be safe guarded.

I'm not sure if I'll go up to level 12 or not yet, Tessa mentioned earlier this week that I had about a 50/50 shot but assured me if I don't make it this month, I definitely will next. It was about this time last year that I advanced to level 11, so I'm definitely due for an upgrade. But the higher you advance, the harder it is to keep advancing. But even still, as a general rule of thumb, you should advance one level a year.

"In level 3: Clarissa, Embry, Diana, and Jasmine. Congratulations, you may begin your level 4 Initiate training." I can't help but grin as the chosen girls begin to jump up and down, squealing and hugging each other while the rest of their group tries to hide their disappointment. The girls who progressed immediately begin scoping out the girls of the next level. Of course, everyone knows everyone in the conclave, but you tend to look at each other differently when Athena now considers you equals and competition. And on it goes, through all of the levels until it's time for us.

"Level 11: Zoe, Sierra, Rachel, Rose, and Caitlin. Congratulations, you may begin your level 12 training."

I try to hide my surprise, but I'm sure the shock shows on every inch of my face. The rest of the girls are just as confused as I am; I'm the leader of our group. The top of our class. No one has ever progressed ahead of me. No one has ever been ready before I have. I shove the shock aside and turn to my sisters-in-arms, bringing the first two fingers of my right hand to the spot between my eyebrows while dipping my head slightly— our salute.

"Congratulations. Your hard work for our goddess shines through." My voice is slightly detached sounding, but there is only so much I can do about that. They return the gesture numbly, clearly not sure what to make of this situation. I'll have to find time to speak to Tessa but I'll not make my friends moment about me so I clap along with everyone else. The other two girls in our group: Kore and Elpis also did not advance, which is also quite shocking as they have consistently been #2 and #3 in our group since we were level 5's. Kore, in particular, is surprising. As my second in command so to have us both overlooked is unheard of. But they, too, congratulate the rest of the girls and clap with everyone else.

Antiope raises her hand for a third time, and with a knowing look in her eyes begins to speak again.

"Level 11: Aristomache, Kore and Elpis. Your devotion and hard work in the name of our goddess shines through. Congratulations. You may begin your Level 13 training." A beat of silence. Then an uproar around the room. The rest of the girls pounce on us, screaming and shaking us. Tessa is pushing her way through the crowds, grinning from ear to ear

13

and I can't believe it.

Tessa brings us in, hugging us all to her chest before pulling away and saluting, smirking.

"You're gonna give us leave for tonight, right?" This is Rose, hanging over my shoulder, staring Tessa down with a glint in her eyes. The rest of us laugh as Tessa rolls her eyes, unsurprised by our priorities, before she waves us off, giving us permission to tear up the night.

I feel like I could eat the whole world raw.

2

Chapter 2

The air is filled with laughter and excitement as we're all dismissed. Girls of all ages hold hands and lock arms with their friends, bursting with joy as they revel in their advancement. Speaking excitedly for what the future may hold. Even those who did not make it to the next level can't sulk for very long before they're sucked into the infectious atmosphere that surrounds them. Not making level is part of this world, if you sit and feel sorry for yourself you might as well leave the conclave as you'll never advance with that attitude.

Girls race along the paths as we filter back to the dorm, jumping on and off of them as they try to gain the advantage. I think about my own advancement as we walk. This is more than I ever expected to get out of my career here, to skip a level is unheard of. My own mother never did. A whirlwind of emotions swirls inside of me, as the laughter of my friends swirls around me. A fierce and raging pride warms me from the core of my heart to the tips of my fingers. However, a creeping, cold sense of doubt leaves my feet tingling with uncertainty. Do I truly deserve this honor? No woman in my family has ever been granted this before. What makes me so special?

But, I can't deny the relief I feel either. My whole life has been carefully mapped out in front of me, written out by my mothers careful and meticulous hand. Be the fastest, the strongest, the smartest. The best. Work harder, run faster, be deadly. Maybe I've finally fulfilled the plans she has laid out for me, as the greatest warrior our family has ever seen. Aristomache Kallis. The spear of Athena. Maybe she'll give me a break now... probably not though. Somehow she'll expect me to be greater than this still.

The sun is just starting to fall behind the trees, giving us a break from the light in our eyes. Rose still has her arm linked with mine. Her smile takes up her whole face as she humors a 17-year-old who was just cleared to begin her level 5 training and talks animatedly about what her upcoming training may look like.

Back in the dormitories there's even more chatter and excitement. Tomorrow we will be given the day off so there's no need for hasty showers and early bedtimes. Girls run from dorm to dorm, trying on others clothes and playing games of Stealth: a game which could be considered a combination of hide and seek and tag. The goal is to hide, and then to run from hiding spot to hiding spot as the girl who is "it" either finds you hiding or catches you as you're moving. The more people she finds, the more people who are "it". There are no rules as to where you can hide or not, leading to some creative and ridiculous hiding places.

Tonight, the older girls have been given passes; permission to dance and drink and cause general mischief out in society with the mortals and otherworldly beings alike. The youngest of the girls mill about our dorm, jumping on our beds and playing in our clothes. The sight hits me with a strong wave of nostalgia. I remember being that young and doing that exact same thing, as though I thought being in the mere presence of such skill and honor would bring it to me as well. Remembering that brings an adoring smile to my face as I tease and play with the girls who cross my path as I mill about.

Our dorms are simple things, typically filled with bunk beds; though ours contains only a dozen single twin beds, with an open wardrobe on one side and a small nightstand on the other, and an armor stand on top. For the most part the wardrobes contain our daily uniforms: fitted and flexible black pants, tight dark gray long sleeve shirts that tuck into our pants with black combat style boots to really tie the "post Apocalypse" look together. But those of us with more privileges are allowed a space at the bottom of our wardrobes to keep "fun" clothes in.

It's in there I dig now, looking for my favorite red dress and the black, red-bottom heels that were so expensive my mother almost killed me when she saw I had bought them. My younger sister, Alena, who, at eleven years old, hasn't been inducted as an Initiate yet and won't be for some time. So in the mean time, she lounges on my bed as she talks at about a mile a minute. It's as though she's afraid she won't get everything out that she's trying to say.

"Do you think Medusa is nice? Or cranky? Cause if I had snakes for hair, I'd probably be pretty cranky but that is because I do *not* like snakes. No ma'am. Not me. Or maybe she has a snake for a tongue! And she doesn't talk because she's self-conscious? Do you think maybe that's a thing, Aris? Cause if I had a snake for a tongue, I'd never say single word!

17

Not one, not ever! How embarrassing! Do you think our Lady Athena will choose you to replace Mama? How cool would that be! You'd be, like, the sixth woman in our family to be chosen! I wonder if maybe I'll get chosen. Do you think I might get chosen, Aris?" I give an exasperated smile as she continues on, now laying on my bed with her head hanging off the edge. She's a stunning young beauty with traditional Greek looks, tar black hair and rich brown eyes, she, and I, are the spitting images of our mother. I've got the dress and shoes but continue to kneel next to Alena as she continues to prattle on. My staring at her does nothing to stop her from talking: "Actually, I'll probably have to work on the fear of snakes thing first, huh?"

Finally, I interrupt her. "Alena, how do you have enough words in your head to talk this much?"

She sits up suddenly, flipping her long hair over her shoulder. She looks down her nose at me, completely unphased by my comment, as I knew she would be.

"I don't know Aris, I'm just talented like that, I guess." I snort as I stand and get dressed.

Alena whistles as I zip up the dress, a rich red with an open back and plunging neckline, it's a statement piece for sure. "I hope you don't plan on moving too much, Aris. Cause it looks like your tits are about one good jump from popping out of your dress." I give a disbelieving laugh, and hear some of the other girls let out their own cackles, as I kneel on my bed and begin tickling her.

"Alena Kallis! Who taught you how to talk like that," I demand as I continue tickling her. She squirms and screams and yells at me to leave her alone. Which does nothing to stop me. Finally she manages to gasp out, "The level six's we were

18

training with!"

"Ah!" I gasp knowingly as I shove her back onto my bed, "that explains so very much about your behavior." Alena gives me a look so filled with attitude I can't help but smile adoringly at her. I know that look well. I should, she clearly learned it from watching me over the years.

"No, Aris. Having you as a sister explain so much of me. The level six's are just bonuses for my bad behavior."

I throw back my head and laugh at that, and hear Elpis and Zoe join in.

"You are just mischief itself, aren't you!" Zoe exclaims from where she sits, facing a mirror and putting on her make up. Dozens and dozens of black braids fall long down her back, swinging hypnotically as she turns back to the mirror. Alena smirks at what she clearly considers a compliment and goes back to jumping on my bed; as she does a young girl comes tearing into our room.

I barely managed to twist myself out of her way as she skids to a stop and looks frantically around our room. Finally, she flings herself at Zoe's feet so she can hide under the desk that we use to put on our makeup when we go out. Zoe obliges the girl and moves her feet to help conceal her. I'm pretty sure her name is Isabel, a level 2 Initiate. Just as they're getting settled a handful of other girls, more level 2's, come flying in, breathless in their hunt. They don't bother asking us where the girl hides. They know we won't tell them. Instead they begin a systematic search of our room, which are some of the skills they are supposed to be learning from this game. They're just starting the sweep of Sierra's bed when Isabel takes a gamble and bursts out from under Zoe, sprinting off as fast as her legs can take her. Her hunters tear off after her, calling out taunts, which mean very little until they actually catch her. We all share a laugh and remember our own games of Stealth, pulling up old grudges of supposed cheating and bad sportsmanship.

"Whatever!" Elpis exclaims, flipping her hair over her shoulder. "I literally skipped a whole level in training, I definitely was kicking all y'alls asses in Stealth."

"Have you lost your *mind!*" Rose demands, freezing in the middle of pulling her skirt on. "You literally cheated all of the time!"

"Lady Athena didn't think so," Elpis disagrees, studying her nails.

"Oh yeah," Sierra chimes in. "That's why you were chosen to skip a level. Because of your domination of Stealth when we were kids."

Zoe and I begin to laugh at that. I have to dodge a shoe thrown at me from Rachel.

"You think you're all that too, huh Cap?" She demands, fighting her own laughter.

Hearing Rachel call me Cap, the nickname I was given when I was made the equivalent of a Captain in our ranks, brings the memory of a sour look to Elpis's face. Always prone to jealousy, Elpis didn't react well when i had been given the promotion. She's mostly over it now but the wound still has the memory of the sting. If she hadn't been promoted along with us tonight, she'd be in a mood for the next two weeks. Minimum.

"Aris, can I sleep with you tonight? When you get back?" Alena asks, completely unphased by the chaos around her. I feel a flicker of fear as I wonder how Alena will cope when I graduate training. I shouldn't. She's already proven herself to be an exceptionally capable young girl who will achieve great things in her life. But my whole life has been keeping her safe and I can't help but worry. Me, and the others, advancing early makes me sure that I'm on the short list for those next in line as Protectors. But what would that mean for my mother? Would she be forced into retirement, or brought back as an Instructor? Booted out of her place of honor by her own daughter? Would she still call me her pride then?

"Of course, but you better be fast asleep before I'm off compound property." She rolls her eyes at this, displeased with a bedtime when there's so much excitement going on, but eventually nods in acceptance and plops down on her butt before wiggling under the covers obediently.

"Atta girl," I tell her as I adjust the blankets for her, before kissing her forehead. "We won't be out too long." She smiles so sweetly up at me and says, "Okay, Rissy. Have fun." My heart squeezes in an odd way. She's getting to the age where she's more likely to roll her eyes at you than smile so I treasure these moments. I try to shake off the feeling.

"Good night, sweet dreams."

"Good night, Aris." She burrows down into the blanket further and closes her eyes. She tries to hide the fact that she's peeking out from under her lashes as she waits for me to leave so she can get up and join the fun again. I don't deny her this childhood memory. The gods know my mother denied me plenty of them, I won't deny my sister of them. Not if I don't have to. By the time I was her age, my mother had me running full circuits of workouts and able to masterly handle a whole armory full of weapons before I knew how to braid my hair. I had to learn how to be a woman second, because I am a spear of Athena first and always. I didn't want that for Alena. My biggest fights with my mother now revolve around Alena's training and how I've let her fall short. Despite the fact that Alena is leagues above any other girl in her age group.

When women in the conclave give birth to girls, they spend the first year at the conclave with their baby before they go back to whatever assignment they've been given. If they have a boy, they either have the boys raised by family or they leave the conclave. After Alena's first birthday, our mom went back to work as Medusa's protector. That's when she left me as Alena's guardian and in charge of her training. I shake off the memories and complicated feelings.

I turn and see my friends raring and ready to go, and raise an eyebrow at them, smirking.

"Shall we, ladies?"

Whoops and laughter answer me as we leave the dormitories, hungry for the night.

* * *

"Rock, paper, scissors, shoot!"

"Athena, give me strength." I say, raising my hands dramatically to the sky.

"Rock, paper, scissors, shoot!"

"This is getting out of hand." Sierra whines to me, all but stomping her foot in frustration. "Both of their choices suck."

"Rock, paper, scissors SHOOT!"

"Okay. Honestly." Elpis groans. "Sierra is right. The convertible isn't practical and the Mercedes is tacky." I'm not the only one who snorts at that.

"ROCK, PAPER, SCISSORS, SHOOT!"

"I'm giving you guys one more opportunity and then I am

intervening!" I announce in loudly. They ignore me, their brows furrowed in frustration and concentration alike.

"ROCK, PAPER, SCISSORS, SHOOT!" Rose and Kore scream at each other, yet again throwing the same sign.

They both let out yells of frustration before my previous words finally seem to sink in. Eyes wide, they snap to look at me, hands still held out towards each other, their rocks still prominently displayed.

"Let us try again!" Kore pleads. "We'll get it this time, we swear Rissy!"

"Have some humanity!" Rose chimes in, now removing her rock to clasp her hands in front of her, a physical testament to her begging.

"Hell no!" I tell them, planting my hands on my hips. "You guys have had so many chances to solve this like the literal adults we are and instead you chose the one game you *know* you guys always tie in. So no. I will not be having humanity. I will be enacting a dictatorship. Final decision. We're taking the bikes."

"No!" Comes the collective groan.

"Yes!" Sierra pumps the air, jumping around and laughing wildly. "Aris chose the bikes! Aris chose the bikes! You took too long to choose and Aris chose the bikes!" She singsongs as she runs over to the security station where all the keys for the various vehicles are kept.

"I need four bikes please!" She announces giddily, tapping her hands rapidly on the counter, in her excitement.

"I hate taking the bikes," Rose grumbles to Zoe. I brush past her, shrugging.

"Sucks to be you. Should've been more efficient." She swears at me under breath.

23

"Hey, Ris." The desk worker greets me. I nod to her as she reaches out to slap my hand. "Major props on the promotion. Skipping a level? Fucking legendary." I grin and accept her hand slap.

"Appreciate that, Lindsey. Between you and me, I'm just glad those early morning training sessions paid off. If I never seen a 4:00AM agility ladder again, it'll be too soon."

She laughs as the computer finally finishes loading, opening the safe with the keys. She pulls out four sets of keys as Sierra enthusiastically signs the log book for vehicle check out.

I give Lindsey another hand slap as Sierra dances off with her keys. "Have a good night."

Lindsey waves back easily and turns back to her work.

Elpis tosses me a set of keys as I approach.

"You're driving." I snatch them out of the air.

"Damn right I am." I agree, as I swing my leg over the bike. It roars under me, bringing a savage grin to my face. The bike next to me revs and I know before I look that it will be Sierra.

"I fucking love these bikes!" She yells out joyfully. I laugh as Elpis swings on behind me, grumbling to herself as she does.

But even in joy filled moments like this, our training shows itself always. I watch the women around me check their weapons and eye the area around us suspiciously. The garage that holds all of our vehicles is built underground and the scent of the damp earth tickles my nose. The ramps that leads up to the surface opens slowly, allowing a rush of fresh air to surround us. As we drive up the ramp and into the night, the women on the back of the bikes heads snap back and forth as they scan the area around us. We will never be able to be wholly carefree women. We will always be Initiates of Athena's conclave first, and women second. I think maybe that's why we get so excited when we get to get out into the world. Just for a second, we can pretend to be normal women, out for a night on the town. We can shed our responsibilities and worries and just get to enjoy being alive.

Of course it can't last forever, but then nothing can.

3

Chapter 3

"No, don't!" Rachel squeals, right before I do cartwheel and then throw myself into several backhand springs. A real feat considering I'm wearing stiletto heels and have consumed enough alcohol to put an elephant on its ass. "You're awful!" Rachel admonishes when I stop, and wraps an arm tight around my waist to prevent me from preforming my trick again. I laugh freely as I sling my arm over her shoulders, letting her guide me.

We have one more stop of the night; a must for those of our world. We've been dancing and hustling mortal men at bar games for the past several hours but now seek the company of those of our world. Gambling and flirting with mortal men is fun. Mostly because the Mist that surrounds us tends to confuse them more than anything. They'll flirt and buy us drinks but the second their attention wanders, their eyes take over a glassy, confused look as we're erased from their immediate memories. We like to play a game to see how many times we can get the same guy to introduce themselves to us or buy us drinks before their buddies finally intervene. It always takes them a while, which is equal parts sad and amusing.

To mortal eyes, it looks like any other condemned factory in the city, but those of us with the Sight are able to see it for what it is. A hot and ready night club, with a heavy bass shaking the sidewalks outside of it. A glamorous building with open windows that young and beautiful beings hang out of, calling greetings to those of us below. I grin up at them, eager to get inside. A shadow figure greets us at the door, appearing out of nowhere. There's a group ahead of us, dryads by the look of them, and they must be first timers, or just very drunk, because they give involuntary squeals at the arrival. Anyone who frequents here expects this security check. The shadow regards them for a moment before gliding to the side and allowing them to enter. Then it moves back in front of the door as our group approaches. I pull my hair back and show it my ear.

Although, it's not my ear he's looking at, but the earring in it. A gold ear crawler earring, it's an owl with its wings spread wide and covers the bottom of my ear lobe but the top edge of the owls wing begins to transform into olive branch leaves, those finish the crawl up and over my ear, with the last leaf resting at the end of my crus of helix. This earring is a pendant only given to those who serve Athena at the conclave, and is infused with magic that allows us entry into our base. To try to enter the conclave without this earring is to sign your life away. Even if you did manage to get past the heavily armed and highly trained guards. Even I don't know exactly what would happen if someone were to try. I asked Tessa one time and she only laughed and asked if I was that eager to learn the scent of burnt human flesh.

The shadow regards us for a moment before something, that

we previously decided is its arm, raises to what must be its head, in our traditional salute. We return the gesture as it moves to allow us entry.

Inside is electric. Beings of all kinds dance to a beat that rumbles our chests and knock back drinks that would burn any regular mortal from the inside out. I drink in a greedy breath as we move through the crowds. There is so much energy in here, it's almost as intoxicating as the drinks they serve. Those who are not totally lost to their drinks and other activities recognize us, either through our pendants or from our frequent visits here, and salute us. We don't return the gesture but nod at those we make eye contact with. I used to think it was so weird, how many beings would salute us when they saw us. Now I know it's self-preservation, eagerness to stay on our good side and away from our bad side. I can't say I blame this instinct since our bad side usually involves the tips of our spears somehow.

"Don't bother me for the rest of the night," Kore half yells into my ear. Her fingers dig into my arm. "I skipped a god damn level and I'm partying like a *god* tonight!"

I laugh loudly at this. "Save some fun for me!" I yell back over the music. Her grin is savage as she shakes her head, backing away.

Not a chance, she mouths to me. I laugh again and watch as she finds a minor god in the crowd and pulls him to the dance floor with her. He can't hand his drink off to grab her waist fast enough.

"Grab me a drink!" I instruct Rose, as a hand grabs my own and begins to spin me to the dance floor. She waves a hand over her shoulder, already making her way to the bar. I have one last glimpse of my friends finding their own dance partners before the crowd closes around them.

* * *

I dance until I cannot and find myself sitting at one of the bars, nursing a drink called *The Golden Arrow* named after Apollo, for its bright and golden hue. It shimmers and glitters in my glass and fills my chest with the warmth of the summer sun with every swallow. I rub absently at my sore feet while surveying the dance floor. Most of the girls still occupy the dance floor, though Caitlin and Rachel have found other ways to fill their time. I didn't have a great view but it seemed Rachel was entertaining one of the dryads who came in right before us and Caitlin has allowed herself to be wooed by some rugged-looking demigod on a quest to earn his godly parents approval or some other. I haven't seen Kore since we got here, I hope she's drunk off her ass and dancing her life away. She deserves some fun. I smile into my drink at nothing in particular as I continue to people-watch around the room. Although, maybe I should call it being-watch, because nothing in this room is human. Even us in Athena's conclave are considered demigods. I admit it's an odd pastime to sit in a club and consider the extent of one's mortality, but I have definitely done odder things in my life.

Although Initiates can begin training with the conclave when they are as young as five years old, they are not official members of the conclave until they come of age and choose to join. When someone is old enough to choose to join Athena's conclave, around thirteen, we undergo an ancient ritual where we receive Athena's blessing to serve in her honor. It is simply called the Choosing and it is not a pleasant experience. It begins with having to down a nasty concoction that a potion maker has made for you to drink. The best I can describe it is if someone had poured milk into mud and seasoned it with a half rotten onion, stirred it all up and left it in the hot New Mexico sun for a few months, before garnishing it with fresh, bloody cow liver and gave it to you to drink. I plugged my nose and chugged the thing. Then spent the next several minutes fighting the urge to violently throw it all up.

After you drink, you're laid on a stone slab, inlaid with the markings and sigils for who knows what types of spells, and the Priestess's of Athena chant some weird magic stuff over you and Athena fills you with the mental and physical strength befitting someone who honors her in service— of course such a blessing is a painful one. Some people, like myself, might call it torturous. I screamed myself hoarse when I went through it, couldn't talk for three days after. But we leave the slab smarter, stronger, faster, more agile and are given a few face marking to show us as one of the chosen. Mine are two parallel lines under both of my eyes, a little less than an inch long and two over my nose: one goes from one side clear to the other and the second one is parallel to the first but about half the size and just covers the bridge of my nose. All of the girls have exactly the same tattoos under their eyes but the secondary tattoo is always different, chosen personally by Athena. No one but the Priestess know what they mean, and they take those secrets to their graves. If one of us were to ever dishonor Athena, she can revoke this blessing. It involves a process that I am told is ten times more painful than receiving it. Thinking about the ritual and my mortality, or lack thereof, depending on who you ask, gives me a headache, so I turn my attention back to being-watching.

I'm enthralled by a pair of nymphs doing some complicated looking dance when I hear someone sit on the stool behind me.

"Fancy seeing you here," The voice is deep and honeyed and immediately I know who it belongs to, even though I have not heard it in a while. It's hard to forget or mistake. "Though, I must admit I'm surprised. I didn't think you'd be allowed to come near here, let alone in." I roll my eyes as I turn, the man sitting behind me is already grinning, pleased with my irritation. With deep blonde hair and stunning brown eyes, he's definitely easy on the eyes; just not the headache I have brewing. He brings his right hand to his brow, while dipping his head in a salute. An odd picture of respect after a disrespectful comment, but I return the gesture. In all honesty, I like Lord Herakles. Even if he can be an insensitive prick sometimes. He provides aid to us on missions if necessary and has proven to be an invaluable ally. Plus, he's an excellent distraction and I think I've earned the right to some lighthearted flirting.

"Lord Herakles," I intone haughtily, "I'm not entirely convinced that you think at all." Herakles grin turns wolfish at that, pleased I'm participating in the game. A minor god of strength and heroes, you'd think he'd have more important things to do than troll around random bars, but you'd think wrong. Some of these gods... I wonder if they serve any type of real purpose at all. Lord Herakles is one of those, no matter how pleasant he is to look at.

"Ahh Aristomache," his smiles deepens as a scowl crosses my face, "always so pleasant." I bite back a laugh at this comment and instead put a sickly sweet smile on my face and bat my eyelashes.

31

"Oh yes, My Lord. For it's my every goal in life to be pleasant company for you." This earns me a good eye-crinkling, belly laugh from him. Which, I hate to admit, is an appealing sound from an already appealing looking being. It makes it that much harder to keep my scowl in place.

Once he's had his laugh, Herakles winks at me and takes my drink from my hand. "As it should be, Initiate" his eyes stay locked with mine as he takes a drink. "Quit distracting me, Aristomache. I came over here for a purpose. That was, before you so rudely began to bully me." Now it's me who's laughing as I snatch my drink back from him and take another drink. "My godly sources tell me that you were cleared to begin level 13 of your training."

I smother my laughter. "Your *godly sources* informed you correctly, Lord Herakles." I say coolly, taking another sip of my drink.

There's an appreciative look in his eyes as he regards me. "That's impressive. Very impressive. You and the other two are the youngest to make level 13 in... how many years?" I shrug and reply nonchalantly, trying not to seem too vain.

"Ever. We're the youngest ever. By three years." Herakles nods slowly, holding out a hand for my drink again. I don't even think twice as I hand it over, already falling into an easy and familiar pattern.

"Very impressive." He repeats, taking another swallow of my drink. "And the first to ever skip a level?"

I shrug airily, though pride rages inside my chest like a wildfire. "Something like that, anyway."

His dark eyes seem to swallow me whole before they flit quickly to look over my shoulder, and then back to me. I cock my head at him and raise an eyebrow. Waiting for his next move. He seems to be weighing his options for a moment before he holds out a hand to me. "I wonder if you'll let me have this dance. To celebrate properly, of course." I smile knowingly as I place my hand in his.

"Of course. A proper celebration." I agree, smirking. I can feel my mothers rage from wherever she is right now. She hates that I go out to clubs so frequently, that I dance with any man who has a nice smile and pretty eyes.

You are a spear of Athena, she would hiss. *Act like it!*

So what if I am, I think, as Lord Herakles leads me to the center of the dance floor. I train harder than anyone else at the conclave. My mother included. What is the point of being the best of the best, the greatest of my family line and this generation, if I cannot reap the benefits of it?

The music is fast and Herakles hands are so warm and so strong, it's easy to lose myself in dancing with him. To let him drag his lips up my neck to my ear to ask me again and again for another dance. *Just one more. One more. One more.*

I know I should tell him "no" but every time he asks I seem to forget every word but "yes". My mother would kill me if she saw me like this and I admit that's part of the appeal of Lord Herakles attention. I've spent my entire life dedicating every part of me to my mother, my goddess, my conclave. If I want to spend sometimes lost in the arms of a god, I think I've earned that. After all, I've just made conclave history. I can have a little fun.

Lord Herakles is a fantastic dancer. Confident and a good leader. We make an attractive pair, twirling and moving with and around each other on the dance floor. I'm vaguely aware that we are being watched by other beings in the room but find I care little for them at the moment, not when all of my senses seem to be full of Herakles.

The final song ends with a flourish and we come to an abrupt stop on the dance floor, my hands braced against his chest. Herakles hands are heavy on my hips, so hot I can feel them burning through my dress, and grip them tight enough my skin gives under his fingertips a bit. I'm slightly breathless as he leans in to give me a lingering kiss.

"Thanks for dance, sweetheart," he's smirking and I can't fault him for it. "Congratulations again and best of luck."

"Thank you," no matter how much I try my voice is still a little breathless. Which is undoubtedly part of the reason why he's still smirking as he salutes me and then starts to make his way through the crowd.

"Hey," I start slightly as Zoe appears laughing slightly and grabbing at my shoulders. "You ready to head home?" I smile at her disheveled state, leaning into her side as she wraps her arms around my shoulders.

"Let's go," I tell her as she tells me the others are outside waiting for us and off we go, pushing our way through the crowd.

* * *

"How is it," Elpis is exclaiming as we make our way back to our bikes, "that every immortal being you come across is making every effort to get between your legs?" The others cackle and agree with Elpis while I just roll my eyes. Which, admittedly, is not a great starting argument because I know the others can smell Lord Herakles on me as well as I can. Godly cologne, or whatever it is, is hard to get rid of.

"Lord Herakles wasn't trying to get between my legs, not

for real. He's in a pissing contest and I was his latest tactic."

"He can use me in a pissing contest anytime he wants," this is Rose, her gaze faraway, suggesting she's thinking about what, exactly, she'd allow Lord Herakles to do to her.

"Ew," I groan and laugh at her, giving her a light shove to call her back to reality. She shakes her head as though to clear it and gives me a rueful smile.

None of us are surprised by the gawking crowd that surrounds our bikes, they are stunning things. Even those who don't know bikes would impressed by these beasts. Top of the line 2024 MTT 420-RR's. Top speed clocking in at 273 miles per hour.

In the wise words of Tessa: only the best for the best.

"Excuse us," I call out to the group admiring our bikes. But they're way too engrossed with the things to hear us. Sierra elbows her way through.

"You fuckers better not have laid a single finger on these bikes!" She barks out. Her sudden appearance and the tenor of her voice sends them all reeling back, allowing us to finally get to them.

She gets protective over her bikes.

Laughing, I swing my leg over my bike, pulling my helmet over my head. Elpis rides with me again and climbs on behind, pulling on her own helmet. Zoe rides behind Kore, Caitlin behind Sierra and Rachel behind Rose. None of us are dressed properly for riding, except maybe Rose who's wearing leather pants and a leather top, but that kind of stuff doesn't matter to people like us. The engines growl under us, filled with speed and power. We walk our bikes backwards from the curb as we rev the engines, and I think I hear one of the guys on the curb actually let out a small moan of envy when we do.

"Remember Aris," I can barely hear Rose over the engines, "this isn't a race."

I bear my teeth in a grin at her, revving my engine again. "Of course not, Rosie. I wouldn't dream of it." I holler, so she can hear me above the roar of our engines. She rolls her eyes as I, predictably, hammer down my throttle and take off like a rocket down the street. I hear someone let out a whoop as another engine revs high and loud after me and I can feel the approach behind me.

Elpis laughs loud in my ear. "It's Sierra and Caitlin!" She shouts and I feel her twist to face them, her fists high in the air as she screams with joy. In the next second we're flying down the empty highway in precise formation.

Me in the front, Sierra to my left, Kore to my right and Rose bringing up the rear: exactly as we've been taught to ride. It's always so exhilarating, riding like this; flying down an open road with no one and nothing to stop me. With my sisters by my side. I take in a deep breath and rev my engine higher, pushing us faster. I hear the other three follow suit and can't help but let out a wild laugh into the night.

Sometimes I imagine this is what it is to be a god.

We slow as we approach the outskirts of our compound. Only someone raised here would see the signs all around us: a mound of dirt and bright wild flowers where a sniper lies in wait, a divot in the dirt where a fall pit lies, trip wires strung up between rocks and plants, and all kinds of other hidden horrors. We salute the guards who remain hidden as we pass, weaving the complicated path around the traps. A part of my brain always wonders if they salute back. I don't think I would if I were them, what's the point?

Ahead of us part of the ground opens up, creating a ramp

36

down underground, which we ride down without hesitation. The growl of our engines echoes and reverberates all over the walls around us, making them sound even more impressive. A couple of girls, I think they're level 7's, working the night shift greet us, pointing to where they want to bikes parked. We nod and salute and park them where they indicated.

"Good night out?" One asks as we hop off.

"Ohhh yes," Rose replies, grinning from ear to ear. The two girls grin back, enjoying living vicariously through us for that brief moment, and bid us goodnight. We walk down the long corridor before walking up about four flights of stairs— I made it up about one and a half flights before I had to stop and take my heels off— before we make it back to the surface. The cool night air raises goosebumps on my exposed skin. Kore wraps her arms around me as we rush back to our dorm quickly.

All around us is the sleep sounds of the other girls and women. Their open windows let us hear the light snoring, muttering in sleep, and slight wheezing from some level fives who have a cold going around their dorm. It's all very comforting, I feel my body relaxing as we walk down along the path.

Our dorm room is the last along the path, which normally I love, except for moments like this. When all I want is to be in bed and off my aching feet. But we get there eventually, tiptoeing in so as to not wake the other girls.

Desma's bed is empty. But then, it always is, after Match Days. Either she sleeps in the infirmary or wanders the halls all night. Too ashamed to show her face to the rest of us. I worry about her a lot, no matter how much she infuriates me. She's my sister too, under the oath of Athena, and I want her to be happy. It can't be easy trying to fill the shoes that her mother has left behind. I know how much I struggle to fill the shoes my own mother has left me.

Alena is curled up in a tight ball on my bed, hogging all of the covers, as usual. I gently place my shoes in the bottom of my wardrobe and slip out of my dress, groaning quietly in relief, rubbing absentmindedly at my skin where the dress was a bit too tight or rubbed weird.

I pull on some pajama shorts and a tank top and finally pull the blankets back from Alena and crawl into bed. I sigh as I sink into my mattress and gently slide my left arm underneath Alena's small body and pull her back to my chest. I drape the other over her and feel her hands hold my one in both of hers. I press a kiss to the back of her head and hear her sleepy mumble, "Did you have fun?"

"Mhm," I murmur, "loads."

She sighs and wiggles a little, trying to get comfortable. "Did you see anybody cool?" My lips give an involuntary twitch at the earnest wonder in her voice, despite the sleepiness that fills it.

"Mm, well I saw Lord Herakles again. Does that count?"

"I guess so. Was he a tool bag, like last time?"

"Nah, not nearly as bad this time. He actually congratulated me and gave me a compliment if you can believe it."

A big yawn and quiet sigh and she's mostly asleep when she answers again. "Oh... that's good of him."

I give a ghost of a laugh before plunging into sleep myself.

4

Chapter 4

I dream of the day my mother presented me to the conclave. We were in the room we use for the Choosing ceremonies. A circular room with a large whole in the ceiling, about 15 feet wide, that opens to the heavens to allow in light. It's dark outside but there's a full moon and the room is ablaze. The room is the barest in the conclave. All that is in it is a door and the stone slab. And, at that moment, about two hundred of Athena's chosen.

I was just five years old— very, very young for an inductee, the youngest ever, in fact— and trying to be brave. My mother, barely twenty-five, was the most impressive thing I had ever seen. She stood before the stone slab used for the Choosing, her arms crossed in front of her. She was so tall. So strong. Lean muscles everywhere you looked, her hair was full and shiny, a black curtain enveloping her as a stray breeze lifted it around her. Her rich brown eyes were filled with a crazed type of fervor as she called to her fellow sisters to allow me entry.

I felt too small. Too weak. I was surrounded by the best of the best for that generation; all hand picked by Athena. All covered in marks that detailed the glory they had brought forward to our conclave in Athena's name. How could I ever dream of being worthy of standing beside them? Tessa stood behind me, still actively taking missions at this time, with her strong hands on my shoulders. Though I didn't feel relieved by her presence then, as I do now. No. Then, it felt as though she was my prison guard. Holding me hostage until the rest of the conclave could decide upon my fate.

"She is the blood of my blood! Honor and courage is all her mind and body knows! Even at her age, if she is not deemed worthy, then how can any child after her?" My mother is a born leader, steel and grit fill her voice. But, then so are all of the other women here.

"She is a child!" One exclaims. "She is nowhere near ready to begin menstruating and could very well be killed by the training she would have to complete!" I feel my body start to tremble ever so slightly at that and fight to stop it; I don't want Tessa to know I am scared. My mother scoffs and waves a dismissive hand.

"Athena has filled my dreams since the day I found out I was pregnant with Aristomache. She will be one of our greatest warriors. If not *the* greatest. She will lead us to a new generation. Look at her and see! See the strength and potential!"

"Potential." It was not a whip that had said this, but Antiope. Who had been standing, listening intently, back towards the door. "Many children have potential. Whether or not that potential shines through into actual skill is another question. Should we allow this girl entrance and that potential does not blossom, we risk dishonoring our goddess." *This girl.* She could not even say my name. What I didn't know then, but

40

that I do now, is that Antiope never liked my mother much. It started with some grudge between her and my grandmother, after my grandmother, Lydia Kallis, had been given some high level job over Antiope. Antiope was sure my grandmother had been given this job because of our family heritage and not skill or worth and resented her for it. That resentment seeped into my mothers generation, showing itself through general irritation and the doling out of undesirable jobs. This fact, coupled with her trying to deny my entry, does not escape my mother.

Leaping onto the stone behind her, she raises her fist into the air. Her eyes locked on Antiope, blazing with a fire that only a mother can withstand.

"Aristomache is the *blood of my blood*!" My mothers voice is thunder. It is steel. It is pride. "She will be the greatest warrior for Athena this conclave has ever seen and will *ever* see. To deny her entry *is* the greatest dishonor to Athena. Hear my words sisters, and hear their truth!"

My brain freezes on that image of my mother. Standing, fist raised, eyes wild, a voice filled with so much passion you feel as though you will choke on it. I had been filled with such a strange feeling then, listening to her talk about me in such a way. A bubbly type of warmth in my chest, almost. But that feeling did not linger, as it moved out and away from my chest, it was no longer warm and light. It was cold and felt as though steel had been injected into my veins. I know now it was pride I was feeling. Pride and resolution. Even though I was merely a child I became hell bent on becoming the woman my mother dreamed of me being. I wanted to be the pride of Athena.

I wanted to be the pride of my mother. Despite the complexity of our relationship, all I have ever wanted was to make my mother proud and to bring honor to the Kallis name.

I wonder if she knows I was cleared to begin Level 13 training.

She must.

I wonder if she is proud of me.

I hope.

5

Chapter 5

Pain.

Everything hurts.

It's disorienting and it takes me longer than normal to get my bearings. I have not been asleep long, this much I can tell. My body still aches in a way that tells me it has not gotten near enough rest. Lights are flashing and alarms are shrieking so loud I can feel my pulse behind my eyes. But that is not the pain. No, the pain is my ear. My pendant. It feels like red hot needles, dipped in acid being stabbed into my ear over and over and over again. I gasp through my teeth, my one hand raised to cup lightly over the pendant. I'm afraid to touch it. As though it might burn my hand as well as my ear. I hear the groans of the others and know they are feeling it too.

This is the second time in my life I've ever experienced this. Not the alarms. Those go off pretty frequently, someone or something will get too close to the compound and the alarms will go off, rousing us from bed or classes, summoning us to the safety of the arena room, while a team is dispatched to examine the threat. The last few times the alarms have gone off, I was a part of the dispatched team.

But when our pendants burn, that means one of us, some-where, is in serious danger. It is a call to arms, a summons that cannot be ignored. The first time had been about nine years ago, when a pregnant Inductee went into labor by herself, during a freak tornado about 70 miles from here. She had gotten herself through the labor All right, but was bleeding out fast and had set off the alarm calling us to aid her and her newborn son. I had wanted to go and help but Tessa wouldn't let me. Said I needed to focus on my archery lesson I had been in the middle of practically flunking. Elpis got to go though, since she was being trained as a healer.

"Oh gods," I hiss in pain as I fumble around, feeling for my armor. I don't bother getting dressed as I slip my armor over my pajamas. My, thankfully, well practiced hands tighten the straps without thought. So I can give my effort to staying focused through the dizzying pain. I grab one of my spears from where it rests leaning up against my wardrobe and reach back for Alena, who had been sitting on my bed looking shocked and terrified. She grabs my hand with both of hers, squeezing so tightly I imagine her knuckles are white.

"Aris, what's happening?" She tries to hide the shaking in her voice but can't quite manage it.

"I don't know," I tell her. "Let's go!" I bark to others, who finish donning their own armor. Grimacing and groaning, they grab their weapons and fall in line behind me. The paths are chaos. Scared girls with questions and overwhelmed leaders, in too much pain to give much of any answers. Most of these girls don't even have their pendants yet, forget having ever seen their leaders crippled by the pain of them. Seeing us in undeniable pain is only increasing their fear. We are supposed to be fearless and incapable of being hurt. I force Alena to drop my hand so I can let out a wolf whistle, which somehow makes itself heard above the alarms.

"TO THE ARENA! MOVE! GO, GO, GO!" My message gets passed along and finally we start making progress down all the pathways. I stand to the side, ushering girls past me, doing a mental tally of all of them, trying to make sure everyone is here. Alena has reclaimed my hand and I can tell she's watching me out of the corner of her eye, so I force calm on my face, despite the blinding pain, and tighten my grip on my spear.

The arena is more chaos. Hundreds of girls and women gathered. All talking over each other, all filled with uncertainty and an undercurrent of fear. They clutch each others hands and arms and shoulders. Leaning on each other as we are taught to do. The night air has turned chilled and I fight off a shiver. The only bright side is that once everyone is here the alarms turn off, though the lights still flash from them, and our pendants stop burning. *Thank the gods none of us are epileptic,* I think randomly. Our head Instructors stand in a tense circle, speaking in lowered voices and periodically glance over at a weathered, wood door. So innocuous it practically blends into the wall. Though, if you look close enough you can see an owl taking flight, with a spear clasped in its claws, engraved on the front.

"Oh my gods," I murmur.

"What?" Rose demands. And again when I don't answer. "*What?*"

I'm in a daze and must look as though I've been struck dumb. I *feel* as though I've been struck dumb. I can feel my mouth held slightly open and all I seem to be able to do is blink. Rose scowls at me and pinches my arm, hard.

"The Council," I finally manage to gasp out. "I think the Council is here." The girls around me gasp as they too look to the strange wooden door.

Most of us in the conclave know very little of the Council of Athena. Just rumors, mostly. Like supposedly, they're all immortal and have been granted godhood by Athena.

What we do know for sure is this: the council is made up of 12 women who were hand chosen by Athena herself. They had to have been previous members of the conclave (thus the immortal theory, since no one alive today seems to know them personally) but they do not live at the compound. No one knows where they live.

I was actually sent to deliver them a message one time a few years ago, a scroll from Antiope, and delivered it to a mail box somewhere in Kansas. A random mailbox in the middle of a random wheat field with no other buildings or anything around for as far as my eyes could see. I had driven along this road when all of a sudden, like a heat mirage in the desert, this mailbox appeared out of nowhere. I had whipped my head around, sure someone would show up and call me a witch or something. But no one did. I had put the scroll in the mailbox and as I drove away, I watched it shimmer and disappear in my review.

The Council only come to the compound when we're experiencing times of extreme uncertainty or a threat of some kind. The last time they were here was not even in my lifetime. Not even in my grandmothers.

Sometimes I have these moments where I don't feel as grown as I actually am. Like I'm still a little girl playing dress up in my mothers clothes. I'm having one of those moments now as I watch the Instructors, still huddled together, and wait for one of the older girls to walk over and start asking what was going on. I stand there, waiting, for a while, before I realize I am the most appropriate one to go over and get some answers. I take a deep breath while removing Alena's hand from mine and march over, trying to look calmer than I feel. I don't know why I have such an unsettled feeling in my chest. Like I'm teetering on the edge of a cliff that I can't see.

Tessa's eyes find me before I reach them and something flashes deep inside them. I could almost swear it is pity. The other instructors won't meet my eyes but make room for me to join them in their circle. I stand there for a moment, looking from woman to woman, waiting for someone to say something, but no one does. Irritation flashes deep inside me, like flames licking around my stomach. I plant my fists on my hips.

"Well?" I finally ask. "What the fuck is going on?" No one will look at me. The fire swells bigger. Tessa meets my eyes finally and must see the anger, and underlying fear, that fills them. She closes her eyes, taking a very slow, very deep breath and tilts her face back to the ceiling, as though she's praying. She tilts her head back up and releases her breath just as slowly as she inhaled it, and looks at me for another moment. All of a sudden, I don't want her to say anything. I become so scared of what has her so nervous that I never want Tessa to say anything ever again. Her eyes are unreadable as she stares at me.

"That was a distress call from the Protectors. Someone hit the emergency button and now no one can get a hold of any of them." My breath freezes in my lungs and I would swear to my Lady Athena that it feels as though concrete is encasing

47

my heart.

"My mother is not answering the calls." My voice sounds odd. With a start, I realize it sounds like Tessa's. Simple, with no real affliction. Without realizing it, I've adopted some of Tessa's mannerisms, which really shouldn't be that surprising to me. Not when one considers the amount of time I have spent under her teachings. It's with another start I realize that Tessa's voice, like mine, was frozen with fear. We have just entered uncharted waters with a storm brewing on the horizon and no one is sure if we know how to swim.

"No." Now it is Tessa who cannot meet my eyes. "No one has heard from your mother since it was her turn for radio duty, twelve hours ago." I press a hand to my stomach and fight back the nausea that simple sentence brings. *My mother is dead.* The thought is quick and undeniable and as soon as it enters my mind I feel bile rise up in my throat. I force myself to focus on the issue at hand.

"Is the Council meeting right now?" I nod over to the wooden door. Tessa and the others look uneasy and glance at the door again too. One woman, Ruby, a Level 5 Instructor, nods.

"They showed up just seconds after the alarm's started going off."

Another gives a small shudder. "They just glided in, so quiet you might have thought they were ghosts. They told us Lady Medusa was in danger—the lights and alarms didn't even seem to phase them— and that they would take Council before instructing us on our next steps." I fight the shiver that threatens to run down my spine. As worried sick as I am for my mother and the other Protectors, and Lady Medusa of course, I can't help but feel a sick sense of curiosity. I'll be one of the few Inductees to ever lay eyes on the Council.

As though they could feel my eagerness, the door opens and one of them enters the doorway. I'm almost disappointed to see that she is just a woman.

She appears to be in her 40's or 50's but is aging incredibly gracefully. She has mouse brown hair and eyes to match. She's wearing beautiful, flowing gray silk robes that ripple around her even as she stands still. Even with the plainness of her appearance, one can't help but feel intimidated by her. Something about her aura radiates power and knowledge and something, innately, tells me I am in the presence of one chosen by Athena. The room falls silent in a wave, as more and more of the girls become aware of her presence. She regards us all for a moment before she speaks.

"Aristomache Kallis. Kore Drivas. Elpis Laskaris." Her eyes find each of us in the crowd and my feet seem to move forward on their own accord. I hear rustling behind me and feel relief in knowing that Kore and Elpis are coming with me.

The Councilwoman steps aside as we near and I find it difficult to look into her eyes. So instead I keep them fixed on the ground. Inside the old wood door is a stone slab, much like the one used in the Choosing ceremonies, though this one is much larger and oval in shape. The stone is inlaid with runes and symbols. Runes and symbols that are possibly older than the volcanic walls we stand in, and I feel the ghost of a shiver run down my spine.

The power in this room is palpable.

The woman who called us in goes to retake her place along the table. I suddenly find myself under the impassive gazes of all twelve Councilwomen. All of them, different races and ethnicity's but still, somehow, all exactly the same. They all

49

sit with their hands interlocked and resting atop the table, their eyes unfathomable as they stare us down. We stand at the end of the table, me in front, Kore to my right and Elpis to me left. We bow our heads as we salute them and wait. One of the women to the right, an Asian woman with a Bronx accent speaks up.

"The safe houses of Lady Medusa have been compromised." Her wording catches my attention and my head snaps up, Kore and Elpis do the same and I see them exchange an uneasy glance from my peripheral.

"Excuse me," I begin, stunned. "Safe *houses*? As in more than one?" Another woman straight ahead answers. Based off her looks and her accent, I think she's Romanian.

"We have reason to believe that all of our current safe houses have been compromised." Not for the first time tonight, I feel as though the air has been sucked from my lungs. It's Kore who speaks next.

"How?" Her voice is loud in my ear and she seems to realize this is not the question to be asking because she immediately asks another, "What do you need us to do?"

A different woman answers again. It's a dizzying effect trying to keep up with all of them.

"We have heard a great many things of you three." Her black eyes stare us down intensely. She pushes a few of her dreadlocks off, her shoulder before continuing. "Fast climbers in the levels of your training. All of you have already completed several smaller missions, successfully, in the great name of Athena and you all have the skills we believe will be needed to be able to solve this mystery. We do not know how this compromise has occurred and that is most worrying of all."

I fight the urge to laugh. Not because I don't think she's

right but I because I can't help but think of that old cartoon: Scooby Doo. A gang of ragtag individuals off solving mysteries together. But I don't laugh. I salute them instead.

"You honor us," I tell them. "Tell us what Athena requires of us and we will do it. In Her Honor."

"In Her Honor." Elpis and Kore repeat beside me, also saluting. All of the women stare us down again. I can feel my heartbeat in my throat. I wonder if they can hear how it pounds in my chest.

"You must go." One finally speaks. "Go to the safe house and ascertain what is going on. If you can, you are to retrieve Medusa and bring her here to the conclave so that she may be better protected while we figure out how the locations of every single one of our safe houses was leaked."

I freeze and feel the others do the same.

"You—" I lick my lips and try again. "You honor us greatly."

"You feel as though you are not ready," this is the one who called us into the room. She stares at us impassively, her head tilted to the side slightly. Something in the way she looks at us makes me think she is not seeing me but every decision I have ever made and will ever make. Suddenly I am sure they must be immortal. "No one ever does when they are called forward by the Fates."

The thought of the Fates calling me anywhere makes me feel nauseous again, though I dare not say that out loud. I take a breath.

"If this is what our Lady Athena requires of us, then that is what shall be done. Regardless of what we might be feeling in this moment." I see several of them nod, pleased by this answer. I lick my lips again.

"If I may... what of my mother? And the other two protectors? And Lady Medusa, of course." The lady from the Bronx gives a somewhat dejected sigh.

"I wish we could soothe your worries for the safety of your mother and the others but even we cannot See what is going on. Another reason we are worried so."

I make a quick mental note about the implied capital "S" on see for an argument on why I think they are immortal the next time Sierra tries to say they aren't. Then I deal with the wave of despair and anger that washes over me but nod in thanks to the Councilwoman who answered me. It's her who speaks again, desperation fills the foundation of her voice.

"You will be given an allowance to aid your travels and access to any of the vehicles in the garage," is that an approving look in her eye? "Though I am told you prefer the bikes, Aristomache. You will leave before sunrise and head North. Coordinates for the location of the safe house will be programmed into whatever vehicle you all decide to take. You must hurry. Who knows what has happened. If Lady Medusa has been kidnapped there may be hope yet for a recovery. Or if her Protectors have taken her on the run from potential death or kidnapping, I'm sure your reinforcements would be both necessary and appreciated."

The idea of my mother, or any of the Protectors, needing our help is a laughable one. But I can see in the eyes of the Councilwoman.... I can see how truly they mean it. I've grown into the warrior my mother desired me to become without even realizing it. I went from looking to my mother for aid to becoming her aid.

I startle myself when I feel tears prick the back of my eyes. We salute as they stand silently.

"We will leave immediately." My voice is firm, not betraying the unsteadiness I still feel in my eyes. They return the salute. We see ourselves out. As the door shuts behind us, I hear a faint whisper of wind in the room behind us and know, that the Councilwomen have withdrawn again.

I say a fervent prayer to Athena that I never see them again.

6

Chapter 6

None of the girls are in the arena room when we come out and wonder vaguely what they were told. Tessa, Antiope and a few other Instructors still wait for us, tense and ready. It feels as though I'm floating underwater. Everything is muted and foggy. Nothing in my surroundings quite make sense to me.

"The safe houses have been compromised," I hear Elpis say, but again, it's muted under the roar of my blood in my ears. I think Ruby gasps, her hand flying up to her mouth. "All of them, they believe," she continues, before they can ask.

I massage at my chest, at a spot over my heart, trying to rub away the aching that fills it. I can feel my heart racing under my hand and my eyelids flutter as I fight another bout of nausea. My breath is quick and unproductive, ripping through my chest.

My mother is probably dead.

These words do not make sense to me. They do not sound like words of any of the languages I know. My mother, strength and life incarnate... dead? I squeeze my eyes shut, trying to calm my breathing, which is bordering on hyperventilation. I think of the last time I saw my mother.

It was the winter solstice and Alena and I had been allowed to visit. Their safe house had been somewhere to the Northeast of the country. We sat in some small town in Northern Vermont, in a mom-and-pop diner all day. I had borrowed a car from the conclave and driven us up there myself. Alena had been bouncing full of energy the entire car ride, I don't think she had slept at all. We pulled into the small town, so small it was practically on deaths door, but was somehow surviving despite the tourist traps that surrounded it.

And there she was. Leaning against the side of a pickup, just as strong and beautiful as the last time we had seen her. Her face had lit up into a huge smile when our car came into view, she began waving and jumping up and down: as though she was stranded on an island and we were the rescue boat that she was terrified would not see her. Alena had rolled the window down, hanging out the front, her smile the younger version of our mothers, waving as well.

"My girls! There are my girls!" There was so much joy in my mothers voice, I feared, for a moment, that she would drown in it.

"Mama! I started my spear training!" My mother's wordless squeal of excitement answered Alena's announcement. Alena was out the door and into my mothers arms before I had even stopped the car properly, her skinny arms wrapped tightly around her neck. Though I was not far behind her. My mother reached out a hand to me, and pulled me to her fiercely. I wrapped my arms around her and buried my face in her neck, like I did when I was younger. A small part of my brain was surprised to note that she and I are the same height. Tears welled up in my eyes.

"Mama," I murmured. "I have missed you."

"Αγάπες μου," she whispered over and over again. Αγάπες μου. Αγάπες μου. Αγάπες μου. My loves. My loves. My loves.

I'm not sure how long we had stood there, embracing like that. Before finally my mother pulled back and made Alena get down before she cupped Alena's face in her hands and studied her for a very long moment, before she kissed her forehead and released her. Then she did the same to me. She held my face in her hands and stared into my eyes, as though they were telling her my every secret. My hands came up and gripped her forearms so tightly my fingertips were white. I stared into her eyes, my eyes, for who knows how long before she pressed a lingering kiss to my forehead and pulled away.

"Ελάτε, αγάπες μου," she says. "You must be starving."

She took our hands and we walked into the diner together, we spent the rest of the day there. Ordering whatever we wanted, talking and laughing and making friends with the staff there. I remember my mother, how she looked then. So full of life. So beautiful. Her smile. Her laugh. How she'd reach across the table, laughing, and grab my hand whenever I said something particularly funny.

I think of Alena. How she stared at our mother with the utmost adoration. With borderline worship.

I think of how she looks at me that very same way. I open my eyes and feel the wetness on my lashes.

"I won't go." My voice is barely louder than a whisper. But, oh, they hear me. The room becomes deathly quiet. For a beat, no one says anything. No one even breathes. Then:

"You cannot refuse Athena." Antiope says harshly.

"This is the life, Aris." This is Ruby, contempt filling every syllable. "You do not have a choice."

I do not care. I am not listening. All I can think about is the look on my sisters face when I tell her our mother is most likely dead and that I am probably heading in the same way. I think of my mother again. On the day that Alena was selected to join the conclave.

She had stood before the Choosing slab, just as I had, and my mother had advocated for her joining, just as I had, but my mothers heart did not seem to be in it. Not the way it was when she called for my service. When she called for me, she had been filled with a fervor so intense it seemed to border on insanity. With Alena, it seemed she almost hoped they would deny her entry. I had been the one to stand behind Alena, as Tessa had stood behind me. I was nineteen, already a level 8, and was already quickly on my way to being everything my mother had dreamed for me to be. I was the fastest, the strongest, the smartest, the most devoted. I was the perfect warrior. Alena, barely seven years old, had stood in front of me, twisting her fingers together. Eventually the conclave accepted my mothers plea and Alena was allowed entry. As is our tradition, she was lifted up and crowd surfed around the room. Everyone chanting: "Alena! By Her Honor!" Alena was a giggling mess the entire time, filled with so much relief as having been allowed entrance. When I had been allowed entry, my mother had run alongside me in the crowd, screaming louder than anyone: *Aristomache! By Her Honor!*

She did not do this, then. She had stood as still as a statue, only her eyes moved as she watched Alena work her way around the room. I made my way to her, though I knew I should join the crowd. *Mama?* I had asked. My mother had not looked at me, keeping her eyes locked on Alena. *You must promise me you will protect her when I cannot.* There had been such gravity in her voice, a tone I had never before heard from her, that I did not argue or ask her what was worrying her so much. Instead, I saluted her. *I swear it on my honor, Mama.* Her shoulders seemed to relax a bit at my promise. At my vow.

My eyes find Tessa and I am not surprised at the disgust that fills them.

"Your mother would be so disappointed in you." She says viciously. Hoping to hurt me. Hoping to wound me into obedience. She should know better than to try that with me. The knowledge that I will never again, in this life time, hear my mother's laugh has made me cold. Immune to the words that would otherwise scar me. The pain in my mother's voice as she pleaded with me to protect my sister echoes in my ears.

"My mother is dead," I hiss back, savagely. "And I will not follow her same path. I will not leave my sister alone in this world while my mother and I are burnt at the pyre— if there is even a body *to* burn." I stare her down. My mentor. My instructor. Never before have I defied her. "I will not do it. My mother is dead and you cannot— you *should not*— ask this of me."

"Mama is... dead?" The voice breaks halfway through its sentence. I whip around, a hand grabbing at my throat as though I can pull my words back into it. Alena stands there, still in her pajamas and her feet bare. Her eyes are swimming in her tears, though she has not let any of them fall. I fall to my knees as I reach for her. But she stands firm and does not come to me. "Is mama dead?" She demands.

"I don't know," I whisper, too shell shocked to speak normally. Filled with too much hurt and confusion to elaborate.

But she deserves an actual answer so I swallow hard and force the words out. "No one knows. All anyone knows is that the Protectors sounded the alarms. They want us to go and check. See what's wrong." What I do not say is there is no way my mother is not dead. For her, or any of the other Protectors, to set off the alarms and then not answer any calls means they must be dead. There is simply no other explanation.

"You don't know for sure if she is dead, but you won't go to her?" Alena demands. "What if she's alive and she needs help?" I close my eyes in frustration. I open my mouth to retaliate but she beats me to it.

"You will never forgive yourself if you don't go." She vows, her tiny voice filled with steel. "*I* will never forgive you." My eyes snap open as I regard my sister. Her eyes are too serious for someone her age. I wonder if that is how my eyes looked at that age. So young, trying to be so grown up. Sometimes it's too easy to forget she is not a regular girl, that she is being raised with the same warrior mindset that I have been. Yes, she may still crawl into my bed when she has nightmares but she is being trained on how to be her own kind of nightmare. She steps forward and holds my face in her small, cold hands.

"You have to go help mama," she whispers pleadingly. "I'll be okay, Rissy, I swear it." I close my eyes again as she falls into me, hugging me fiercely. Tears are welling up again in my eyes as I feel her strength in her hug.

"Okay." I whisper to her. Then, reluctantly, to the group. "Okay. I'll go." I hear several quick exhales of relief.

"Get packed," Tessa says to the others. "She's right behind you."

And I am. Alena has cleared my thoughts of the soul gripping fear and I have remembered myself. If only for her sake.

"Aris." I open my eyes to find Tessa kneeling in front of me. "This will challenge you to your very being." I nod at this. Tessa nods in return, contemplating something. She is silent for a long few moments before she speaks again. "You must use your advantages to help all of you survive. *All* of your advantages." Now I'm confused because what does she mean by all of my advantages? There is only one thing I can think of and that is the fact that my family has been members of the conclave since the day our Lady Athena created it. Not only have I endured the blessing of Athena but I am born of a woman, who was born of a woman, who was born of a woman who had endured the blessing. Making us almost genetically perfect. I have also been training at the compound since I was five years old, this is another advantage that I have over every other girl here. But something in Tessa's face tells me it is not any of those things. Tessa nods again, seemingly bracing herself to say the next words. "Go to him. Get some answers."

Oh. *That* advantage. I sigh heavily at the thought of mixing two different parts of my world.

"Yes, ma'am." I respond. I squeeze Alena once more before I release her and stand. "I'll go right now."

* * *

The dorm is chaos. Kore, Elpis and I trying to pack. The others trying to help us. Other girls trying to get answers for what is happening. Alena sits on my bed, looking pale and terrified but strong. I try not to think about how not even 24 hours ago, she was sitting in that same spot full of energy and pride, eager to begin the next phase of her training. So, I focus on my packing. Three pairs of pants. Three t-shirts. Six pairs of underwear and six pairs of socks. Three bras. My spare set of boots. Gods, what else do I need.

"Here," Sierra says, setting a Ziploc bag full of toiletries on my bed. "Last thing you need when serving Athena is shit for breath." I give a breathless laugh at that and shove the Ziploc into an end pocket of my duffle bag. I stand for a moment, overwhelmed, and press my fingertips to my eyes. My knife. I dig in the drawer on my bedside table and pull out 18 inches of black steel, wicked sharp and begging to be used; and the sheath that goes with it. I quickly get dressed in my actual gear, black pants, gray short sleeve, armor over top. I strap my knife to my thigh, patting it a couple times when I'm done; a nervous tic I thought I got rid of years ago. My spears, enchanted by Hekate, sit around my wrist as five plain gold bracelets when I'm not using them. All I have to do to "activate" them is to yank them off my wrist and they come undone. Growing into a two meter long, weapon of war. Topped with a bronze spearhead, shaped like a leaf, it is a weapon I have trained with since the day I joined the conclave. On my other wrist is another gold bracelet, this one with a round pendant dangling off of it, with the head of Medusa engraved on it. One snap of my wrist and it becomes my shield. I grab a necklace off my nightstand, a gift from my mother. There are only three in existence. It's a gold locket, with a picture of my mom and I together on the day I was allowed entry on one side and the three of us, together at the last solstice on the other. I squeeze it tightly in my fist for a moment before I finally put it on. I place my hand over it again, where it rests over my heart and take a deep breath.

Rose comes in with some excitement in her step. She skips to a stop and hands me a set of keys.

"I got the good one," she tells me with a wink. I look at the key fob and then look at Rose with an eyebrow raised. I get a mischievous smirk in return. 'The good one' is a 2024 Jaguar E-Pace. Black with burgundy leather seats. The 'good one' is an understatement. I grin back at her as I shove the keys in my pocket and zip up my duffle bag, letting out a huff.

"Come here," I kneel down, motioning to my sister. She moves to sit in front of me on my bed. Her brown eyes filled with tears but also with resolve, she knows I cannot stay, so she does not ask me to. No matter how much she may want to. I hold her face in my hands. "I'll be home before you know it."

She nods as a few more tears escape. "Just promise you'll be careful." She mumbles as she scrubs at her eyes. Ashamed at showing her weakness.

"Promise, promise." I murmur as I pull her into a crushing hug. "Remember to let the tears out, so they don't poison you." She gives another tearful nod as she throws her skinny arms around me. I rub at her back for a few moments, blinking back tears of my own.

"Okay," I whisper, pulling away. "Okay, be good." I plant a kiss on her cheek, then her forehead, then the top of her head as we both stand. Rose wraps an arm around her chest, holding Alena to her.

"I'll make sure she's okay, Rissy." Rose tells me solemnly. "Don't worry." I nod once, in gratitude, before turning to the others.

"Ready?" I ask. Kore nods, giving the zipper on her duffle a sharp tug as she stands and moves towards me. Her long black hair hangs loose around her, with an eagle feather braided into her hair on one side. The seven-pointed star of the Cherokee

62

people is tattooed under her left ear, she has her usual silver make-up surrounding it to highlight it. Elpis, so pale she often looks like she's glowing, already has her bag slung over her shoulder. Her short white-blonde hair is pulled back into several braids in her attempt to keep it out of her face.

"Ready when you are, Cap," Elpis replies. I heave a sigh as I look around the room one last time.

"We're gone," I say. I say a prayer to Athena, begging her for patience as we try to complete this. Failure is not an option, not only for Lady Medusa's sake, but for all of those who would be affected by the wrath of our goddess.

7

Chapter 7

"How do you know he'll be in Las Vegas?" Elpis asks from the backseat. She has a bit of an attitude when she asks, which is not surprising but still aggravating. I don't want to answer her, mostly because she really will have an attitude when I tell her why I know we have to go to Las Vegas and I so do *not* want to deal with that. I readjust my grip on the steering wheel and keep my eyes forward. I can feel, more than see, Kore side-eyeing me from the passenger seat, also curious. I steel myself before I answer.

"Because I met with him there last weekend and he told me he'd be there until the UFC fights are done, which isn't for another 4 days."

"You met with him again?!" Elpis seethes from the backseat. "Aris how *stupid* could you be? No seriously! How is this supposed to end, girl? Like c'mon! There is no happily ever after here! You told us you were done with him!"

"I imagine he's a hard habit to kick," Kore mutters, her eyes faraway. Elpis reaches up and smacks the side of her head for siding with me, Kore quickly turns around to retaliate.

Normally this would irritate me, but right now I welcome the distraction. Elpis's reaction reminds me of my mothers and that wound hurts like nothing else right now.

Three years ago, I was running a reconnaissance mission for the Protectors. Someone had gotten too close to their old safe house, they had since moved locations and the mystery person got away, but not before they shot a tracking device into the bag he had been carrying. I had been tasked in finding him and establishing his threat level and, if deemed necessary by the conclave, eliminate him. I started tracking him from where the conclave sits, in the Mark Twain National Forest, and wound up in Downtown Charleston, North Carolina.

I found myself in a tight spot when a harpy with an attitude decided to pick a fight with me. We were at the back of some nasty alley. The thing was fast, but I was faster. I finally killed it but not before it had gotten a few good scratches on me.

I was swearing under my breath as I took a knee to clean and bandage the wounds on my side when I felt it. It was as though my breath had been frozen in my lungs, while my heart raced so fast I wondered if it was about to burst out of my chest. Chill after chill after chill raced down my spine; a sense of dread and primal, raw, unfiltered *fear* filled my mind and body. I was gasping, clutching the front of my shirt, trying to slow my breathing down. I had never felt so afraid in my entire life. I thanked Athena that we had been trained to fight this level of psychological warfare; because there was nothing else this could be *but* psychological warfare. How fear could feel natural and artificially created at the same time, I will never know. I closed my eyes and forced myself to focus. I felt my heart slow down infinitesimally when:

"Impressive." The honeyed voice was gravelly. "Very

65

impressive." A new wave of terror rolled through me followed by a whole body shudder. I had shot to my feet picking up my shield and yielding a new spear at the threat. "Ah, you're one of Athena's." Now the voice was appreciative. I bared my teeth in the direction of the voice.

"Who are you? Where are you?" I demanded. "Show yourself, coward!" A chuckle. A new wave of fear that made my knees buckle and bile rise up in my throat. It was only years of training that had kept me on my feet. When the voice realized I had not knelt, the laughter stopped. The air shimmered and he appeared in front of me. Tall, with night black hair and eyes, lean and muscled, he did not look inherently imposing. But something about him made me feel terrified to the very core of my being. He regarded me for a moment and when he spoke I saw his canines were longer than a typical human's, and a little bit sharper than a typical human's.

"What is your name, Initiate?" I bared my teeth again, in response. He cocked his head to the side, studying me. "You're right. How rude of me. You asked me first." He spread his arms as a black smoke began to show around him, growing bigger and darker by the second, tendrils reaching out of it like fingers. I could hear the rats squeaking with fear, scurrying around, trying to escape as the smoke reached them. My heart was racing, so fast I could barely feel it pounding away in my chest anymore. My eyelids fluttered as I fought to stay conscious. My palms broke out in a sweat, I readjusted my grip on my shield and spear and prayed to Athena I would not drop them. Just when I thought this display of power would never end, it did. Like he flipped off a light switch. The darkness leaves and the light from the street was able to reach me again. My heart began to slow. I locked eyes with him but I could not read the blackness within them.

"I am Deimos," he announced. I resisted the urge to swear, suddenly wishing I did not know who I was dealing with. "God of dread, fear and terror." He gave an ironic little bow. "At your service, my lady." I huffed an exhausted laugh at the display of mock-manners. My body felt as though I had just run seven marathons back to back. Deimos raised a perfectly shaped, pitch black, eyebrow at me. He nodded to where the harpy had been behind me.

"Impressive skills," he remarks. "I'd love to take some lessons from you."

In the moment that I met his eyes for the first time, something shifted. I felt as though I had met him before. I cock my head to the side, my brows furrowed in confusion. I try to keep my head. Deimos is a god, one who needs to be taken seriously. I won't allow myself to be swayed by a pretty face. But it's not just that he's attractive that has me off-kilter. There's that feeling of knowing, of remembrance. The poets might say we had known each other in a past life, and that's the way it felt. As though I had known him in a past life. It's as though my mind and body has already forgotten the terror that Deimos had inflicted on me. He's obviously powerful but, as we stand there regarding each other, I'm struck by the ridiculous notion that he won't do that to me again. He had his show of power and I had mine. Lord Deimos stood there, grinning savagely, watching me do this mental math. Before I know it, I'm answering his grin with a tentative one of my own.

"I am Aristomache Kallis," I tell him easily, holding out a hand for him to grab. "Level 9 Initiate in Athena's conclave." He smirked as he stepped forward to grab my hand. I tried to notice practical things, like how his skin is the same olive tone as mine and not how pretty his full lips looked while smirking at me.

"It is *very* nice to meet you, Aristomache." He murmured as he bent down and kissed my knuckles.

It had not taken long for a relationship to form. Deimos was fun and easy to talk to. He was one of the only men (could you still call him a man? Probably not.) I had been around who wasn't intimidated by my strength and power but also wasn't obsessed with it. He let me remember there is more to the world than the conclave. I had spent my entire life as the creation of my mother, the spear of Athena, a leader of my conclave. That type of life takes a toll on a woman. It was right around my twenties that I started to feel run down by it all. My relationship with Deimos was the break I needed. At first it was purely physical but it didn't take long for the lines to become blurry. He quickly became my confidant. Nothing that had to do with the conclave, which made the relationship all that more appealing. It was as though I was living my own personal double life. One where I had the weight of the world, literally, on my shoulders. Where my days consisted of beating my scores from the previous days and guiding those younger, or lower rank, than me. I bore their hopes and dreams and defeats and soothed over rivalries and had no time to think about how I was feeling. The other side of my life was so much easier. Freeing. I wore revealing clothes and drank until the rooms spun and relished in the feeling of Deimos's warm and strong arms around me. I never had to make decisions or worry about anybody but myself. In fact, I barely I had to worry about myself.

Both were my lives, both were easy and hard in different

ways and both made me feel alive in different ways. I wanted the best of both worlds and I know I can't have it.

It's like the world's slowest heartbreak.

The others hated it, couldn't make sense of it. What was I, doing hanging on the arm of the god of terror? I always told them I just liked his attention, when they would ask me what I saw in him. That he was a distraction with a pretty face. And at first that had been completely true, but it didn't stay that way.

My mother had flown into a rage when she had found out.

She had come home for a visit, surprising us. I had been with Deimos for a free long weekend and had spent all four days at his palace with him. She was sitting on one of our desks when I returned home.

"Where were you?" She had asked, cold steel in her voice.

I remember sighing as I threw my duffle bag onto my bed. "Hi mom, nice to see you too. I've been good thanks for asking. How was your drive?"

"Don't play stupid, Aristomache Kallis." She shot back, her arms folded tightly over her chest. "Alena says you were gone all holiday. Where were you?"

I planted my hands on my hips, narrowing my eyes. "Sounds like you already know where I was."

"Tell me you weren't rolling around in the sheets with him?" My mother stood slowly, anger blazing in her eyes. "With the son of Ares."

I jutted my chin out at her. "And if I was?" I don't feel as tough as I sound. My stomach is in knots and I can feel my pulse in my fingertips. I hated challenging my mother. Mostly because I was always afraid it would come to blows and at that point in my life I genuinely didn't know who would win. Now

69

I'm even more afraid that I would win.

"You," she hissed, stepping closer to me. "anonyma! You're throwing everything away over a *god*?"

"What, pray tell," I snapped right back, my fear vaporizing in my anger. "Am I throwing away? We're just having a little bit of fun!"

She threw her hands into the air. "Everything we've been working towards, Aristomache! Here you are, spending your long weekend partying and drinking when you could have been training instead! I don't care how much *fun* he is. This is the stupidest thing you've ever done, daughter."

"Deimos isn't a thing," I snarled at her. "And even if he was, he sure as hell isn't the stupidest one I've ever done."

Her eyes went wide and furious at the implication and what would have been a nice visit, quickly dissolved into our usual fight. She said I wasn't training enough, I said I was training too much and needed a break. She said I was sabotaging Alena's training with my neglect. I told her it didn't matter what she thought because she had left me in charge of Alena and her training. Finally, my mother went to storm out but stopped at the door and whipped around.

"He's using you. For your status as an Initiate. And you're a fool if you can't see that."

I hadn't bothered with a retort as she stormed out of the room, but as I had laid in bed that night, quietly fuming, I replayed our long weekend together. But what had stuck out to me more was the sense of injustice brought on by my mothers wrath. Because I was so sure she was wrong. I *knew* she was wrong. I had spent all weekend laughing and dancing and enjoying Deimos's attention and never once did I feel like an Initiate. I only ever felt like a woman. Did I want to live that way? No, I didn't think so. But it was a nice break from the daily grind of training and more training.

"Yes," I tell them, interrupting their squabble. "He is hard to quit." For some reason this quiets them.

"I'm sorry," Elpis says quietly. "I know it's complicated... I shouldn't hound you about it. I'm trying to be supportive of you, I swear." Kore does not say anything but reaches over to pat my shoulder. I keep my eyes on the road and do not say anything until the lump in my throat has passed.

"Thank you, Elpis." I murmur thickly, not quite in control of the lump. Kore, in an effort to break the tension, changes the subject.

"Game plan? After talking to Shadow Boy?" I snort at her subtlety. And at her use of the group nickname for Deimos.

"Depends on what he tells us. Tessa was adamant that whatever it is he tells us is going to change how we approach this."

"How much could he tell us that the Council could not?" Elpis grumbles, still displeased with having to go to Deimos in the first place.

"Because," Kore interjects before I can snap, "Shadow Boy is still a god, whether we like it or not, and has the *connections* that our Council does not." Kore seems to have a displeasing thought and turns to me, eyebrows knit and with her lips pursed together.

"Will Elpis and I even be able to get into wherever Mr. Boy is?" I shift in my seat. Her eyes narrow as she recognizes my discomfort. "Well?" She demands. I fight the urge to flinch at the tone.

"You will if you're with me." The car erupts at this again.

"OH MY GOD!" Kore yells, suddenly.

71

"DOES THE WHOLE SEEDY UNDERWORLD KNOW WHO YOU ARE?!" Elpis screeches, leaning up between the seats.

"I can't stand you sometimes." Kore tells me fiercely.

"Look at me, I'm Aris, I can go wherever I want because my super scary lover will literally *stop your heart with terror if you so much as look at me weird!*" Elpis makes a motion like she's gagging herself.

"*Oh!* Wait until I tell Zoe!" Kore fumes.

"And it's okay if I decide to dump him because I have *Lord Herakles, the hero of all heroes* waiting in the wings!" Elpis continues her rant, her eyes burning.

"I can't *stand* you!" Kore repeats, her eyes rolling.

I roll my eyes. "How about you guys get some rest? We have like five more hours until Vegas— might as well get some sleep." They both grumble some more at me before finally shifting around to make themselves comfortable and falling asleep, as quickly and efficiently as we are trained to do.

I take a very deep breath, reveling in the first moments I've had by myself in what feels like forever. I wonder how Alena is doing, Rachel told me she would let her sleep with her, if she got scared. Will Alena take her up on this? My instinct tells me no, Alena will want to be tough. She will want to represent our family well. She will not seek out, what is considered, childish comforts. My head starts to hurt again. I twist my head this way and that, sighing, trying to work out the seemingly permanent kinks in my neck. In the silence I find myself praying, almost constantly, to Athena.

Guide us on our quest.

Let my sister find peaceful slumber, if she cannot have peaceful days.

Keep my friends strong and my conclave devoted.

72

A single tear runs down my cheek, kissing at the corner of my lips.

Please...do not let me be the one to find my mother's body.

8

Chapter 8

"The streets are alive". That's the type of stuff that people always say about cities like this. That they were *alive*. That's so stupid, they're not alive. If anything I'd say they're contaminated. Vomit and alcohol and smoke, from who knows what, sting my nose. Men with leering eyes and quick tempers stand in dark corners, waiting for the perfect opportunity. Women in miniskirts laugh loudly, clinging to their friends as they bounce from bar to bar, oblivious to the danger that surrounds them. Men with too much cheap cologne try to convince themselves that their wives won't find out what they did in Vegas and antagonize their friends to make one last bet before they leave. We shoulder through them easily, they do not even notice us, grimacing slightly as their sweaty skin touches ours. We walk in a tight formation, so tight we'd step on each others heels every other step if we were not so practiced at this. But we are, so we don't. My eyes bounce around, constantly on edge. These mortals pose no real threat to us but it is not just mortals that fill this night.

Sure enough, it does not take long before a creature of the

Underworld, sensing our power, seeks us out. He's a minor spirit, probably a servant of some minor god, just looking for some street cred. His skin is a bright red, his eyes all black with no whites or pupils, and small horns stick out the top of his bald head. He's no taller than me, though he is certainly acting as though he is. He must have planned his big reveal, maybe rehearsed in front of his bedroom mirror in case he ever got the opportunity to confront the best of the best. He was standing on the other side of a bus stop and as we approached, stepped out from behind it, so quickly that I barely had time to register his appearance before we were nose to nose. He barely had time to open his mouth to perhaps quip the one liner he had practiced, before I have unsheathed my knife, and pressed the tip firmly under his chin.

It's almost funny how quickly he goes from arrogant to astonished.

"What?" I purr, enjoying playing with my meal. "Owl got your tongue?" Tilting my head to show him my pendant. He closes his eyes and mouths a curse, I feel him swallow hard against my knife. I toss my hair back over my shoulders and press my knife in harder, just short of drawing blood. "We're in a bit of a hurry so you get a pass this once. But if you ever question the might of Athena's best again, or even dream of challenging us, I will obliterate you in such a way that you will never regenerate. Do you understand me?" I feel his "mhm" vibrate against my knife. He must be scared to nod against it.

"Good boy," I purr again. "Now scram." In a puff of sulfur he's gone.

We share a laugh and quick high fives as we continue down the street.

We finally reach the casino that we need, it's neon sign

makes my eyes throb but it will not be ignored: The Labyrinth Casino. Behind me, Kore snorts.

"Little on the nose, 'doncha think?" She mutters, twisting her bracelets anxiously around her wrist. I give her a small smile over my shoulder. Elpis reaches forward, brushing the small of my back lightly, also displaying her anxiety. The feeling of tension and anger is so prominent, yet so subtle, in the air it gives one a feeling of...*wrongness* without being able to figure out why. Having been exposed to this type of environment several times, I do not feel it as keenly as my sisters do, but enough still that all of my sense are on edge.

We approach the door to find it blocked by a bouncer. One that is 9-feet tall, has goat legs and huge horns that curl over his head, the pupils of his yellow eyes are slit sideways like a goats too.

"Password?" his voice is raspy and unsettling, like nails on a chalkboard. I roll my eyes.

"Pyl, do I appear as though I have time for this?" I ask snottily, planting my fists on my hips. I hear Elpis and Kore catch their breath. Pyl makes a noise like a chainsaw being run through mud: laughter. Pyl works for Deimos and is very familiar with me, allowing me to speak to him more easily. He steps to the side, sweeping his arm out in a grand invitation in. I give him a small smile and pat his arm as we pass. "Always nice you see you, Pyl."

"Likewise to you, Ms. Aris." He pats the top of my head clumsily a couple times as I pass, making me laugh. Kore gives a shudder as soon as we're through the door.

"I don't know how you're so calm around them." I shrug, thoughtful. They've never really bothered me the way they do the others, the Underworlders.

"Oh my gods." This comes in unison from them as they get a look around them. I can't help but laugh. The room is decorated somewhat stereotypically: red and black leather furniture, fog rolling throughout the room, bones and chains used as decoration. I don't need to look at the bar to know at least one vampire is being served a drink of some blood cocktail nor do I need to look over to the hot tub swamp in the corner to know I'll see a creature straight from Swamp Thing. We've barely made it into the club when a voice calls out.

"Initiates!" We stop as one, closing in on each other, fingering our bracelets. I feel the mistrust carved onto my face as the man approaches us.

He's about our age, maybe a little older. There is absolutely nothing remarkable about him so I know immediately he is not a god and but maybe a demigod. I've met a lot of people and beings in my years of gallivanting across the country and I'm sure he has never been one of them. He has dull, lanky blond hair that he is continually pushing out of his eyes.

He steps in front of us, slightly breathless. His watery eyes flicker across all three of us and back again.

"What is it?" Elpis asks him.

"My name is Jason," he tells us. "and I'd like to offer myself to be of assistance with the conclave."

I don't bother to keep the disdain off my face as I rake my eyes over him.

"Is that so." I drawl in contempt. "And what is it, Jason, that you would be able to offer us?"

He purses his lips together as he glances at me, anxiety filling his eyes.

"Because of the god I serve," he clears his throat. "I might be able to help."

77

"So nothing of your own value?" Kore sneers at him. "I think we'll pass."

We do just that, and shoulder our way past him. Anger flashes in his eyes at our dismissal, but his bruised ego is the least of my concern.

As we make our way through the crowd, more and more regulars nod to me, raising glasses and clearing paths. I nod back and try not to notice Elpis and Kore's response to them, though it is difficult to tune out them whispering to each other. When we reach the VIP lounge I know Deimos will be in, I suddenly find I do not want them with me. But asking them to wait without me would be cruel and I would never hear the end of it. So I grit my teeth and don't even glance at the bouncers outside as I make my way in. They know me well and make no move to stop me.

Minor gods and spirits dwell in here, not wanting to mingle with the "dust bunnies" that fill the floor. So called that because they are low born monsters and beings, ones that haunt nightmares and hide under beds to scare mortal children. These beings also laugh loudly and often, as drunk as gods can be off their nectar. They also know me and unlike the dust bunnies, acknowledge me loudly. Hollering greetings across the lounge, raising sloppy glasses that they spill all over as they do. But they do not touch me, oh no. They will start to, they will reach out to ruffle my hair or pat my back or pull me into a rough hug but will remember where they are and who I am, and let their hands fall empty.

He knows I'm here of course. He sits at a poker table, fingering the rim of something that glows acid green, staring at his cards as we approach. Phobos, Agon, Alke, Caerus, even Lord Dionysus, who has made a rare appearance, give me familiar and easy greetings. I nod to all of them, and stop to allow Deimos's brother, Phobos, to give me a and give me a brief kiss on the cheek. As I move on, I give Lord Dionysus a proper salute and make my way to Deimos. Even under the scrutinizing eyes of my sisters, I cannot force my body to be casual, cannot hide how much I ache to be with Deimos. As I approach him I drag my hand along his upper arm before resting both it and my other hand on top of his shoulders.

"Are you winning?" I ask him casually, eyeing the cards over his shoulder. He swears in Ancient Greek.

"With Agos playing? No shot, gorgeous." I smile at the genuine irritation in his voice but quickly become serious. I give his shoulders a squeeze and lean over to whisper in his ear.

"I need to talk to you." He tilts his head towards me, helping to cover my lips and what I say with his jaw. "Now." He reaches up to squeeze my hand before motioning for his friend, Dolos, to come take his spot, who does so eagerly, but not before throwing me an acid filled look. I level my own nasty gaze back at him. Dolos and I can't stand each other. Oblivious, Deimos stands and motions for me to lead the way. In turn, I motion for Kore and Elpis to stay put, they're plenty safe where they are and walk a few meters away to a private room. Sometimes the VIP will get private shows from exotic dancers, both mortal and otherworldly, for special occasions. Thank the gods it's empty right now. I push the door open and walk in without hesitation.

It's a simple room, round with plush red velvet couches all along the edge and a pole with a small stage at the center. Deimos takes a seat on the stage and motions for me to sit on couch in front of him.

We simply stare at each other for a moment and in that moment I cannot believe that I ever thought his black eyes to be expressionless, they are screaming at me right now and they are screaming nothing but pity.

"How much do you know?" The pity in his eyes has made my voice hard and flat. Deimos knows better than to take my attitude personal, he just rubs his hand along his jaw, never breaking eye contact with me. Finally he moves, so that he is kneeling in front of me. One hand rests on my hip while the other comes up to cup my face, forcing me to look at him.

"I know that you are in danger and I am once again on my knees *begging* you to please—"

I push roughly at him, which admittedly does not actually move him much, but it gets my point across.

"Deimos I cannot keep having this same conversation with you!" I hiss, my eyes wide and serious. "I have given you my answer and it is not changing!" Deimos meets my eyes for another moment before sighing in resignation. "Now. How much do you know?"

He rubs a tired hand over his face, before grabbing at the back of his neck. He moves to sit beside me and braces his elbows on his knees before motioning in exasperation towards the door. "I know you should call your friends in here." I stand and move quickly to the door, poking my head out. Elpis and Kore are standing in the exact spot I left them, looking supremely uncomfortable. They meet my eyes and I wave them in. They jump at the opportunity to be away from the beings that surround them and stride over quickly.

I make room for them to push past me into the room. Despite the gravity of the situation, I hear Kore give a tiny snort of laughter as she sees the stripper pole. They move to stand on either side of me, arms crossed, faces blank.

They will be swayed by no god.

Deimos smirks at the open display of hostility but, thank the gods, does not make a comment. His hands are braced on his thighs as he regards us.

"There is a traitor at the conclave," he says suddenly.

A hiss goes up around the room and it takes me a beat to realize it's coming from the three of us.

"You're lying," Kore bites out savagely, her entire face full of mistrust and disbelief. To his credit, Deimos takes the accusation well, spreading his hands as though to show there is no lie hidden in them.

"I wish I was. But I'm not. There is a traitor. She has sold out the locations of the safe houses to whoever would buy them." He takes a deep breath. We are statues. "Now it is a race to whoever can get to Medusa first."

"How do you know this?" Elpis demands, her eyes full of distrust. Deimos levels his gaze at her.

"Because they tried to sell them to me." Another hiss, as we all unconsciously reach for our spears. Myself included.

"And what did you do?" I snarl, betrayal threatening to coat my heart. Now his gaze is annoyed and vaguely insulted as he turns it to me.

"I declined it, Aristomache." He wields my full name like a shield, reminding me he has the right to use it and that right comes with trust. "Have some faith." I bare my teeth at him in response. He rolls his eyes before continuing, speaking quickly as Elpis opens her mouth furiously. "No. Before you ask. No, I don't know who it is. Whoever it is masked themselves greatly using some serious magic. I acted like I was interested and tried to figure out who it was but they must

81

know I have other loyalties and wouldn't bite. Just told me to fuck off if I wasn't a serious buyer." He shrugs as though to say, *what else can you do*?

I groan quietly as I push my fingertips in my eyelids. A traitor. Gods help us, what are we going to do?

"You talk like there is still hope of saving Lady Medusa," Kore notes. I take my fingers off my eyes in time to see Deimos shrug again.

"If Medusa were killed or captive it would be huge news, particularly in the Underworld. There has been nary a peep nor a pipe about the death of Medusa so one could probably, safely, deduce that she is still alive." Now he gives a noncommittal tip of his head. "Though for how long that remains true has yet to be determined. Like I said, there were some eager buyers. Mostly those pesky male heroes seeking eternal glory that you Initiates despise so much." He says this last bit condescendingly, having previously admitted to me he thinks our protection of Medusa is overzealous. Normally this would earn a smartass comment from me but another thought has just occurred to me that outweighs his dickish attitude.

"She'll be executed. Whoever this traitor is." I murmur to myself, almost wonderingly. "It'll be death by the board." Kore and Elpis blanch and Deimos's eyes become wary.

"They still practice that?" He asks cautiously. He flexes his wrists unconsciously in discomfort at the thought of the ancient punishment. I nod once, still shell shocked. Boarding, also known as "bloodless crucifixion", was popular in Ancient Greece. Criminals had iron rings placed tight enough to cut off circulation, around their wrists, ankles and neck and then stretched over a large wooden 'X', slowly suffocating to death as all blood is cut off. It is a slow and painful death. It hasn't been used in I don't even know how long. We don't get many traitors at the conclave.

"I can't believe any one of us would turn our back on the conclave," I give a half laugh of surprise, still thinking hard. "Especially knowing that would be our fate."

"We need to get going." Elpis says suddenly. "Now." Kore and I nod, immediately turning to go.

"Be careful." Deimos's cuts in, suddenly. His voice is oddly soft as we go to leave. I look back at him questioningly. We do not, as a rule, show such affections in public. Me sitting on his lap, flirting and making out, those are fine. But to show just how much we care for each other... that is not allowed. Too many would be eager to use it against us.

His hands make a helpless little gesture before rubbing the back of his neck awkwardly. "I'll keep an eye out for you lot, when I can." I nod, my eyebrows pinched together in confusion before turning and hurrying after Kore and Elpis, who wait just on the other side of the doorway; looking impatient.

* * *

We make our way back through the casino in daze. I barely register where I'm walking and narrowly avoid running into anybody. A traitor. This has never happened in the history of the conclave, at least not to my knowledge. I shake my head in disbelief as we hit the door.

Pyl is still working as bouncer and is shifting his weight anxiously as we approach. He's one of Deimos's personal guards so he knows me well and would know what's going on. He has also grown attached to me, and me to him, as mine and

Deimos's relationship has progressed. He twists his meaty hands together as he addresses me.

"You will be safe?" I can't help but smile at Pyl's concern and grasp one of his large hands in both of mine. His clutches mine, like a child scared at the doctor. His other hand covers mine, dwarfing them.

"Yes, I will be safe." He swallows hard, shifting from hoof to hoof.

"You will call? If not safe?" His yellow eyes are filled with concern. Even with everything that's going on, I feel my heart warm at the sight of his obvious affection. I squeeze his hand.

"I will call." He lets out an anxious snort at that and squeezes my hands one last time before dropping them. He looks to Kore and Elpis and gives them a salute.

"Be safe, Athena's Warriors." They look stunned but return the gesture without thinking.

"Thank you, Pyl." Elpis says, sincerely, surprising me.

He watches us walk away, continuously taking his hand from his left shoulder to his ribs on his right side and then shoving both his hands out: the ward against evil. Again and again and again he does this. Which begs the question: what does he know that has him so afraid for us?

II

Part Two

9

Chapter 9

We ride in silence for a while; Kore is driving now, me riding shotgun, Elpis still stretched out in the back, all of us quiet. Each of us trying to gather our thoughts. I look out the window, my mouth pressed against my fist, seeing nothing. It feels as though there will be smoke coming out of my ears before long with all the overtime my brain is working. Kore's fingers are tapping out a random, anxious beat on the steering wheel. I can feel her peeking at me out of the corner of her eyes. Finally, I sigh and sit back in my seat again. This seems to be a signal of some kind for the others, who both defrost, becoming animated and agitated at once.

"*Who* would do such a thing?" Elpis marvels, at once. "Who would risk it? Knowing the board is your fate?" I give an involuntary blanch at the thought of the board. We are all shown depictions of what it looks like when that punishment is utilized and even my ghost will have those images burned into it.

"I've been running through every girl and woman in the conclave," I say, rubbing my hands over my face harshly. "I would never think any of us capable of something like this."

"That's if Deimos is telling the truth," Kore blurts out before eyeing me again. "I'm sorry Ris, but that is definitely a possibility we need to be considering."

"No, I know," I agree. "I already thought about it and I really do think he is telling the truth. He has nothing to gain from lying about this."

Elpis groans from the back. "I was afraid you were going to say that. I was really holding out hope that you were going to tell us there was a possibility he was lying to us."

I shake my head slowly, sighing.

I want to tell them that there's no way Deimos is lying. That he has nothing to gain from lying to us about this and that, honestly, it's just not his forte. He's also a terrible liar, he always bites his lip after he lies, but that's besides the point. I want to reassure them that he's not lying but a voice nags at the back of my head. One that says, *how do you know it's not them? How do you know they're not the traitor?*

The thought has bile rising up my throat, disgusted by the thought alone. Shame also floods my body. Who am I to trust the word of a god, the god of terror no less, than my sisters? The ones I have grown up alongside, trained beside and defended for years now. What would my mother say? I wonder. But then I remember my mother is most likely dead and feel my heart harden. Deimos has given me no reason to doubt him, but now, suddenly, one of my sisters has. It's a hard pill to swallow. I shake my head to try and clear it of the doubt and fear.

"We should call Antiope, give her an update." Elpis says, bringing me back to the present.

"Should we?" I question. The other two look at me, startled.

"I mean it. Should we tell anyone what we know right now? *We don't know who to trust.*"

I don't even know if I can trust you two, I think sadly.

Kore swears under her breath as she realizes I'm right. Elpis, however, seems torn.

"We can trust our Instructors," her voice sounds small and hurt and full of doubt of the words she says.

"Athena forgive me, but I don't think we can!" Kore objects. "Aris is right, I mean Tessa is the one who told her to talk to Deimos in the first place!"

My head whips over to her at that, my mouth slack with shock.

"Gods…" I murmur. "I didn't even think about that. But you're right. Why would she have any reason to tell me to talk to Deimos? She hates that I'm seeing him."

"We have no idea who is safe." Kore stresses, smacking her palm on the steering wheel in emphasis.

"We can call the others," I allow, seeing the look of heart-break on Elpis's face. "Fill them in, let them start snooping around and decide who's safe to talk to."

"Yes!" This helps settle Elpis's nerves. "That's a good idea."

Kore nods in agreement. "Yes, at the very least they can give us a starting point."

My phone is connected to the Bluetooth so I pull it out and open my contacts.

"Who're you calling?" Kore asks as the line begins to ring.

"Rose, she's the most discreet," I reply. "And she actually answers her phone."

"Good call," Elpis agrees. "On both counts. I couldn't tell you the last time Sierra answered one of my phone calls" I

89

snort as Rose's voice fills the car.

"Thank the gods. Are you guys okay?" We can hear the sounds of daily drills going on in the background.

"We're fine, Rose. But you need to find a reason to go to a quiet corner to talk. Now."

"That's going to be hard," Rose admits. *"The Head Instructors have been watching us like hawks since you all left. Asking us if we've talked to any of you, or have any updates. It's very weird. They've definitely already noticed me on the phone and are going to, correctly, assume I'm talking to you guys."*

The three of us exchange loaded looks.

Rose correctly interprets our silence. *"What's going on?"*

"Rose you *have* to get away," I urge. "We cannot talk to you with so great a chance of being overheard." Rose sighs, annoyed at the prospect of sneaking away. All of a sudden the noises go muffled.

"C'mon, c'mon, c'mon," I mutter under my breath. For five long minutes we sit there, waiting for Rose's voice to come back on. Just as we're starting to think the worst, she's back and the background noise is gone.

"Okay, be quick." Straight to the point then. Kore and Elpis both look to me, waiting for me to deliver the news. Sometimes I hate being in charge.

"There's a traitor at the conclave," I state. A sharp intake of breath from other side of the phone. "We have no idea who, Deimos told us, yes I believe him. Said the traitor reached out to any takers, male heroes, Underworld creatures, minor gods, whoever might want the glory of killing Medusa and sold the safe-house locations to whoever could pay their price. They tried selling to Deimos, he denied them, again I believe him, but that's how he knew. He also thinks Lady Medusa is still alive, says there'd be a lot of chatter in the Underworld if she had been captured or killed. So there's hope. Not much. But some."

We sit in silence for another beat or two. Then Rose begins swearing in rapid Ancient Greek, one swear after the other, overlapping like some symphony of the profanity.

"*Oh, Athena* have mercy!" She groans out finally. I nod, impressed at the creativeness of her swear words. I think she may have even invented a few new ones.

"Yeah that's pretty much how we reacted." I state. Rose swears a few more times.

"*Okay, okay,*" Rose gushes out. "*What do you need us to do? Start putting out feelers for who it might be?*"

"Yes," Kore tells her. "That's exactly what we need you to do. Get the others to help but this *has* to be on the down low, Rosie."

"*Yeah, of course.*" She agrees. "*Do you guys have any leads?*"

"Well," Kore sighs, eyeing me. I give an exasperated wave of my hand and then begin gnawing on my nails. If I don't die on this mission, I'm going to go prematurely gray. "Tessa said something weird before we left. She told Aris to seek out Deimos, talk to him. Said he could point us in the right direction. And he could, he's the one who told us about the traitor. But the question stands..."

"*How would Tessa know that Deimos knew that?*" Rose interjects. "*Yeah, that is super weird. Especially considering how much she hates that Aris is even seeing him to begin with.*" I press my fingertips into my eyes again. This headache is never going to go away. "*Okay, I'll get the girls on it. I have to get back to training. We're still on red alert. Antiope says we're staying that way until check in from you guys. So I'll tell them I*" *talked to you but that you had no new information."*

All three of us nod at that.

"That's definitely for the best." Elpis agrees.

"Okay, be safe. I love you all. Come home safe."

"We love you too, give the others our love too." Kore speaks for us.

"I will, and don't worry Aris, Alena is doing All right." I breathe a sigh of relief as the line goes dead.

We sit in silence for a several miles before Kore turns to Elpis and I and tells us to get some sleep. Neither of us object and after some maneuvering and adjusting we both go still and are asleep in seconds.

* * *

There's no relief in my dreams. Of course not; that would be too helpful. I spend the entire time chasing some shadow figure, I'll get close to it, close enough that a persons features start being identifiable, and just as I'm about to grab them, the features shift and the smoke filters through my hands. I'm looking around, trying to find it again when all of a sudden, I can sense the shadow behind me, getting closer. But every time I turn around there is nothing there. I'm running through nothingness when I feel it creep up behind me again. I can feel it breathing down my neck. It's reaching out for me, to grab me.

"Aris." My eyes snap open immediately. I'm curled around myself, my arms folded tightly across my stomach, my head resting on the door frame. It's Elpis who woke me, her bright eyes tense as she leans up from the back to shake me awake. "We stopped for gas. Come on. Let's go stretch our legs and grab some food." I nod mutely and stretch, feeling the kinks all over my body from sleeping so contorted.

She and I step out together, Kore is already inside paying for the gas.

"Where are we?" I murmur. Wherever it is, it's small and desolate-looking. Scraggly bushes and dirt instead of grass. It's very late, or early I guess depending on how you look at it. Maybe three... four in the morning. I could get my phone out and look but walking seems to be taking up all my focus and to be honest I don't care that much.

"Jackpot, Nevada." Elpis informs me. "Small-ass town on the Nevada-Idaho border. Hey," this is to Kore, who has just come out of the gas station with a small plastic bag of snacks and drinks. "I'll drive now." Kore just nods, having just taken a huge bite of a protein bar.

"We're making good time," I remark as we enter the gas station, a tiny, rink-a-dink thing that's more dirt than anything else. A grubby man sits behind the counter, eyeing us just as suspiciously as we are eyeing him. A town this size, I imagine they don't get many visitors so any outsiders are automatically untrustworthy. And we're trained to always assume someone is laying a trap for us somehow, so it's a psychological showdown of mistrust. Some may call us paranoid but what can you do about it.

The bathroom is disgusting and I try not to think about it too much, which is thankfully pretty easy considering how badly I needed to go to the bathroom. I wash my hands, trying to tempt some soap from the ancient looking soap-dispenser, while Elpis goes to the bathroom.

"Yuck," she mutters under her breath as we step out. "We'll be lucky if we don't catch the plague from here."

I snort under my breath and go to grab myself a couple of drinks and some snacks. The old man stares us down as he rings up our stuff, pausing occasionally to spit into an empty water bottle, I do my best to make sure he knows I am not impressed by his tough guy act.

We make our way back out to the car and find Kore already stretched out across the backseat, passed out. Elpis gets behind the wheel and the car purrs to life as I'm fastening my seat belt.

Elpis and I ride in easy companionship for about a few hours, I nap off and on for the first couple of hours but soon I'm well rested and full of energy. We play a game of "Don't even get me started" where we're given random topics (like rocking chairs versus laZboy chairs) and have to argue as to why one is better than the other. But we can't play long because we get too into it and will start arguing for real, which leads to us becoming absurdly defensive of the random topic we are given. We're playing a game of I Spy when I notice them.

"What?" Elpis asks tensely, immediately noticing the change in my behavior.

"We're being followed." I tell her, still staring intently out of the side mirror. She swears under her breath as she studies the car behind us in her review.

"Are you sure?" She asks, glancing at her speed now, which she is slowly increasing.

"Yep." I say and I turn around, pretending as though I'm getting another drink from the cooler we have filled back there.

"Kore." Her eyes are open immediately, but no other part of her body moves. "We're being tailed." She swears softly under her breath and immediately begins to rub the sleep from her eyes. I sit back up and glance in our rearview mirror again.

"We need gas again anyway." Elpis tells us. I nod and look at our GPS.

"How long was I asleep?" Kore asks, still laying down.

"Uhh," I look at the clock that now says 10:00 AM. "About six hours."

"Shit, at least I'll be well rested for this shit show we're about to hit."

I laugh at that. "You and me both. I'm actually kind of excited for this. I definitely need to stretch my legs."

"Oh yeah, it'll be nice to get the blood pumping." Elpis agrees. "Okay, we'll stop in a town called Pendleton and get gas. We'll go from there as to how we want to handle this."

"Where's Pendleton? Where are we now?" Kore asks.

"Northern Oregon. We're about 40 minutes from there now." I tell her, looking at the GPS again. "When we leave Pendleton we'll go Northwest for about 15 minutes. There's a tiny cemetery there that should be remote enough for us to do what we need to without anyone seeing us." The others nod their agreement.

"Ugh okay I'm sitting up now," Kore groans as she sits up and rolls her neck around. "Do we think there's a tracker on us, or they got lucky and saw us somewhere and started following us then?"

I suck my teeth, shaking my head. "No way to know, we'll just have to shake this, get them taken care of and go from there. We'll have to search the car still anyway, of course."

"Gods, I hate car searches," Kore complains. "They are just so damn tedious. And these new cars have soo many hiding places in them."

I snort while pulling my hair back in a braid. "First world

problems." Kore laughs, high and excited, as she begins to braid her own hair.

"Can we count it as a first world problem if we are not *technically* of that world?" She asks.

"Kore. We are driving a brand new, sports SUV thingy. We're counting it." Elpis tells her firmly. Despite the severity of our situation I laugh loud and long at this and am still fighting the residual giggles when we pull up to the gas station half an hour later. Then the seriousness, the impending fight, becomes real again.

"Someone stays with the car always. If it hasn't been bugged, no reason to give them an opportunity." I tell them. They nod once, and both quickly dash inside, leaving me to pump the gas. I'm just inserting the nozzle when I see them. A charcoal gray GMC Denali pulls smoothly into the gas station, a low bass pulsing out of it. I make careful notes of them, committing the plate to memory, while being as sneaky as I can. I count six men, all close to our age, except for one who looks like he's in his mid 30's at least; their leader I'd bet. Elpis returns to take my spot.

"GMC. Six men. No visible weapons." I murmur as I pass her.

"Got 'em," she whispers back.

I hurry inside to go to the bathroom and pass Kore, who's buying a cheap handle of vodka. I blanch and say a quick prayer to Athena we won't need it. I try to be as quick as possible, the GMC was getting gas too and their tank is bigger than ours. If we can get back on the road and out of their sight before they've finished that can help us figure out if there's a tracker or not.

The others are in the car waiting for me when I return,

Kore driving, Elpis in the back looking through her medic bags. I quickly slide in the passenger seat and see one of the men making motions to the others to hurry up. We pull smoothly out of the gas station as they start to rush around. The cemetery we're heading to is already in the GPS system, so now it's just time for the longest fifteen minute drive of my life. I put on my armor in the car, feeling better once it's on, and then help Kore with hers as she drives. I feel my pulse start to thrum and my leg won't stop bouncing. The nerves in my stomach flutter and kick around. One look at Kore, whose lips are pressed so tightly together they look white, tells me she's feeling the same way. I'm dimly aware of Elpis wiggling around all over the backseat but assume she's looking over her medic bags still, so I pay little mind at first. But then she keeps making noise and looking all over. It's when she kneels on the seat to look over into the trunk area that I say something.

"El, what are you *doing*?" She's frowning a little, as she turns back to us.

"Do you think there's a crowbar in here?" she asks.

Kore slams her palm on the steering wheel and whips around to glare at Elpis.

"What is it with you and crowbars?" She demands. "A crowbar will not solve all of your problems!"

"Yes it will!" Elpis says adamantly. Kore groans in aggravation and twists to face the road again. "I have a problem," Elpis makes an exaggerated frustrated face, putting her fists on her hips, "I give it a couple of whacks," she mimes hitting something, presumably, with a crowbar— "and then: *boom*." She throws her hands up, smiling. "No more problem."

"You are a *healer*," I admonish.

"Yeah," she agrees. "A healer with a crowbar." She looks

97

around again, a frown on her face. "Or a healer in need of a crowbar... do we seriously not have one in here?"

"I am *not* answering you." I tell her as I too, turn back to the front, folding my arms firmly over my chest. "And put your armor on."

"All right, be that way." She says coolly, but obediently begins pulling on her armor. "But I don't want to hear any whining when we're in the middle of this fight and one of you is getting your ass kicked and you're like 'Ah, Elpis help! Elpis! Your crowbar!' cause I won't have one." I pinch the bridge of my nose, heaving a sigh. Kore shakes her head in disappointment.

"A highly trained warrior of Athena," I say in disbelief, refusing to look at her. "And you want to go into battle with a crowbar."

"Oh hell *yes* I do," Elpis says enthusiastically, miming swinging her crowbar again. "How sick would that be!"

"I am not answering you," I mutter petulantly.

10

Chapter 10

We pull into the drive of the old, forgotten cemetery in silence. The rusted iron gate tells us this cemetery belongs to a Methodist church. We've settled into a familiar and easy silence, now that there's a job at hand, a job we have trained to do for years.

Kore pulls the car off into the shade of some trees, where it will be easier for her to cloak it. We step out under the cover of clouds. I glance at the sky and say a prayer that it does not rain.

"Ugh I hate cemetery's," I grimace, looking around. Elpis and Kore both nod, looking around with the same distaste as me.

"So weird to think about your body rotting underground," Elpis says, shuddering.

"Oh yeah, chuck me on a pyre and be done with it." Kore agrees, nodding. Then she rolls her shoulder and cracks her knuckles. "Want me to cloak this bitch?" I smirk and motion for her to do her worst, then I cross my arms over my chest and settle in to watch the show. Taken in as a child and trained under Hekate for several years, Kore is the best Initiate at wielding magic. Her ability to manipulate the Mist and other forces is beyond anything else I have ever seen, short of the magic goddess herself. Her coming to the conclave to train was in payment of a favor that Hekate owed Athena.

Kore holds her hands out, palms to the sky, eyes closed in concentration, and begins to mutter a spell so old I fear it may raise the dead that lie around us. A dialect of Ancient Greek so forgotten I'm not sure if any historians today even know of its existence. Continuing her muttering Kore brings her hands up and cups them around her mouth, speaking fast and harsh into them. A dim smokey gray light glows so faintly from between her fingers. Then she opens her hands and blows harshly against the gray. It spreads out from her hands and flies towards the car; coating and clinging to it. Blending it in perfectly to the trees and shadows around it.

I nod, impressed, giving her a brief round of applause. Elpis gives a couple whoops of excitement before we freeze, hearing tires on the gravel road around us. Immediately we melt in our surroundings, I kneel behind a particularly overgrown bush and see Kore and Elpis find large trees to place themselves behind.

Sure enough, a car large enough to be the Denali we saw, pulls into the drive, so slow it's basically crawling. It hesitates for a moment before parking right at the gate.

"You fucking idiot," a booming voice swears.

"Keep your voice down, Eddie! They could be around here somewhere."

"Of course they're not! According to the tracker their car should be about 200 feet in front of us, do any of *you* numb nuts see a car 200 feet in front of us?"

Ah. So we are being tracked. Well, that's helpful to know. So nice of them to announce it like that for us. Men. I swear.

"They probably found the tracker and ditched it here, now we have no way of knowing which way they're going." Another voice chimes in. The one that told Eddie to be quiet speaks up again.

"Listen, we know there's a safe house way up north somewhere in Washington. I say we make our way to the general vicinity of where we were told it might be and wait. We'll see them sooner or later." Mutters of agreement go up, until finally the booming voice agrees.

"I think I'll use that snake bitch's head as centerpiece on my table," a new voice says thoughtfully while the others laugh and joke about taking turns displaying our Lady Medusa's head in their homes.

Any hope I might have had of avoiding a fight here is gone. They know too much and are too motivated. They will die here today.

One is walking towards the bush I'm kneeling behind, scanning the area. Every muscle in my body tenses as I focus all of my energy on listening to the footsteps that come closer and closer to me. I hook a finger around one of my bracelets and wait.

"Hey, Zach, c'mon man, let's get back on the road." A voice calls, near the front gate.

"Don't you guys think we should at least search the area fir—" He comes around to look behind the plant I currently hide behind.

And gets my spear lodged in his eye socket for his trouble. His words cut off in a scream, which turns guttural as I rip my spear back out. His screams cut out as I attack again, this time burying my spear in his throat. I rip out my spear again and he's dead before he hits the ground.

"You snake-loving *bitch!*" I turn just in time to block the blow aiming for my neck but the man manages to twist his arm in a way that gives him open access to my leg. Now it's my turn to scream as his knife slices my thigh. White hot pain sears up my leg and immediately hot blood begins to flow. I'm cut bad, I can tell without even looking at it.

"COWARD!" Kore roars, jumping in to begin the battle with the man who was brave enough to attack me from behind. Elpis holds one of the men in a headlock, using him as a shield in front of her as his bullet proof vest guards her from the rounds fired off by his comrades. The moment they stop to reload, his neck is snapped and her spear is off and buried in the neck of one of the men. Mine follows quickly, taking out the other shooter. Everything is quiet when all of a sudden an engine revs and gravel begins to kick up.

The older man we saw at the gas station. He's making a run for it. Kore gives a mighty battle cry and launches her spear, lodging it in the grill of the car. An impressive amount of smoke begins to immediately spill out of it. The engine begins to stall and fight to turn over as he tries to turn it back on over and over.

We sprint over, Elpis throws one of her spears through the windshield, which she then rips out, along with the entire windshield, as she leaps onto the hood of the car. Kore follows quickly behind her, dropping to a knee as she levels her own spear at the man's head. I rip open the door and am met immediately with a pistol leveled at my gut. The man does not hesitate to pull the trigger. I don't even have time to look shocked.

Immediately the lock action opens and I realize a half second before him that he's defenseless. That half second is all I need to bury my fist in his face and crunch his nose beneath it.

"Ah, you bitch!" He cries out thickly, covering his nose, from which an impressive amount of blood is already beginning to flow.

"Find a new insult, fucker." I growl as I rip him from the car. "'Bitch' is not the insult you idiots seem to think it is."

The moment he's out of the car he begins to try and fight us. It's almost pathetic how weak of a fight it is. The three of us have him slammed up against the hood of his car as we wrestle his arms behind him. The smoke still pouring out has us coughing and makes it hard to see at times, depending on how the wind is blowing, but it stops neither him nor us as we battle for control. He tries to kick back at us, step on our feet and such. For his valiant efforts, Kore buries her spear in one of his feet, pinning it to the ground. His swearing becomes intermixed with screams but he does stop trying to kick us. We use that moment of distraction to clamp his arms behind him, as Elpis quickly shoves his hands through a pair of zip tie hand cuffs. Kore pulls out her spear, which prompts more swearing, before Elpis and I haul him away from the car.

Kore uncloaks our car as we throw the man down on the ground beside it.

"If you think you're going to get anything out of me, you snake-loving bitches are wrong." His voice is thin and grates on my nerves immediately.

"Get. New. Insults. You limp-dick, scrotum-breathed, waste of space," I groan as I lean against the front of our car. Now breathless with the pain that my adrenaline previously masked from me. My leg feels wet and sticky from the amount

103

of blood that coats it. All Initiates have accelerated healing but that doesn't mean we don't feel the pain in full force before the healing happens.

My hand trembles as I probe around the wound. It's deep and blood pours freely from it. I've been injured before of course, but never to this severity and never on a mission so crucial. I curse at myself in my head, I can't believe I was so stupid to get injured in such a moronic way. I should have known he'd have a buddy with him.

"Get those pants off, Ris." Elpis orders, as she rushes around to get her med packs from the back. I grit my teeth as I undo my belt and steel myself. I take a ragged breath and pull my pants past my wound as fast as I can, biting the inside of my cheek to keep from groaning.

"Sorry, Ris." Kore tells me as she sidles up next to me. She grabs a hold of one of my hands. Before I can ask her what she's talking about, she dumps half of the cheap Vodka I had seen her buying, on to my leg.

"Ohh fuck you! Fuck you, Kore." I swear, clutching her hand, as fire races down my leg. She pours more down, unapologetic. Every single muscle in my body is clenched as tightly as they can be; I force myself to relax each part, one at a time.

"I know gorgeous, I know. But who knows what those dirty fuckers have got on their weapons and you are *not* allowed to die before me." I give a breathless laugh at that, my head tipped back as I focus on my breathing and not being a baby anymore.

"You will all die, nameless and forgotten." The man's thin voice calls out.

"Shut *up*," Kore tells him, turning and aiming a kick at his stomach. Ugh. Even his coughing is annoying.

"Kore, get her pants all the way off. Ris, deep breaths. This is going to suck... like a lot." Elpis's voice, usually halfway to a laugh, is as serious as I've ever heard it. She's in her domain now. She's in charge and she will not let us down. I feel a surge of pride run through my chest. I grip the still warm metal of the hood under my hands and burying my face in the top of my shoulder as Kore quickly works my boots off, followed by my pants.

"Athena guide my hands," Elpis prays as she preps her tools, kneeling in front of me. "May they be steady and light as I heal those who have been harmed. As I heal those who have been called to your service. May those at my hand forgive me for the pain I must cause, to heal their pain. Athena guide my hands."

Elpis wipes the blood off my leg, then disinfects it properly, leaving it a stained orange color while Kore trains her spear on the man. Protecting us while we're vulnerable. Thankfully, he keeps his mouth shut, maybe he's curious as to how we do things. Maybe he's getting sick of being hit. Anyone's guess really.

Elpis swears under her breath in Ancient Greek.

"This thing is deep. I'm going to have to do a couple layers of stitches here, Ris."

"Do what you need, El." I gasp out through gritted teeth, my knuckles white on the hood.

No anesthetics for me as Elpis's needle digs repeatedly into my wound and my flesh, stitching it shut.

Time passes slowly as, stitch after stitch, Elpis makes my leg whole again. I keep my lips pressed tight together and meshed into my shoulder. After a while the pain becomes much easier to ignore and I'm able to keep my breathing quiet and mostly even.

Finally, *finally*, Elpis swipes some antibacterial ointment on it and wraps it in clean white cloth before handing me a new pair of pants.

"I'd tell you to stay off it and not irritate the stitches but, ya know." She jokes, standing. I grin back at her, now bending over stiffly to put my boots back on.

"Yeah something tells me that'll be hard to do, El." I test my weight out on my leg. "Good work, feels right as rain." I tell her, slapping her on the shoulder as she passes me.

"All right, you," I groan lightly as I kneel down on my good leg in front of the man, stretching my bad one out to the side. "Who sold you the information about our Lady Medusa?"

He, predictably, spits in my face.

I, predictably, punch him in the windpipe.

"Thanks." I mutter as Elpis passes me a towel that she has in her med kit, in case she has a need for a makeshift tourniquet. I sit and wait for a moment for his gagging and coughing to let up. He takes a rasping breath and grins at me, apparently changing tactics for how to best intimidate us.

"You know," he drawls arrogantly, "you will never catch all of us. There are so many more of us than you that if we were to invade your precious training space right now, we would slaughter you all." I fight the urge to smile, especially as I hear Kore and Elpis quietly groan behind me, knowing my love for history and one liners better than anyone else. I cock my head to the side.

"Sorry, what?" I ask, playing dumb.

"If we invade your previous little conclave you will all die!" He bellows, laughing manically.

"*If.*" I tell him calmly. He has only a moment to look confused before I bury my knife under his jaw.

"Shut up," Kore says, already stalking away from me.

"I *never* get to use that one!" I say delightedly as I stand carefully. The towel that once cleaned the man's spit from my face now cleans his blood from my knife. "I feel like a bad ass Spartan."

Kore opens her mouth to retaliate but I'm spared from hearing whatever scathing remark she has in store for me when Elpis cries out, "Guys! They have a crowbar in here!" She comes running around the trunk of the Denali, which she had apparently been scavenging, waving her war prize in the air, grinning like a jackass.

"Oh for *fucks sake.*" I say.

"I can't." Kore waves her wand over her shoulder as she crawls into the backseat of the car, to start the interior search for the tracking device.

"Woo hoo hoo," she crows as she skips to a stop in front of me. "Check me out, bitches." She swings the crowbar back and forth as though it's a sword before moving on to mime as though she's going to hit me.

"Oh yeah!" She says, suddenly halting her fierce assault on me. She holds her hand out, in her palm sit three red pills. "Take these, they'll help with inflammation. You'll already heal faster than normal, being an Initiate and all that jazz, but these will just make it that much easier." I nod to her and take the pills from her.

"Thanks. Now are you done," I motion to the car, "so we can get back to our mission?"

"Oh, yeah sure." She says easily and goes, with a bounce in her step, to begin the exterior search of the car. But first she carefully and lovingly sets her newly acquired crowbar in the back of the car. I shake my head as I watch her get started before casting my gaze around the graveyard; which is now littered with more bodies than we had found it with.

I sigh to myself as I go to the car and slowly lower myself to the ground and wiggle my way under the car. It's a slow and tedious process, searching a car. Car search training was one of my least favorite categories. The Instructors seemed to know the best places to hide stuff. I once spent six whole hours searching a pickup for a tracking device smaller than the size of my thumb nail. It took days for my body to quit aching from how contorted I had been while looking in every nook and cranny.

Kore wasn't lying. These new cars just have so many nooks and crannies that stuff can get stuffed and hidden in. Slowly but surely, I reverse army crawl under the car, shining my pocket flashlight all over the place. I grit in my teeth as my movement pulls on my fresh stitches. So much for taking it easy. We have a small metal detector we could use but most detectors nowadays aren't made from real metal so it'd be a wasted effort. I'm swearing under my breath in a near constant stream as we look, both from impatience and the pain of my leg. Periodically I glance at the watch on my wrist. We're spending too much time here, we need to get back on the road but we can't until we find this damn bug. *This is the fucking worst.* I think to myself over and over again.

"Got one," I call out after too long of searching. I unsheathe my knife from my hip and use it to pry the device off. I turn it over in my fingers a few times as though it will reveal some of its secrets to me.

"I got one too," Elpis calls, kneeling behind the trunk, her hand reached under the tailgate. She pulls her off and I watch her boots make their way over to me. "Come out, come out wherever you are, Rissy." She croons, grabbing my ankles and pulling me from under the car. I can't help but give a snort of laughter as I'm pulled back under the sky.

"None inside," Kore reports hopping out of the front as Elpis hauls me up to my feet.

I nod once, heaving a sigh, and check my watch and then glance at the cloudy sky, then roll my eyes at myself for checking the cloudy sky since it has no distinguishable time telling features. Elpis and I set our respective devices on the top of one of the bigger headstones, then bring the butts of our knives down on them, hard. It takes a couple good whacks to alleviate my anxiety that they are completely destroyed but eventually they lay in pieces on the old stone.

"We've been here way too long," I tell them. "We've done what we can for now. It's time to get back on the road. And from now on, one of us is always with the car, we don't have time for this shit to keep happening." Like the highly trained soldiers they are, they nod and jump to obey. Immediately packing away what little we still have left out before hopping into the car. Elpis takes her turn stretched out in the back while Kore gets herself settled in the passenger seat. I give a huff of pain as I slide into the drivers seat and adjust myself as comfortably as I can get.

I take care to avoid the newly added bodies as we pull out of the cemetery.

11

Chapter 11

The wind whips my hair around my face as I walk back to the car. Kore kneels beside a gas pump, filling two newly acquired gas cans while Elpis fills the car. Time seems to be standing still, even though the wind will not stop howling. They glance up at me as I approach, nodding. I nod back, but say nothing.

Now is not the time for words.

Somewhere, about an hour into the forests of the North Cascade National Park, is the answer we have been waiting for. We spent the seven hours up here debating back and forth between calling Antiope and the rest and giving an update. Eventually we decided against it, we still have not gotten an update from Rose and we don't want to risk our phone being intercepted or something. We texted Sierra, simply saying "still alive", but that has been the only additional communication we've had since calling Rose the day before.

Elpis drives, Kore rides shotgun, I take the back. Not for long though. As soon as we're safely hidden from the public eye by the towering and plentiful trees, I roll down the window and make my way to the roof, taking a knee on top, my spear brandished. Kore sits on the windowsill of the passenger seat, her shield held in a semi defensive position.

The roads in the park are in horrible shape because of the constant rain, which left large potholes in its wake that make the driving slow and tedious. I keep my head on a swivel, constantly pushing myself around in circles, eyeing the green around us.

Nothing. It's almost too quiet.

Finally El stops as a sudden break in the trees appears to our left. Distinct tire impressions that lead up a particularly steep section of hills, so far up you can't see the end of it.

"Why aren't the tire marks cloaked?" Kore whispers almost inaudibly, as El turns carefully onto the road. I can only shake my head in return. There's no reason for the marks to not be cloaked. Every Initiate knows a simple cloaking spell. Hell, even I, with my rudimentary magic skills, could cloak the marks without second thought. If these tire marks are not cloaked then that means the Protector that cast the spell is dead or too wounded to maintain it. There are iron weights in my stomach, my fingertips are tingling with the adrenaline that pulses through me.

Too soon, I can tell we're approaching the cabin. The trees begin to thin slightly, allowing a little more natural light to penetrate, and there are more signs of human, or near human, habitation. A pile of logs that have been chopped for a fireplace. Clothes hanging on a clothesline swing in the light breeze.

Built in a natural clearing of the trees, there is an old, traditional log cabin. Two stories high, with four rocking chairs around a table on the porch. Wind chimes tinkle softly in the breeze from where they hang. The window and door frames are painted a soft mauve color, and a matching welcome rug sits in front of the front door.

The open front door.

The open front door where the bottom half of a body lies. I leap off the top of the car before Elpis has even come to a stop, with Kore not far behind me. I hear her boots crunch hard and fast on the gravel of the driveway. As I approach I can see that the body, wearing the traditional uniform of an Initiate, is face down. I can smell blood on the air. The woman has dark red hair and for one wild and horrible moment I think it is Desma. Before I realize—

"Melenthe!" I gasp, casting my spear aside as I kneel next to her still body. She is cold and stiff under my hands.

So much blood. There is so much blood around her.

It matches her hair, I think wildly.

My fingers flutter around the back of her head where she has a blunt force injury, which is also caked with dried blood. "Melenthe." I repeat again. I know I will not get an answer, but I can't stop myself from calling for her. I can hear Elpis running up to join us. I grab Melenthe's shoulders and roll her over, and immediately clap my hand over my mouth to keep from screaming. Her green eyes are wide and stare me down, her mouth slightly open, as though in shock. But this is not what has me threatening to throw up my breakfast. No. The horrific gash across her throat is what churns my stomach. So deep I swear I can see part of her spinal cord.

"Oh my gods," Kore murmurs. Elpis opens her mouth to say something when a board creaks from somewhere in the cabin. We all go still. I silently pick my weapons back up.

Communicating using only sign language, we begin to search the cabin, room by room. Evidence of a fight is everywhere. Curtains in front of broken windows blow freely in the breeze. We take extra care not to crunch the glass under our feet. Tables are turned over with legs broken off— possibly used as makeshift weapons. Two bedrooms, a bathroom and an office with the communication center set up in it, occupy the ground floor.

I stare at the comm center, like it's something you'd see in a sci-fi movie— fantastical and hard to believe. But that is not what makes it so hard to look away. No, the bloodbath inside is what captures my attention; a bloody hand print that covers the panic button and smears off onto the floor is what has tears burning the back of my eyes. Someone sacrificed themselves to set off the distress signal and it cost them their life.

I force myself to turn away.

We all keep our shields up and ready as we approach the stairs, my spear held tight in my hand. I lead the way, Kore brings up the rear. Elpis, as our healer, is always in the middle of any formation, so she can be best protected. Slowly, we begin to make our way up the stairs, managing to avoid any creaky stairs.

As we near the top of the stairs, I brace myself against one of the walls and peak around, down the short hallway. To the left side, there's nothing but another broken window and an overturned chair. To the right...the fractured stone body of a man. I step into the hallway, facing the remains and direct Kore and Elpis to search the remaining rooms.

The man's right arm is broken off from his body and a large fracture runs across his face. Slowly I begin to inspect around him and freeze when I see the material of something I am sure belongs to a hijab. I know from my mother and lessons that Lady Medusa wears a hijab to cover her snakes. The others

113

finish searching the other rooms and are motioning to me that they're all clear when they see the look on my face. I tighten my grip on my spear. I ground my teeth in frustration. We don't know enough about the emergency procedures the Protectors had in place, the code words and meet-up spots they undoubtedly had. We're at a complete disadvantage here and there's a good chance we've just walked right into a trap that will claim our lives. I exhale slowly through my nose, trying to force the uncertainty out with it. I have no other choice. No other good one anyway.

"Lady Medusa," I call as calmly and clearly as I can, talking into the air since I have no real way of knowing where she is hidden. "My name is Aristomache Kallis, daughter of Atalanta Kallis. I am an Initiate of Athena's conclave and I was sent her along with my two sisters-in-arms, Elpis Laskaris and Kore Drivas, to recover you and bring you to the conclave for safety."

We wait, heartbeats in our throats, before, suddenly, there is a click of a lock directly next to me, where I stand next to the man. A door, hidden so seamlessly in the wall I never would have found it, opens a millimeter. Our spears are raised and leveled at that infinitesimal gap in an instant.

"Don't look," comes a terrified whisper. "I'm not covered." I grind my teeth again. It goes against my every instinct but I close my eyes, trusting my other senses and instincts to protect us. "Are they gone?"

"For now, My Lady, but we must expect more to come," I respond tensely. Light, quick footsteps step around me and past Kore and Elpis, running into the room closest to the broken window.

"Okay," comes the almost inaudible whisper. "I'm covered." I open my eyes and barely manage to keep the shock off my face. I knew the truth of Lady Medusa but it is not something you can be fully prepared for. Standing before me is not the seductive and alluring body of a woman out to scorn her Mistress. No. Before me stands a girl, no more than fifteen. Slight with dark brown skin and a habit of biting her lip when she's nervous. A mauve colored hijab, her favorite color I'm guessing, is now wrapped securely around her head. Her electric blue eyes study me just as closely as I study her.

"You look just like your mother." Her whisper is almost inaudible but it still causes my heart to squeeze in a painful way, but I manage a smile. She turns to greet and address Kore and El, I turn to her panic room.

I open the door all the way and am greeted with a bright and blinding light. The entire room, about 10-feet all the way around, is covered with mirrors and a single light bulb at the top of the ceiling. The ultimate defense for Medusa.

"What happened with him?" I ask her, motioning to the man on the ground. She bites her lip again.

"He chased me up the stairs. Atalanta screamed at me to run," tears fall fast and unyielding from her eyes. "But she could only help so much, she was battling two men by herself. Melenthe was long dead and I don't know what happened to Julia, she was out in the yard fighting the last I saw her. He got his foot in my panic room door before I could close it and started to pull me out. I just panicked I didn't know what to do. He was grabbing at me and then he grabbed my hijab and I just reacted and helped him pull it off and I just... looked at him." Now she gets very quiet. "It's been a long time since I've had to kill a man. He broke when I pushed him over to close my panic room door."

"My Lady, how long ago was my mother here?" I ask quietly.

"This happened yesterday... so sometime around then. I'm not sure what happened to her. I'm sorry. This is all my fault." She sobs. All three of us move in to comfort her. Murmuring reassuring things and rubbing her back.

I can't help but glance around nervously, Kore and Elpis mirroring my behavior. We need to get out of here.

"My Lady," I murmur, taking her hands in mine. "You are not at fault for this but we *must* get moving. It's not safe and we need our other sisters to help us." She nods in understanding and begins to wipe her eyes. "All right. Atta girl. Let's get out of here. You have a go bag? Good. Grab it." She darts back into her room and returns not even a second later with a black duffle bag ready to go.

I summon my spear and shield again and lead us back down the stairs. No new disturbances. We move quickly to the front door. As much as it pains me we cannot stop to burn Melenthe, it would take far too long. I kneel and place two gold drachmas on her eyes and murmur a prayer of rest and rites over her but that is all we can do.

"Oh Melenthe," Medusa sobs quietly. Elpis wraps an arm around her shoulders and gently, but firmly, guides her out of the cabin.

"My Lady, lay on the floorboards in the back. We will lay our shields over you." Kore instructs her. Medusa hastens to obey. I ball up a blanket for her to lay under her head before laying my shield over her and reclaiming my spot on the roof of the car. Kore quickly follows suit, now kneeling beside me. We kneel hip to hip, facing opposite directions, covering each others backs, while Elpis drives faster than she should to get us out of here.

"Are you okay?" She asks me quietly.

"No." I answer honestly.

Kore says nothing in return. What can she say? Nothing.

So instead she leans her weight into mine, letting me feel her warmth and strength.

Giving me hers when I'm not sure I have any of my own.

12

Chapter 12

I sit next to Lady Medusa , knife drawn, while El drives and Kore navigates the dark back roads we travel down. The sun has long set and we have not even managed to leave Washington yet because of how slowly and carefully we had to drive when leaving the safe house. We knew the area would be on high alert with our descriptions and couldn't risk drawing any attention to ourselves.

Lady Medusa proves to be a girl of formidable resolve. She now sits quietly and tearless beside me, staring out the dark window of the car. She does not fidget or squirm, does not ask where we are going or how long it will take. I want to ask a million questions but she does not ask me any, so who am I to initiate the questioning? Instead, I use my knife to tap out an anxious beat on my thigh.

Finally she speaks, "What will happen to the traitor?" I glance at her out of the corner of my eye. We had long since filled her in on the happenings that occurred to force her to flee her home.

"The bloodless crucifixion, My Lady." I answer. She nods

thoughtfully and does not speak again.

"We need to call in," Kore tells me after a few more minutes of silence. I sigh heavily.

"I know," I use my free hand to rub at my eyes, my knife beats more insistently on my leg. "I know. The next time we stop I will."

"Well you better start practicing your speech because the next motel I see we're stopping at. We all need to shower, El needs to check your leg and they won't expect us too. It'll throw them off."

I can't argue with her logic and just nod my understanding of the plan.

Twenty minutes later we pull into the parking lot of a decent looking Motel 8, which is not saying much since the standards for a Motel 8 are already exceptionally low. El goes to get us a room while Kore and I stand guard. She's back out in mere minutes, our key card in hand.

We all grab our bags, Kore carries Lady Medusa's, and all but sprint to the room, my hand wrapped tightly around Lady Medusa's bicep, eager to be out of the public sight. I help the others sweep the room before excusing myself and step back outside.

I spend the next few minutes psyching myself up and forcing deep breaths in and out. I pull out my phone and dial.

"Aris. Where are you guys?" Antiope's voice is full of relief.

"Antiope, we found Lady Medusa. She's in our protective custody. We're bringing her home. We've stopped to rest somewhere along the Oregon/Idaho state line." Antiope gives a breathless laugh at that, sounding as though she may be fighting tears. Now that I'm talking I can't stop. I don't want to ruin that feeling of momentary peace she is feeling but if I

119

don't get these words out I fear I may choke on them.

"Melenthe is dead." The breathing cuts off suddenly on the other end of the line. "Probably my mother and Julia as well, though we couldn't find their bodies and we did not have time to search the surrounding forest." I thought I would cry, when giving this report. But it actually feels as though someone has carved my heart out of my chest and replaced it with a cold, hard stone.

"Aris— Aris, I am so—" All of a sudden I can't bear to listen to her apologies. Especially when I think about her history with my family.

"Have you gotten any closer to figuring out who the traitor is?" I cut in, my voice somewhat harsh. A frustrated sigh answers me. Whether it is with my interrupting or the situation is anyone's guess.

"We have a few ideas but nothing concrete and sure as Hades nothing concrete enough to punish for." Now it's my turn to sigh in frustration. "Get her back here. Get yourselves back here. We'll regroup and go from there. That's all we can do."

I nod even though she can't see it.

"Yeah, all right, Antiope. We're moving as fast as we can."

"I know you guys are. Just come home to us." Then the line goes dead. I sigh and let my head tip back to the stars. Forcing slow and deep breaths in and out of my body. I stare at the moon and find my mind oddly blank. All I seem to be able to think about is getting back to the conclave. It's as though there is no room in my head for grief right now.

Or maybe Athena knows once that dam breaks not even Poseidon would be able to hold back the tide and keep me from drowning in it. I take care to wipe my face blank and head back inside.

El is just exiting the bathroom as I enter, towel drying her white blonde hair. All three women look up expectantly when I walk in.

"No news. They're narrowing it down but still no solid evidence for who the traitor is." I tell them, my voice flat. Kore and Elpis swear, Lady Medusa bites her lip. The frustration sits on the air for a moment before Elpis claps her hands together and instructs me, yet again, to strip my pants off. Normally I would roll my eyes at her for being annoying about it but I can't seem to find the energy to fight with her.

Kore hops in the shower while I take off my pants and lean against the television stand. Lady Medusa eyes us keenly as Elpis begins to unwrap my bandages.

"You were injured?" When she's not whispering her voice is melodic and soothing. All of a sudden it strikes me what a wonderful Priestess she would have been. Her prayers and intonations would have been magic to listen to.

"Yes, but it's just a scratch. I'm All right." I reassure her. She raises her eyebrows as she studies the thick stitches that hold my wound together. All Initiates have accelerated healing so the wound is half-healed and a puckered and tired looking red.

"Yeah," she drawls. "You look right as rain." I give a laugh at that.

"It looks worse than it is and, as I'm sure you know, I should be mostly healed by morning."

Elpis's well practiced hands probe at my wound without irritating it. Satisfied with what she sees, she tells me she'll rewrap it after I shower. I nod and go to trade places with Kore.

The water, while not as warm, still feels amazing on my muscles. I've been cooped up in the car too long, I feel as though I have a permanent hunch back. I take care when cleaning around my leg but feel confident in my estimation of my healing time. Not for the first time I thank Athena for giving us this blessing. I couldn't imagine having to complete this mission with one of my legs all but out of commission.

I finally get out of the shower, but hustle to get dried and dressed, desperate to avoid catching my reflection in the mirror. I couldn't say why, but the idea of looking at myself right now puts knots of lead in my stomach.

Out in the main room Kore and Lady Medusa are already curled up and fast asleep on the bed furthest from the door. Kore, who sleeps next to the night stand, has her hand wrapped around the handle of her knife. Elpis motions me over silently. I stand before her and stare hard at nothing in particular while she swipes antibacterial ointment across my stitches. I don't think I've ever been this drained and exhausted in my entire life. I feel like I could sleep for a lifetime.

El lightly smacks the side of my leg a couple of times after she's rewrapped it, calling me back to reality.

Should we take turns staying up? Keeping watch? Elpis's fingers fill the silence that stretches on. I groan quietly under my breath as I stretch.

Probably, I admit, signing back. *But to be honest I don't know if either of us could stay awake long enough, or well enough, to actually provide adequate protection.* Even as I sign this to her, I can see her eyes struggling to stay open and I know mine must look the same. *We're all light enough sleepers. That'll have to be enough. None of us have actually slept more than a few hours in too long. Might as well get what we can, while we can.*

Love that plan, oh captain, my captain. Elpis responds before turning to crawl into bed. I sigh heavily as I crawl over her, taking the spot closest to the door, and wiggle under the covers. Following Kore's lead El and I both unsheathe our knives and hold them tight in our hands as we drift off to sleep.

* * *

Why am I awake? I ask myself as my eyes snap open again, my hand automatically tightening its grip on the handle of my knife. The exhaustion in my mind and my body makes it obvious something woke me up. I lift my head from where my chin is tucked against my chest and look out the window. Nothing. Something shifts against my back and feel my pulse trip for a moment before I realize it's just Elpis. She has a habit of fusing into whoever she sleeps next to. I can feel the warm spot on my neck that she has been exhaling onto for however long.

I slowly scan my eyes across the room and freeze as I see a figure sitting in the desk chair. But relax just as suddenly as I realize who it is. I slip silently out of bed, knife still in hand, and walk on careful feet across the room.

"My Lady?" I whisper. She starts slightly, her back to me. I hear a quiet sniffle as she tries, in vain, to discreetly wipe the tears from her eyes.

"I'm sorry," her voice is thick with her sorrow and her tears. "I didn't want to wake Kore so I got up." I shake my head even though she can't see me and move to sit in front of her.

"No need for apologies, My Lady. Are you All right?" She claps a hand to her mouth, fighting to keep her sobs silent. Fresh tears pour from her eyes and into her lap. I can hear the quiet hiss of agitated snakes and fight the shiver that electrifies my spine.

"They're all dead," she whimpers. "And it's all my fault." I press up to my knees and clasp her hands in mine.

"No," I murmur soothingly. "No, this is not your fault, My Lady. The traitor who betrayed their Goddess and their sisters is to blame. Protecting you is our lives. Our cause. Every one of us would pray to Athena as girls. Pray that she would find us worthy of protecting you. To die in service of Athena, as chosen Protectors for her most beloved Priestess?" I shake her hands slightly, urging her electric blue eyes to meet mine. "There is no greater honor." Her eyes hold mine for another moment more before they squeeze tightly shut again, tears racing down her face. She takes a ragged breath and wipes her face. Then she smiles tremulously at me. The hiss of snakes sounds almost comforting now.

"You'll have to forgive me. But you do remind me so much of your mother." The stone in my chest feels colder still, but I force a smile to my lips.

"You honor me, My Lady. I can only hope to be half the woman my mother was." Was. Ice floods my veins as I register that word. How easily I refer to her in past tense. As though I truly have accepted the loss of my mother. Which, I guess I have. Lady Medusa doesn't seem to notice my inner qualm.

"I think you can rest easy, knowing you have achieved that. I see your mother in you, in many of your words and your actions. You are truly your mothers daughter."

Fire burns my throat, but I force another smile to my lips.

"You honor me," I repeat, before shaking her hands once more. "Let's get you back to bed. Long day of driving for us tomorrow." She smiles gratefully at me, wiping the remnants of her tears off her face, as I escort her to her bed, pulling back her covers. She crawls in, looking her age in that moment, and allows me to place the blankets back over her. "Sweet dreams, My Lady."

She smiles up at me, already drifting back to sleep.

I walk slowly back over to my bed, as though in a daze. I scrub my hands over my face harshly for several moments. It feels as though the stone is spreading and is locking my muscles into place. Vaguely, I wonder if I will ever be able to smile without forcing it again.

I sit on the edge of the bed, my elbows braced on my knees, hands clasped in front of me, and stare at the floor.

I never truly thought I would live in a world without my mother. But I must now accept that fact. For it must be just that. A fact.

What am I going to tell Alena? I think desolately. I quickly shove that thought away. I cannot think about those things now, I have a job to do. I rub my hands over my face, twisting my neck this way and that to crack it, telling myself to get back to sleep.

Instead I press my thumbs into the corners of my eyes and focus on my breathing. The urge to cry swells up like a wave inside of me. But I don't have the luxury of tears. No. I hold other peoples tears, giving them the space to break down. No one gives me that same space, no one thinks I need it, I guess. No one accept Deimos. I force another steadying breath in and out of my lungs. I remember a cartoon I saw as a child. There's one episode where the character knows only "fine dining and breathing". I feel like that's me, but all I know is fighting and breathing. I sit back suddenly, taking a deep breath, as though to remind myself that I do, in fact, still know how to breathe properly. I sigh to myself once more as I swing my legs into bed.

I'm just getting comfortable when Elpis slides up to me again. I've never minded that she does this and welcome it especially right now. It's like I need the reminder that I'm still alive. That I'm still here and fighting. That I have a job to do and other people to return home to. Because right now I feel like a puppet, having my strings tugged around as I'm pulled through the motions of daily life.

I'm just drifting back to sleep when I feel it. The ground shaking with muted, too heavy steps. My pulse trips for a second time as I watch a shadow pass across the curtains of our window. *Please let me be being dramatic and paranoid,* is a prayer I never thought I'd pray but here I am repeating it so fast that even my thoughts are blurring together. The shadow is simply too big, too *almost* human but also not quite human at all. The shadow seems confused. It shuffles back and forth, I can hear it snuffling at the air. *It's tracking us,* I think.

Fuck. I think next. I keep my eyes on the shadow as it continues to walk back and forth in front of us, but slowly reach my hand back, reaching for Elpis. She gasps quietly as I pinch her side.

"What?" she breathes out. When I don't answer her she slowly lifts her head up to see what I'm looking at. I can feel her quick breathing on my ear. "*Fuck!*" She and I are both up in an instant. I quick throw on my armor while Elpis wakes up Kore and Lady Medusa.

"My lady, I'm sorry," I hear her murmured apologies as I pull out a spear. "We have to move." I hear the quiet shuffling as everyone begins pulling on armor and shoes and getting ready.

"Kore," I whisper. Her dark eyes flash up to mine from

where she is pulling on her shin greaves. She pulls the leather tongs tight and is by my side in a moment. "Take Lady Medusa, take the car. It looks like it's just one of whatever it is. I'll hold it off while you guys get away. Shut up. Listen. I'll hot wire a car and meet you guys when it's safe."

She purses her lips in a way that makes it clear she does not like this plan but it is also clear we do not have time to argue, nor does she have the authority. She rolls her eyes but nods.

"Can we go out the bathroom window?" This is Lady Medusa who has sidled up to our sides at some point. I can't get over how short she is, how eternally young.

"Yes, My Lady," Kore tells her. "And that's exactly what we're going to do."

"Let's go, let's go, let's go," I mutter hurriedly herding everyone in front of me to the bathroom, glancing behind me to the window. The shadow seems to have finally decided that this window is the one it wants to be in as it's now sniffing around the edges of the window and the door.

Kore has the bathroom window open and is ducking under the window frame and dropping to the ground in an instant. I hear the soft thud that tells me she has landed.

"Um," Lady Medusa murmurs, wringing her hands anxiously, her eyes flit from face to face.

"Don't be afraid," Elpis tells her, her voice strong and sure. Together, the two of us help her crawl up onto the windowsill and, each of us clasping a hand, lower her as far as we can. Kore's ready arms down below. Her terrified eyes bore into mine as she dangles in the air.

"Be brave." I tell her as we drop her. A squeak of fear catches in her throat in the split second that she is falling, before she lands safely in Kore's waiting arms. Kore grunts with the effort but other than that, seems unphased by this trick. I grin down at her, the badass. She sets Lady Medusa down, who immediately begins fussing with her hijab, ensuring it's where it's supposed to be.

"Okay," I tell El, who immediately swings herself onto the windowsill. "Make sure—" The sound of breaking glass a roar that shakes the ground cuts me off.

"GO!" I scream, all but shoving Elpis out of the window. She swings down, landing hard. She rolls with a swear as I drop down right behind her.

Elpis almost rips my arm out of socket as she hauls me up from the ground. We fall automatically into protective stance, a semi-circle with Lady Medusa in the center. Our shields locked, spears raised we move on quick and silent feet around the back of the building.

Once we reach the end of the wall, Kore peers her head around the corner before nodding to us. We're almost to our car when a shadow leaps over a different car, standing in front of us, their own spear brandished.

"Hello, ladies," the voice sneers from the shadows.

"Oh my *fucking* gods," Kore and I groan as the shadow steps out under the light of a lamppost. A familiar figure stands, smirking at us. Samuel Jones. Local legend-wannabe. He's picked more than his fair share of fights with conclave members at local bars and clubs. Looking for loose glory laying around for him to lay claim to. He's a demi-god, of which god, I couldn't even say. I know whoever his parent is refuses to acknowledge him because he's done nothing worth acknowledging.

"Ugh, it's you," Elpis murmurs in disgust, her nose wrinkling.

"Sam." I warn, stepping forward with Kore, as one. "This is not like when you talk shit to us at the clubs. We will not just break your nose and leave your ego wounded but your body alive. If you raise your spear to us right now, you will die."

He gives a braying sort of laugh that sets my nerves on edge. Before deliberately stepping into a fighting stance and raising his spear.

"You lot always were so arrogant." He sneers.

"Hope you've got your coins for the ferry man," Kore says simply as we move in.

It's not a long battle. He swings at me first. I duck under easily, swiping at his back. His roar of pain tells me I hit exactly where I aimed.

This idiot doesn't even have armor on. While he's grimacing from my wound, Kore steps in for the kill.

He begins a wet, choking sound as Kore's spear lodges in his throat. He stops as soon as she rips it out, dropping to the ground.

"What a fool," she mutters, toeing his dead body. I don't disagree.

"C'mon," I call, falling back into our protective stance.

We jog the rest of the way to the car. Kore and I quickly check in and around the car, making sure Sam didn't have backup waiting. Predictably, he did not. Didn't want to risk sharing the glory.

"What if it's bugged again?" Elpis asks as Lady Medusa crawls into the back, laying on the floor again. I sigh in frustration, shaking my head.

"We'll have to deal with that when it comes up. Odds are it wasn't and he was doing this alone and called in that thing," I jerk my thumb back to our room, where we can still hear it bellowing, "as back up. He wouldn't want to risk sharing the glory by calling in anyone else."

She nods, satisfied with this explanation and quickly makes her way over to the driver's side. Kore stands half in, half out of the passenger side, spear still drawn.

"Be careful." She says, eyes serious.

I grin back at her. "Who me? C'mon. You know me, 'careful' is my middle name."

She's not amused by my joke.

"I'm serious. Don't be stupid. We need you." Her tone is grave as she continues to stare me down. I feel my own gaze soften. Ever since I was named Captain and I named Kore my second-in-command she's become particularly worried about something happening to me. Says she can't handle the responsibility without me.

"Of course I'll be careful," I assure her. "Look after them. I'll meet up as soon as I can."

She nods before sliding the rest of the way in the car and slamming the door.

"Wait for me to engage before driving off." I tell them, already jogging backwards.

I see their thumbs up of understanding before turning and running full tilt back to the thing that's still destroying our room.

13

Chapter 13

I take the stairs three at a time. Not only do I not want this thing following the others, but I don't want to risk some mortals getting in its way. It will not discriminate in who it kills. I sprint hard along the exterior corridor and skid to a stop as I approach our door. I can hear the thing ransacking the room. I fight back the urge to gag as the smell hits me before the sight does. Rancid and sour, like a rotting carcass that was soaked in vinegar and left in the desert sun for a moon cycle... or seven. Spear brandished, I come around the corner to the main room and swear at what I see.

At least eleven feet tall, wearing only a worn leather loin-cloth, with gray mottled skin and a single eye on his forehead, he's definitely one of the ugliest Cyclops I've ever laid eyes on.

I whistle hard, just once. "You looking for me, you poor, ugly bastard?"

He turns faster than I would have thought possible. His gray eye is full of malice as he trains it on me. His following roar feels as though it may have ruptured my eardrums.

He wastes no time in beginning the battle, swinging one of his large fists at me. I jump forward, managing to flip over his extended arm, land easy on my feet and jab my spear into his armpit.

He roars in pain and swings at me with his large wooden club. And so it goes. Fighting these battles is what I was born to do. I begin an easy dance, twisting around his bumbling limbs, parrying his attacks and answering them with a blow of my own.

Time after time his roar of pain shakes the Earth around me. Time after time I dodge and dive around his club. Until something catches my eye. A person, I'd swear, peering through the open doorway. A human. *Shit*, I think. I turn, without thinking, to look properly. I don't see anyone and when I look back I see I'm about to pay for my lapse of attention. The thing is mid-swing and this time I'm not fast enough to dodge it. He is much faster than I would have given him credit for. Because of this arrogance, he hits me square in the chest, sending me flying into the wall above the beds where we slept.

The drywall buckles under the force of me, scratching up the back of my bare arms. I'm sure plenty is buried in my hair too, judging by the hot blood that begins to flow down my scalp. He's also broken several of my ribs, that much is immediately evident by the pain that blazes through my chest. I bounce of the wall and onto the bed where I land, bouncing slightly on my feet.

"Well that was just plain rude." I tell him, rasping a bit. He roars back at me. Ignoring the searing pain in my sides, I lunge out with my spear. I don't hit him but I manage to make him jump back enough that I can get off the bed.

He's immediately on me again, swinging his deadly club. I take a few steps and dive into a roll under his spread legs, turning quickly and coming up on one knee as I swing my spear, hacking at his Achilles tendon. His following bellow shakes the walls, making picture frames fall to the ground and shatter.

I forgot about he'd still have one good leg, which he promptly lifts and kicks back at me like an irritated horse, sending me flying back and through the hotel door.

My mouth opens in a silent, agonized cry as I'm thrown against the wrought iron fence that surrounds the upper level hotel rooms, my arms caught over the top of it. For a second the pain is so blinding I can't move, and in my panic I'm sure he's paralyzed me. I gasp as my whole body releases as one, leaving me half hanging against the fence. That doesn't last long though as I re-orientate to the situation. With a frenzied gasp, I throw myself over the fence as, with a bull-like roar, he charges at me, club raised.

I land hard on the ground, rolling several times to try and dissipate my weight and movement. I come up on one knee and watch as my opponent rips the iron in half as though it was a twig and stepped off the third story, landing as easily as though he was walking down a flight of stairs.

"Oh, you've got to be shitting me." I swear to myself, breathless. He meanders slowly towards me, confident and arrogant in his victory.

I take a few hard and fast breaths, psyching myself up before I give the mightiest paean—a battle cry— I can manage.

I charge at him, swinging my spear hard and fast, trying to disorient him with the flash of glowing gold in the night sky. Our battle becomes a dance of a kind, he swings at me, kicks at me, roars at me as I twist and turn and jump and parry at him. The scratches and stabs I'm able to hit him with annoy him more than they do wound but they're something. Slowly but surely his blood begins to water the ground around us.

When he lifts one of his massive legs at me for one split second I actually think: *is he about to fart at me?* before he brings his foot down with the force of a dozen bull elephants. The resulting shake is enough to knock me off balance for a moment. Just a moment, but that's all he needs as he swings his club at my open chest again. I go flying through the air and land hard, face down, on the gravel. My spear lays in splinters around me, some of them have buried themselves under my skin. New wounds have appeared on me where it broke, jagged and hazardous, against my body. When I begin to cough I can feel the heat of my blood on my hands, can taste the iron of it on my tongue. My hair, now loose, sticks in odd ways to my face, whether by blood or sweat I can only guess.

I push myself to my hands and knees slowly, too slowly. If he wanted to, he could kill me easily in this moment. I'm so defenseless right now, I couldn't fend off a kitten. But he's gloating, openly laughing as he watches me struggle, enjoying playing with his meal. My breath shudders in and out as I force myself to my feet. I snap off a new bracelet, feeling the reassuring weight of another spear in my hands.

He's still laughing as I charge at him, arms spread wide open as I approach. I level my spear, and then I hit the ground hard, sliding under his legs before jumping up and leaping towards the old pickup parked just behind him.

I put away my spear midair, drawing out my knife instead (a trick that took me months to master). Planting my feet hard against the side of the truck, I push off, soaring towards my opponent, knife in hand. Although he turned in time to see my attack, he's not expecting the change of weapon and is not prepared to defend himself against a knife rather than a spear. Because of this, I soar right through his outstretched arms and sink my blade up to the hilt, into his one and only eye. I drop through his flailing arms and roll as though my life depends on it— which, ironically enough, it does. He wails around, the golden hilt of my knife shines bright in the night, his hands too large to pull it out.

He begins swinging his club around wildly, roaring and reaching out for me in vain. But he's big enough and angry enough that this poses a big enough threat to me. I have to continue our one-sided dance, leaping back and somersault-ing onto the ground to avoid another blow from his club. I'm honestly not sure I could survive another blow.

Finally I see my moment. He swings his club as though it was a baseball bat, as it swings past me I grab a hold of the massive head of it, letting him swing me around. As he pulls me up by his head I release my hold. I hover there for a moment, feeling free in my weightlessness, before I snap off a spear, and bury it where the monsters neck meets his shoulder. With a bellow, he explodes in a puff of dust.

I land hard, coughing before I fall backwards against the truck, waving the dust away from my face. As it clears I brace my hands against my knees, trying to breathe through what remains of my chest. Every breath sears like fire, until it becomes almost excruciating to breathe. I can feel my sides are swollen and I don't need to touch them to know they are tender as well. I brace my spear in the dirt, leaning on it as though it's a walking stick. A small whimper breaks through my lips, which are sticky with the half dried blood that coats

135

them, as I raise my other hand to my side against my better judgment. A pained hiss comes out through my teeth as I feel the heat under my armor and shirt.

I press my lips together as I look back over my shoulder into the cab of the truck I lean against. Then I look back to the pile of dust that was the Cyclops, which is already spreading across the wind. I was never the best at this but I hold my hand out to the pile, close my eyes and concentrate. I feel for the pull of the weight in the pit of stomach, for the string to tighten, reminding from what, exactly, I come from. I'm beginning to regret this almost immediately. I become dizzy and nauseous as I use this power. I groan and focus on that string, which goes up from my stomach, through my body, following my arm and filling my hand with a burning heat. Once I feel that I open my eyes, gasping and straining to maintain my hold.

"έλα σε μένα," I rasp. The dirt pile shifts as my knife comes flying from the rubble back to my palm. I close my eyes, breathing heavily through my nose, my knife clenched in my hand. I rest my head on my hand and feel reassured by the warm metal I hold tightly in my grasp. I reach my free hand around my ribs, as securely as I can, then twist and smash the hilt of my knife into the corner of the driver's side window, shattering it.

Glass tinkles all around me as I reach inside the window and unlock the door. I grit my teeth as I drag myself in, beyond caring about the glass that digs into the back of my thighs. Grunting, I close the door and steel myself for a moment before reaching down and popping off the cover for the wires under the steering column. Bending as low as I can while biting off gasping screams, I pull free and cut the wires I need, twist them back together and am rewarded with the rumble of the old engine underneath me. Sitting back up, I brace my hands against the steering wheel as hard as I can, willing the blinding pain in my ribcage to alleviate.

Finally, accepting that the pain level is as good as it's going to get, I carefully put on my seat belt and put the car into drive. As I'm driving away, I see the mess start to shift and morph itself as the magic that surrounds our world tries to explain to the mortals what happened there. From what I can see of the mess now, it looks like some sort of gas explosion. Humans love blaming things on gas exploding.

One of my hands gropes at a pocket along my calf and unzips it. I pull out my phone and am so relieved that, while the screen is broken, it still works, that I almost crash. Elpis is the first name I see. The ling rings barely twice before her frantic voice fills the other line.

"*Where are you?*" I try not to groan as I hit a pot hole.

"Just pulling out of the motel parking lot. Where are you guys?"

"*Keep going South, once you've driven out of town you'll see County Road TL on your left. Turn down there and keep going for 17 miles. You'll see an old, empty barn on your right. We're in there.*"

I nod to myself as I force myself to remember what she's saying. "All right, I'm on my way. And El?"

"*Yeah, Aris?*"

"Be ready. I'm hurt bad."

Quiet on the other end of the line.

"*I'm always ready, darlin'.*" Comes the response, finally. Then the line goes dead.

I toss my phone to the side as I focus all of my energy and thinking on driving. I can't collapse until I am safe and I won't be safe until I'm with my sisters and I won't be with my sisters unless I can pull my head out of my ass and quit being a baby. I do my best to ignore my rasping breaths that burn like fire through my chest. It's harder to ignore the blood I continually cough up but somehow I manage to do that also.

"Turn left... on County Road TL..." I whisper to myself, a half an hour later, as another coughing fit starts up, blood splattering my hands on the steering wheel. Thank the gods the roads are practically empty because I do not take any care before I make that turn. There could have been a semi coming and I doubt I would have noticed. "Now 17 miles... an old, empty barn... on my right."

It's as though my body knows it will soon be able to rest. It's becoming harder and harder to stay conscious, to stay aware. More and more blood fills my mouth. I begin spitting it out without a thought of where it will land and soon there is a blood-soaked spot on the seat beside me.

When at least I see the barn I almost pull off the road and into a ditch in my haste to be safe with my sisters again, to see them, and Lady Medusa, and be reassured I did not endure this for nothing. But I keep my head, only just, when I see one of the doors open and Kore motioning me in, frantically.

Somehow, I steer the truck in without issue. I barely manage to put the gear into park before my door is ripped open and hands reach for me. Based off of the horrified gasp that Kore gives me, I must look as bad as I feel. Elpis just swears under her breath. They haul me out of the truck, my arms over their shoulders, their arms around my waist. I offer no help as I dangle, limp between the two of them. The pain of their arms around my ribcage puts black spots in my vision and makes me vomit. I'm still coherent enough to notice that a concerning amount of blood comes up with it as well.

"Medusa," I breathe out, half delirious with the pain. "Lady Medusa."

"I'm here." I hear her voice but cannot see her until she steps directly in front of me, holding my face in her hands. "I'm safe."

"Good, good," I mutter almost incoherently, my eyes trying to roll back into my head.

I can't help the scream that rips through me as I'm lowered to the ground. Kore holds me, murmuring apologies and soothing things, while Elpis hauls her medical kit over to where I lay.

I'm shivering, half laying in Kore's lap, cradled against her chest, watching Elpis prepare to work through hazy eyes. Kore cuts my shirt away and immediately claps a hand to her mouth at what she sees.

"Athena give me strength," Elpis mutters, her hands falling still in her lap, dumbfounded by what she sees.

"What?" I mutter, trying to pushing off Kore's chest to sit up right. "What?" I finally manage to prop myself up enough to look down at my ribcage and almost puke again at what I see.

My whole ribcage is a mottled black and blue. I can see the broken ribs sticking up every which way, barely contained by my skin. My abdomen is a hot looking red color, blotchy and bruised in a way that tell me it holds at least one, but probably more, ruptured organ.

Actually, wait. There is a rib poking through my skin. My finger pokes at it, almost in wonder, before Kore slaps my hand away, making a distressed and disgusted noise. Elpis's eyes are wide and serious as she scoots forward and holds my face securely in her hands, her ice blue eyes drilling into my own brown ones. The look in her eye is enough to cause another flutter of fear to fill my stomach. Elpis is rarely so serious. I've only seen it a handful of times in the decade I've known her.

"I'm going to have to use magic."

Dread fills my stomach and, for the first time since being injured, tears fill my eyes.

"No," I whisper, too worn down to feel shame at my tears and my fear.

"I'm sorry," she insists. "It has to be magic, there is too much damage. Listen to me Rissy, there is too much damage. There's just too much."

"No, no, no, no," I cry, causing more searing pain down my sides. I know she is right. I know in my mind she is right, but in my heart I know I cannot endure this. To be healed by magic is a weighty thing. It's a sacrifice, the cost for defying nature in such a way.

And all sacrifices come with a cost. Namely, in this case, otherworldly and excruciating pain. As a general rule of thumb, the level pain that is healed is endured tenfold during the healing process. That is why it is used so sparingly and only in the direst of circumstances. Most healers aren't even trained on how to do this. And with the extent of my injuries, healing this will make my Initiation into the conclave look like a dislocated shoulder on the playground.

"Please, Elpis, *please*! I'm not strong enough right now, I can't, I can't." I'm sobbing, terrified at the thought of enduring that right now. She tightens her grip on my face.

"You can! You have to! You will die if I don't do this. Do you hear me , Rissy? *You. Will. Die!*" But my exhaustion and fear has taken root and I cannot listen to reason. I begin to cry in earnest, thrashing in Kore's arms as much as I can, throwing up from the pain of my thrashing and opening up half clotted wounds. Blood flows from my head into my mouth, making me gag on it. I hear Elpis's frustrated and exasperated sigh. The resolution in her voice. "Kore. Hold her."

Kore obeys immediately. One arm wraps around my torso, securing my arms to my sides under it, my back tight to her chest. The other comes up to support my head, holding my forehead, both to comfort and restrain. I cry and struggle against her but there is no use, I am too weak, too far gone to fight anyone off right now. She lays her head on mine, her tearful apologies hot in my ear. I open my mouth to beg for mercy and Elpis takes the opportunity to shove a belt in my mouth and begins to work.

She lays one hand along my ribcage and the other she shoves between mine and Kore's bodies, pressed heavy and strong on my back. Kore doubles down her grip on me as Elpis begins to chant. I can feel the heat from her hands as her magic fills them. Immediately, it is pain unlike anything I have ever known. I thought I knew what it was to hurt. What it was to endure pain. But the gods surely laugh at that hubris now as half choked screams tear their way out of my throat and my still-gagged mouth.

Is this what it is to be bathed in lava? I wonder. Is this what Achilles endured when he was bathed as a babe in the River Styx? It must not be my sister, Elpis, who lays her healing hands on me but Algea, the goddess of pain. For surely only she could deliver a blow so large, so lasting. Not even the best of Athena could withstand this pain. My eyes try to roll back in my head, desperate to lose consciousness, to shield myself from the memory of this pain. But that is part of the sacrifice in being healed by magic: you will remember every moment of it.

How long does this go on? It feels like an eternity. My throat feels raw from my screams and I have long run out of tears to cry. After some time I become vaguely aware that, while the healing pain continues without pause, the actual pain in my body is receding.

Finally, just as suddenly as the torture began, it stops. Panting slightly, Elpis gently takes the belt out of my mouth and Kore lowers me slowly to the ground. My hand, braced against the cold stone floor of the barn, shakes and my rapid breaths blow dust and straw around me with every huff. The cold of the floor feels like heaven against my fevered skin and I'm suddenly so exhausted I could sleep right there without issue.

Hands, light and jittery, like a sparrow, flutter against my back, my arms, my hair.

"Aristomache," she mutters concernedly. "Aristomache, Aristomache." I don't even try to lift my head or hand. I know I will not be able to. The most I can do is flutter my fingers in a truly pathetic way, murmuring back *I'm all right, My Lady. I'm all right.*

Kore and Elpis are back. El strokes my hair from my face, leaning down to press her head against the back of mine.

"I'm so sorry, Rissy. I'm so sorry. It was the only way." She's half crying as she continues stroking my hair.

"I know," I barely manage to whisper. "I know." She strokes my hair one last time before moving back to allow Kore to grab my shoulders and roll me over. She squats behind me, holding under my armpits and around my chest, so that

I'm half sitting up between her legs. My head lolls useless, I can barely keep my eyes open, let alone my head up. Elpis squats beside me, wrapping her arms around my thighs.

"One, two, three…" they mutter together, lifting me up. I want to protest. *I can walk. I can do it myself.* But it's a feeble argument and even I know it. I don't even think I could walk anywhere, forget about raising my spear.

They lay me down on a straw bed, covered in the blankets we brought from the conclave. They smell like the conclave still, like the wildflowers we grow all over the place to bring sunshine and happiness to our underground home and fresh baked bread and polished steel. If I weren't so exhausted the scent alone would make me cry again. But I am too tired to do anything but lay there and slip gratefully into oblivion.

The last thing I'm aware of is Lady Medusa using a wet t-shirt, as a washcloth to gently wipe the blood and dirt from my face, the soothing hiss of snakes lulling me to sleep.

14

Chapter 14

I come to dazed, and more than a little confused. I'm no longer laying on a straw bed in a barn. No. I'm watching four women as they sit around a table, playing cards. They're laughing and smiling as they deal cards and take turns playing. It's late, very late. It's pitch black outside and I can hear rain pelting the windows but no one seems eager to head to bed.

"You are such a *cheater!*" Melenthe exclaims, throwing cards across the table. Julia snorts, collecting her new cards.

"Don't hate me cause you ain't me, sugar," She replies, looking haughty. Lady Medusa giggles into her fist while my mother *tsks* and lays down her own cards.

I wonder closer, tears filling my eyes as I stare at my mother. Her black hair shiny and pulled back in a complicated braid. Her brown eyes alight with mirth and mischief as she gets ready to put the winning hand down.

I look around the cabin and find it well loved and lived in. Throw blankets are draped over the furniture, a fire crackles merrily in the fireplace and a half-empty, now cold, cup of coffee sits on the coffee table, a long dried ring under it.

It's clear this is a familiar time for them, reminders of old cheating instances are brought up and inside jokes are thrown to the air with ease. I watch as my mother's phone lights up in some kind of alert and find a lump in my throat as I see the picture on her background. It was when Alena passed her agility training. She did it so fast she shattered Kore's previous record. In the photo, she's sitting atop my right shoulder, my right arm covering her legs like a seat belt, my left fist raised in triumph. Alena also has her hands raised to the sky, a proud smile fills her entire face, I'm in the middle of chanting Alena's name, an excited type of fervor covers my face.

The same picture is my phone's lock screen.

"What's that about?" Melenthe nods to my mom's phone as she checks the alert.

"Mm, motion along that back stream again," she responds nonchalantly, pulling up cameras to double check it's nothing to be concerned about. But the cameras don't load. "No signal?"

Then chaos. Multiple alarms start going off, loud and piercing. The Protectors stand as one, fierce and determined. They summon their spears but before they take a step the window in the living room shatters and a smoke bomb is thrown in. Lady Medusa screams, covering her ears. Julia charges out the door to head off the attackers. I run to the door and see Julia wielding her spear like it was an extension of her arm. She takes out one of the attackers before I have time to blink and then launches her spear into the thick forest trees, I hear the wet squelch and following thud that tells me she hit her mark.

Melenthe runs out to the porch to check on her, Julia yells at her to *protect her! Protect our Lady!* Her voice is almost lost in the rain but she is heard somehow. Melenthe nods and turns to go back inside but stops as someone walks along the porch towards her. They wear a long deep green hooded cloak, which drips water all along the porch. They have the hood over their face in a ridiculous way that masks their identity. Even still, I know that I must be looking at our traitor. There's a purposeful look to their walk. Like they know the path they walk is one that will get them killed but they know it's too late to change course now. Melenthe levels her spear at them and goes in for the kill but stops short as the person lifts their head— it must be enough for her to see their face. She blinks, as though in shock and appears dumbfounded by what she sees.

"What are you doing here? What's goi—" She grunts as someone else brings the butt of their knife down onto the back of her head. They grab a fistful of her dark red hair as her knees buckle and takes advantage of her momentary disorientation. A flash of black then a shuddering gasp. The legendary Melenthe has finally met her end. Whoever wields the knife pushes her limp body away, she collapses in the doorway, just as we found her, and moves no more.

"You hesitated." A male voice accuses, wiping Melenthe's blood from his black blade. The traitor does not move, just studies the body for a moment before, suddenly, spitting on her face. White hot rage boils inside me. Not only did this traitor betray our Lady Medusa but she helped murder one of her sisters. And then she spit on her body.

I think I will spit on hers next.

"My Lady! *RUN!*" I have never heard my mother's voice sound like that before. Terrified and desperate and lost. My blood chills as I wheel back inside and see my mother fighting in vain. I catch a glimpse of a mauve hijab whipping up the stairs and out of sight. One of the men waits until my mothers back is turned and follows. The man who killed Melenthe comes in, knife ready. My mother uses the end of her spear to pick up the coffee table, spins and kicks at it, sending it flying into the mans chest. She's locked in close combat before she manages to jam her knife into one opponents chest. She's panting and wildly looks around, she must realize one of the men is no longer here for she tears up the stairs.

She skids to a stop, gasping as she hears Lady Medusa crying, sees just her arms as she tries to push the now stone man over. She squeezes her eyes shut, wraps her arms around the statue. Groaning she pulls him far enough back that his foot is no longer in the door and Lady Medusa can now close it. She pushes him over, breaking off his arm and causing him to land on the torn off hijab.

"Stay in there until one of us comes for you, My Lady!" My mother orders her. She does not wait for a response before running back down the stairs. Without stopping, she runs for the command center.

A scream of horror builds in my chest as I watch Melenthe's murderer melt out of the shadows and follow my mother silently. I don't want to see this but my feet seem to move of their own volition and before I know it I stand in the doorway of the comm room.

He's no fighter, that much is obvious. He should be no match for such a highly trained and experienced warrior such as my mother. I can tell she's surprised by the effort it is taking her to touch him. For every blow she lands on him, he lands three on her. It does not take long for her to be bleeding and worn out. This also does not make sense, she has not been battling for that long. Her endurance, and the endurance of all the Protectors is unheard of, she should not be this tired. Something is draining her.

As I look I can see something, almost like a heat mirage on the road during the summer, surrounding the man. I'm confused for a moment before the horrible truth fills me.

"The blessing of a god," I whisper to myself. I should not be surprised, there are a great many gods who would love to claim the warrior who has finally managed to kill Medusa. But now this means we have another foe to deal with. I turn my attention back to the fight in time to see my mother, exhausted and bloody, plant one of her feet in the mans stomach and send him flying back into the wall.

My own recent injuries cause me to flinch and wrap an arm around my now healed ribs.

She takes that moment to turn and smack her hand on the big, red emergency button. At this moment dozens of Initiates are waking up in agony, myself included. The man roars in frustration. I don't think he knows exactly what the button does, but he probably has a good guess. Just as my mother goes to turn back towards the fight, he rushes her, grabbing a fistful of her hair and smashes her face down into the console.

I hold my breath and I wait. I wait for him to bring his horrible black blade across my mother's throat the same way he did Melenthe's. But he doesn't.

First he tries to take off her Initiate pendant but roars in pain and snatches his hand back. One of magical defenses, if anyone but certain Priestess's of Athena try to take our pendants from us, it will feel as though they have just soaked their hands in acid. The more they try, the more it hurts.

Clearly infuriated, the man bashes my moms face into the

148

console again.

I will eat your heart raw in front of your *mother,* I think at him savagely, tears silently fall from my eyes. I cannot see his face, the gods deny me this knowledge. But this will not stop me. I will be the death of this man. *Athena hear my vow.*

"Fine," he snarls, as he hauls her out of the room. "We'll do this the hard way."

* * *

There's heat on my side and wetness on my cheeks. The heat is so much so that for a second I think I must be injured again. But as I wake up properly and my eyes adjust to the bright sunlight, I realize it's just Kore. Not a lot of space and a lot of body heat has left me sweating in my sleep. Or maybe that was the nightmare. I shift away from her slowly so as to not disrupt her and sit up tentatively, wiping the tears off my face with my other hand.

"How're you feeling?" Elpis asks from where she sits beside Lady Medusa. They sit side by side on the tailgate of the truck, near the big barn door. Her eyes are filled with guilt and worry. I nod stiffly and slowly rock forward so I'm kneeling in front of my makeshift bed. I groan quietly as I stretch, stiffness filling every nook and cranny of my body. I rub the sleep from my eyes and stand in one sudden, fluid movement. "Here." A water bottle is held out in my direction and shaken enticingly. I make my way over to the pair on careful feet, not wanting to move too fast, too soon. I give a nod of thanks as I take the water and twist the cap open. I take a mouthful and swish it around before spitting it out to help get rid of the stagnant taste in my mouth. I do that a few more times before actually swallowing several large mouthfuls.

I wipe my mouth as I force myself to take a break. "Thanks." My voice is slightly hoarse, which immediately puts me on guard. "How long was I asleep?" I ask, thinking of my dream. I watched the whole thing, which is no small feat.

"About 15 hours," she tells me, and seeing the look on my face presses on. "And before you bitch, you would have done the same for us and there is nothing else we could have done. If we had put you in the car and moved and been attacked we would have been stuck between protecting you *and* Lady Medusa or protecting Lady Medusa and leaving you for dead." I can't argue with this and she knows it. "Besides, this way all of us were able to actual get a good amount of sleep for the first time in too long." Again. No way for me to argue. I raise my hands in concession.

"All right, you're right." I tell her. She nods, pleased. "Thank you."

"For saving your life?" She questions with her eyebrow raised. "That's my whole job, Rissy. I'm just sorry I had to cause you so much pain to do it."

"Nah," I shake my head, taking another drink. "It didn't hurt that bad. You know me, I was just being a drama queen."

This startles a giggle out of Lady Medusa, who looks torn between being scandalized at my words and amused at them. Elpis nods at her knowingly.

"No she's right," She tells her solemnly. "Biggest drama queen I know. You should see her with a splinter in her foot." I grin and shove El's shoulder as Lady Medusa gives an actual laugh at that. "Speaking of that, I went ahead and took your stitches out of your leg while you were out, hope you don't mind I took your pants off."

I roll my eyes in exasperation.

"Why do you have to say it like that?"

"I'm just saying that—"

"I'm up!" This is Kore sitting up suddenly in a daze. We all laugh at that as I toss my half empty water bottle at her, which she catches, startled.

"Good morning, Sunshine," I tell her. She rolls her eyes at me as she drains the rest in a few mouthfuls.

"Now that they're all up, you can go if you'd like," Elpis tells Lady Medusa, nudging her lightly with her elbow. Lady Medusa hops up, grabbing a blanket she had beside her and skips to the back of the barn where a patch of sunshine burns onto the ground through a window. She sets the blanket on the ground, kneels and begins to pray.

"Morning prayers to Athena," she tells us as Kore joins us. I shake my head.

"I had a dream." I have their attention, they know it must have been a message from the gods or I wouldn't bother sharing it. "I saw it. The attack on the cabin. I saw Melenthe die and my mother was beaten near to death after she managed to sound the alarm. I saw the traitor but I couldn't see her face and there's a man, human but maybe a demigod or blessed by a god who's working with her. He had a blessing that surrounded him when he was battling my mother, it's the only reason he didn't die."

They stare at me, eyes wide.

Finally Kore closes her slowly and horror fills her voice as she whispers, "What are we going to do?"

I can only shake my head again.

"We keep going. We get Lady Medusa back to the conclave." Elpis says, shrugging. "It's the only option right now. Who was the man?"

I shake my head again, "I don't know. Whoever gave me the dream wouldn't show me." Elpis sucks her teeth as she folds her arms in agitation.

"Who do you think the god is?" Kore asks, her voice hushed. "The one backing the traitor?"

I look pointedly at Lady Medusa.

She nods sagely. "Poseidon."

"Seems too obvious," Elpis chimes in, looking doubtful.

"Yeah, cause the Sea God is so well known for being stealthy," I reply back sardonically. "It makes the most sense, obvious or not."

"Well we can't—" Elpis is cut off by the return of Lady Medusa, who is all smiles after a good night sleep and prayers to her goddess. "Ready to hit the road, My Lady?"

"Absolutely," she beams.

I motion for everyone to load up. Time for discussion is over.

15

Chapter 15

For the first time everyone is well rested and awake. In this comfort it turns out Lady Medusa is a bit of a chatter box talking about anything and everything that comes to her mind. She's a natural at Don't Even Get Me Started and gets Elpis so fired about which burner on the stove is best that Kore has to intervene.

I can almost pretend as though this is a normal road trip, some girls out to experience the world. But when my mind strays I see the blood pooled under Melenthe's lifeless body, see the stranger bash my mothers face into the console, and feel myself harden back to reality.

"How're you feeling?" Elpis asks from her spot next to Lady Medusa in the back. I glance at her in the review mirror. "Stiff?"

I shift automatically in the drivers seat.

"Not terrible," I tell her. She nods, smiling. Pleased with her work. I turn my focus back to the road. I startle slightly when Lady Medusa grabs the back of my seat, leaning forward.

"Can we stop at Wendy's for lunch?"

I can't help but laugh at the child-like joy on her face and outright cackle as she adds, "Atalanta would never let me. She said it was garbage on a bun."

I tell her we can stop for Wendy's.

We're waiting in the drive through when my phone rings, I see out of the corner of my eye who it is and go to grab it before the others see but it's too late.

"Oh you *anonyma*!" Elpis cries. I whip around, my jaw dropped in indignation.

"An anonyma?! Who do you think you are calling me that! I am *not* an anonyma!"

"Who was it?" Lady Medusa asks keenly, straining to look at my phone screen. I ignore the call before she can see it.

Kore clucks her tongue, shaking her head.

"Ooh!" Lady Medusa exclaims. "It was the god you're seeing wasn't it? I remember Atalanta mentioning that!"

I whip around again, agitation flooding me.

"My mother said *what!*"

Lady Medusa seems oblivious to my agitation.

"Yeah! When she found out you were seeing, who is it again? Deimos? Yeah! She was like 'What does she think she's doing? She's going to give me gray hair.' She said more too but that was the nicest of it."

Kore and Elpis are cackling at that but I cringe, remembering the verbal lashing my mother gave me all too well.

"She called me an anonyma when she found out," I admit. Then immediately regret admitting as Elpis is no longer making any noise as she laughs, tears leaking out of her eyes.

"She didn't!" Kore exclaims, half laughing herself. I roll my eyes, sucking my teeth in agitation as I remember the fight.

"Her petty ass, yes she did. One of the women she graduated Initiation with saw us out at some club so of course I was... not dressed as modestly as I might typically be and was with Deimos, so my mother called me an anonyma." Kore claps her hand to her mouth, trying to stifle her giggles.

"That is just not nice of her." She says, trying to make her tone as serious as she can. Elpis is just gasping intermittently as she slowly dies of laughter. Lady Medusa is in stitches just watching Elpis. We pull up to the menu and I place our orders, ignoring Elpis and Lady Medusa in the back.

"She apologized later," I remember, as I collect our food and drinks from the worker. "But she made it very clear she did not, and would never, approve of me seeing him. She goes, 'I don't care how much fun he is, this is the stupidest thing you've ever done.'" Finally pulling herself together, Elpis wipes the tears from her eyes and face.

"What did you say to that?" She asks, mirth filling every syllable. I press my lips together, fighting a smile as I remember. Kore leans forward, half smiling.

"You never did tell us about this fight, you just said you had one." There's awe in her eyes and her voice. "What *did* you say to that?"

"I said," I glance in my rearview mirror, stalling. "That I was fairly certain that Deimos was not a *thing* and, even if he was a *thing*, that he was certainly not the stupidest one I had ever done."

Kore howls with laughter while a half scandalized, half amused laugh escapes Lady Medusa before she covers her mouth with her hands. Elpis takes up a mockingly scandalized tone.

"Aristomache Kallis! I cannot believe you would make a *sex joke* to your *mother*!"

"Well, you know what!" I defend myself. "She shouldn't have been asking. Fuck around and find out, that's what I say. I'm not going to lie to her and she knows that, so ask me questions at your own risk!" Kore has pulled her shirt up over her face and I can hear her quiet giggling, gasps as she tries to collect herself. With a deep breath she emerges, still fighting to keep her voice even.

"That seems like a very fair boundary to have," she says, smothering her laughter.

I can only shake my head at the memory of irritation as I pull back onto the interstate.

We make it the next several dozen miles with nothing interesting happening and I actually start to think that maybe getting Lady Medusa home will be a piece of cake. That all comes crashing down though.

"Ris," Kore mumbles from beside me, eyes hard on the side mirror.

"I see it," I mumble back so that Lady Medusa, who prattles away happily in the back about her french fries, won't hear. I meet El's eyes in the rearview mirror again, she furrows her eyebrows in question. I shake my head minutely at her, cutting my eyes to Lady Medusa.

"What're we gonna do, Ris?" Kore asks.

"Okay," I exhale slowly. "My Lady?" Her eyes, still full of excitement from her excitement of fast food, flit up to mine. They immediately become more wary as she reads the tenseness in my own eyes.

"What's wrong?" she asks nervously.

"There's something in the air," I tell her. "Following us."

Immediately, fear floods her eyes as she begins to try and

156

look out the windows.

"Don't!" Kore instructs, as Elpis drags her back from the windows.

"What is it?" she asks breathlessly.

"I have no idea," I tell her honestly.

"We're never going to get home at this rate," Kore mumbles to me. My eyebrows furrow even more.

They're going to get stuck like this, I think vaguely. I shake off that thought, forcing my face to relax.

"Armor up," I tell them. "We're going to—" I don't get to finish saying what we're going to do as something dives down and hits the side of our car like a battering ram. Tires squeal as I fight to keep the car on the road.

Lady Medusa screams as Elpis covers her body with her own. Kore rolls down her window so she can sit on the ledge and aim her spear at whatever is assaulting us.

As another one dives down, Kore fends it off with a jab of her spear.

"Harpy!" She spits at me.

I growl under my breath as I try to evade the worse of the onslaught. Fucking harpies! You can't spit on a shadow without running in to one and I've yet to meet one that wasn't a bloodthirsty bastard. Half a dozen harpy's take turns dive bombing us, doing everything they can to crash us. It's everything I can do to keep all four tires flat on the road.

One hits the back of the car, sending me into a tail spin. Lady Medusa's terrified screams fill the air. Kore hangs on for dear life as I try to fix our course. Finally I get the car stopped and punch the gas again, just missing a harpy who was aiming for our windshield.

But that isn't the only concern. More than once, as I've

swerved away from the harpy's I've swerved towards another car, almost crashing us.

"Son of a—" I growl. Kore cries out from where she still sits on the windowsill. I reach out and grab the belt of her pants, yanking her back in. There's a massive cut down the side of her face.

"Bastard nicked me before I got him," she mutters distractedly, swiping at the wound with the back of her free hand. She moves as though she's going to go back out.

"Kore don't even—" I snarl at her.

"Look!" Elpis cries, pointing out the side window. As we watch two, three, four harpy's fall from the sky, arrows piercing them between the eyes.

"What the..." I say in wonder, looking around. "Oh you've got to be kidding me."

A dozen motorcycles pull up along side us, motioning for us to pull off the next ramp. I wave them away, telling them I understand.

"Who are they?" Lady Medusa whispers fearfully.

"They're friends, my Lady," I reassure her. "Annoying friends, but friends nonetheless."

"Are they friends right now though, Ris? With the company we have right now?" Kore asks me quietly.

"That is a good question," is the only answer I can give her.

16

Chapter 16

We pull into a campsite, filled with both tents and luxurious RV's. The bikes keep a respectful distance as they pull in behind us.

"Does she stay in or come with us?" Kore asks.

"She stays in," I order. "You two stay with her."

They both open their mouths to complain but I'm out the door before they can properly start. As I walk away Aris throws herself onto the windowsill again with her spear in hand. The look on her face dares me to object.

"Airr-riss," the leader drawls as he dismounts his bike. Tall with brown hair and hazel eyes, he's not disappointing to look at. I smile ruefully at him as I approach.

"Hey, Charlie." I greet him easily. He kisses my cheek.

"Howdy, gorgeous. How's it going?" He asks, leaning back from me with his arms folded over his chest. The rest of his buddies still sit on their bikes but give me friendly waves. I return them before motioning to our car behind me.

"How's it look like it's going?" Charlie heaves a sigh.

"Yeah... yeah sorry for intervening but you were getting

creamed out there."

I snort. "Yeah, that's the understatement of the century."
Charlie spreads his hands out to me.

"Darlin'... what is going on?" Charlie asks softly.

I always liked Charlie. A son of Hermes who linked up with
other demigods or children of demigods and formed a biker
club. The Hellions of Hades, they call themselves. I admit
I was jealous when I first heard of it. I even asked Tessa if
we could form our own club, form an on the road section of
Initiates. More protection for Medusa and all that. That idea
was swiftly shut down.. much to my intense disappointment.
Even without the formal section, I've run into the Hellions
more times than I can count while on the road. They've always
been helpful and tend to mind their own business and stay
out of godly business. Even with this knowledge, I hesitate
to confide our situation in Charlie. I hear Kore's voice in my
mind. *Can we trust them, right now?* I can't know for certain.
He can sense this hesitation and sighs as he puts his hands
heavy on my shoulders. Reassuring and understanding.

"Oh Charlie..." I sigh. "I can't tell you. It's too time sensitive.
Too serious."

Charlie nods as he studies my face. "Ris, those harpy's were
out for blood..." I can only nod in response. "Just promise me
you'll be careful."

"Course I will," I agree easily. "You know me." Charlie
smirks and pulls me in for a hug.

"I know you won't tell me what's going on. But I've heard
the rumors. Rest here for the night and we'll clear the air for
you while you're resting."

I hesitate. This is a fantastic offer but part of me wants to
say *forget it*, and truck on home. But we need to check over the

car and Lady Medusa is more than a little shaken up. Maybe a few hours rest will be okay.

"Okay," I tell him, pulling away. "Just for a few hours."

He pats my shoulder before turning back to his group, motioning for them to circle up and head out. The answering rev of engines is deafening.

Dust fills the air as the bikes leave the campsite. Several of the members wave as they leave.

I hear gravel crunching under feet as the others run up to me.

"What'd they want?" Elpis asks breathlessly, clinging to my arm.

"To help," is all I say. Kore makes a disbelieving noise. I ignore her. Kore doesn't like the Hellions, doesn't understand how someone can know of our world and not be involved in it. Elpis doesn't trust the Hellions because they have no affiliation to anything to hold them accountable. I think those reasons are why I like them so much. They have the freedom to do as they please and for the most part they choose to be helpful. Every once in a while they get rowdy and loud and might cause some trouble that we have to intervene in but for the most part, they're not a concern on the conclaves radar.

"We're gonna camp out here for a few hours. Dig out the sleeping bags. Catch a few hours sleep if you can."

"Here?" Kore asks. I shrug.

"Might as well. We're already in an empty slot."

Kore makes another noise in the back of her throat, but goes to do as instructed without question.

"You staying up?" Elpis asks.

"Yeah," I tell her. "You get some rest, I know you didn't while you were watching over me. I'll stand guard." She smiles and nods at me and accepts the sleeping bag from Kore.

I'm watching a couple across from us as they play a game of badminton when I hear Kore gasp, followed by the sound of her spear materializing.

I whip around to find someone new watching us.

"Easy, killers," he greets easily. All at once, we all deflate. Lady Medusa even waves. I plant my hands on my hips but a smile, instead of a scowl, covers my face.

"My Lord," I greet. "To what do we owe this honor?"

Ares steps forward with a grin, returning Lady Medusa's wave.

"I was actually wondering if I might speak to you privately, Aristomache?"

I raise an eyebrow at this request.

"Of course, my Lord." I agree. I turn to the others who both hold spears. Their eyes are wary but agreeable. Kore gives me a nod, telling me it's okay to go. I nod back to her before turning back to Lord Ares.

"Shall we take a walk?" He asks, motioning to the walking trail that surrounds the campsite. I shrug and fall into place next to him.

"I hope you'll forgive my interference." Ares begins. "But I simply couldn't stand by and let this play out... Fates be damned."

"You honor me, My Lord." I respond, completely non-plussed by what he's talking about. "What can I do for you?"

"You could hear me out," Ares tells me. "You can let me aid you in your journey home."

A startled laugh escapes me.

"Aid us?" I ask him. "My Lord, you must know we can't accept this."

Ares growls low in his voice. He steps in front of me, bringing us to a stop. I blink in shock at him.

"Lord Ares!" I admonish, my hand twitching to reach for my spear.

"Here's the deal. You need my help," Ares insists.

"My Lord, why would you want to help us so badly?" I ask. "I know we have had a good working relationship over the past several years but we are not sworn to you. You are not bound to help us."

"I don't want to help you all. I want to help *you*, Aristomache Kallis."

"My Lord?" My eyebrows furrow again, the feeling of being caught off balance slams in to me.

"I have watched..." Ares begins, oddly hesitant. "For a millennia, as woman after woman in your family has been chosen as an Initiate of the conclave. Every single generation of your family has had at least one... but usually more... women who have been chosen to serve Athena."

I nod. I know all of this.

"Yours is *only* family that has had this." His tone is one of wonder and amazement.

"My Lord," I interrupt, holding up a hand. "Not to be rude, but I know all of this already." Studying our extensive history is all but a requirement as a Kallis.

"Of course, of course I know that but still! It's just... amazing. All of these other legacy families have one, maybe two generations that are inducted before someone doesn't qualify and breaks that chain. But not your lot! Not those magnificent Kallis women!" He gives a wild laugh and his black eyes become filled with an excited fervor. It's a strangely endearing thing to see. I think of the Amazons of the old times, honorary warrior daughters of Ares. It's said he loved them for their bloodthirstiness and, above all, their passion. In a way, I suppose it would make sense that he would be drawn to our conclave as well. "As I've watched, I've seen the women in your family surpass greatness time and time again. They have.. they've drawn the attention of the most selective of gods, they've even been called to serve on your elusive Council! And I just can't understand it."

I cock my head reflexively to the side in question.

"What makes your lot so *special*?" He rushes out, his voice getting louder. His curiosity drives it out faster, his words rushed and tripping in his haste. "How has your family managed to achieve the standards of the conclave *every single time*? Again, your lot is doing this while other families can't hold a torch to you. So *how?*"

This is not what I thought this conversation was going to be about. Though, if I'm being honest, I never dreamed of having much of a conversation with Lord Ares to begin with. I take a moment to think and collect my thoughts before answering.

"Well... I cannot say for certain." I brush my hair out of my face as I think. "Some speculate that the men we choose to father our children plays a role, they tend to be superior type of men so that helps us be superior." Ares makes a noise that's a combination of disbelief and disgust and waves his hand impatiently. I find myself nodding with him. "Yeah, no woman in my family has ever put any stock into that theory. Some think it's just good genetics that have been finely tuned across the years, on top of the expectations that have been set before us." I shrug. "My grandmother always believed it's the blessing of Athena and the fact that we have all endured it, multiplied across so many generations has made any child one of us carries more likely to be destined for success and greatness, no matter if they choose the conclave or not. I think that's the most popular one."

Ares makes a face, like that theory makes a little more sense to him, but that he still wasn't completely satisfied with it. He opens his mouth but I beat him to it.

"You said you don't want to help us," I remember. "But me."

"Yes," he admits, his black eyes unfathomable. As I stare into them I see the echos of every battle I have ever fought and the battles of my ancestors. A chill races down my spine, despite the heat of the day. "The fate that has been laid out before you... I wish to meddle in it. I would like to see what you might be capable of as you grow older and settle into your world more."

"Fate?" I interject. "What fate?"

He ignores this completely. His stare becomes far away as he continues. "The women of your family fascinate me. Always have, since your first ancestor picked up her first knife. And you have shown yourself to be the greatest of them that I have seen, to date.I have watched you survive battles and wounds that should have crippled you. I have watched as you have proven to be a formidable partner for my son. Your skill, and the skill of your family, constantly amazes me. So uniquely stunning in a way that only mortals can be. I should like to see how this plays out for you. To be a Kallis woman seems to mean your are destined for greatness and you... Aristomache Kallis..." his mouth seems to caress my name. As though he's relishing the time he has to say it. "Well I think the Kallis woman who stands before me might find herself to bet he new standard to which every Kallis woman after her is held to. That

165

is if you'll let me aid your journey home."

There is so much information to sift through. Too much. My head throbs again.

"My Lord, you honor me. But we cannot accept your help." I tell him bluntly. Another thought comes to me. "Wait. I literally can't. Gods can't interfere in demi-god quests."

"Ah!" He begins happily. "Initiates are not actually demigods! Although most agree your lot is demigod *enough*. But, according to your Lady Athena herself, you are not demigods but mortals with a godly blessing." He bounces on his toes, pleased with his loophole. A small smile flits across my face.

"Even still," I say gently. "We are servants of Athena. We cannot accept aid from another god."

Ares heaves a sigh so deep it flutters my hair around my face.

"I wish you would reconsider, Aristomache." He tells me sincerely.

"It's not as though I wish to say no, Lord Ares, it's that I *must* say no." I insist. He nods slowly, studying me intensely. I can feel my skin prickle under his gaze.

"Well," he says. "I knew this already. But I hoped we could come to an arrangement."

I smile sadly and raise my hands in a shrug. Lord Ares heaves another sigh.

"I wish you all a safe journey home and long and satisfying lives." He says, his eyes locked onto mine.

"You honor me, Lord Ares," I murmur. "Thank you."

"Aris..." he hesitates. "Go straight home. No more stops. If you won't accept my aid, accept my advice. Please."

All I can do is nod.

I avert my gaze as Ares reveals his true self, the light warming my skin. And just as suddenly as he appeared, he's gone.

17

Chapter 17

The whole encounter leaves me reeling and shaking my head as I make my way back to the others.

"What was that about?" Kore asks as I approach. I press the heels of my hands to my eyes, rubbing them, trying to get rid of the confusion.

"I have no idea," I tell her sincerely, dropping my hands to my side as I stare out over the campsite.

"We're looking at this the wrong way," Kore says suddenly. Her eyes fierce on mine. "None of this makes sense. The attack on Lady Medusa, the traitor that hasn't actually given any critical information. Your mother being taken. It just doesn't add up. We're missing something."

I laugh incredulously and make a helpless motion with my hands. She's right though. None of this makes any sense. This was supposed to be about Medusa and those who would kill her for a scrap of glory. A traitor was confusing enough, but the longer this mission goes on, the less it feels like it's about Medusa. Part of me wants to tell them about what Lord Ares was saying about my family. We tell each other everything. Especially Kore and I. But something holds me back. Fear or uncertainty of what, exactly, Lord Ares was talking about. I tell myself I don't say anything to spare their feelings. Everyone at the conclave knows my family line. We're practically considered royalty. There's no reason to rub this in their faces, telling them Lord Ares sought us out because he was curious about my family and wanted to help me, not us, because of it.

That's what I try to tell myself. I don't do a very good job of it.

But even with all of that to think about. It still doesn't make sense. Why would the man take my mother? They knew Lady Medusa was in the house, why not burn it down? Flush her out? Kore is right, we're missing something. And I'm terrified that the something we're missing has to do with what Lord Ares was talking about.

"What other way are we supposed to look at this, Kore?" I respond, exasperated and overwhelmed by the whole damn situation. I snap a spear off my wrist purely for the satisfaction of driving it into the ground.

"Well that was dramatic," Kore remarks. I glare at her disparagingly.

"None of this makes any sense!" I insist. Kore looks as though she has a headache brewing. She pinches the bridge of her nose, her eyes squeezed shut.

"We just need to get home is all. Lord Ares is telling us to go straight home, no more stops. Then we're doing just that. Straight home. No more stops. "

"It just doesn't make any sense, Kore." I can't help but repeat again. I feel her hands on my shoulders, shaking them to get me to look at her.

"I know it doesn't," she tells me, her eyes and tone reassuring. "But we'll figure it out. Together. Right?" I give a huff of a laugh and smile wearily at her.

"Right." I affirm.

"All right, you ass. C'mere." She pulls me in for a hug, the stress of the meeting with Ares weighing heavily on us both. I pull away after a few moments.

"Let's get out of here." I say.

"Gods, yes please." Kore begs. I pull my drama spear out of the sand and put it back on my wrist as we head back to the car.

"I'll drive," Kore tells me, heading to the drivers side.

"All yours, babe," I say, tossing her the keys.

Lady Medusa has been quiet throughout this exchange. Her eyes flit from woman to woman like she's watching a tennis match.

"Do you trust him like that?" She asks finally.

"I don't." Elpis sneers. She's never liked Lord Ares. Claims it's the healer in her. "He's just a warmongering bully."

"I trust him, but there's a lot of our situation that just doesn't make sense. Too much is not adding up." I twist my neck this way and that, forever trying to work the knots out. "And watch your words please, Elpis. He's still a god and I don't need you getting smote for your mouth." I frown as I think that over. "Smote? Smiten?"

"Smote," Kore agrees but then frowns. "Oh hell, I don't know." She thinks is over for another second before sighing in defeat. "We're just gonna say it's smote."

"Smote sounds stupid though," Elpis pipes up, brow furrowed as she thinks. Or because she got reprimanded. Anyone's guess really.

170

"I vote smote," Lady Medusa chimes in, raising her hand as though someone is tallying a vote. I shrug and raise mine as well.

"All in favor of smote?"

"Aye."

"Aye."

I nod, winking at Lady Medusa. "Motion passed."

Before long we've pulled back onto the interstate. The car is filled with silence as we drive along, all of us lost in our own thoughts. It's a long time before any of us speaks again. Lost in the confines of our minds.

None of us notice the black storm clouds forming overhead of us as we drive south. When at last I realize the sun is gone, I frown outside the passenger window, looking up at the sky.

"Where did these clouds come from?" I wonder aloud. Kore swears from beside me as she snaps out of her own thoughts.

"Probably nowhere good." She gushes out in frustration.

"Where are we?" Elpis asks, leaning forward.

"Uhh," I confer with the map that lays across my lap. "Just outside of Monticello, Utah. Way, way South Utah. Almost to the Colorado border." As soon as these words leave my mouth a torrential downfall begins to fall from the black clouds of the sky.

"Oh you have got to be kidding me!" Elpis exclaims, her hands pressed against the glass as she watches the storm. Immediately a howling wind begins to shake the car as we drive. She jerks back from the window, pressing her back to her seat. "Okay. *Now* you're kidding me." I allow myself a moment of dramatics, thumping back against my seat and covering my face with my hands.

"Ohh you have got to be fucking kidding me!" I moan, my

face still covered with my hands. I pull them away as I turn to Kore, who is, arguably, the best driver in the entire conclave. "Can you drive in this weather?"

"Can I drive in the rain? Yes. Can I drive in the wind? Yes. Can I drive in this clearly-created-by-a-god-who-is-trying-to-stop-us-from-taking-Lady-Medusa-to-safety-weather? Not for very long."

"What do you mean?" I tease her absently as I do a compulsive check over of my armor and weapons. "You're the only person I know who I would trust to drive us through weather clearly created by a god who's trying to stop us from completing our mission." She gives me a tight smile, her tone sardonic.

"You honor me, Sister Aristomache."

"You honor *me*, Sister Kore."

"You honor me, Sister," I hear mockingly from the back. I turn back to swat playfully at Elpis when a particularly strong gust of wind causes us to swerve several feet, I jerk back around, gasping.

"May Athena grant me steady hands and a steady heart." Kore prays, her voice tight.

"You're doing great, Kore," I tell her, my voice low, as though I don't want the storm to hear me. Maybe I don't. "Do what you can. If we have to stop, we have to stop." She nods and glances at me, grateful, out of the corner of her eye.

"If we stop, will you have to fight, again?" Lady Medusa asks, anxiously.

"Probably," Elpis tells her. "This isn't a natural storm. This is someone trying to stop us. If we have to stop and battle them we may be able to stop the storm."

"*May* be able to." I emphasize, my grip white-knuckled on

the door. "That is why Kore is going to get us as close as she can and maybe we'll be able to call in an escort for the last part of the journey."

"What? An escort?" Medusa demands. "Why haven't you called for an escort sooner?" Her fear erases her manners, making her tone clipped and full of venom. I'm already shaking my head, however.

"It doesn't work like that. We were given a quest to complete. A quest is three. Three is the strongest number. To send more than three is to send an army, which we can't do without a declaration of war. Which we cannot do without a direct order from Lady Athena herself." She's got a pout to her lip as I explain, clearly she had been fantasizing about the might of Athena's conclave coming to the rescue. I continue. "But there's a loophole. If we're within a certain amount of miles or time or whatever from completing a quest we can call for an escort, which is an additional six warriors. So if we can get close enough we can't call for *reinforcements* but we can call for an *escort*."

"I guess that makes sense," Lady Medusa pouts, sitting back and crossing her arms. I smile sympathetically at her.

"I know. It's frustrating but we must obey our laws." She finally gives a conceding nod and plants her elbow on the windowsill before mashing her face into her fist and settles in to watch the storm.

Kore swears, her knuckles white on the steering wheel, as sheets of rain come down, blocking her vision and the wind pushes us from side to side.

"As far as you can, Kore," I murmur comfortingly. "Just as far as you can."

She nods tensely muttering under her breath, "just as far

173

as I can", as though it's a prayer. Almost immediately a car comes out of nowhere almost swerving into us.

I grab the assist handle and mutter a real prayer as Kore swerves to avoid the car. She manages to dodge it but sends us into a hydroplane. I want to close my eyes like Lady Medusa, who has her face buried in El's shoulder, and Elpis who has her eyes closed and looks as though she's bracing for impact, but I can't get them to cooperate. Like Kore my eyes seems frozen up in fear, my lips press tightly together to keep my scream inside. Seconds later, or maybe eons later, who knows, she manages to correct and keep us heading in the right direction. The right direction being, namely, not wrapped around a guardrail.

"Good job," I whisper.

"Thanks," she whispers back shakily.

And so this dance continues on, cars come flying at us, invisible to us until they are right on us. Time after time Kore saves our asses, pulling off some truly remarkable saves and adjustments. The more progress we make the more fierce the storm gets. We have long accepted having to drive at an angle since driving in a straight line no longer is an option. But Kore keeps us true on course. I watch the odometer, watch the miles tick by slowly, willing them to tick by faster. I keep up near constant encouragement and praise to Kore, stowing my fear just as she stows hers. Finally, after a very, *very,* close call with a semi Kore calls it.

"That's it," her voice just on the edge of frantic. "I have to call it, it's getting worse by the second and I can't keep pulling off these miracles."

I lay a reassuring hand on her shoulder.

"Do what you need to, Kore," I assure her. "We'll figure it

out from there." She nods gratefully, looking exhausted.

"There." I point to the exit coming up. Directly off of it is a large gas station. Kore's mouth twists distastefully but she begins to move the car over to the exit.

"Back parking lot?" She asks.

"Yeah, the less people we're around the better." She nods curtly, carefully making her way down the exit.

"Oh I hope this doesn't come back to bite us in the ass," Elpis whispers.

"Better wear your big girl pants just in case," I mutter to her, my hand tight around the handle of my knife, still securely in its sheath.

* * *

Immediately the wind and rain begin to let up, the closer we get to the gas station, the lighter the wind and rain become. By the the time we park the car, the sun is shining and the heat begins to dry the sidewalks. I give a humorless laugh as Kore takes us to the back parking lot and parks. Kore raises her eyebrows as she looks outside, then glances at me out of the corner of her eye.

"Ohh this is going to suck so bad." I remark simply, looking around as well.

"What do we even do?" Kore asks, frustrated. "Sit here and wait for the attack that is *clearly* coming or go and seek it out to head it off?"

I don't answer for a moment, thinking hard, my pointer finger tapping an irregular beat on the space between my eyebrows. Finally I sigh in defeat and motion to Kore.

"Suit up. All your armor. Shin greaves too. We're seeking it out." Kore jumps at my orders, eager to be doing something. None of us do *stillness* very well. I turn to look at the pair behind me. "I'm sorry, El. You gotta stay here." She's not pleased but she understands. As healer she has to take the backseat more often than she would generally like to.

"What do I do?" Lady Medusa asks, eagerly. I give her a hard look that quells her excitement enough that she studies the floor mats in the backseat.

"You do whatever Elpis tells you to do." She folds her arms and huffs under her breath but doesn't argue with me. "Kore will stay in the area, so she'll be around for reinforcement."

"Speaking of reinforcements," Elpis drawls, flipping a hand in the air. She looks peeved. Whether that's about having to stay in the car, or something else, I doubt even she knows. "We're not close enough to call for them."

"I'm aware." I snap, my eyes hard. Sometimes Elpis toes the line of rank too much. She will sometimes step out of line and need a good reminder to remember what her place is in our world. I rarely feel the need to remind any of my sisters-in-arms that I outrank them and that my orders are just that. Orders. But out of all of my friends I swear Elpis is the one that brings it out of me the most. "Kore did what she could and now we'll have to do what we can. I didn't see *you* offering to drive in the storm."

Shamed, Elpis just glares out her window, arms crossed tightly over her chest. I hold my stare on her for another moment, letting her feel the weight behind it, before motioning to Kore.

We come around to the front, adjusting armor straps and survey around us.

"I'm sorry," Kore bursts out as soon as we're alone. I look

over at her, startled. She seems confused by my confusion, because she elaborates slowly. "For not getting us closer."

I wave her off dismissively, rolling my eyes a little. "Ignore Elpis. You know how she gets when she's cranky. You did a phenomenal job. Better than she or I could have ever done."

She still looks unsure but she also knows I don't hand out false compliments so eventually she nods her thanks and gestures around us.

"How're we playing this?"

"Honestly I have no idea. But, if we keep doing stuff, stuff has to keep happening."

"Shit, it's worked for us so far."

"Has it though?" I ask curiously, as Kore pulls her hair into a ponytail.

"Ha! No." I give a good laugh at that, before pointing with my spearhead.

"I'm gonna go search around, see if anything looks weird. Kinda come stand out here so you can see both me and the car and then just stay there. I'll call if I need help. You know the drill, Lady Medusa is priority, always." I order. She nods, pulling a spear out.

"That's a big 10-4, boss lady, I read you loud and clear." She mimes holding a CB radio up to her mouth as she says this. I regard her for a moment, utterly dumbfounded.

"You are," I tell her matter-of-factually. "Just so strange. Just the oddest little duck I ever did see."

"I know." She beams, twirling her spear around her.

"All right," I mutter, striding away.

Anyone who has ever done recon in a public, somewhat crowded space knows it is the most awkward thing to do. I walk around, peaking under cars and poking bushes with my spear, looking for enemies, but none jump out at me. The bastards. The worst is when I'm checking around the parked semi's, full of drivers catching a much needed nap.

I squat down underneath the trailers, peaking between cabs and trailers and generally just being a menace. Thank the gods for the Mist that covers me. Without it, I have no doubt that someone would have called the police on me for loitering or suspicious behavior. I probably look like I'm having a psychotic break, poking around everything like this. That or I'm some criminal who was sent to pick up ransom money but I can't remember where I told my victims to put it.

"Are you a hostile enemy in disguise?" I ask an agitated pig, who is impatiently in a livestock trailer for its driver to return. "Because if you are, legally, you have to tell me." I take its squeal to mean that it's not a hostile enemy but definitely a hostile pig and continue my walk around, feeling more ridiculous by the minute.

Sometimes when I'm doing stuff like this I wonder if Athena is watching us, just shaking her head. It makes me feel like throwing my head back to the heavens and screaming *I promise I was inducted for a reason.* Just that reason was not to covertly search random gas station parking lots. Or now I guess it is. I walk over to the edge of the building to peek around the corner. Before I go around, I catch Kore's attention and sign to her that I'm checking the other side and that I'll be back in no more than five minutes. She signs back, saying she'll come check if it's longer than five minutes. I give her a thumbs up before moving around the corner. Immediately, a dark pressure washes over me. I feel my breath rush out of my lungs as the concrete disappears from under my feet.

III

Part Three

18

Chapter 18

"Oh what in the name of Athena?" I swear, blinking wildly as the air returns to my lungs. A deep bass shakes my chest and people mill about, drinks in hand. More than a few of them immediately begin to eye me with interest. A few who recognize me wave friendly, albeit confused, hands to me.

I look back behind me but see only a long bar, made of gleaming walnut, that is currently very packed with people waiting for their drinks. A dance floor lies in front of me, packed with even more people. No, not people. Gods. Demigods. Spirits. Shit. VIP booths line the back wall with a private room in the back right corner of the room. Strobe lights fill the room with their neon glow, causing odd reflections on the teeth of those who occupy this space.

I scan the room quickly, but stop when I see a group of empusa. I have definitely pissed them off a time or two before. They stand around a table, nursing drinks with blue flames flickering around the rims. As servants of Hekate, empusa have no real beef with Initiates. But on one of my last missions one of their sisters got lippy with me and tried to take a chunk out of my side during a disagreement about her lipiness. She got a spear in the stomach for her troubles. Her sisters did not much appreciate that, despite the fact that even their Lady said the kill was justified. Even with the severity of my situation and the panic that is threatening to boil over, I can't help but throw a taunting smirk at them. They bare their teeth in response, one even moves as though she's going to come over to me, but is stopped by another one of her sisters with a hand on her arm. A full grin fills my mouth and I bite back a laugh. I force myself to quit being petty and actually focus on the issue that is at hand.

"Shit," I mutter under my breath, as I look around. "Shit, shit, shit."

I've been to this club before, last year with Deimos. It's called the Fates and Furies, not quite an Underworld bar but not quite a "upper" bar either. The fact that I'm in this bar is not what's distressing me. No. The fact that this club is in Los Angeles, is what's distressing me. Hundreds of miles away from my sisters and my Lady. I try to remember the layout, where the door is namely, but I had been pretty drunk the last time I was here and honestly, not paying attention to anything that wasn't Deimos's arm around my waist. I pick a random direction and begin to walk as fast as I can, without drawing more attention to myself, as I look around.

I startle as a hot hand grabs my bicep, pulling me to a stop.

"What are you doing here?" I almost collapse with relief. "Lord Herakles!" Never did I think I would be so happy to see him. "Please, I have no idea what's going on. I have to get back to the others!"

"C'mere," he mutters, pulling me behind a support beam. I have never seen him look so serious and... is that fear? I'm

182

not sure that's what it is as I have never seen Lord Herakles look afraid before.

He glances around several times, his hand still tight on my bicep, before turning back to me. "Now. What is going on?"

The events of the last several days come pouring out of me. Lord Herakles is not a friend but he is certainly not an enemy. He has actually helped the conclave with dozens upon dozens of missions across the years. I myself, have worked with him four separate times and have developed a good rapport and working relationship with him. The last time I saw him, well the time before the last time, he ended up saving my skin on said mission. He was an ass about it, but still. He's earned my trust for sure.

His eyes grow impossibly wide when I tell him of how Elpis had to use magic to heal me and his hand on my arm becomes comforting rather than constricting. He's seen us healed by magic before— he knows what that burden entails. When I get to the storm that forced us to stop, his eyebrows knit together, furrowing deeply in the middle.

"And then I walked around the corner to clear the other side and when I did I walked in here instead!" I finish, throwing my hands in the air. "And now the girls are probably *freaking* out for more than one reason and they could be getting ambushed right now and I have no way of knowing or helping or—"

"Okay, okay, okay," Herakles interrupts, actually covering my mouth with his hand. Normally I would bite him for doing that, but I'm still too relieved to have someone that I know and trust with me right now, that I allow it for the moment.

Allies, I think suddenly. That's the best word for mine and Lord Herakles relationship.

"We have got to get you out of here *now.*" He stresses,

adjusting his grip on my arm and begins to pull me away. I don't fight him at all and actually keep pace with him, eager to be out of here and back with the others. Maybe I can convince him to magic me back to the others when we get out of here. I can't understand why he's so stressed though. He can't care *that* much for the fate of Lady Medusa or Kore and Elpis, for that matter. And I know he doesn't care *that* much about me. But he is. Stressed. His fingertips dig into my skin so hard that I think might be leaving bruises. He's biting his lip (*I have never seen him do that*) and scanning his eyes across the club so fast they're almost blurring. I want to ask him why he's so nervous. Because he obviously is. I don't waste my breath because I know he won't tell me but seeing it on his face leaves a hollow feeling in my stomach. My own breathing comes quicker and my eyes follow the same route as Herakles', flitting all around the club.

"Aristomache Kallis." I skid to a stop, startled by this new voice calling my name. Herakles drags me for several more feet, ignoring both the voice and my stopping, before something skips ahead and plants itself in front of us. Herakles swears loudly, finally forced to come to a stop.

The man in front of me looks vaguely familiar. It takes me a second to place him.

"Jesse?" I ask, perplexed.

Something primal and raw flashes in his eyes. He quickly smothers it, like a flame deprived of oxygen.

"Jason," he reminds me. *Okay dude*, I think snarkily. *I do not care that much.*

"Could I have a moment?" He asks me, smiling vacantly. His voice is immediately forgettable, especially when compared side-by-side with Lord Herakles who leans forward, teeth bared and eyes threatening.

"We were actually just leaving." The man, Jason, is un-phased by this open display of hostility. An odd smile works its way to his mouth. His head cocks to the side, like he's spotted an interesting puzzle he'd like to try and solve.

"Are you interfering with my conversation, Lord Herakles?" The wording of the question is weird. But what's even weirder is the way that this automatically seems to defuse Herakles. His snarl disappears and he straightens up as though he's had an electric shock run through him. His eyes go from hate-filled to oddly empty. Defeated, almost. I have an odd sense of deja vu as I look at his face. With a start, I realize it reminds me of Lord Ares's when we denied his help. Resigned and more than a little upset. It only lasts for a heartbeat or two before Herakles snaps out of it, but for as long as I live I will never forget seeing that look on his face.

"Only if Aris wants me to interfere." He sneers, recovering from whatever shock he had just endured. He stands his ground, hand still gripping my arm. He and I lock eyes and his are filled with silent begging. It's clear he wants me to say yes. He's telling me to let him interfere. Even without this silent message, I would be asking Lord Herakles to take me out of here. Something about this man sets my teeth on edge, and not just the odd conversation. Something nags at the back of my head, a voice that I can't quite hear but know I need to obey. That, coupled with the fact that I trust Lord Herakles with my life, because he has earned it, has me ready to tell him to interfere without question. I'm just opening my mouth to say *yes, I want to leave,* when the man speaks again.

"Aristomache," something about the way he says my name, my full name, causes bile to rise up in my throat. "It might

185

help you make your decision if you know what it is I want to speak to you about." I just barely see Herakles close his eyes in defeat as mine snap to the stranger, distrustful and more than a little hostile. "I have information about your traitor." I freeze. Herakles clamps down on my arm in response to my response and now I know he is leaving bruises. My arm grows hot and numb in his grip, but even still I don't try to pull myself from it.

"How could you have that information?" I demand, all bite and teeth. "How do I know you're telling the truth?" He shrugs nonchalantly.

"You'll just have to trust me," he says, smiling and holding out his hand. I bare my teeth at him in a snarl and make no move towards him. In fact, I lean back so my shoulder is just slightly pressed to Herakles chest, seeking comfort in familiarity. Not a single part of me trusts this man. Every instinct I have is screaming at me to run this runt of a man through with my spear. But, for reasons I don't fully understand, I stay my hand.

"No shot." I reply acidly. "I trust no one and nothing except for my Lady Athena and those of us who serve her with honor." I turn my head to Herakles to try and ask him, again, to take me out of here. But again, I've no more than opened my mouth before the man speaks again.

"The god I work for bought the information she was selling," he relents, his words rushing and tripping on their way out. He pushes himself onto the balls of his feet and his arm twitches as though he's fighting the urge to reach out to me again. "I had to coordinate with her to make sure it was worth the price she was asking."

I narrow my eyes at him. I can feel my heartbeat in my throat.

Or maybe that's Lord Herakles death grip on my arm that has me feeling that way. I fight the urge to spit on this man and swallow the curses I want to throw at him.

"Which god are you in service to?"

He's already shaking his head, a coy smile on his lips.

"Sorry, I can't tell you that. Oaths and all that. But what I *can* tell you is not only *who* the traitor is, but *where* she is." Well that narrows the list. There are only so many gods who demand silence in their oaths of service. And it also makes my decision very easy, just as he knew it would. I want to scream in frustration. I want to deny this man, send him off with his tail tucked between his legs. But, like at the cabin where I couldn't know if it was a trap or not, I feel as though there is no good decision for me. It feels as though the Fates have taken every choice in front of me except for this one and I swear I can hear their ethereal voices hissing in my ears, *take his hand. This is the only way.*

"Why would you want to help us?" I ask guardedly. His eyes become soft.

"I sympathize greatly with your Lady Medusa. As do more than a few women in my family." Ah. We've seen this before. Male heroes who will offer us aid or a tip once in a blue moon to help ease their own guilty conscious. All at once, I feel better about this whole exchange. This is familiar ground. Maybe more so than Lord Herakles aid.

"If you're lying to me or give me bad information," I tell him, my voice calm and serious. "I will kill you."

Inexplicably, he grins at me, then he holds his hand out again.

"Please." Herakles begs suddenly, grabbing my shoulders in his heavy and hot hands, yanking me around to face him. I try not to think about how less than a week ago those hands were on my hips, twirling me around a dance floor. "Please, just let me take you back. You don't need to know."

I look at him in incredulous anger and, for the first time, attempt to move out from under his grip. Attempt, because I don't actually go anywhere.

"How can you say that?" I shoot back at him angrily. "You *know* I do. You know I have to know. You know I have to *bring her in*. We have *laws* that I have to obey, Herakles. This is not solely about honor or vengeance. This is also about my duty to my goddess! You know, the goddess Athena? The one I have sworn my entire life in service to? It is *treason* if I don't bring this woman back."

I think he is going to yell. That he is going to use his godhood card to curb me into submission. He is not used to being denied and he's not known for taking it well. But what he does instead shocks me to my core.

He leans down and rests his forehead on my shoulder, the conclaves sign for respect, for a moment before shifting and resting his forehead on mine.

"Please trust me. Let her go. Ignore him." His voice is insistent. Desperate. "You don't need to know."

But, despite my confusion, and rising fear, so is mine.

"I can't. You know I can't!"

He sighs, pulling back to look at me fully. His face goes wholly blank and his eyes become unreadable. Without warning, he leans forward and presses his lips to my forehead, keeping them there for a moment or two before pulling away from me completely. Then he slowly, with great effort, peels his fingers from my shoulders and without another word, he turns and disappears into the crowd.

I suddenly feel naked without his heat next to me.

I catch a glimpse of something, deep in the man's eyes as I turn back to him. But he quickly smiles at me.

"Thank the gods that buzzkill is gone, right?" He tries to joke with me.

"Who is the traitor? Where is she?" I demand, ignoring him completely. I absentmindedly rubbing my sore bicep where Herakles had first grabbed me. He mock pouts at this and I resist the urge to cringe.

"In such a hurry! I thought we could get to know each other a little." His voice has a whiny edge to it that has me fighting my lip to keep it from curling in disgust.

"If you're telling the truth then you know what type of information the traitor sold and you know that I am kind of busy at the moment. So how about you just tell me what I need or I'll go find Lord Herakles again and have him take me home," I retort.

"Lord Herakles," Jason, snorts. "You know it was me who made the portal that brought you through."

I'd swear by his tone that he's trying to impress me with this information. It almost does, too. Creating portals is weighty magic, similar to the magic needed to heal wounds because of the strength and energy it requires. I'm not sure if even Kore could create one. Or maybe I should say has never been curious enough to attempt it. Magic always has a price, which usually becomes evident after the magic has been completed. And more than once, people find themselves in a situation where they are not always ready to pay up. So instead on impressing me, this information causes me to regard him warily. *What price were you willing to pay?*

"How is it you can make portals?"

189

He seems delighted by my question.

"A perk of the god I service," he says, winking. I blink in surprise at how nonchalant his behavior is.

"How about you just tell me your information." I tell him, disliking his behavior more and more by the second. "Name your price. I don't have time for these games. I have places to be."

Jason shakes his head, waving a dismissive hand.

"No price. Like I said, I sympathize with your Lady. I want to help, even if I can't do much. " He laughs at the look on my face. "How mistrustful you Initiates all are! Follow me to get your answers!" He motions for me to follow him again. This time I do, careful to keep him a few steps ahead of me.

I watch him with open hostility as we weave through the crowd. Every muscle in my body is coiled tight in anticipation. I do not trust this man, but then I do not trust anyone outside of the conclave. Not Lord Herakles, not even Deimos. *Deimos.* I think. *Maybe I should call him and see if he can help get me back to others.*

Eventually I realize he's leading us to the VIP booths in the back. They sit up a few steps from the main floor and are blocked off with velvet ropes. We stop just short enough that the spirit on bouncer duty has no reason to accost us. He stops so suddenly I almost smack into him. I skip back on light feet, putting some space between us.

He turns, grinning at me as though we're co-conspirators. He keeps standing too close to me. His cheap cologne stings my nose, making it itchy.

"Well?" he asks, gesturing to the booths. "See anyone you recognize?" I stare him down for a moment, distrust seeping from every pore on my body. He seems to find this amusing, his smile widens and he gestures again to the booths. Pressing my lips together I begin to scan the booths. After the first several I'm ready to keep my promise of killing this guy for being useless. There are plenty of people and beings I recognize. I've been all over our world on missions and traveling with Deimos. More than half the demigods here I met at a summit meeting last winter when Lady Persephone was refusing to leave her Lord Hades and her mother was pitching a fit, killing crops all over the globe. We met to decide if our intervention might be necessary. The longer I look, the more my fingers itch for my knife handle. Again, he seems to be amused by my attitude, watching my fingers twitch.

"No, not that one," he keeps up continually goading as I scan. "Nope! Close but not quite. Keep looking."

Finally, suddenly, my entire body goes deathly still, the blood draining from my face. I think my pulse even stops for a second. Until that moment, there was a part of me that was still in denial about everything. Part of me that thought I would never find the traitor because there was *no way* she could actually exist. But she does. And there she is. The blood comes roaring back to my head, a rushing sound echos in my ears as it does. My breath comes in quiet, hissing gasps through my clenched teeth. I still haven't moved.

There she sits. Lounging, Smiling. Laughing. Tucked under the arm of a god. I recognize him immediately. Lord Dolos. He's one of Deimos's friends. Or as close to friends that you can get with the god of treason and treachery. How fitting of a match for her. As I watch, she raises a glass, toasting whoever is sitting next to her. She raises her glass high, yelling something I can't hear over the music.

Finally, the hold on me breaks. A low hiss breaks through

my teeth. Her eyes snap to me as though she heard the hiss echo over the chest-rattling bass of the music. Her face goes even paler than normal as the blood drains from it, her mouth falls open in horror.

"Desma." I growl. I watch her lips move in return.

Oh shit, Aris.

Dolos sits up suddenly, his neon green eyes flash to mine. He and I bare our teeth at each other simultaneously. We never did like each other. I turn to Jason but he's gone. I swear and turn back to the booth, reaching for a spear. But instead, I gasp as I come face to face with someone. I don't even have time to register who it is before they shove their hand at my face, muttering something in Ancient Greek. I feel the ground shift beneath me and the air rush out of my lungs as I go flying, disoriented.

* * *

I grunt as I land hard, rocks and scraggly grass dig into my skin.

"Where the *hell* have you been?!" Someone screams before grabbing my arms roughly, pulling me to my feet.

I cough several times, my hands braced against my knees. Someone thumps me hard on the back. I stand up suddenly making everyone around me jump back.

"Oh thank Athena," I cry, gathering them all into my arms. "Oh thank the gods." Three sets of arms pat my back as I squeeze them all for a moment. The gentle lull of snakes hissing brings me back to my senses. I step back from them, wiping my eyes harshly. "I was so worried."

"*You* were worried!" Kore yells, shoving my shoulders.

"You just straight up disappeared, dude! What in the name of Athena happened?"

The disorientation is wearing off quickly. I pat my pants pocket and swear when I find it empty. I look around and see I've landed a dozen or so feet from our car. I dash over and throw open the drivers side door, digging around for my phone.

"What are you doing?" Elpis demands as I triumphantly dig my phone out from under the passenger seat. Lady Medusa watches me curiously, peeking around Kore's shoulder on tiptoes. I don't bother answering as I dial the phone furiously.

I put the phone on speaker and fidget in the drivers seat with each ring. Finally, Antiope answers.

Do you need an escort? I don't bother with a greeting or to answer her question.

"Antiope, I know who the traitor is."

Gasps echo from everyone around me.

Hang on, comes her reply, then silence.

"Is that who took you?" Elpis asks, her voice hushed. I shush her and shake my head.

Okay Aris, you have the Instructors. Fill us in.

I take a deep breath to steady myself.

"It's Desma. The traitor is Desma."

More gasps. Horrified tears fill Kore and Elpis's eyes, no doubt remembering, as I am, what I said about the traitor spitting on Melenthe's body. Or maybe they are remembering the last decade we have spent learning, growing and fighting with each other. Maybe they are remembering sharing a room with her, how everyone of us knows she talks in her sleep. Maybe they are remembering what a fantastic musician she is. How she can play the harp and sing so beautifully that many of us joke that maybe Apollo, rather than Athena, is her patron god. Maybe they are remembering their sister that they love, despite everything she has done.

Maybe they are thinking about how she will now die.

That's what I'm thinking about.

Are you sure? Comes the reply finally. I shake my head in irritation.

"I wouldn't be telling you about it if I wasn't sure," I snap. "I don't have time to explain everything now but *yes* I am sure." Horrified silence fills the other end of the line.

Where are you guys? Tessa's voice fills the other end of the line suddenly, voice sharp.

"About an hour from the New Mexico border," I answer. Her reply is immediate, as though she knew this would happen and has been planning for it.

You lot carry on, your escort team has been in position to meet you along the border for the last day. Rendezvous with them. Normal spot. Once the meet with the escorts is complete Aris you will *go hunt that rat down and bring her home. Alive if you can, but dead if you have to. Eliminate this threat.*

Kore, Elpis and I exchange loaded looks.

Is there a reason you're hesitating on your order, Initiate Kallis? Comes Antiopes voice. Using my title. As though to remind me of my oaths. I do not need reminding.

"No ma'am. We understand." I answer. "I understand."

Good, comes her curt reply. *Get it done. We'll see three of you by the end of the day. Aris. Do not come home until this job is done.* I nod even though she can't see me as the line goes dead.

"Load up. I'll explain on the way." I slide all the way into the drivers seat and start the car up. Kore flings herself into the passenger seat with Lady Medusa and Elpis taking their spots in the back.

"How long was I gone?" I ask them as I peel out of the parking lot.

"Twenty minutes," Kore answers immediately. "Max."

"What *happened?*" Elpis asks, her eyes wide as she leans up by my seat.

"This weird dude made a freaking *portal*—"

"*What!*"

"—And pulled me to this club in L.A.. I ran into Lord Herakles and *he* was being super weird and telling me I needed to leave immediately and I thought he was being super weird about us getting Lady Medusa home but *no* he and this dude who stopped us definitely had some kind of beef. He was talking super weird to Herakles and was like, 'are you stopping me from talking to her' or something like that and it was all just *so bizarre.* And Herakles was like "I'm not stopping anything unless she wants me to' and he kept looking at me, clearly telling me to ask him to stop this and I kept trying and each time before I could this dude would say something weird and cryptic and make me want to hear him out. Anyway! Get this! The dude who made the portal was that random blond dude we met in Vegas when we met up with Deimos."

"That guy again? You're kidding!"

"And he starts talking about how he was in service to one of the gods who bought the information being sold."

"Which god?" Kore asks immediately.

"Don't know," I answer curtly before jumping back in to the story. "Says he felt bad for Medusa because of some of the women in his family and was working on his good karma with the Fates or something like that. I don't know dudes, he was a freak for sure. But anyway, he tells me he knows who the

195

traitor is and where they are. He was weird for a while and I had to resist the urge to stab him like a dozen times, but then finally took me to the back of this club, like the VIP section and there, curled up under Dolos—"

"The god of treachery and treason?" Elpis interjects. "How fitting!"

"That's what I said," I tell her before promptly going back to my story. "Anyway she's all comfy and cozy with the god of whole ass treason and she sees me and I see her and the weird Jason dude disappeared and I went to grab a spear and kill her ass right then and there but then someone got in my face, I have no idea who, and must have opened a new portal and sent me back."

"Athena guide us," Elpis swears, thumping back against her seat. Lady Medusa's eyes are still wide as she stares at me. Kore has her eyes closed, her fingertips pressed tightly against them.

"How're you going to get back to Los Angeles?" Kore asks, her fingers still pressed to her face.

I exhale slowly, weaving in and out of traffic. "Great question. Might try a tracking spell, but we all know I'm shit at those. Might ask Lady Athena for guidance but who knows if she'll give it." Kore finally takes her fingers off her eyes and turns her head towards me, already looking as though I'm breaking her heart in two.

"Please let me come with you. I can do a tracking spell in a heartbeat. And you shouldn't even be by yourself anyway."

I feel my heart cleave in two. The hardest part of being a leader is making the calls no one wants to make. But being the leader of your friends? It makes those hard decisions even harder to make.

Selfishly, I want Kore to come with me. I don't want to face this alone. I want her to share this trauma with me. But that is not my right, not my fate. I will protect her, and every other woman in my conclave, at my own expense. Every single time I will make that choice.

"I'm sorry," I say. And I mean it, I very much want Kore to come with me. We're stronger when together. We always have been. "But you can't. You know you can't. You have your orders and I have mine. Trust mé and trust our Lady. I'll be fine and we'll be rid of this traitor once and for all." Can she hear the lies that coat my tongue like Novocain? I can taste them, heavy and numbing each time they cross my lips. Elpis heaves a sigh in the back, sounding as though she's fighting tears.

"I can't believe she'd do this," she says, wiping her nose. "If she was so unhappy why didn't she leave? Or she could've gone noncombatant!"

"She could never." I shake my head, fiercely. "Melenthe would have disowned her in a heartbeat and she'd have nowhere else to go that her mother wouldn't have say over her."

"You think that's why she helped kill her?" Kore's voice seems to have dropped an octave. It takes me a very long time before I can answer. My own grief coats my throat, leaving me unsure of my voice.

Finally, "I think it was probably a motivating factor." I think back on her behavior the last several weeks. The evasiveness, how she was never in her bed at night. Always off by herself, not even with her Level. The bags under her eyes... the strain on her face..."I don't know, maybe she was swayed by a god. But that would be damn near impossible."

"What do you mean? Why would that be impossible?" Lady Medusa asks. I glance at her in the rearview before looking back to the road and swerving around a minivan who doesn't understand the fast lane is for those who are trying to break the sound barrier.

"Gods can fill the dreams of mortals and demigods, sway them to do their bidding, earn their loyalty or sew seeds of doubt in their current relationships. But the conclave has protection all around it to prevent that from happening, even Athena herself struggles to fill our dreams when she so desires to do so."

"But you think maybe one did?"

I heave a frustrated sigh. "I don't know much of anything anymore, My Lady. All I know is this is going to be the worst mission I'll ever have to complete."

A heavy silence fills the car as no one seems to know what to say to that.

19

Chapter 19

Do you ever regret our lives?

Desma asked me that once. When we were younger. I think we were around thirteen. I had just been inducted as an Initiate, a month or so before hand. Desma had not. We were still friends then. Confidants in each other. As daughters of active members, we understood the pressure our families put on us to succeed. It drew us into a natural alliance, though our Instructors tried to turn us into competitors. We were never interested in completing against each other though, never saw the point in it. That changed later of course, but then so many things changed. A bunch of us were sitting around, wrapping our hands and feet, waiting for some training on hand to hand combat to start. I lounged, leaning back on my elbows, and watched Desma struggle with her wrappings.

Regret? I had asked, finally sitting up and taking over her wrappings. *Like this*, I reminded her, showing her, yet again, how to wrap herself properly.

Yeah, regret. Maybe wonder what you would have been if this hadn't been your life. She didn't look at me as she spoke, just watched my hands go round and round her limbs. I remember laughing a bit, shaking my head in amusement and disbelief both.

Gods no, can you even imagine me doing anything else? I was bred, born and raised for this life. I gestured to the Marks I had been given during my Induction ceremony. The ones that marked me as a legacy Initiate. *Generations of my family were bred, born and raised for this, I'm just carrying on the torch.* Desma nodded, still not looking at me as I finished wrapping her up. Her eyes had been filled with such sorrow. I pressed my lips together as I looked at her, my heart squeezing in worry and fear for my friend.

Hey, I had said, grabbing her elbow, her eyes darted up to mine, startled. I smile at her, telling her without words that I understand what she's trying to say. That I understand what she's feeling. *It will get easier. Have faith.*

She hadn't answered me. Just smiled tearfully and wouldn't meet my eyes again.

But it didn't get easier for her. She just wasn't meant to be a warrior. She didn't have the ruthlessness needed to be successful in our world. Tessa spoke to Melenthe several times about letting Desma transfer to a noncombatant role. Melenthe had vehemently denied it, made it clear that no daughter of hers would step down. She struggled with training's that were easier than breathing for the rest of us and steadily fell behind. Her depression grew and none of us could do anything to help her. Eventually she stopped seeking us out for comfort, started hiding herself somewhere in the compound during our rare moments of free time to avoid being around us. Nothing we did made a difference.

It was several years later, when she called my name for the

first time as her challenge for Match day. I remember staring at her, stunned, from across the arena. Her green eyes bore into mine, unrelenting. Full of so much rage. Kore had turned to look at me in disbelief too. We were eighteen and Desma was only just starting to act truly weird around us, distant and short-tempered. We'd invite her to come out with us, or make space for her to sit with us during meals. She'd all but snarl at us as she either flat out ignored us, or hurled insults at us.

"What's she playing at?" Kore asked me quietly. I could only shake my head in response.

Hesitantly, I accepted her challenge and stepped into the arena with her. It had not been a long match. Though it had been brutal. She refused to yield, forcing me to continue beating her.

That night I visited her in the infirmary. She looked bad, with her split lip, black eye and broken ribs.

She didn't look at me as I sat on the edge of her bed, just kept her gaze on the wall next to her. Her face was eerily blank.

"You going to tell me what that was about?" I finally asked her.

"I don't know what you're talking about," she muttered, her fingers clenched and unclenched where they rested in her lap.

"Des," I gave a disbelieving laugh. "Why would you challenge me? What were you playing at?"

"Why is it so hard to believe that I could be a challenge to you, Aris?" she asked quietly, her voice trembling. I was dumbfounded. And hurt. "Why couldn't I be considered worthy or standing across from you in the arena?"

"Desma," I began, reaching out for her. I stopped when she recoiled from my stop. I pulled my hand back completely as

I listened to her hiss in pain. "Des, we've talked about this. The arena is not where your strengths lie. That is not a bad thing, it just means you were meant to serve our goddess in a different way."

She didn't answer me right away. She shook her head slowly, still avoiding my eyes. I watched as she opened and closed her mouth a few times but swallows whatever she was going to say.

"Please leave," she finally whispered. Her voice broken and lost. My heart shattered and I open my mouth to argue with her when I caught the healers eye. They shook their head at me and jerked it towards the door. My mouth twisted in displeasure but I stood.

"I'll talk to your mother about you going noncombatant again," I promised her, knocking my hand on the end of her bed.

"Whatever," I think I heard her mumble into the pillow.

20

Chapter 20

"Aris!" Elpis's voice calls me back to the present. I shake my head, trying to shake off the ghosts of my past. Soon to be the ghost of my present and future, too. "You're gonna miss our exit!"

"Sorry," I murmur, signaling to move over a lane. I can feel all of their eyes on me. I can feel their pity. At least I'm assuming that's what's making my skin crawl. Concerned hissing fills the silence, leading Lady Medusa to patting her hijab, now sky blue, reassuringly.

Elpis opens her mouth but stops at the sharp look she's given by Kore. I want to be annoyed by this exchanged but find I'm relieved at this interference. I do not want to talk about this.

More mixed emotions flood me as we pull into the Four Corners Monument, for surely I will face more ill-disguised pity.

They sit on their bikes, all restless energy and longing as we exit the car. They jump up as we near, rushing over.

"Thank Athena!"

"Oh, we've missed you guys!"

"Never let us leave you guys again!"

"Come, My Lady," I murmur, placing a gentle, guiding hand onto her back. She's nervous. I can't say I blame her. Initiates are designed to be intimidating, even to the one we are meant to protect, and so many of us can be overwhelming.

"My Lady," Kore calls for her. "Please, come meet our sisters!" Her eyes flit to mine, filled to the brim with anxiety and uncertainty. I smile encouragingly down at her and nod for her to join the others. All except Zoe and another Initiate who break away and make their way over to me. Zoe has me swept up in a rib-crushing hug before I can even open my mouth.

"I'm okay, it's all right." I murmur to her, rubbing her back as I feel her tears wetting my neck. Zoe always was the most sensitive of us. She draws back, scrubbing at her eyes.

"I know," she says thickly. "I know, but it sucks." Well I can't disagree with her so instead I turn to the other girl.

"Miranda, thank you so much for agreeing to be a part of the returning guard." I say, saluting her. She returns the gesture with a small smile.

"Honored to be here, Aris." Miranda is a level 13, competent but not showy. Flagged to return to the conclave as a language Instructor after completion.

The others drift over slowly, still chatting animatedly. I give and receive many perfunctory hugs as I fill everyone in on their roles for the last stretch home.

"Yeah, Rissy, we got all that," Sierra chimes in impatiently. "But what are *you* going to do?"

Rose reaches for my hand, concern flooding her eyes.

"It doesn't feel right, leaving you to fight this on your

own." I give her hand a squeeze back before making a point of dropping it.

"This *is* mine to fight alone. This is the burden our Lady has asked of me and I will not deny this call. Desma must face her atonement."

"You didn't answer Sierra," Zoe points out, arms crossed, eyes narrowed.

"Well first thing I'm going to do is find some place to eat. I'm starving and if I'm going to perform a tracking spell—"

"Beg your pardon." Rachel says. An insulting amount of disbelief colors her tone. "You're going to what?"

"Rissy, you have a lot of skills but magic is not one of them." Sierra says matter-of-factly. I try to bury the irritation that flares hot and heavy in me. Try to. I do not succeed. I've been burying my irritation for several days now and I'm running out of places to put it.

"Oddly enough, I am perfectly aware of this. But unless anyone else has a better idea for how to track her rat ass down across the entire world then this is what I'm working with." I don't mean to snap at them, but my grief and stress are boiling over. I make eye contact with each and every one of them, my stare harsh. "So since no one is saying anything I'm going to assume that means that no one else *does* have any better ideas. So that means I'm going to find a quiet spot to have some lunch so I can do this fucking tracking spell without passing out for several days."

All nine women around me wear identical looks of fear and pity and suddenly all I want is to sleep. But I can't. Not yet. Not until I finish this. I rub my hands over my face before gesturing to the road.

"Go on, get. Get home. Get her safe. I'll see you all in a few days."

They shuffle uneasily in response. I outrank them all, so technically my words are not words, but orders to be obeyed. They teeter, unsure if they have been given parting words from their sister, or orders from their leader. I shoo them away. "Now! Go! Get our Lady home safe!"

They all, with the exception of Lady Medusa, snap into a salute that I quickly return. After one last round of hugs, Zoe hands me the keys to her motorcycles, as she's taking my spot in the car. The rest will lead and follow on bikes. Lady Medusa stands in front of me and clasps my hands firmly in hers.

"I will see you soon." She says simply. Her voice steady and sure.

Again, I think of what a tragedy it is. That she will never be a Priestess of Athena again. I would have loved to have sat and listened to her speak, pray, sing. What a fate she was given. A talented and striking Priestess, cut down before she had a chance to bloom because someone else felt entitled to her. To her story and her fate. I feel that grief, *her grief*, in the deepest part of my heart. I force myself to smile back at her. She squeezes my hands before dropping them and running lightly back to the waiting car, Kore and Zoe right on her heels.

I stand there with one hand raised up to shield my eyes from the relentless sun and watch them drive away. I keep standing there, watching their dust recede and then stand there for a moment more before I dig my cellphone out of my pocket.

I dial the number without looking.

You screening your calls now? Is the greeting I get. I can't help but smile, almost in relief.

"Want to get lunch?"

* * *

An hour and some change later I pull up to some tiny mom-and-pop diner in some tiny no-name town in Utah. He's already there waiting, leaning up against his own bike black as night with ancient sayings scrawled into the side.

His eyes are also tight with worry but his does not inspire anger. I think it's because I'm too relieved to see him. Or maybe it's because I know I can scream awful things at him and he will let me. I pull off my helmet and set it on the back of the bike.

"How're you doing, gorge—" he cuts off with a grunt as I throw myself at him.

The weight of what I'm about to do, of what we have gone through, slams into me suddenly and I screw my face up against the grief that threatens to drown me. My breaths, half smothered into Deimos's chest, become ragged and wet. For days now I've been burying my worry and grief and anger. I've had to. I'm the one in charge, the one the others look to for support and guidance. It won't work for them to see me like a mess. That's another one of the reasons I fell for Deimos. I didn't owe him my composure. He wasn't following me so it didn't matter if I was in no condition to lead. I could grieve around him.

His arms come around me at once, strong and familiar. One of his hands stroking my hair. He doesn't say anything, thank the gods. He knows there is nothing that anyone could say that would bring me comfort right now. Instead, he presses his lips to the top of my head, warming the skin of my scalp with every breath.

It takes me longer than it should to get myself under control and I find I don't want to look at Deimos as I pull away, wiping away the evidence of my weakness. I'm opening my mouth to apologize when his hand comes up to cup my face, his thumb wiping away my tears.

"Don't." He says. I glare fiercely at him. He doesn't react to the anger, just finishes wiping the last of my tears away. "Don't you apologize to me. I thought we were past that."

"Old habits," I mutter, unable to stop myself from leaning into his hand.

"C'mon, Killer," he grabs my shoulders, leading me inside the diner. "Let's get you something to eat."

The diner is small and the locals regard us somewhat warily, but are friendly enough as we slide into an empty booth. Our waitress, an older gal with a name tag that reads *Brenda,* greets us with a genuinely warm smile and hands us our menus while rattling off the day's specials. She asks what brings us to town. *Oh just passing through, we can never resist stopping at proper diners such as places like this.* Oh the town is always so happy to have visitors, even for just a little while. Now what can I get you darlings to drink? *Oh just a couple of Cokes would be fantastic.* Would Pepsi be All right? *Oh yes ma'am, that's no problem at all.*

"Peppy woman," Deimos remarks with affection as Brenda whisks away, promising to be right back with our drinks.

I nod in agreement, a real smile filling my lips as I look over the menu.

"Why are you looking at that thing?" He teases me. I don't deign that with an answer and idly flip the menu over. "I'm serious, you already know what you're getting. The same thing you get every time we go to a place like this."

I look up at him, self-righteous. "And what if they don't

have it? I won't know unless I read their menu!"

He blinks once at me before erupting into laughter. A hearty chuckle that has no business coming from the god of terror, but it soothes me anyway. I feel the knot in my stomach loosening, as I sit and listen to it.

"Shut up," I tell him, grinning. He wipes his hand across his mouth, trying to stifle his laughter.

Brenda returns with our drinks, which she sets deftly onto the table before planting her fists on her hips.

"We know what we want? Or do we need some more time?"

Deimos raises a teasing eyebrow at me, smirking. I make a face at him before turning to Brenda.

"Could I please get a bacon cheeseburger with extra pickles and no mustard or onion?"

"Of course you can, sugar. Fries with that?"

"Please." I hand her back my menu.

"And for you, sugar?" She turns to Deimos.

"Same as the lady, please." He tells her, smiling as he hands over his menu as well.

She beams at both of us as she moves on, checking on her other customers, lingering to chat with some.

"So." He says after a moment, reaching across the table to hold one of my hands. I clutch it like a lifeline. It's all the prompting I need. I close my eyes as the severity of my situation slams into me. My chest becomes tight with my grief all over again. My throat feels hot as the tears fight to escape my eyes. The situation, the full situation, is finally hitting me as I sit, safe with Deimos and I can't deal with it. I don't want to deal with it. I'm so tired, so tired of all of these battles, so tired of the adrenaline coursing through my veins. What an odd thing for a spear to think.

"It's Desma, Dei," I whisper raggedly. "She's the traitor."

"Shit," he mutters, his eyes wide.

I swallow hard, choking on my next words. "And I've been ordered to deal with her."

He leans forward suddenly, clasping my hand in both of his.

"Aristomache," he murmurs so lowly, so tenderly, I almost don't hear him. A fresh wave of tears come to my eyes. I lean forward and rest my forehead on our hands. "I am so sorry, ἀγαπητή. I am so sorry."

I sit up and wipe my face on my shoulders, not wanting to let go of his hands even for a second.

"Everyone knows we weren't the best of friends but our issues only began the last couple of years. We used to be friends. I used to spend hours with her, helping her with her training, helping her advance." I tell him, my voice thick. "We all did. She's our sister. We love her. We protected her. We celebrated her." I look at him, tears blurring my vision and wetting my cheeks.

His stare is tortured as he gazes back at me. Knowing I am hurting, knowing there is nothing he can do to stop it.

"How could she do this to us?" I sob, clapping a hand over my mouth. My eyes squeeze shut as though that may keep the tears inside them. It doesn't work. They fall fast and frequently down my face. I can taste the salt of them on my tongue. I don't need to look to know that the hand that clutches at Deimos's is white with the strength of my grip.

"Desperate people do desperate things, ἀγαπητή ." His voice is bleak as his free hand comes up to wipe away my tears.

Normally, I do not cry this often. But it has been a partic-ularly trying week and I know better than to push this wave down. It will drown me if I do.

"*Gods!*" I breath out in a huff, grinding a fist into my forehead. "How am I going to come out of this whole, Dei? I've killed before, I'm not afraid of that. But *how* am I supposed to kill one of my sisters without losing a part of my soul?"

"I wish I could answer that for you, Aris." His voice is rough and gravely, distressed by my distress. But his hands are not as he continues to hold my hand, stroking his thumb over my skin. I cover my eyes as another sob breaks free, and I allow myself one more moment of weakness. Of dramatics. Then I drag in a deep breath and pull my other hand free to wipe harshly at my face with both of them.

"And don't get me wrong," I continue raging. "She deserves to die. She killed her mother. She betrayed her goddess and her family but by the might of Athena why must it be me?"

I go silent after that, staring at nothing outside the window. I focus entirely on slowing and steadying my breathing, ignoring the pathetic hitches that come every so often.

Recognizing that I'm attempting to get ahold of myself, Deimos fishes an ice cube from his drink and, after sucking on it briefly to get the soda off of it, hands it to me.

"Ah, thank you." I tell him gratefully, if still somewhat tearful. I rub the ice around my eyes to help with the puffiness. That and the cool water helps soothe my flushed skin and ground me back in reality. I pop what's left into my mouth after I'm done and realize just how thirsty I am. I quickly crunch up the ice so I can begin to drain my soda.

"So where do you go from here?" He asks, helping me focus on the task at hand. I finish off my soda before I answer him.

"She was in Los Angeles as of a few hours ago." I tell him. "With Dolos." I add my tone acidic, as I give him an I-told-you-so look. He closes his eyes as an irritated sigh huffs out of his lips, his heading rolling back.

"One time." He tells me, his eyes still closed.

"You know the rules," I say arrogantly. Sighing in frustration, he lifts his head up and looks me in the eyes, his expression already peeved.

I make sure we have solid eye contact before: "I told you so."

His eyes roll all the way back into his head. "Happy?"

I shrug. "It helps. Anyway, I don't know if she's still there or not. Dolos might have whisked her away somewhere else. So I need to load up on carbs and sugar," I gesture around us, "so that I can preform a tracking spell— yes I know I'm ass at them, please don't remind me, I think you'll find that I don't have many options— to figure out where she's hiding."

He regards me for a moment, sighing deeply before switching his full soda for my empty one.

"Better drink that too, then." I smile ruefully at him as I wrap both hands around the glass.

"Here we are," Brenda half sing-songs to us, laden with our plates. After she sets them in front of us, she plants her fists on her hips again. "Anything else for ya?"

"No ma'am, this looks prime. But some refills would be fantastic." Deimos tells her, his smile dazzling. I grin at her as well.

"No, thank you," I echo. She beams at us again, telling us she'd be right back with those refills, and makes her rounds again.

I immediately begin to devour my burger, not realizing how famished I was until I had the food under my nose.

"The Fates know I love a woman who's not afraid to eat in public," Deimos tells me, winking, trying to get a rise out of me.

I glare balefully at him, my mouth too full to give a verbal response. I eat most of the burger before coming up for air. I take several mouthfuls of soda before speaking again.

"Gods," I say, wiping my mouth with my napkin. "I didn't realize how hungry I was."

"You humans and your need to eat," he teases, then be-comes more serious. "You've been running all over the place, getting into fights and not sleeping. I'm amazed you're functioning as well as you are. But maybe I shouldn't be with the whole blessing of Athena thing you Initiates got going on."

"You make some good points," I breathe as I pick up my burger again, polishing it off in a few more bites.

"Is that actually any good?" He asks, wrinkling his nose a little.

"It's delicious," I tell him with relish, now working on my fries.

It doesn't take long before those are gone too and Deimos swaps my now empty plate for his full one.

"*Where* do you keep all this food?" He says wonderingly as I sink my teeth into his burger too. I smile at him, all teeth, mouth all full.

"In my muscles." I tell him slightly muffled by my burger, pulling up one of my arms in a flex. Showing off a well defined bicep. He nods knowingly as I flex for him. His eyes get serious as he stares at me.

"Let me put a blessing over you, before you go." He says, suddenly. I stare at him, and equal mix of regret and irritation.

"You can't, you know you can't. Not while I have the blessing of Athena."

"The *passive* blessing of Athena. Dormant. Let me give you an active one."

"It's not me denying you, Dei. I'm telling you it won't work. Other gods have tried to bless us on other missions and they don't work. They don't take. The blessing of Athena cancels them out. Or worse."

He gives me a hard stare for a moment before finally rolling his eyes in annoyance and turning his gaze out the window.

We finish my meal in silence.

Brenda comes over as I'm finishing off my second helping of fries, asks us how everything was.

We beam and heap on the praise, not exaggerating, these people know how to cook a burger. She's clearly pleased with our enjoyment, her smile takes up her entire face.

Deimos hands over some crisp dollar bills, more than plenty. It took some explaining but he understands how tipping works now and takes joy in tipping wild amounts. Her eyes widen and her mouth opens, to protest judging by the look in her eyes.

"Keep the change," I tell her firmly. Her wide eyes swing over to me. "Please. We insist." She purses her lips together and her eyes begin to look a bit misty.

"Well. Well then. You guys be safe out there. And if you're ever in the area again, you be sure to come on in." We beam back at her and assure her we'll do just that.

"You feel ready?" Deimos asks as we stand by our bikes. Putting off goodbye. I nod, pulling on my riding gloves.

"As ready as I'll ever be, anyway." I answer. Deimos nods, then steps forward, taking my face in his hands. We study each other's eyes for a moment before he leans in to give me a lingering kiss. My one hand comes up to cover his, while my other grips his forearm.

"I'll be All right," I try to reassure the fear I see looking back at me. He doesn't say anything for a while, just continues to stare at me, stroking my hair back from my face, studying me, before nodding slowly.

"I'll see you later, then." He says, finally pulling away and sitting on his bike. I smile at him, and can't resist reaching my hand out to stroke his face one last time before I go.

"Stay breezy, Dei."

"Stay safe, ἀγαπητή."

I see him in my side mirrors. He sits and he watches me drive away until I'm long gone from sight.

21

Chapter 21

I hate doing this. I grumble to myself. I manage to find an old, forgotten gas station along some old, forgotten highway that I pulled into to suit my needs. My bike sits nearby, the hot engine ticking at me, as though reminding me that I am on a deadline.

I sink onto a flat spot of the ground, my legs crossing underneath me. I roll my neck out, trying to chase away the eternal stiffness.

"Okay," I mutter, trying to psych myself up. "This is going to suck. Make your peace with that now and get this over with."

I'm stalling. I fully admit this to myself. But this really is going to suck. Finally, I shake the nerves out of my hands and plant them firmly on the ground in front of me.

I begin to chant the spell hard and fast, muttering under my breath. I can feel the magic, sluggish to respond to me, swirling under the earth. I grit my teeth, agitated that this is so hard for me, and repeat my spell again. Louder. Firmer. I will not take 'no' for an answer.

Show me. I call. *Show me where she is.*

I begin to get flashes in my mind. Brief glimpses that tell me I'm on the right track.

The magic fights me. My stomach churns and I close my eyes against the black spots that beginning to flood my vision.

Unworthy, hisses up at me. Maybe from the earth, maybe from my subconscious.

Show me! I now demand. My breath starts to come quicker, gasping through my teeth. *Show me!*

Unworthy! Unworthy! Unworthy!

SHOW ME! SHOW ME! SHOWMESHOWMESHOWMESHOWME!

Saliva floods my mouth as I fight the urge to puke. It feels as though someone is stabbing behind my eyes with an ice pick. But finally, the magic bends to my will and allows me glimpses of what I'm seeking. Slowly the images start to come more frequently. More usefully. They become longer and more defined.

With a scream, I give everything I have. I send it out into the Mist, calling for the magic that is *my right*.

Finally, she erupts, crystal clear in my mind. Lounging and unconcerned, as she sits laughing and knocking back drinks. With a gasp I sever the spell. I don't want to risk someone detecting the magic and giving her a heads-up. The after math of using magic is immediate. A dull ache fills my body and nausea turns my stomach.

With a groan, I roll onto my hands and knees and fight to keep my meal down. I dry heave several times, truly battling the nausea. I stay that way for a while, longer than I should but using magic this way drains me to my very core. It's always been this way, no matter what training's or blessings I received. I lean forward so my head rests on my hands, my breath swirls desert dirt around me. I can taste it on my tongue. I rock my head side to side, attempting to chase the aches away. It takes longer than I would like it to, but eventually I mange to get myself under control. I sit back on my heels, pressing a hand to my stomach, willing it to stop churning. Scrubbing at my face, I stand and make my way to my bike.

Ready or not, Desma, I think viciously as I mount up. *Here I come.*

A dull light on the horizon calls to me as I kick up dust, flying down the road. Like the illumination of a far off city. But it is not a city that is calling me.

My mind drifts as I drive. I wonder if she knows I'm hunting her. She must. But she was certainly not acting like someone who thought they were being hunted. Laughing carefree and wild. She looks like her mother like that.

Her mother who she helped murder. Her mother whose corpse she spit on.

Red hot anger flares inside me as I twist my throttle, my bike growling underneath me.

* * *

I drive straight through the night, stopping only when absolutely necessary. Part of me wants to drag it out, maybe stop in a hotel for a night and deal with this ugliness tomorrow. Or maybe the next day. Or the day after that. But I don't. Because it has to get done eventually. And it's been decided that I'm the one who has to deal with this and me stalling won't convince them to change their minds.

Too soon, I see it.

Lord Dolos's mansion.

I stand atop a a seaside cliff, binoculars pressed to my eyes. The full moon gives me plenty of light to see what I'm doing. It looks like he's having a party of some kind, our dear Lord Dolos.

Down below, on a bluff of the cliff, sits the mansion. Gods and spirits of all kinds fill his balcony, inebriated on drink and power both. I recognize some of the demigods that mill around them, both as servants and as company. My heart squeezes. I don't want to fight them. I keep scanning, looking into open bay windows and more patios.

I know she is here. The dull light hovers over the top of the mansion, calling me to notice it.

I see you jackass, I think venomously at it. *Just not my target.*

I see guards at the doors, gods in the halls, demigods trying to blend into the shadows. No red-haired traitorous bitches. Just my luck.

"Oh you raggedy *bitch,*" I say out loud, my frustration growing. "Where are you hiding from me?"

I'm just accepting my fate that I'm going to have to go in blind and flush her out when something catches my eye.

"Gotcha," I murmur, freezing like a dog whose caught a scent. Not Desma. Dolos. Shirtless and sweaty, opening a window on the third floor. The blood red curtains (*tasteful decor, Dolos)* flutter in the sea breeze. As they do I catch a glimpse of red hair being thrown over a pale and skinny shoulder.

Now I really do feel like a hunting hound. I can feel the call of the hunt. It sings to me. Begs me to join it. A savage grin fills my face as I put away my binoculars and ready myself. I always was best at this part. Seeking out my prey and then eliminating them. How many missions have I done like this in the past? Too many to count. Somewhere along the way of my training, in my desire for the hunt, I almost became a hit-man for hire. Gods and other creatures alike would earn Athena's favor just to ask to borrow me. Most of them were denied, but some were granted. Artemis, Hera, Demeter, they would all call to me to avenge those who worship them. Those who were ravaged just as my Lady Medusa had been. They couldn't excise justice themselves, so they hired Athena's spear in their stead.

Even my Lady Athena would send me out in her name. When her temples were violated and desecrated.

Avenge me, she would whisper in my dreams. *Raise your spear and strike down my enemies.*

I have found I am very good at raising my spear. Putting it down however...

I take my phone out of my pocket (and quickly answer the text from Kore telling me they made it home safe) and stow it in my duffle bag, which I just leave sitting on top of my seat. After strapping on my armor, I check my spears, counting them off in my head.

One, two, three, four, fi— damn. I forgot to ask one of the girls to borrow one of their spears after mine broke while fighting the cyclops. Oh well. I twist my shield bracelet around my wrist a few times and then reach for my locket, squeezing it tight in my grip.

I release a slow, deep breath. Then I begin picking my way down the small trail that leads down towards the mansion.

The moon provides the perfect amount of lighting and I say a fervent prayer to Artemis, thanking her for this. I have to take care as I pick my way down the trail, it's thin and rocky and while a fall wouldn't kill me, it would slow me down a little and piss me off more than a little. So. Probably better to avoid that.

Finally I do some side stepping climbing move to get onto the bluff where Dolos' mansion sits. I pick up at a run again and as I near the mansion the air shimmers as the Mist shifts to reveal a 20-foot security fence that runs all the way around the property. I huff in annoyance, rolling my eyes as I skip to a stop.

I look around briefly, praying in vain that there's a tree I can scale but suck my teeth as I realize I'll have to do this the hard way.

I jog back until I'm about 100 feet away from the fence. After, I stand for a moment holding up my hand to help me gauge the distance. Then I take several striding leaps forward before working up into a sprint. I leap at the wall, managing to find traction on it, and run up it before reaching out with my hands. I dangle from the top for half a second before I finish, swinging myself over the top and landing soundlessly up and over to the other side. I grin, pleased with myself before taking off at a sprint across the large yard.

Loud voices and laughter surround me as I slow. I crouch down as I near the mansion, which is honestly unnecessary. There's no way any of them can see me with how much higher up they are. Still, I don't relax until I've hidden myself in the shadows, pressed up against the walls of this massive place.

I'm just thinking over how I'm going to get inside this place when a sudden light and an increase of voices sends me ducking behind a rose bush. But it works out in my favor. It's the door to the kitchen. One of the cooks dumps something out of a pot into the bushes and ducks back inside.

I'm trying to figure out what the odds are that I'll be able to get through the kitchen without being seen when the door swings open again. Mortals and demigods alike pour out, happy to be done for the day, chatting about the rudeness of the guests they had served.

Moving fast, I mange to catch the door before it fully closes behind the last girl and slip in before any of them can see me.

The kitchen is a wide and open space. I'll be the first to admit, it surprised me. I was absolutely expecting a dungeon. It's the cleanest kitchen I've ever laid eyes on, including the one at the conclave. Although, we were never afraid our instructors would kill us if we didn't clean it right. So I guess these guys have better motivation.

I make it out of the kitchen and down the long hallway to the service stairs without encountering anybody or anything. I make sure to close the door to the stairway silently behind me and swear under my breath as I see the stairs I'll have to run up.

Unsheathing my knife, I get to work. Running stairs was one of the most popular workouts for us, an easy way to build stamina and strength. Desma, of course, struggled with it. She would trip over her feet and the stairs constantly. It hurt me to see her struggle so much. As I climb I try not to think of the countless mornings I ran stairs side by side with her. Slowing my pace to match hers, muttering encouragements under my breath at her, reminding her to breath correctly, looping my arm with hers to help her keep her feet. I shake my head to clear it of the memories and force myself to climb faster.

I pause, listening hard, when I reach the door for the third floor. Once satisfied, I crack open the door, peering down the hallway as far as I can see. Again, when satisfied, I slip out from the door and make sure it closes silently again. Immediately, two guards, harpy's by the look of them, come out of an adjoining hallway.

Fortunately for me, and unfortunately for them, their backs are to me as they continue their patrol. On light and deadly feet, I advance.

I whistle once as I'm a few feet away. One of the guards starts to turn— and immediately gets my knife stabbed into his throat for his trouble. He explodes with a *bu-kawk* and a puff of sulfur and feathers.

His partner swings his sword without looking, without hesitating. I drop to a knee, then pivot so I'm behind my opponent. Rising, I cover the guards mouth with my hand before burying my knife into his spine and jerking it up sharply. Another cloud of sulfur and feathers and he's gone too.

I stoop to pick up a discarded key card, shoving it into my pocket. Could be nothing. Could be something.

I stalk down the hallway, head swiveling back and forth down hallways and into doors. It feels as though this hallway is going on forever and I'm growing more frustrated as more time goes by. My teeth seem permanently ground into each other and I can't seem to remember how to relax them.

The door behind me opens suddenly, filling the dark hallway with light. I snap off a spear as I twist around. A grating male voice breaks the silence of the hallway.

"Don't bother getting up, babe. I'll be right back. Those stupid servants don't know how to do anything right." Dolos steps out, still shirtless, and closes the door with a sharp *snap.*

He turns and immediately sees me. Sees how I'm dressed. How I hold my spear. His voice is nonchalant, although his body language is not.

223

"You were stupid to come here. You should have waited until she left to attack. She's under my protection here and you," he points a pale, mocking finger at me, "are not under Deimos's."

I sneer, cocking my eyebrow at him. "You think I need Deimos's protection? Unlike that spineless whelk you have warming your bed right now, I fight my own battles. And after I take you out, she'll fight her own too."

"You're as predictable as you are arrogant, Aristomache. You think you could defeat a god?"

I level my spear at him. "I think it is what I was born to do."

He opens his hands and a shining bronze spear materializes in them. He levels it at me.

"You always were a bad gambler, Dolos." I say, stalking towards him. Armor appears on his body as he countermoves against me and we begin the age old dance of combat. "Always backed the bad ponies. Never could pick the winning hand. And now look at you. Defending a girl who is slated by the Fates to die. If not by my hand then by the hands of our conclave. She will die nameless, guilty of matricide, forgotten by our goddess and her sisters. And you will forever be the fool who supported her."

His lip curls and with a yell of fury, he closes the gap between us, swinging his spear at me.

I taste the metal as it flashes in front of my face. Grunting, I parry his attack and make for any weak spots I see. He is a god yes, but he is not a god of battle, or of strategy or strength. He is the god of betrayal and treachery and it's a lot harder to betray someone when you're already engaged in combat with them.

His eyebrows furrow in frustration as he realizes I'm an

equal match for him. As he realizes I meant what I told him.

I was born to fight gods.

Not that he doesn't get some lucky hits in. It's with a cry of surprise, mingled with pain, that I realize he managed to slash my face. He made the smallest amount of contact but still, hot blood coats my cheek and neck.

With a frustrated cry I lunge at him, my attacks frequent and lightning quick. His anger makes him sloppy. Mine makes me vicious. He's stumbling over his feet as I push him further and further back. Vases and other art pieces shatter around us as we duck and dive around each others blows, leaving them to take the damage.

Taking a move from Kore, I feint as though I'm aiming for his face and, when he goes to defend against it, drive my spear down into the top of his foot. He bellows in pain, reaching out to grab at me. I use my spear as a vaulting pole and flip neatly over his head, pulling out my spear as I go. Before he can turn, I find another weak spot on the back of his thigh and swiftly bury my spear in it. His following roar echoes in my ears.

He manages to grab my braid before I can dance back out of reach and throws me bodily down the hallway. With a grunt, I land and roll several more feet before I manage to get my feet back under me. The blood on my cheek feels sticky as it dries. I've rolled through a broken vase and mutter a curse as I pull a particularly large piece from the back of my arm.

Dolos limps at me, swearing as he does, staining the lush carpet with his golden ichor. Again, I revel in this part of my destiny. While a *god* limps towards me, exhausted and wounded, wounded by *my* hands, I feel as though I've been taking a stroll through the park. Despite my injuries, I'm still light on my feet and full of energy.

"You're not tired already, are you, Lord Dolos?" I taunt, twirling my spear around me. I suck my teeth at him in mock disappointment. "I sure hope your stamina is better than this in bed. Poor Desma. Not only is she a traitor, but she's a traitor getting bad sex? I almost feel bad for her now."

With a curse, he lunges. But he's slow and clumsy. Even more so than usual. The swipes of his spear are almost too easy to dodge and block.

I summon my shield and catch his spear against it. With one sharp movement, I snap it. His eyes grow large and I feel a thrill as I see the fear in them.

He summons another one just in time to block my next blow. He spins his spear around and manages a sharp jab with the butt of his spear to my stomach, which sends me skidding backwards a few feet. It does him no good. With a yell I run those few steps at him and leap into the air. My spear is buried in his clavicle before he can blink.

I pull out my weapon just as suddenly as I put it in and keep up my violent attack on the god of traitors. He's just barely managing to block my attacks as he keeps backing up, retreating from the onslaught. When I glance behind him a savage grin fills my face.

I twist my spear in a sinuous fashion before plunging it into his thigh. He barely has time to cry out before my foot connects with his chest, sending him flying out of the window behind him and down 60 feet to the ground.

Putting my foot on the broken windowsill, I peek out down below. He lays there, groaning quietly, ichor flowing freely from his wounds.

In a blink he's gone. The only proof that he was there is the gold-stained grass.

Satisfied, I turn away from the window and stare down the hallway. She knows I'm here. No way she didn't hear our fight. Yet she didn't come out to help her lover. How odd.

I begin making my way back down the hallway. Slowly. Peacefully. She knows I'm coming. She had her opportunity to run or to help kill me and instead the coward chose to hide.

Does she know I'm coming to kill her? Or does she think my orders are to only take her into custody? I try not to think about what this might do to me. To kill someone is a weighty thing. To kill one of your sisters... I shake my head to chase away the thought as I come to a stop in front of the door. I can see the light underneath the bottom of it. She didn't bother to turn it off.

My hand seems separate from me, like it's another person's hand I'm watching, as I reach for the handle. Silently I twist the cold, metal knob and swing open the door.

22

Chapter 22

She doesn't turn as I walk in. Choosing to keep her gaze focused outside. She sits on the bench of the open window, the curtains flutter in the breeze as she sits with her knees to her chest, arms wrapped loosely around her shins. She looks perfectly unbothered at the situation she finds herself in. I take a few more steps in before the sound of her voice stops me.

"I was planning on jumping," her tone is nonchalant. As though she's asking for my opinion on her hairstyle. "Before you got to me. I just couldn't seem to follow through with it." I nod even though she's still not looking at me.

"Yeah, that probably would have been a lot easier for both of us if you had." She gives a watery chuckle and I hear her sniff as she unwraps one of her arms to drag the heel of her hand across her cheeks.

She gives a groaning sort of sigh as she leans back against the wall. "Is it weird that I'm relieved?" I plant my spear on the ground, leaning on it as though it's a walking stick. I know she's stalling by talking to me this way but I can't seem to stop myself from answering. In fact, I find I'm grateful for the delay.

"No," I tell her honestly. "I imagine spending whatever time you had left looking over your shoulder for us wouldn't have been much of a life." She nods at this, looking peaceful suddenly.

"Yeah," she murmurs, almost to herself, "yeah that's what I thought to." She turns to face me, moving so she's sitting cross-legged on the bench. "Ask me."

I know immediately what she's talking about. I shake my head slowly, never taking my eyes off of her. "No, I don't think I will, Des." Anger flashes across her face.

"Oh I think you will," she says mockingly. "Because you can't kill me until perfect little Aristomache has the answers she needs."

I throw her a look.

"Desma, why are you doing this? You can't delay the inevitable. Dolos isn't coming back to protect you."

"No, it sounded like he got his ass handed to him pretty good."

She agrees with an ironic laugh as she stands, staring intently at me. "I tried to warn him. Tried to tell him what it's like to be on the other end of your spear. Your mighty, mighty spear."

I can only shake my head at her, warning her, begging her, as she fingers her own spear bracelets, twisting them round and round her wrist. But she won't be stopped now. This has been building up in her for who knows how long.

"But it's a hard thing to describe. How do you describe the feeling of worthlessness and inadequacy that you will only feel while having generations of perfection and excellence lunging at you? While realizing you are *nothing* compared to them?"

"Desma you're not noth—" I begin, but a manic look fills her eyes as she snaps off a spear, pointing at me with the tip of it.

"YES! YES I AM NOTHING! I AM NOTHING COMPARED TO YOU, ARISTOMACHE!" Spittle flies from her mouth as she screams at me. I blink once in pure shock. I've never even seen Desma raise her voice, let alone become unhinged like this.

In the next second, though, she's fine. She lowers her spear and stands up straighter. Her face goes blank and that, more than her screaming, sends a chill down my spine. "That's what my mother told me, you know. During her last visit."

It takes me a second to remember Melenthe's last visit. It was two years ago, for Desma's 21st birthday and the whole conclave had been very excited about it. Melenthe is a legend for the missions she's carried out for the conclave. She was the youngest person to ever be selected as a Protector for Lady Medusa, selected when she was twenty-five. She had come in time for a Match Day and had stood, arms crossed and impassive as Desma fought.

She had, of course, chosen me for her fight. Although it had been one of her best fights, undoubtedly pulling out all the stops to impress her mother, it ended the same as the rest of them: with her bloody and exhausted in the sand and me standing triumphantly over her.

Desma nods, watching me remember.

"Yeah," she drawls out slowly. "Yeah, you can imagine what a disappointment *that* fight was to see. She came to talk to me in the infirmary. Stood at the end of the bed with her face twisted like she had something rotten under her nose. And while she stood there, just staring at me, I apologized. Can you believe that? You shattered, like, three of my ribs and *I* was apologizing to *my mom* for it. But I did. I apologized and promised her I'd get better. Promised her I'd advance in my training. That I'd make her proud. She just *stood there* while I laid in front of her, injured, crying, begging. Finally she held up a hand and said 'I don't know who you're kidding. You'll always be nothing compared to that girl.'"

I don't know what to say. We all knew that Melenthe was incredibly hard on Desma, but she's a legacy. That's how it is when you're a legacy. My own mother was sometimes incredibly harsh with me about my training. It's just a part of the life. But even I could never imagine my mother stooping so low to say something like that to me, no matter how disappointed she was in me. I open my mouth to say, what I don't know. But before I can decide, Desma begins talking again. Tripping over her words in her need to be heard.

"My mother *hated* me because of you, Aris. She saw Atalanta with her two *perfect* daughters and then she looked at me and couldn't even get herself to not glare at me. Forget about smiling or giving me any kind of affection. No. No it was easier for her to pretend that I never existed. So *say it* Aris. I know you saw it. The night we came for them." I fight the nausea that rolls over me as I remember the vision shown to me. "I admit, I was hesitant to show it to you but then I had my eyes opened and realized we *needed* you to get angry and stupid and come after us guns blazing! The Kallis way!"

I want to refuse. Tell her she's crazy and that she will die by my spear but instead what comes out is, "Who was the man?"

Now it's her turn to blink in shock at me. Whatever she had wanted me to say or expected me to ask, it was not this. Her answer comes fervently. "You don't need to know that, Aris. I know you have no reason to trust me, but trust me on that. Forget about him. Kill me, take me back to the conclave and leave it at that but leave him be."

I gape at her, furious and bewildered that she'd protect a man in such a way while simultaneously condemning her sisters. "You killed your own mother, Desma. You *spit* on her dead body! That's between you and the Fates but I have not and will not forsake my mother in such a way."

This takes her aback. She straightens suddenly as her head cocks reflexively to the side.

"What does your mother have to do with him?" she asks. Her eyebrows knit together as she looks at me.

I stare back at her, dumbfounded. She can't be serious.

"He *took* her, Desma! She didn't die that night with Julia and your mother."

Now she's the one shaking her head, but this time in denial rather than anger, her eyes growing wide in horror. She takes a step back from me.

"No. No. He wouldn't do that. He wouldn't risk our plans like that! He said she's dead."

A wild, incredulous laugh escapes me. "You'd trust that scum of a man over me? She's not. She's not dead. Your little buddy took her and I *will* find her."

Anger flashes hot in her again. Her eyes lose the confused glaze as they snap to mine.

"Damn it, Aris! Why won't you listen to me?! Leave it alone!"

"Why won't I listen to you? Do you even hear yourself? Why won't I listen to you?! Gee, I don't know Desma! Maybe because you helped *kill your own mother!*"

With a snarling shriek, she leaps at me.

I summon my shield and deflect her blow, following it you the shaft of my spear to her ribs.

"You just don't get it!" She screams, angry tears in her eyes. "You'll never get it! With your perfect scores, your perfect genetics, *skipping a level!* Do you have any idea what it was like? Trying to fill shoes my mother left behind?"

I gape at her. "*Yes!*" I say emphatically. "Yes I know *exactly* what that's like! You know what my family's like! You think they would accept anything less than perfection?"

With a shriek that makes me jump, Desma grabs at her hair, her eyes wild. "No, you don't! No you don't, because you've never been anything but perfect! You were the perfect little star and I was left to rot in your shadow!"

Even though her behavior is setting me on edge, I can't help but respond back to her allegations.

"Are you seriously kidding me?" I ask her incredulously. "That's the angle you're taking? Desma, you chose to live in the shadows! You think we didn't know how your mom was? Why do you think I spent all of my free time helping you with your battle training? Why do you think Rose spent hours upon hours helping you with your language skills? Why else would Kore coach you in your agility and balance? Because we *loved you*! Because we knew how hard it was for you and we were just trying to get you through so you could be done and live your life the way you wanted! But you played your little pity game, your little "boo hoo no one likes me" and completely snubbed us. Desma we loved you. We cared about you. We only wanted to help you."

"No, but you didn't!" The manic gleam is back in her eyes. "I thought you did! I was so grateful, for so long! I worshiped

233

the ground you guys walked on because you were the only thing keeping me from getting kicked out of the conclave and disowned by my mother! But then they showed me the truth! They showed me how you guys were just trying to keep me down so you could excel faster! They showed me the truth! They showed me the light. They filled my dreams and helped me see there's another way, a better way for me to live."

"Wait a minute," I say. "They filled your dreams? What do you mean? Who? How?"

"Wouldn't you like to know," she leers. "I've learned stuff you could never even imagine."

I resist the urge to rolls my eyes at her childish remark.

"But I've seen the light. I've seen what real glory looks like. And it's not in Her honor." There a gleam in her eye that I've never seen before. One that promises blood and suffering. "No. Not in hers. You'll see. And you'll *weep*."

"You're crazy." I spit at her, before drawing myself up to my full height. I am the spear of a Athena and I was sent her to do a job. I put all of my authority into my voice as I level a hard gaze as the woman who was once my sister and friend. "Desma Osarke. By order of the conclave of Athena, you are hereby found guilty of matricide and treason. You have been sentenced to death by bloodless crucifixion. Submit for custody."

She bares her teeth at me, becoming more unhinged by the minute. "I'll spit on your body just like I did my mothers."

Then she lunges again.

She's not human as she fights me. I'm surprised by her skill level. Never before has she gone blow for blow with me. But she does, she blocks my attacks and counters them with moves of her own. I grit my teeth in concentration as we move around each other, trying to figure out where these new skills came from.

It's not until she does a trick move that opens up my ribcage for her to aim a kick at, that I realize what's happening. Even through my armor I'm sure she's at least cracked one of my ribs.

She takes advantage of my moment of weakness and closes the distance between us, trying to get behind me. Her impatience always was her greatest weakness. She thinks I'm going to grab my knife, holstered on my thigh. She's braced for that, waiting for that. She's not anticipating my elbow in her face.

I hear the satisfying crunch of her nose as I drive my elbow home. Blood gushes out immediately. She's still trying to get her spear back into an offensive position so I quickly jab at her mouth before kicking at her chest, sending her flying backwards. She falls into a wooden chest at the foot of the bed.

As she lays across the chest, trying to regain her bearings, I see them. Almost like gnats flying around her head. In the quiet I can hear them buzzing.

"The *maniae*." I whisper. Desma's eyes shoot open and she clambers to her feet. "You host the spirits of the maniae? Have you lost your entire mind, Desma?"

To take on the blessing of another god, or host a spirit that has not been sanctioned by Lady Athena is to reject the blessing of Athena. To reject the blessing is to choose death. Her body will start trying to overcompensate for the lack of the blessing. It'll make her heart and lungs work harder and harder. Eventually it will be too much and her heart will just stop.

"Mind your own business, Aris." She tells me, a little

frantically. I shake my head in wonder.

"You've chosen death either way." I tell her. She bares her teeth at me again. They're coated in her blood.

"I am above death! Death is nothing to me! Death cannot touch me!"

Now I am the one baring my teeth as I lunge at her again. The duel picks up again, but it's evident that the manic energy that the maniae brought is already waning. Her moves are becoming sluggish and more predictable. When I snap her spear the same way I did Dolos's, I can see in her eyes that she knows her death is approaching.

"Aris," she pleads, standing before me empty-handed. It's too late for begging. With a yell, I smash the shaft of my spear into her knees, hitting her so hard it snaps with the effort. With a cry she falls. As she tries to catch herself I throw away my broken spear and lunge at her, tackling her to the ground.

Straddling her chest, I begin to bring my fists down on her. Over and over. It's not until I open my mouth to speak that I realize there tears falling down my face.

"You're a traitor!" I scream at her, her eyes already beginning to swell under my assault. "How could you do this to our Lady? To your sisters?" I grab the front of her shirt, lifting her up to shake her. "HOW COULD YOU ABANDON US LIKE THIS?! HOW COULD YOU FORCE ME TO KILL YOU LIKE THIS!"

A defiant scream is her only answer as she manages to grab the top of her broken spear and stab it into my leg. My adrenaline dulls the pain of the stab but does nothing to brace me for her punch to the side of my head. With a grunt I go flying off her. I roll once and quickly spring to my feet. I can feel the hot blood coating my thigh as I pull out the spear. Damn it. That's deep. She scrambles to her feet yet again, watching me hungrily as I inspect my wound.

"Do you see?" She says to me, crazed. "Do you see the greatness they've given me? Eucleia blesses me in ways I never could have imagined! She has allowed me to wound my greatest enemy!"

"Greatest enemy?" I whisper, more than one kind of pain fills every syllable. "Desma I was your greatest supporter until you pushed me away."

"No!" Her movements are frantic as she paces back and forth in front of me. "No, no, I pushed *off of you* and when I did that I pushed myself *onto* greatness!"

She's insane. Rejecting her blessing is taking effect. There will be no reasoning with her. I know this in my head but in my heart I still see the girl that raced down the hall with me as we played Stealth together and I don't want to be the one to kill her.

"Desma." I call to her, breathless and begging. "Enough. Let this be done." Something about my words seems to cause something to snap in her. Her eyes become possessed and terrifying. I swear she starts to foam at the mouth.

"I DON'T NEED YOUR PITY, ARIS!" She shrieks, not even sounding human as she lunges again.

It's too easy.

Too easy to sidestep her lunge. Too easy to reach my left arm out to catch her around the chest. Too easy to hold her wriggling body against mine. Too easy to stab my knife into the chink of her armor under her armpit.

She gasps as the knife plunges in. Her eyes grow wide and her mouth falls into an almost childlike 'o'. Now she clutches at me rather than claws as I slowly lower us to the floor.

Her green eyes, now filled with fear, lock onto mine. Her

trembling hand reaches to probe at her wound.

"No, no don't touch it." I murmur to her, catching her hand and holding it tight. I cradle her in my lap, rocking back and forth as though she is a fretful child I'm trying to soothe.

"Aris." Her voice cracks.

"Shh," I murmur. "Shh." She shakes her head at me.

"I'm sorry. I'm so sorry. I don't— I don't know what I was thinking. It was like— they just got in my head. I couldn't get them out. I tried at first. I swear I did but I just couldn't. And then I started to like the things they were saying and I couldn't—" Tears fall from her eyes as she coughs up blood. I can feel it splatter on my face but I can't bring a single part of me to care.

"Who, Desma?" I urge her, stroking her hair back from her face. "Who turned you against us?" She presses her lips together and squeezes her eyes shut, shaking her head.

"No, Aris." She sobs. "Just go home. Swear to me, you'll just go home."

"You deserve justice, too!" I whisper fiercely. She smiles at me for a moment, suddenly looking so much like her mother I think she must already be a ghost.

"You gave it to me." She whispers raggedly, struggling more and more with each breath. "You freed me. Now it's time to free yourself. Go home. Go be with our family."

I can see the light leaving her eyes and a child-like fear fills me fiercely and suddenly.

"No, no, no, no. Desma! No! Keep your eyes open! No, Desma, please!" All of our training is about protecting. Protecting Medusa. Protecting the conclave.

Protecting each other.

It's an instinct I can't—won't— ignore. No matter what

she's done. No matter how angry I've been at her. She is my sister as much as Alena is. I can't stop myself from begging her to stay with me. Even as her breaths become shallow gasps.

"I'm going home." She tells me, almost silently. Then, all at once, she goes limp in my lap. Her chest stops moving and her eyes stare blankly at nothing. My own breath catches in my throat as I register this change. My hand comes up to cover my mouth as I fight back a sob.

"Oh gods." I sob to nothing and no one. "Oh gods, please." Somewhere, in the back of my head, I know there is no point to this begging. No god is listening. Even if they are, they are certainly proud of me for fulfilling my duty.

Gently, I lay Desma onto the ground and wipe the tears from my face, but more follow quickly. In this moment, in my solitude, I allow myself to grieve. Pulling my knees to my chest, I shove the front of my shirt in my mouth and bury my face in them. I wrap my arms around the back of my head, shoving my face harshly into the boniness of my knees, almost relishing in the pain it brings.

And then I scream.

I scream until my throat is raw and aching. Scream until I'm sure that every god and goddess on Mount Olympus has heard my grief. Scream until I'm sure that every Instructor has heard my anger.

Just as suddenly as I started, I stop. Coughing and gasping, I release my hold on myself. I scrub my face harshly as I gaze down on the corpse that was once my friend. I stand quickly and move over the the lush red curtains. After making a slash in the fabric I rip off what I need and make my way back over to her.

Kneeling beside her, I adjust her limbs so she's laying as

though she's on a pyre, taking care to fold her hands gently over her chest. I wish I could wash away the blood that covers her side but there's only so much I can do in this moment. With great care, I close her eyelids with my fingertips. Then I dig into my pockets and breathe a huff of relief that I still have some drachmas in them. I fish out two and cover her eyelids with them and then take my strip of curtain and cover them, tying it off to the side, to ensure they stay on her eyes.

I can't give her full funeral rites. I'm forbidden. Not only because she's a traitor but because I'm not a Priestess. They're the only ones permitted to give full rites. But I can give her a burial.

All along the top of the headboard for the bed, are candles, I make my way over and pull a few off, and gather them into my arms.

My eyes are dry, painfully so, as I lay the candles around her. I spend a few careful moments lighting them. Their soft, flickering shadows dance around us. Fishing another golden drachma from my pocket, I hold it tightly in my hands and press it to my lips.

"Lord of the Underworld. Lord of the dead. Mighty Lord Hades. Hear my plea and accept my prayer. Give her her rites. Let her burn so she may be judged as is her right. Lord, aid me. If I have ever done right by you and your Queen, aid me. Lord I beg of you. She was led astray. She deserves proper judgment. Lord, aid me, please."

I bend my hands down, holding the coin over the flame of the candle. I can feel when it's been accepted. It pulls against my grasp, growing unbearably hot. I let go and watch it hover in the flame, flickering with black flames until it disappears.

I'm just beginning to wonder if he'll actually help me when

a shudder rolls through the earth. The ground below me shakes and, as one, all of the candles fall forward, their flames reaching out for Desma's body.

At once a roaring black flame consumes her body, obscuring her from my view. With a cry, I leap up and away from the flames. I watch, eyes wide, chest heaving, as the flames grow smaller and smaller. Until, just as suddenly as they erupted, they cease. Leaving behind nothing but the scorch marks in the carpet and the memory of a troubled woman.

Dazedly, I gather myself and walk, almost blindly, from the room. It's not until I've made it all the way down the hall, into the stairwell and take my first step down that the fire that races up my thigh, reminding me of my injury. Hissing, I lean against the handrail and probe around my wound.

Damn. I'm going to have to stitch myself up. It's still putting out a good amount of blood. No way I can get all the way back to the compound without resting it. *Damn!* Gritting my teeth, I force myself to carry on. Nothing I can do about it right this second anyway.

When at last I make my way back to the kitchen I came in through, I find myself desperate for fresh air. I shove my way through the door, almost tripping in my haste, and stand for a moment, with my hands on top of my head, forcing slow and deep breaths in and out.

Opening my eyes, I remember the climb up the cliff side I have to do to get back to my bike. I swear under my breath as I drop my hands. *No one ever tells you about this part of the stories and myths*, I think wryly as I begin the climb.

23

Chapter 23

"Ooh girl, who'd you piss off?" The receptionist crows when I walk in. Flamboyant and nosy. Not a great mix.

I throw my I.D. and a wad of cash onto the desk.

"I'd like a room please."

"Ooh, of course, Miss Ma'am. My mistake for making conversation." He snarks as he snatches up my license to inspect.

"Dude," I sigh, "as you've already pointed out, I've kinda had a hell of a night so I'd like to shower and go to bed. Not endure the Spanish Inquisition."

He makes a sass-filled face as he begins putting my information into the computer. "We only have one available right now. The Presidential Suite." I wave his words away.

"That's fine. Whatever you have, I'll take." He eyes me up and down.

"Honey, no disrespect. But I don't think you heard me. This is our *premium* suite." An exasperated laugh bursts out of me.

"I have more money in my pinkie finger than you'll see in your entire life, *honey*. Now give me the damn room and charge the damn card. Please."

An almost comical look of shock seems stuck on his face for a moment before he resumes typing my information in.

When he finally puts my card information in, I can tell he's waiting for it to decline, so he can have his *I told you so* moment. But it doesn't. So he doesn't.

"Here you are, honey," His smile is as fake as his lips but he holds out my room card and that's all I give a damn about.

I give him an equally nasty smile as I pluck the cards out of his hand. I snatch up my duffle bag, using it to hide my leg, and march over to the elevator, which a man in a hotel uniform holds open for me.

Hearing the whole conversation, the man doesn't ask what floor I need. Just pushes the right button and then pushes the close door button and off we go in silence. A few moments later the door opens to our floor. He turns to me and softly lays his hand on my arm.

"Those who wearily travel shall always find safe shelter," He tells me solemnly. A Hermes worshiper. My hand goes up to my ear. He nods at my understanding. "If you require anything, my lady, you call housekeeping and you will have it. Those who fight the just fight deserve rest too." Tears well up in my eyes as I clutch the mans hand.

"Thank you," I whisper. He smiles at me in a way that I imagine a grandfather would smile at his grandchild. But that falls off his face when I try to hand him cash.

"No, no, child." He tells me, pushing my hand away.

"You wouldn't believe the day I've had," I tell him, smiling in exhaustion. "Please let me thank your kindness."

We battle with our eyes for a moment before he relents and pockets the cash. I smile in victory as I step off the elevator.

243

"I'll have room service sent up. My treat." He tells me, laughing, as the doors close. I roll my eyes but can't help but smile before making my way to the door at the end of the hallway.

I'm sure the room is grand but I take no notice to it. Once in, I strip off my clothes and cast them aside. Standing before the mirror I can't help but gaze in horror at my naked body.

The wound on my thigh is an angry red and gaping. The slash across my face from Dolos is trying to clot but I keep aggravating it, leaving red droplets to streak randomly down my face. Bruises dot my ribcage and the gash on the back of my arm from the vase is deeper than I originally thought. That'll need stitches too.

Throwing my duffle onto the desk I dig around in it until I find my hygiene bag and then the small medical bag.

It takes me a minute to figure out how the fancy shower works, but once I do, I take a few minutes to sit on the shower bench and let the hot water roll over me. It feels magnificent on my aching muscles as I slowly undo my braid.

Finally I force myself to stand up and begin the long process of scrubbing away my sins. Blood and dirt swirl around my feet and down the drain. Little pieces of glass and vase join it as I scrub at my hair. I take great care in cleaning my leg and arm. The cleaner our wounds are, the faster they heal.

It takes me forever to feel clean again but finally I get there. I reluctantly turn the water off and wrap myself in a towel.

I open my medical kit and make sure I have everything I need before hopping on the bathroom counter. Biting my lip in both pain and concentration, I begin to stitch together the wound on the back of my arm. While it's long, it's thankfully shallow and a single layer of choppy stitches does the trick. I swipe antibacterial cream on it and cover it with a large band-aid before carefully lifting my right leg onto the counter.

This time I take a bit more care, this wound is much deeper and I'm not trying to bleed to death or get an infection. I follow the little note card full of step-by-step instructions that Elpis left in our med kits in the event that something like this ever happened, carefully consulting it before each move I make.

It takes me longer than it would take Elpis but I have less practice. Finally, about 15 minutes later, I'm gasping and my lip is raw from me gnawing on it, but I'm stitched.

I lean back against the bathroom wall, holding my hands over my face, just trying to focus on my breathing. I turn on the facet and gather some cold water in my hands to splash on my face. After my moment of dramatics I swipe on ointment and wrap up my leg and hope off the counter, groaning as I put my weight on my leg.

Flipping off lights as I go, I make my way to the bedroom. I don't bother to get dressed as I crawl into bed. Let them charge me for damages if I get blood on their sheets. Once I'm settled I grab my phone and dial a familiar number.

Aris, thank Athena!

Where are you?

Are you all right?

Are you hurt, child? Do you need assistance?

Rissy? Are you coming home now?

It sounds like I'm on speaker with the whole conclave. Voice after voice after voice overlap into a blur of concern and longing. The homesickness hits me suddenly and I'm not surprised to find that my next breath comes ragged and wet.

"It's done," I tell them thickly. "She's dead. I tried to bring her in but she—" I stifle a sob and wipe my face.

Oh, Aristomache. Comes Tessa's voice.

"I got hurt. Had to stitch myself up a bit. Thanks for the manual El, really came in handy." I try to make light, but since I'm still crying I don't think it comes across the way I want it to. "I got a hotel for the night. Gonna rest and I'll head home in the morning."

An escort team will be waiting at the border for you too. Get your ass home, Initiate so we can care for you properly. This order from Antiope is not up for debate. I find relief in it, rather than annoyance.

"Yes, ma'am." I answer.

Get some sleep, Ris.

We'll see you soon!

I love you, Rissy!

Come home to us.

* * *

My dreams are chaotic and confusing, as they often are when I'm outside the compound. Flashes that come fast and furious as various beings call for my attention, trying to earn my favor to run errands for them.

I see my sister during her agility training. Kore stands off to the side of the course, watching as Alena runs through the obstacles. Her lithe body finds no difficulty in the moves, twisting and twirling in the air, through hoops, across beams. She finishes the race with a huff and a proud look on her face. It's a solid six seconds before any of the other girls finish. Kore gives her an approving nod and a wink before Alena skips off for a water break. A gold hair clip, a heart with an arrow through it, that I got for her when I was sent to Greece last year is fastened in her hair.

I see the day my mother was selected as a Protector. We all gathered in the Choosing ceremony room, my mother and four other Initiates stood a top the stone. I was seven years old and was standing as close to the stone as Tessa would let me get, bouncing on my toes, shaking with pride. The Priestess stood behind the five who were contesting to be Protectors with a scroll. Sealed by the magic of Athena, only this Priestess had the ability to open it. *In the name of Athena our Lady has chosen Atalanta Kallis as the next great Protector of Medusa. In Her honor.*

My mother tipped her head back to the heavens. Her hands covering her face as she laughed. *In Her honor!* Rings out around the room as her sisters-in arms raise their fists to the sky. Then she looked for me and reached out for me. I didn't hesitate to launch myself into her arms. She nuzzled her face against my, laughing and crying at the same time. I knew this meant she would have to leave me but I also knew what an honor it was to get chosen. *I'm so proud of you, Mama.* I told her, hugging her fiercely.

But then it gets weird. It starts as another dream. The time mama, Alena and I went to the beach. We were all playing in the water together, pretending we could talk to the animals and were calling sharks and mighty sea creatures to come to us. Alena, just five or six, kept squealing both in fear and delight as fish and stuff would touch her foot— convinced it was the monsters we were calling to us. I dive away from my family, feeling the pull of the current under the surface.

When I surface, my mother turns to me, terrified. *Aris, wake up!* Now I'm confused because that's not what happened. When I surfaced my mother was smiling and laughing and had asked me if I had seen the Nereids from Lord Poseidon's court. I start to get scared. Why is my dream veering off course? *Mama, what are you talking about?* I ask her. Now she and Alena both, who is cradled in my mothers arms, are staring at me. Eyes wide and terrified. *Wake up! Aris, you must wake up! WAKE UP! WAKE UP WAKE UP WAKE UP!*

I don't want to be here anymore. I try to wake myself up but I can't.

Finally I feel it. Hands on my body. On my physical body. Someone is in my hotel room and touching me. With a yell I force myself awake. Alarmed and loud voices greet me as I begin to thrash against the hands that hold me to the bed. Something has been shoved in my mouth and my screams come out muffled and useless.

"Hold her!"

"You hold her, damn it!"

"Come on, come on! Give me her hand!"

I bring my leg back and kick out, making contact with someone. I'm rewarded with a grunt and a curse but am punished for it when someone grabs my leg and puts their hand on top of my stitches. They bear down on my leg with all their weight and strength. My cry of pain is muffled by my gag.

Something sharp jabs into my arm followed by a victorious "got it!". I don't make the connection of what they got until I feel myself start to lose consciousness.

IV

Part Four

24

Chapter 24

I'm groggy and disoriented when I come to. My pulses spikes and thrums in my neck before I'm fully aware. My eyelids flutter, fighting me to stay closed, wanting to stay sheltered and unaware. After several seconds of struggling, I win the battle and force my eyes open. My vision swoops around me, the walls spinning, the floor rocking like a ship at open sea. My breathing starts to edge towards hysterical, sharp and gasping. This is no good, I can't focus on what's going on if I can't even breath correctly. So even though I don't have the time to spare, I spend a few precious moments focusing on my breathing, working them towards slow and even. Once my breathing is even I shake my head sharply, willing my vision to quit swirling around me. With my fists clenched by my sides, I use the pain of my nails in my palm to help me focus. Finally, *finally*, the world stops spinning. Whatever they drugged me with seriously messed with my body.

Once I've managed that, I slowly sit up, nervous to move too fast and send the world spinning again. Once sitting, the first thing I notice is that someone has clothed me. For a moment,

IN HER HONOR

I'm completely bewildered by this, which only increases when I realize I'm wearing a sports bra and a pair of biker shorts from my own duffle bag. Realization sets in as I finally connect the dots of all of this. I blanch at this new type of violation, feeling bile rise up in my throat. I raise my hand to touch at the fabric, as though I need to physically confirm that they're real, but when I do, I freeze. Never before have I felt like a wild animal caught in a steel trap, but I imagine this is what a coyote feels like right after the trap closes around their leg.

As quietly as I can I lift my hands up. The soft rattling of the chains fills the air. My heart is racing again as I take in the shackles that encircle my wrists. The metal is tar black with gold engravings covering them, different spells, that I don't recognize, are carved into the metal. My eyebrows pinch together, the shackles would be enough themselves, why would they need magic as well?

"What the fuck?" I whisper as I continue to look around. I'm laying on a cot, barely long enough for my body, covered in a thin mattress. The room is a perfect square, maybe fifteen feet all around. There's a window on the wall behind me, with a beautiful oak desk beneath it, which is covered by thick metal bars. An empty, open wardrobe sits on the wall opposite of me. Next to the wardrobe is a bookshelf, filled with a few dozen books. Catty corner from me is a small bathroom area, just equipped with a toilet, sink and a shower head, pointed over a grate in the floor. Plain white curtains hang, pushed up against one of the walls to give the bathroom user privacy.

I sit there for quite some time. Staring at the bookshelf. The longer I look at it, the greater my sense of horror is but I can't seem to connect the dots of why the bookshelf scares me so bad.

Suddenly frantic, I spring up and off the bed, and almost immediately tilt sideways into the desk. I stand there for a second, ignoring the throbbing pain in my hip and gain my equilibrium back. Gods, how long was I asleep for?

Once I'm sure I won't pass out, I scramble onto the desk to peer out the window. I'm on a coast line somewhere. Wherever I'm being held is right up against the water. The rocky shoreline is just a couple dozen yards away, seagulls fly overhead, their cries audible even through the closed glass. It looks like I'm still in California but I can't be sure.

As I kneel on the desk that thought sinks in: I don't know where I am. I don't know if I'm still in California. I don't know if I'm still even in United States.

Again my eyes fall onto the bookshelf and before I'm aware of making the decision, I'm leaping off the desk and flying towards the door. I beat on it, hysterical. Screaming and cursing. Calling for Tessa. For Kore and Elpis. For Deimos. For Athena. I beat on the door until my shackled hands are bruised and bloody. Scream until my throat is raw and stinging.

No one answers me. No one is coming to save me.

I back away from the door, clutching my now sore hands into my hair. I think back to the night before. To the men around my bedside. None of them sounded familiar. None of them looked familiar in the brief glimpses I got. My thigh still throbs where the one man braced his weight against my stitches. I rub at my thigh, absently, fighting back tears and panic alike.

"Athena please," I whisper desperately. "Please, please. Give me the wisdom. How do I get out of this?"

As though in answer, there's a loud, mechanical whir as a flap of the door drops down and a tray is pushed through. I leap at the hole.

"Hey! Where the fuck am I?! Who are you? Where am I?" The men on the other side of the door don't answer me. Even though I can only see their midsections, I can tell they're human, nothing particularly special about them. They stand impassively as I scream at them. When I don't take the tray, one of them reaches forward and shoves the tray at me. I catch it on instinct and as soon as the tray is clear of the flap, it snaps upwards and closes again. The loud, mechanical whirring repeats as the flap locks into place again. I scream in frustration and throw the tray against the door. Some type of soup, a roll and a bunch of grapes slam against the metal.

Growling to myself, I begin to pace the room, twisting my shackles around my wrists. Back and forth, back and forth. Slowly the sun begins to set against the seas horizon. If night is falling now then I was taken at least 24 hours ago. The thought makes me snatch up the chair tucked into the desk and throw it, screaming, across the room.

I'm glaring out the window at the sea when I remember my conversation with Lord Ares. With Lord Herakles. With Desma. Their warnings. Their concern. *Go straight home. Don't stop for anything.* Oh my gods. Did they see this coming? Did they know this was what the Fates had in store for me? How could I have been so stupid?! But what else could I have done? I was injured and bleeding profusely. I couldn't have driven in the condition I was in. I needed to rest. I would have crashed my damn bike if I had tried to drive it any further than I did to the hotel. For fucks sake I almost did crash on the way to the hotel! I almost got mowed over by a semi when I swerved into its lane!

"Oh god, Athena please," I cry and fall to my knees, my face buried in my hands. I know it is pointless to call for Athena to save me. Athena does not help those who beg. She helps those who've earned it. But I can't help it. Never in my life have I known such terror and uncertainty. How am I going to get myself out of this?

I didn't think I knelt there for long but when I pull my face from my hands the sun is fully set on the horizon, leaving only the full moon to give me light. Wiping my dramatics from my face, I get up and begin examining the room. I walk the length of the room. I was right, about fifteen feet. I climb up on the wardrobe, hissing as it agitates my stitches, to examine the concrete ceiling. Whoever did the sealant here better have been paid well, because it's a hell of a job.

Swearing like fiend, I jump down from the wardrobe, hitting the ground heavy before leaping back over onto the desk. Groaning, I push and pull at the bars. They don't even shift a little bit. I slam my fist on the bar with a frustrated grunt. I might eventually be able to grind these down but then what? The glass feels really thick under my fingers, it's probably shatter proof. And even if it's not, it'll take ages to work the bars enough to get them loose.

As I stand atop the desk, I see a shadow appear under the door. There's a mirror at the top of the door but now looking at it properly, it must be a two-way mirror because all I can see in it is myself. Which means someone is watching me right now. Even though I know they can see me, I still freeze. I slowly drop to a knee and reach to hook a finger under one of my bracelets.

Horror, however, bleeds through my body as I realize that my spears will not snap off, no matter how hard I pull on them.

I bare my teeth, feeling like a wild animal, and stare down

whoever is on the other side.

"Come on out," I call out, tauntingly. "Let's chat!"

The shadow under the door doesn't answer. Just continues to stand there for a few more minutes before walking off without a word. Huffing with frustration I jump down from the desk and try to ignore the crawling sensation of my skin.

Raking my hands through my hair, I think of something that makes me feel like an idiot.

My pendant.

"Please, please, please," I murmur as I raise my hand to my pendant, squeezing it so tightly I can feel the impressions it's leaving on my skin. I murmur the spell to call for aid, repeating it over and over. Nothing happens. My pendant stays cool and unaffected under my hand. No one is coming to save me.

I can't even bring myself to cry at this development. I just feel numb. Like I had known what would happen before I tried. Maybe that's why it took me so long to think of it, because it I knew that no one would hear me.

I stand and stare out the window, pulling on my spears incessantly. Praying to whoever might be listening.

25

Chapter 25

I spend the next several days the same way. I wake up and do my daily inspection of the room, looking for weaknesses that may have appeared or that I missed.

I get hungry enough that I stop throwing my food against the door, instead wolfing it down hungrily. Then, I spend the rest of my day praying for guidance and working out, pushing myself through extensive high intensity interval workouts and round after round of core workouts. I end each day sweaty and tired. The manacles around my wrist make things difficult but I won't let them stop me and I won't let whoever is holding me captive think I'm giving up.

Every night, after the sun has fully set, the shadow comes back. It never speaks, never comes in. Just stands there and observes me. Each time it does I can't help but reach for my useless spears.

At night I lay in my cot and try not to cry as I think about Alena and my mother and my other sisters in the conclave. I think of the way the sun shines down in the Choosing room, warming the stone slab beneath it. I think of the way the sand of the fighting ring felt on my bare feet as I fought, gritty and invasive but soothing and familiar as well. I think of standing in line at the mess hell, loud voices and echoing laughter as girls moved along in line, their trays in front of them. With a pang I remember I was supposed to be on mess duty. The morning that everything started.

They must be so worried. I was supposed to be home days ago. How many now? I think I've been here four days?

Instead I'm in this damn room. I have no idea what's going on. No one has even talked to me. I have no idea why I'm being held. I assume it has something to do with Lady Medusa but if that's the case, why have they not tortured me for information? None of this makes any sense.

Each day my frustration grows. My workouts become more intense, each one for a longer duration. My responses to what little interactions I get become less and less human. I bare my teeth, almost growling at the men who bring my food. I scream and swear and beat my fists against the two-way glass as the shadow does his nightly observation.

If they want to keep me locked away like an animal, I have no problem acting like one.

Each night, before I crawl into my cot, I hit my knees beside it. Each night, I beg Athena, my ancestors, any god I have ever done a favor for to have mercy on me. To fill my dreams with guidance.

If I have ever brought you honor, I beg them, *please bring me aid.*

My dreams remain hopelessly and heartbreakingly empty. I don't dream at all. Maybe this place has protections like what the conclave has. But even at the conclave I still have normal dreams. I'm not even having those here.

As I lay, curled up on my side, alone in the darkness, I try not let myself lose hope. But I confess, it's an exceptionally hard thing to do. With an exhausted sigh, I pull my thin blanket over my head and let myself drift off again, joining more nothingness that waits for me in my consciousness.

The next morning, everything changes when I decide I should shower. No towels are given to me. Maybe they think I'll hang myself with them. I admit the water feels nice. At least it gets hot, but it aggravates my stitches, which are long due to come out.

After I shower, I wipe as much water off of me as I can and get dressed, still wet, behind the curtain. The cameras in here are not getting a free show. I'm sitting on top of my desk, picking at my stitches, deciding on if I should just rip them out when the door of my cell opens.

Not the food flap, the full door.

My head snaps up and my blood sings at the possibility of a fight. A real chance to get out of here.

That chance diminishes slightly when a half dozen heavily armed, battle-ready men walk in. Still, I won't go anywhere or do anything without a fight.

I push myself to a crouch on top the desk, snarling at the men. Another dozen fill in behind them, crowding the not-very-big room. I'm just opening my mouth to start the show with a smartass remark when there's some shuffling amongst the ranks.

Shoving between the guards, is a young girl. Younger than me by several years. I'm immediately caught off guard. She looks as though she doesn't even have her drivers license yet. When she smiles at me, I see the metallic glint of braces.

"Hello," she greets me. Her voice soft and unassuming.

"My name is Leya. I couldn't help but notice those stitches you have probably need to come out. I'm a medic, if you'll allow me to help you, I'd be happy to get those out for you." The proof in her claims lies in the red bag she carries, with a white cross on it and the nitrile gloves she wears.

I regard her for a moment before turning to the guards in bullet proof vests and carrying guns.

"Seems like a dramatic response for some stitches being taken out."

None of them deign this with an answer. The girl, Leya, looks at the men over her shoulder, her mouth twisting with displeasure, before turning back to me, looking annoyed. I know this girls appearance is by design, a way to sway me some way, I just don't know how yet.

"I told them I would be perfectly fine on my own, but they disagreed." Her dark brown eyes are serious as she looks me over. "Will you allow me to help you?"

After a stare down with one of the men, I nod to her, sitting back down on the desk.

"Wonderful," she seems happier now that she knows she gets to be useful. She actually gives a little skip as she makes her way over to me, betraying her youth. Setting her bag next to me, she unzips it as she frowns over my thigh stitches. "Just a few quick snips!" She informs me, pulling out tweezers and medical scissors. "Who did these stitches?" She asks as she pokes at my shoddy job.

"I did," I answer, somewhat ruefully. She grins up at me at this answer.

"Well that explains why they look like they were done in a gas station bathroom," she quips. I know she must have an idea of who I am and where I've been but I can't bring myself to show any cruelty or abrasiveness to someone so young. Teaching the next generation of young people is a point of pride in the conclave, so many of us genuinely hope we get chosen to stay on as trainers after our time there is complete. I know of several women who went out to be teachers and instructors in the mortal world after leaving us.

"It was a hotel bathroom, actually." I inform her. She snorts quietly and gets to work. She's very efficient and smooth in her movements and in no time at all, she has both my arm and leg stitches out.

"There," she announces, sitting up. "All done. I wish I could stay and chat more but my orders were very clear."

"Seems odd," I say as though she hasn't spoken. "To care for a prisoner in such a way. Decent food, medical care."

"What makes you think you're a prisoner?" She asks, trying to keep her voice light and just failing.

With a pointed look, I eye the guards behind her and lift my shackled hands.

A strained smile has filled her face. "Just precautions. I'm sure you understand."

I cock my head to the side. As we've talked, her entire demeanor has changed and for the first time, real fear shows in her eyes. She may not be chained the way that I am but this girl is as much of a prisoner as I am. Which means all of the showboating I do for her, may have real repercussions on her later.

So I take a breath and force myself to smile at her and give her a nod to tell her I understand.

She visibly relaxes and seems several years younger when she smiles back as she gathers up her things and files out with her entourage.

261

A deep frown comes to my face as soon as I hear the mechanical whir that tells me the door is locked again. Nothing here is making sense. I've been kidnapped but fed adequate food, given decent lodgings and the first time I spoke to someone it was not while being interrogated or tortured, no it was to a teenage girl who came to take my stitches out. A teenage girl who insists that I am not actually a prisoner here. As if I could be anything else.

I turn to face my window, bracing my hands on the desk as I glare out at the sea. As though the sea can sense my anger, the tides gather strength and crash down on the beach time and time again. Pounding the sand into submission. A glance at the dark gray clouds forming in the sky tell me a storm is brewing.

Maybe it will take me away with it.

* * *

Nine days. I've spent nine whole days spent pacing this damn room, inspecting every nook and cranny. At least I think it's been nine days. Even with the window to help me see the setting of the sun, it's hard to keep track.

Wake up. Work out. Screaming at the walls. Eat lunch. Tear up books from the bookshelf. Lounge in total apathy. Repeat.

I start to get bored. Very bored. I begin to have to force myself to do even the simplest of workouts and even stop my daily screaming matches with whoever walks by my cell door. Instead I spend my time sitting on top of the desk, my arms wrapped around my knees as I stare out at the sea.

That's where I'm sitting when I hear the footsteps coming down the hall. That's a new thing. Now that I'm not screaming at everything I can hear a lot more. Doors like mine opening, guards on rotation, screams from other cells. A lot of fun things to hear. I don't even bother turning my head as the footsteps stop outside my door. My interest is piqued when my door actually opens but then I realize it's probably one of the guards bringing my dinner. Since I stopped going to the tray slot to grab my food the last few days, they've been bringing it in and setting it on my bed.

"Hello, Aristomache. I hope you've calmed down enough for us to have a conversation now." A bland voice breaks the silence. Something sets chills off down my spine but I don't realize what or why until I finally turn my head to the intruder.

My mouth falls open first in confusion and then in horror as I look at the man in my room.

"I take it by the look on your face that you remember me this time?" Jason asks, smiling coldly.

26

Chapter 26

I can only blink at him for a moment.

"You're the guy from the bar." I answer him blankly. His face tightens in anger for a moment. With a great amount of effort he smooths it, adopts a playful sort of look.

"Yes, but we've met before then." Now I'm completely nonplussed.

"I'm sorry," why I'm apologizing, I have no idea, "I don't remember. I meet a lot people."

"Yeaaa," he draws out. He walks causally into my cell, his hands shoved deep into his pockets as she gazes around. He circles around to face me, his face impassive. "Yeah I'm probably pretty easy to forget, especially when you couldn't take your tongue out of Deimos's mouth long enough to notice anyone else." His tone turns savage and petulant at the end, his eyes cruel and challenging. He must see my own anger flash in my eyes, see my mouth open defiantly, because he rushes on before I can say anything.

"That seemed to be a common theme for you. When you were around Deimos. You go from this," he gestures to me, "a highly capable, highly trained *bad ass* to a simpering mess. Trailing after a god like a bitch in heat."

I leap off the desk, my chains rattle loud and demanding to be acknowledged. Again I open my mouth to hurl every insult, every obscenity I know at this man, but he, again, pushes on before I can even start.

"Did you know, I was one of Deimos's private servants?" He hurls at me, almost accusingly. "You were at his palace *all the time*. You would coo over Pyl every time, ask the cook how her mom was doing, thank the cleaners whenever you saw them. But you *never* saw me. I begged and I prayed to every god under the sun: *let her see me!* and you never did! You thought you were so much better than me! As though you were too good to be seen with me!"

I tuck my chained hands closer to my chest, not to shield me from his words, but to shield me from him. Never before have I ever been so close to someone who was so clearly and deeply unhinged. All at once, all of my anger deflates, leaving only cold fear behind it. This is entirely new territory, the opposite of what I was trained for. But I have no idea what this man is capable of. Gods and demigods and other supernatural beings have strict laws they must abide by.

This man is not bound by any laws of the gods.

My entire energy becomes focused on diffusing the situation, so I can figure out how to get out of here. But the longer he paces around my room, ranting and raving, the more deranged he becomes, spittle forming at the corner of his mouth.

"Do you know how many times I would sit outside Lord Deimos's room and listen to you moan like a whore for him?! How many times I would come in when you two were finished

265

to bring wine and grapes and cheese for you guys and I would see you." His eyes take on a glazed and dreamy sort of look that makes me feel as though I'm naked right now. "See you naked and sprawled on your stomach, your hair wild, your back covered in sweat," he licks his lips, his gaze faraway and suddenly I'm sure I'm going to throw up on his shoes, "and I would see *Lord Deimos*, sitting beside you, not touching you, not looking at you, not worshiping you like the *miracle* you are. He used you! He used you like a *whore* and you let him! You couldn't spread your legs fast enough for him! And he wasn't the only one! You would tell Deimos you loved him but then at the first opportunity there you were! Grinding your ass into Herakles, letting him grab on you and kiss on you! Do you know how sick it made me to watch you degrade yourself in a way like that!"

He rushes forward and reaches for my hands, which have locked into place, along with the rest of my muscles, and will not budge as he tries to pull them to him. He doesn't seem to notice and clutches at what he can.

"But, but you see *I* wouldn't do that to you! I- I would *worship* you the way you deserve to be! I wouldn't lay beside you, not even acknowledging you after making love. I would feed you grapes or whatever it is you do after having sex!" He gives a wild laugh, clutching at my hands so tightly they begin to lose feeling.

My mouth is so dry it takes me a few tries to swallow.

"You went through—" I lick my lips. "You went through a lot of trouble to bring me here just to have a conversation."

Jason laughs and drops my hands to plant his hands on his hips. A violent wave of relief rushes through me as he puts space between us again.

266

"Aris, you wouldn't even believe what I went through to bring you here. The preparations I had to make!"

"Preparations?"

"Oh gods yeah!" He has a seat on the desk chair, making himself comfortable. "First I had to complete all kinds of quests to get all kinds of favors from all kinds of gods. I might even have more quests than you now, doll face." He winks at me, smiling. It takes real effort to keep my face smooth.

He gestures around us. "One of my favors was this little hidey hole, and this room in particular for you was another favor. Your manacles were like two and a half favors!" He seems to just remember something and smacks his hand on his thighs as though in emphasis. "Did you *know* that you technically qualify as a demigod?"

"All Initiates do, because of our blessing," I respond automatically. He's shaking his head, grinning, before I've finished talking.

"Nope! Remember what Ares told you? That you guys *weren't* demigods and that's why he could interfere? That's not technically true *for you.* Because you have so many generations of the blessing in you, technically you are a demigod! Isn't that neat?

"Well anyway, because you're technically a demigod it actually made this easier for me! Those chains were made by Hephaestus, designed to keep godly beings contained. None of your blessings will work while they're on. Your spears, your pendant, your powers." He raises his hands, complacently. "Now I know, that may seem extreme. But you have been so conditioned to be Miss Independent and resist the teachings of others I knew I had to do something extreme to get your attention."

"Well," I say, "you got my attention. But why did you need Desma's attention too?"

"Oh her," he waves a dismissive hand. "Well I couldn't talk to you while you were in the conclave now could I? And normally when you left you were going to see *him* or you were with other Initiates and I could never get you away from them either. So I sought out the guidance of another god and they gave me the idea. I actually wasn't looking for Desma specifically. I was just scanning for the weakest point." A shrug. "And she was it. Her dreams were remarkably easy to infiltrate and influence. She was a pawn. A pawn who started to second guess what she had agreed to. She didn't know everything I was planning, I wouldn't be that stupid as to tell her, but she was clever. She guessed more than she should have." Another shrug. "She was a loose end."

A pawn. A tool for him to use and manipulate to play out his sick and twisted fantasies.

Just go home. Swear to me, you'll just go home. She tried to warn me. To save me.

"I had to kill her," I whisper, horrified and fighting back tears. "Because of you. I had to kill one of my sisters because you... you couldn't find a way to start a conversation in a bar?"

"No, no, no," he tells me, rushing forward again. "I mean, yes but—but they don't matter, you see?"

"Don't matter?" I ask, appalled. The girl who I spent my childhood with, who I used to spend lazy Saturday afternoons seeing how far back we could stand from each other while tossing candy into each others mouths, doesn't matter? Has no value to this man? She mattered to *us*. No matter how bad our relationship was the past couple of years *she mattered to us*. How can he say she didn't matter? Because she had no worth to him, she had no worth at all? Cold fury rises up in me like a poison, filling my veins and hardening my heart.

"Don't matter!" He reaffirms, his eyes filled with the fervor again. "See, because we're destined to be together! So none of them matter! Just us. Together. That's all that matters! You'll see. In time, you'll see that everything I've done, I've done for us. For our future."

"For our future..." I whisper, revolted. He doesn't catch my tone. Too caught up in the excitement of having me see his plan.

"Yes! Our future! I knew you would see. Knew you'd understand!"

"*Understand*?" I hiss, my fists clenched. He blinks in shock and reels backwards a step on instinct before steeling himself against my advance. "You had me *kill* one of my sisters. One of the people I am bound by the most ancient of laws to protect! You ripped me from my home! Who knows the amount of grief you've caused the rest of my sisters as they sit, waiting for me!" My voice has risen to a shout. The fear I feel for this man, who is clearly unhinged, is still prominent and pulsing through my veins, but his words have pushed me past reason. My grief and anger are mounting, overwhelming me. Maybe if I had more control of it I would have noticed the cold and calculating look on Jason's face as I yelled at him. I would have noticed how close my fury-filled steps had taken me to him. "And what of my mother? I saw you took her! What did you do to her *you monster!*"

Quick as lightning, Jason's hand darts out, fisting his hand in the hair at the back of my head. I cry out, my hands flying up to his, as I feel his grip rip some of my hair out from the root. Since I'm so much taller than him, my head is yanked back so

269

that I'm staring at the ceiling. He pulls my face closer to his. His breath is sour and stings my nostrils. I'm off balance like this, and I fight to keep the panic it brings at bay. His other hand twists my manacles together, immobilizing my hands.

"*I am not,*" he snarls in my face, breathing harshly, "*a monster.*" He tightens his grip on my hair and I refuse to give him the satisfaction of seeing me react to the pain. "You are just a wanton *whore* who doesn't know what's best for her! *You* forced me to take these measures! Do you think I *like* doing this to you, Aristomache? You think I like isolating you? Hurting you? DO YOU?!"

I refuse to answer him. I grit my teeth and lock my lips together.

"Fine," he puffs out. "I should have known you'd make me do this the hard way. You couldn't just let me love you. Couldn't just accept that I know what's best for you! I guess you'll just have to stay here. In this room. Until you're ready to *listen* and see reason."

I try to tune out what he's saying and watch the shadows dance along the ceiling. I pretend I'm home. Laying in my bed. Watching the shadows of my sisters dance on our ceiling as they get ready for bed. If I close my eyes, I can hear their laughter.

A single tear escapes from my eye and my next breath is ragged.

What have I gotten myself into.

* * *

Now that Jason has shown himself, my entire routine has changed. For the next several days, I wake up and stare at my ceiling in quiet desperation until my breakfast is brought to me. It's right around then I realize being pathetic and moping around isn't going to help me, so I force myself to get up and eat my breakfast while I walk around my room mindlessly.

After eating my breakfast I shower quickly, more out of habit than a desire to keep my hygiene up. Once I've showered I consider going through a workout, realize that's the last thing I want to do, and then force myself to do some lunges around the room because I know I should.

By the time I've completed my extensive to-do list, it's early afternoon and I've taken my usual spot on the desk while I wait. I've just settled in when I hear the whir of the lock on my door.

I keep my eyes locked on the waves of the ocean outside when Jason comes in and makes himself comfortable.

"Good afternoon, Aristomache," he always says the same thing when he first comes in, "I hope you've had a chance to think about our last conversation."

"Eat shit," I mumble into my knees as I curl around myself.

He ignores me as he begins his daily rambles. I paid attention the first couple of days he came in, hoping his ranting would give me some insight to him that could help me escape. But it quickly came apparent that these ramblings were just an excuse to hear himself talk. He was tangential and erratic, his speech pressured. The only insight I got was just how unstable this guy is.

"I understand how hard it is. To accept true love." I can't block everything he says out, no matter how hard I try. "Especially when you've never experienced it before in your life. Now I know what you're thinking 'my mom truly loved me!' and you know? Maybe she did! But how often was your mom there? She became a Protector when she was, what? Twenty-seven? From then on you saw her, three? Maybe four times a year?"

And talked to her every morning. I think apathetically. *And sent her photos and letters, and received them in return, of our daily activities.*

"You were left alone! Unloved. Unprotected. It's no wonder you struggle so much to accept healthy and appropriate support and affection." He tells me plainly. "I mean, if I were you I probably would have sought out such unhealthy and toxic relationships too!"

As I stare out at the water I remember when my mom left to be a Protector. I had just turned seven years old and was terrified for her. Even though I didn't know the details, I knew being a Protector was dangerous work. A week or two after my mom left I began to have recurring nightmares of my mother disappearing or dying— ironic given the current circumstances— and took to wandering the halls at night.

One night, I had woken from the usual nightmare, my cheeks and pillow damp from my tears and slipped out of bed, for the umpteenth time that week.

My bare feet padded silently along the stone hallway, heading in no real direction. I wound up in the library at some point. My hands trailed along the shelves of the bookcases, the spines of hundreds of books rippling under my fingers.

"Aristomache?"

I gasped, whipping around at my name. "What are you doing, child?"

"Um," I whispered, unsure if I would get in trouble or not. "I couldn't sleep..." The woman, Miranda, was a level thirteen Initiative, completing her turn of night guard duty. My fingers knotted in front of me, full of anxiety of getting in trouble. I've never been much of a rule breaker, especially when I was younger.

Miranda pursed her lips as she knelt down in front of me, her fingers brushed at the bags under my eyes. Cold, hard evidence of my sleepless nights.

"Patrol has noticed you out of bed a lot lately." While I knew who Miranda was, I had never had a conversation with her before, but in that moment her voice was the most soothing thing I had ever heard, short of my own mothers voice. "Been having nightmares?"

Shame-filled tears flooded my eyes. Initiates weren't supposed to be afraid of silly things like nightmares. Miranda seemed to understand exactly what I was feeling in that moment.

"It's All right," her soft smile was barely visible in the darkness of the library. "I have them sometimes too."

This absolutely floored me. And forever changed the way I viewed being an Initiate.

Miranda regarded me for a moment before standing and holding her hand out to me. "I could use your help, if you don't mind." She told me, simply. "Since you're already up."

My hand was reaching out and curling around hers before I even knew what I was doing. Miranda's hand was warm and reassuring as I walked down the hall with her. I couldn't help but cut glances up at Miranda, in awe of being in the presence of a level 13. She undoubtedly knew I was staring at her, and would smirk occasionally, amused at the wonder and awe of a child. But she made no comments, just allowed me to feel safe in her presence.

Before long we came to the control room. A large, circular

room, the control room holds the radios and a wall of security monitors, and a circular table with various control buttons on it.

"Oh!" Someone cried. "You found our little nighttime wanderer!"

I felt my face flush at this but Miranda just gave my hand a shake as she picked me up and set me on the control table.

"Want to help me out with something?"

I nodded vigorously, eager to be helpful, particularly around so many older and experienced women.

Miranda gave me a clipboard with an inventory sheet and a pen and told me to cross off the stuff she said. I spent the next couple of hours doing just that. Finally, my yawns were frequent and I began rubbing my fists into my eyes that I fought to keep open.

"I think I'm ready to go back to bed, Miranda." I mumbled sleepily. Miranda smiled over at me and set her inventory down.

"All right. Let's go, chickadee." She held her hands out to me, which I fell into easily. "I'm gonna take her back to her dorm real fast." She tells the group at large. "I'll be right back." A few voices answer in affirmative before we slip out into the hall.

The lulling rock of Miranda's gait makes my eyelids even heavier and I'm asleep before we turn off the hallway.

I jolt back awake as I'm laid into my bed.

"You don't have to be ashamed of your nightmares," Miranda murmurs to me as she tucks my blanket around me. "We all have them. They help remind us that, no matter what we endure, we are only human. And eternal peace will find us eventually."

I think I nodded in answer. Miranda stroked my hair back from my face and placed a kiss to my forehead.

"I know it's hard with your mom gone, but we are your sisters. We will not leave you alone in the world."

I barely catch the last of her sentence before plunging into sleep, knowing I was safe and loved. Knowing the comfort was there should I desire it.

After that night I never had that nightmare about my mother again.

I let the echoing love and laughter of my memories drown out the voice of my captor. How can he stand there and say I've never experienced real love when I can feel the memories of it wrapping itself around me? Like a warm blanket on a cold winters night, it seeps into my bones and holds me close.

And when at least he leaves my cell and I'm allowed my solitude again... I sing the lullabies of my ancestors to myself. I let the ghosts of their voices, and their love, echo alongside mine and lull me to sleep.

Chapter 27

Our new routine lasts almost two more weeks. Twelve days. If I've been counting right that is.

Every evening Jason comes in and drones on. Tells me it's to help forge our bond. Says he learned about attachment styles in some intro to psychology class he took and now he's a damn expert on human psyche I guess. Tells me I've never had a secure attachment before and that's another reason I struggle to recognize what's good for me.

Of course according to him, the only good thing for me is him. So. There's that.

So every evening he contaminates my air with his presence and every evening I retreat further and further into my memories. Seeking solace in them. It's becoming harder and harder to keep track of what's real and what's not. How can I be sure it's not my real Grammy, sitting behind Jason making faces as he speaks, coaxing smiles out of me? Or that it's not Tessa walking along the beach outside, sending me signals of their plans to break me out of here? I can't. And I don't try to. It hurts too much to.

The longer these nightly chats go on, the more Jason pokes and prods at me to respond. The bond, he says, can't be properly forged if I'm not a willing participant. If I'm not willing to forgo my old, insecure attachments to create a new, secure one with him. The longer I keep up my unresponsiveness, the more his temper shows itself.

"You know this is a huge waste of your time." It's the first time I've spoken in several days. Jason actually startles slightly as I interrupt him, shocked I'm actually speaking I guess. I turn my gaze away from the shore outside and meet his eyes.

The eyes are the windows to the soul. That's what people say anyway, right? Well then, let him see my soul. Let him see the anger and contempt I hold for him. Let him see how deep the bonds to my people truly are. Let him see how much I pity and despise him.

He sees it. I know he does. I watch as the hope that filled his eyes when I spoke, hope that maybe I was coming around, quickly drains as he reads my eyes. Despair replaces it.

Good. I will never be able to inflict as much pain on him as he has done to me and my family.

"Never," I tell him, my voice filled with steel and hatred. "Will I forsake my family for you. Forsake my birthright. Forsake *my goddess*. Your moronic plan makes no sense. Only a fool as pathetic as you could ever truly think something like this would work. I don't know what god was blowing smoke up your ass or what price you paid to get me here but I hope it was worth it. I hope you've made your peace because when I escape— and make no mistake, I *will* escape— I will send you on a fast pass to the Underworld and you will have to repay that debt. So hear me now, boy.

"You will never get what you want from me. Gods and greater men than you have tried to break me. Tried to corrupt me. They all have failed. Just as you will." A tiny spark of fear ignites in me as I give this defiance to him. I know the consequences of this rejection will be great, but I will not just roll over and submit. "I will spit on your grave before I will share your bed."

I can see him, trembling with rage. His breathing harsh, his face flushed. His hands clench and unclench as though he's struggling to keep them away from my neck. I know I will suffer the consequences but I deliver my final blow anyway.

"You are weak. You will never be worthy to feel my love."

His roar of rage shatters the quiet of my cell. He launches forward, hands outstretched and I think *this is it. He's going to kill me.* Or he's going to try at least.

One fist comes up, connecting with my cheek. In the instant my head turns, Jason grabs a fistful of my hair.

I gasp as I'm yanked off the desk and fall to the ground. My hands fly up to my hair, to cover his hands as I try to alleviate the pressure on my scalp, like I was taught to. But he has the strands of my hair wrapped around all of his fingers. I can't peel them off.

I scream, both in surprise and in pain as he begins to drag me forward. I'm only vaguely aware of the whir of the door's lock as it is opened for us. I kick and scream and swear as Jason continues dragging me down the hallway.

I hear the jeers and catcalls of the guards as I pass them. I can't even find the focus to spit at them. Never in my life have I been humiliated and demeaned in such a way. Never in my life have I been so powerless. The constant rankling of my chains is a reminder of that.

No matter how much I kick and twist, my bare feet can't get enough purchase on the smooth marble floors to give me any kind of leverage.

"You're going to learn." I think he's talking to himself. Crazed and rambling, he's filled with some kind of strength as he jerks me along. "I didn't want to do this but you must learn. You must see."

Finally I give up screaming and my lips feel as though they're fused together with the effort it takes to keep my cries inside. I swear I can feel each individual hair in my scalp being ripped out.

"Open it!" He orders someone. I hear an affirming response and the sound of another door being opened.

"Here." he mutters as we approach the opened door. "Teach you a lesson, you stupid whore. You'll see. You'll see." I redouble my efforts to fight him off. To get loose. I don't want to see what's in that room. Of that much I'm sure. I claw at his hand and arm, drawing blood. I can feel it dripping onto my hands. He doesn't even seem to notice.

"Here! Here, you *anonyma!* Let's give you a taste of what your stubbornness and loyalty will get you!"

I can't help but scream again, despite my efforts, as he throws me bodily into the mystery room. I hit the ground hard, unable to brace myself as I normally would.

"LOOK!" He screeches at me, spit flying from his mouth. "LOOK AND SEE WHAT FATE AWAITS THOSE YOU CALL YOUR FAMILY!"

I can't place the noise I hear, at first. Muffled and rattling. Groaning gasps. No. I've never heard such noises before but hearing them now puts Sisyphus's rock in my stomach. I push myself to my hands and knees and raise my head.

279

And find myself staring at my bound and gagged mother.

"No!" I scream, attempting to launch myself at her. Someone grabs my hair again. I don't pay any attention to who it is. All I can see is my mother. Chained to a wall in the same chains that bind me. A white strip of something shoved in her mouth, tied around her head. I screech and scream and swear as I try again and again to go to her.

She's trying the same. Tugging helplessly on her chains. Working her gag, trying to get it out of her mouth. Tears stream down her bruised face. Old and new bruises. They've been beating her.

"Mama!" I sob, straining against the grip on my hair. "*Mama!*"

She cries something back to me, my name I think, and tugs hopelessly against her chains again.

Suddenly, Jason drops in my eye line, blocking my view of my mother. I ignore him entirely, trying to see around him to my mother. Still calling for her.

"Hey!" He slaps me. Hard. I gasp, wild and frenzied, baring my teeth at him, desperate to reach my mother. He points a finger in my face. "You remember. This is your fault. *You* did this, Aristomache Kallis. You could have just accepted the Fates design! But *noo*. You had to be prideful! And vain!" He slaps me again. I don't even register the pain now. The pain of my body is nothing compared to the pain in my heart. Has she been here the whole time? Yes, something tells me. She has been. Chained and beaten and tortured.

He stands and backs with slow and purposeful steps towards my mother. Realization fills her eyes at the same time as mine. I feel the blood drain from my face. I don't know what he's going to do to her, but I know I don't want to see it.

"No! No, no, no!" I beg him, thrashing in vain. "Please! I'll do whatever you want! Please! PLEASE!"

"It's too late!" He screams, gesturing wildly. "You had your chance to choose me and you chose your past! Well," he takes a deep breath, trying to force nonchalance and shrugs. "You can't choose your past, if you don't have one."

He drops to a knee beside my mother, ignoring her snarling and attempts of lunging at him.

"Your fault." He reminds me, as he pulls a knife from his jacket.

My eyes barely have time to widen in shock before he plunges it into her stomach.

My wordless scream covers the sound of her surprised gasp. A piercing wail that thrums in even my own ears. My whole body feels as though I've been doused in ice water, chilled to the bone, as my mothers eyes widen, as though in disbelief, and she begins to struggle to breath almost immediately. I'm cold to the very center of my being. As though it will never again know warmth. Jason seems completely unphased by any this. He takes his time to clean his knife off before making his way back over to me. Whoever holds my hair uses their other arm to pull my arms behind me.

Jason kneels down in front of me. The hand that he used to plunge the knife into my mother now strokes softly at my cheeks, catches a strand of my hair between his fingers.

"I'm sorry it had to be this way. But it did. Have to be this way." He stands and makes his way quickly to the door. I pay him no mind as whoever holds me finally lets go. I fall forward and begin to crawl towards my mother.

"Mama!" I cry. "Oh gods, please, mama."

She's gasping as I reach her, her face paling under her

usually olive skin. Blood quickly begins to cover her stomach. I lift my manacled hands up and over her so I can wrap them around her. Her chains are just long enough that I can cradle her in my lap, holding her to my chest.

"Aris," I squeeze my eyes shut, shaking it against the intruder to my grief. "ARISTOMACHE!" Startled, I look over at him. He stands in the doorway with his many guards. His gaze and tone are casual as he speaks, as though he did not just murder— because I know she will die— my mother in front of me. He tosses his knife in the air, flipping it around and around.

"You should know, this is the beginning. I gave you the opportunity to make the right choice here and you chose wrong. You must learn that there are consequences to your actions." His voice is matter-of-fact, like he's one of my Instructors during a lesson.

I can only stare at him, uncomprehendingly, as I listen to the rasping breaths of my dying mother. He adopts an overly patient tone, as though I'm a particularly dense child.

"You're confused. I understand, I do. But you need to *see*. You need to come to terms with your destiny. With me." He shakes his head, almost looking sad. "You can't do that if your conclave still calls to you. I'm going to help you get rid of that bond. That sense of loyalty. I'm going to help you." And then he's gone. Leaving me staring at the door like an idiot, until the something cold and soft touches my face. I start slightly before remembering where I am. I lean forward and bite my mothers gag, ripping it out of her mouth.

"Aristomache," she croons to me, stroking my cheeks.

"Oh, mama," I sob. "I'm sorry. I'm so sorry! This is all my fault!"

"No," she whispers, "no, my love. This is *his* fault." I shake my head before pressing my forehead against hers.

"No," I insist. "No, it's mine. You told me! You told me seeing Deimos was a bad idea. This all happened because I crawled into bed with a god. You warned me and I didn't listen! You warned me and Tessa warned me and my sisters warned me. You all warned me! If I had listened none of this would have happened!"

Mama gives a little laugh that turns into a painful cough. "You were 20 years old, my lovely. Of course you didn't listen to me. You had the attention of a *god*. What woman wouldn't bristle with the pride of that? Your mothers opinion became moot."

"No!" I argue. "It shouldn't have though! I should have listened to you!"

Another small smile. Another painful and bloody cough.

"You think I listened to Grammy when I was twenty? When your Grammy saw who I had chosen to have a baby with, I thought she was going to kill me!"

I can't help but give a watery smile at this, as this story is a familiar one. Grammy hated my father, a mortal military man with a high and tight hair cut and an ego the size of Jupiter. She tried to forbid my mother to see him. The idea of this leatherneck being allowed to father the next generation of our lineage disgusted her. But mama swears she knew that that match would produce a formidable offspring. *And I was right*, she would always say when she told the story, turning to wink at me.

"You are my greatest pride, Aristomache Kallis." She whispers resolutely. "You and your sister. My greatest pride and my greatest joy. The best thing the gods ever did for me

283

was to give me you two as my daughters."

I lay my forehead on hers again. "I'm sorry I let you down, Mama."

"Hey," she grabs my chin with as much strength as she can muster. "*Never* say something like that again. What part of 'greatest pride' are you not understanding?"

"This is all my fault! Because I was an anonyma for a god." I insist.

"You are the greatest Kallis woman to ever walk this Earth." Pride fills every ounce of my mothers voice and I can't make sense of this. She should be so angry at me. She's been so angry at me, for so long. Insisting that I wasn't training hard enough, railing that I was letting Deimos distract me from my duties. And what's worse is she was right. It's all my fault that she's dying. It's my fault that Lady Medusa was put into harms way to begin with. Because I allowed myself to be swayed from my mission by a few honeyed words of a god. Tears spill over my eyes and onto her cheeks. She doesn't seem to notice. A fervor has filled her voice, a determined gleam in her eyes. "And it is the greatest honor of my life that I got to be your mother."

"No," I cry harder, shaking my head. "No, if I hadn't started seeing Deimos, Jason would have never even met me."

"Listen to me, *αγάπες μου*." Her nails dig into my cheeks. Hearing her murderers name has brought back some of her fire. "Hear my words, my daughter. *You* are not responsible for my death. Did you plunge the knife into me? *No!* So quit crying and quit blaming yourself. This is *his* fault. And you *cannot* let him get away with this."

Steel fills my veins. She's right. Well, half right. I certainly am to blame for parts of this, after all if I hadn't purposefully antagonized him, Jason would have never been driven to "sever my bonds" but how could I have known this would be the consequence of my defiance. But for a mortal man to take such actions... to think he had a *right* to my love and my body with such intensity that he would commit such an affront against the gods... "No." I whisper. "No. I won't."

"Make him *pay* for this." She levels her gaze me. I try to ignore how her breaths rasp in her chest, how hot and sticky her blood feels on my skin. "You hear me, Aristomache?"

"Yes, mama." I sniffle and wipe my face on my shoulders. "I hear you."

"*Kill him,*" she hisses venomously, her eyes filled with hatred, her teeth gritted against the pain of dying. "You hear me, daughter? You are a *Kallis woman.* The product of thousands of years of greatness and perfection. The daughter of a daughter of a daughter of *heroes*. Do as you were trained! Do what you were *born* to do. Raise your spear and strike down our enemy."

"How?" I can't help but gripe. "I can't do anything with these chains on!"

"Athena will help those who are worthy. And you, my pride, are worthy." She answers solemnly.

I try to find some scathing retort to this. Something like *well she hasn't yet* but before I can my mother begins to cough and gag, spitting up blood in earnest. My panic doubles down, my vision swims and I can feel my pulse in my throat. I cling to her as adrenaline floods my entire body, leaving me feeling numb and electrified and dead all at once.

"Mama," I shake her. "Mama, you have to hang in there."

Her face is pale and blood coats her lips which move sound-lessly.

"What?" I ask, leaning in. "What are you saying?"

"Greatest pride..." she's barely audible. "You are our greatest pride."

"Mama," I whisper, terrified.

Her eyes lock on mine, her voice a hiss as she gives me one last order. "*Kill him.*"

28

Chapter 28

My whole body trembles as I wait for my mother to take another breath. The longer I wait the more frantic my own breathing becomes.

"Mama," I mutter as I lay her gently on the ground. My hands shake as I lift them to her neck, feeling for a pulse. "Mama, mama, mama."

For the first time in my life, my mother does not answer my cries. I feel myself begin to hyperventilate. My hands flutter from spot to spot over my mother, trying to be useful, knowing there is no point.

"I can't—" I gasp, clutching at my chest. "I can't— I can't—"

And it finally happens. The grief that has been clawing at my heart, at my throat, at my lungs, since the moment my pendant first burned my ear finally rips free of my body.

Grief and guilt and rage tears its way out of my throat, leaving a burning and raw feeling behind it. I beat my hands against my breasts, wailing and screeching. So angry at myself for my foolishness I can feel the red hot heat of it, licking around my throat. I throw myself over her, burying my face in her neck, as though I hope my screams will fill her with life again.

My grief is beyond words. All I can manage is animalistic, bloodcurdling screams and sobs. *Your fault. Your fault. Your fault.* I rage at myself. Jason's face floats up in my mind. *But your fault too.*

It takes a while for my screaming to stop. No one comes in, leaving me to my broken heart.

Once the screams are gone all that's left is my pitiful whimpering. Which fills the silence, leaving it heavy and palpable. I've lost the drive to do anything. All I can do is lay across her chest, running my fingers through her hair.

"I'm so sorry, mommy," I sob. "I'm so sorry."

The longer I'm left with the corpse of my mother, the more I have time to think. Think and realize how much guilt I carry, despite my mothers insistence that none of it is mine. I know it is. Jason and I, we bear the responsibility of my mothers death between us. The guilt seems like a living thing, festering in my stomach, eating me alive from the inside-out.

"Athena, help me." I groan when the festering feeling in my stomach becomes too much. I cling to my mother as I beg, clutching her to my chest. "Athena *please* if I have ever brought you honor, *help me, guide me.* Let me avenge my mother."

Athena will help those who are worthy.

That's what my mother told me. But no help has come to me yet and I've been here... how long have I been here now? A month? More? I have no idea, the days have blurred together.

Maybe Athena doesn't find me worthy. And that's why she hasn't helped me.

I sniffle pathetically, continuing my methodical stroking of my mom's hair. No, something tells me that's not right. Athena has never abandoned me before, so why would she start now? I am her mightiest spear. All of her Priestess's tell me so. She still has use for me. So why? What? What am I missing?

My heart stops beating as I hear footsteps coming down the hallway. I begin to pant, clinging to my mom even harder. I freeze as something comes to me. I pull back to look at my mom, at her empty eyes, her slightly parted lips.

"Athena, thank you!" I whisper fervently as I crush my mother to me again. I close my eyes and bite my lip against my grief.

I buckle down and tighten my grip as I hear the familiar whir of the door lock. Heavy boots echo on the floor as they march towards me.

Rough hands grab at me, grab at my mom, pulling us apart.

"No!" I screech, lashing out. "Mama! No! NO!" I can't tell how many people grab at me, picking me up and carrying me out of the room. I thrash in their arms, ignoring their bruising grips, screeching and screaming at them, sounding as though a banshee has possessed my body

"*Ugh*, c'mon let me knock her out. I'm tired of listening to her shatter my ear drums." One of the men complains.

"Have you totally lost your mind?" Another demands. "He'll kill you." The first man swears under his breath in annoyance as I continue my work of shattering their ear drums.

"Open it!" One of the men hollers. I hear another mechanical whir and, for the second time, am thrown bodily into a room.

I give a grunt of pain as I hit the cold, hard ground of my cell. But I don't dwell on the pain, I flip to my feet and throw myself at the door, snarling.

It's quickly slammed in my face. I give it several frustrated kicks before I pick up my old pacing path.

My breathing is fast and harsh as I pace back and forth. I see it over and over again. My mother reaching for me. Jason kneeling next to her, pointing at me with his knife. Plunging his knife into her stomach.

I retch and clap a hand to my mouth. I try to fight back the nausea but the image of Jason plunging that knife in replays over and over in my head, like a skipping C.D.

I rush over to the bathroom and barely make it in time to throw up violently into the toilet. I continue to gag even after my stomach has long emptied. I lay my head on my arm, periodically spitting into the toilet.

What have I done? I've killed my mother just as though I wielded the knife myself. I'm just as guilty of matricide as Desma had been. They should put me on the board. Or they should, if it looked like I was going to get out of here alive. Which it doesn't. Jason is clearly deeply disturbed. How much longer will he tolerate my defiance before he flies off the wall and kills me?

Or worse. How long until I feel the apathy, that envelopes me now, start to shift to a bond with him? I squeeze my eyes shut, shuddering violently against the thought. I'll kill myself before I let that happen.

It's there I still lay when my door opens again. I don't need to lift my head to know who it is who invades my mourning.

I hear him lean up against my desk, groaning quietly as he does so. He doesn't say anything for a while. I can't bring myself to look at him. It would require too much energy and I have none to spare. It seems all of mine has gone into keeping my heart beating, I can't even summon enough to move away from the toilet.

I count, as I wait for him to say something. Because he has something to say. Or he wouldn't risk his life to come in here. No. He has one more point to make and he will not be ignored.

It's seven minutes before he speaks. Seven minutes before he says four words that chill my blood and freeze my muscles in horror.

"Mark Twain National Forest."

My muscles lock into place and I clench my fists, the skin over my knuckles white. Before in apathy, now in terror. I want to look at him but my body won't obey. "It really is..." he heaves a sigh, "such a shame that you couldn't be more amendable to my proposal, Aristomache."

Slowly, I sit up and turn around. Jason's blank face stares back at me. I've never seen a human being have such expressionless eyes.

"I offered you security and devotion and commitment, but you threw it back in my face." I find myself wishing he would yell. This plain and unaffected way he speaks now instills more fear in me than anything else ever has. "Like a child, you couldn't listen. Couldn't behave. Had to prove that you knew best, unable to admit that you needed help finding your way in the world.

"I tried to give you help. Tried to show you how much you were missing in your life. But what did you do? You reacted immaturely. Threw it back in my face. So now I have to be the bad guy. What you need to understand is that you *need* a strong Alpha male in your life to guide you. Protect you. To sit at the head of your table. But the conclave... they've taught you to go against your biological destiny. That you're a big, strong, independent woman who don't need no man! Right? But think of that empty feeling you have whenever you think of your life. That pit in your stomach that tells you, you were missing something. Well. I was that pit. That something. And I understand this is a big adjustment to make— I mean for gods sake you were running around mostly naked in all kinds of night clubs, dancing with gods and all kinds of men! Think of the position you put yourself in! All of the different ways you allowed yourself to be disgraced, how you begged for it even. Oh yes, I heard that too."

Everything about him is casual. He leans against my desk with his hands folded across his chest. His one foot, that sits crossed over the other, bounces to a beat that only he can hear. He gives a nonchalant tip of his head as he continues.

"Maybe I'm not wording this right for you to fully understand where I'm coming from. Let me think..."

I gape at him in horror. All these years, I thought it would be a monster that would take me from my family or my family from me. But whenever I would think about that, it was never this type of monster I envisioned. But I think the one in front of me is the worst type of monster I've ever met.

"Okay. I know!" He announces happily, clapping once. "Think of yourself as a flower and every time you've given yourself to another man you've allowed him to pluck one of your petals away. How many petals do you think you have left now? How many petals have you left for me to enjoy? Do you see how this might be frustrating for me? Knowing that you've given so many of your petals away, leaving me with just scraps? I mean any real man would be upset about that!

That's understandable I think. But don't worry. We'll work through these differences together. But." He raises a single finger in the air, looking down his nose at me. "In order to do that, you need to learn to trust that I know what is best for you."

I think of a million things I want to say to this man. A thousand ways to cut him down to size. To leave his ego shattered around my feet. I want to call upon the anger of my ancestors and show him what I was born to do. But I don't. Instead all that comes out is:

"Why me? There are so many women in the world. Some of them might have even chosen you willingly. So, why me?"

He smiles down at me in a way that he clearly thinks is adoringly.

"Aristomache" He tsks at me. "Pretty girls like you always go for jerks. For the bad boys who just want to take a young girls petals and throw them in the trash. I had to show you what a true gentleman was like. Show you what you deserve in life. That is my purpose in life, the reason the Fates brought me here." I shake my head slowly, ice in my veins.

"Please, let me go home." To beg this man goes against every fiber of my being but it's all I can think of to do. His smile turns sardonic, his tone almost mocking.

"Aris..." he draws out. "What makes you think you have a home to go back to?"

"I don't..." I gape at him. "I don't understand."

He sucks his teeth and shakes his head in mock disappointment. "I knew you weren't listening to me earlier. I *told* you, sweetheart, that I'm going to help you get rid of all of your other loyalties. Do you remember that?"

"I don't understand." I repeat, my voice taut.

"Oh, I think you do." Jason disagrees. "You can't give yourself to me if you're bound to someone else. You can't be bound to someone else if they're gone."

I knew what he was saying. When he was talking earlier before leaving me with my mother. When he came in saying the three words I never wanted to hear, an outsider, a man, say. But to acknowledge it was the worst kind of pain, next to the loss of my mother but now I can't ignore it.

Without warning I leap up from the floor, launching myself at the cowardly excuse of a man that lounges in front of me. Every part of me is begging to claw him, rip him, make him bleed.

I don't get that far.

I should've realized he was too much of a gutless bastard to come in here without a guard. But I didn't. Not until he materializes from the other side of the curtain that surrounds my bathroom area and he was burying the tip of his cattle prod into my stomach. The electric shocks that pulse through my body rattle my teeth.

With a scream, I fall to the ground, but clamber to my feet just as quickly. Teeth bared, fists clenched, I stare down my captor. A flicker of fear passes his eyes, betraying him.

"If you even think of touching my family... I will eviscerate you." I whisper to him. "I will scatter you like Cronus into the deepest pit of Tartarus after I piss on your remains."

My breathing is ragged but my hand is steady as I point an accusing finger at him. "You will never own me. You will never be man enough to be my equal and you will never be big enough to force me to be your submissive."

Jason clicks his tongue and shrugs his shoulders, making a show of his supposed disregard for my fury. "Only one way to find out I guess." He makes his way towards the door. When I shift as though to follow, his henchman crackles the cattle prod at me again in warning.

"Don't worry. We'll laugh about this someday," is that last thing I hear before the door slams behind them.

I stare after him for a long moment, my heart in my throat. He's going to target the conclave. He claims he's earned all these favors of all these gods... is that true? Has he earned enough that he might actually be a threat to my sisters? The mere thought of this failure of a man, possibly being strong enough to take out any of my sisters is laughable by instinct. But he managed to kill, or orchestrate the kill of three of us already. He managed to capture me.

He was right in one sense, we Initiates are vain and ego-tistical. It takes real effort to remind myself that people underestimating their enemies has cost the victory of more than one battle in history. Which means I need to take what he's saying at face value.

Which means I need to get out of here. Someone has to warn them and someone has to help lead my legion into battle.

The sudden calmness that washes over me is a familiar feeling. I've always felt better with an action plan. I've fought plenty of fights before. This one will be no different, truly. First the first time in what feels like forever, my breaths feel steady and sure as I lift my hand up and reach into my bra.

Once cold, but now warmed by my fevered skin, my mother's pendant glints gently in the light of my cell.

Athena will help those who are worthy.

I clench my fist around the metal, feeling the vines of the olive branch dig into my palm.

Kill him. Her memory whispers in my mind.

295

And I will.
In her honor. I will.

29

Chapter 29

That night, I lay curled up on my side. My blanket pulled over my face. I put on the performance of a life time, shaking my shoulders to look as though I'm crying underneath. Sniffling as though I'm desperately trying to hide my tears. Which is dangerously close to being my reality but I just manage to hold them at bay.

In reality, I'm using my mother's pendant to severe the magic of my manacles. Or at least I'm attempting to. It's difficult because everything must be specific. It took me forever to decode the magic enough to figure out where the weakest point is, where that intersection between spells is. Because where that intersection is, is where I need to focus my attention on. If I can break the binding between the two weaker spells, the whole sequence of spells becomes voided. It's tricky and dangerous ,but it's also my only hope. You can't do it to every spell and you can't use just anything to sever the spells. You need to use an item blessed by a god, or crafted by one; it's the only thing strong enough to withstand the spells fighting back against being severed.

Dragging the tip of the owls wings back and forth, I slowly but surely begin to scour the metal. Some spells are surface level, meaning if I just create a scratch between it will be severed. However, these must be deep within the metal because after several hours I've managed to create a small valley in the metal and still they hold strong.

I'm sweating, swearing and trying to ignore the cramping in my hands as I work the pendant methodically back and forth. I'm just beginning to think that this won't work when I hear heavy footsteps coming.

"Shit!" I hiss, shoving the pendant in my bra again. I lay as still as I can, feigning sleep, praying whoever it is will just look through the window and not actually come in.

"Please, please, please," I mouth to myself as the footsteps draw nearer. I hear them stop outside my door and almost allow myself to feel relieved that they're not coming in when I hear the whir or the door.

I have to remind myself to breath and try to look relaxed and asleep as I hear the quiet steps come into my room.

Big, lumbering, trying to be quiet and not get noticed steps.

My blood chills as I realize it is not Jason. This new unknown threat, trying not to get noticed, sneaking into my room is not the evil I have become accustomed to. I hate myself for hoping Jason will notice my intruder and will whisk this strange and new threat from my cell. Unless he sent them to punish me. This new thought stops my heart for a beat and I clamp my teeth down on my lip to keep from screaming.

Athena protect me, I scream in my head. I wonder if Lady Medusa screamed the same thing as she ran to her goddess's temple, all those years ago.

They walk over to my bed and kneel beside me. I bite my lip

so hard I draw blood. The sharp, metallic taste lingers on my tongue.

"Ms. Aris," a low, rasping voice whispers, laying a warm and heavy hand on my shoulder.

With a gasp, I flip over. Hardly daring to believe it. But in the light of the full moon, there he is.

"Pyl!" I cry, throwing my arms around his neck. "Oh, Pyl!" A little voice in the back of my head warns this is a trick. That Pyl is in on it too. That he's a threat. An enemy. But I can't bring myself to listen to it. Especially not when Pyl begins patting my back in the clumsy manner of his.

"There, there, Ms. Aris." He rumbles. "Sorry took so long." I pull back, but keep a grip on his shoulders, smiling and laughing and crying.

"Pyl, I'm so happy to see you!" I whisper tearfully. He smiles back, his yellow eyes crinkling.

"I'm here to help," he whispers conspiratorially.

"How did you find me?" I ask him, amazed he was able to.

"The boy asked Lord Deimos if he could borrow me. Few days ago." He tells me. "Lord Deimos did not want to say yes. He had me looking for you but could not say no. So I came and heard them talking. Talking about the Initiate girl who swears a lot and I thought, 'must be Ms. Aris'. I've been looking but this place is very big. So sorry it took me so long to find you."

I throw my arms around Pyl again. "Don't be sorry, you amazing satyr." I murmur. I pull back to meet his gaze. "Thank you, for caring about me." He gives me his shy, flickering smile and pats my cheek. I hate myself for asking my next question, for pinning my hope of rescue on any other god other than the one I am sworn to, but I can't stop myself. "Did you tell Deimos I was here?"

Pyl shakes his head at me, apologetic. "Could not tell. Rules."

I huff out a breath. I don't know which rule is stopping Pyl from being able to tell Deimos but at the moment I despise it. With that hope squandered, another comes to me.

Suddenly frantic, I dig my mothers pendant out of my bra and hold it out to him.

"I'm trying to sever the spell on these," I explain to him, holding out my manacles to him. "But I think I'm not strong enough to break it on my own. Can you do it?"

He reaches out for the pendant, seeming nervous. His eyes flit up to my ear, and a crease forms between them when he sees my pendant still with me.

"It's my mothers," I whisper tearfully. "He killed her, Pyl. Right in front of me."

An angry growl rumbles in his chest and he takes the pendant.

"Wait," I tell him, suddenly frightened as another thought comes to me. "Pyl, you can't do this. I'm being watched from a camera. They'll see you! I don't want you hurt!"

Pyl shakes his head and takes my chained hands. "No , Ms. Aris. I broke cameras." After a brief moment of shock, a delighted laugh escapes me.

"Broke them?"

"Broke them," he confirms, resuming the path I had begun on my manacles. "They are trying to fix now. They will not."

I tip my head back smiling, tears running down my face.

"Pyl," I tell him, tilting my head up again. "I love you."

"I love you too, Ms. Aris." He replies, simply. "That's why I'm here."

I lean forward and rest my forehead on Pyl's massive

shoulder. Feeling reassured by the presence of someone known and safe and let myself cry. Pyl continues his careful work on my manacles, humming a gentle, discordant tune as he does.

* * *

Feeling relatively safe for the first time in a month, I must have drifted off while Pyl was working because I jerk awake with a gasp as an electric shock races up my arms and down my spine.

Pyl gives a rasping giggle. "I did it!" he whispers excitingly. "I broke Ms. Aris out of jail!"

I stare, dumbfounded and disbelieving as the black metal crumbles around me, covering my legs in its filmy ash. I flex my fingers in wonder. I can feel my strength and blessing come rushing back into my body. It leaves me gasping and wanting, shaking with adrenaline. Pyl stands and backs away from me, wringing his hands together.

I stand slowly. As though I'm learning how to walk all over again. But I'm not and my legs are sure and steady under me. My hands shake as I raise them for the true test.

I hook one of my fingers around my bracelets and give a tug.

My spear springs to life in my hands. Gasping, I stare at in awe. Never have I been so happy to have a spear in my hands before. Never again will I take my blessings and skills for granted. I grasp it with both hands, resting my forehead on the cool metal. The familiar and reassuring weight of my weapon fills me with such relief it almost knocks me to my knees.

"Ms. Aris will kill her enemies?" Pyl asks.

I open me eyes and a savage smile fills my face.

"I think I will, Pyl. Can you open the door?"

"Oh yes," he tells me, immediately going over to the door. "I can open the door."

I follow him on light feet, quickly falling back into the role of a hunter. Of a spear of Athena.

Pyl opens the door to an empty hallway. He goes first, looking up and down the hall before turning and motioning for me to follow.

I can't help but hold my breath as I step over the threshold, expecting another shock from a cattle prod or to wake up from this dream. Neither of those things happen. The cool marble of the floor sends a chill up my body. I shiver both from the chill and anticipation. I turn to level my gaze at Pyl.

"Where is he?"

"I will show you!" Pyl tells me eagerly, motioning for me to follow.

The hallway is shaped like an L. To my left is a long hallway, with several cell doors on either side with one heavy metal one at the very end. To my right is about a dozen or so more feet of hallway before it turns left. This is the way that Pyl motions for us to go. I go to follow before my eyes fall on the other cell doors again.

"Is anyone else being held here?" I ask Pyl, motioning to the doors.

He shakes his head adamantly, stepping towards me to grab my arm and tug me along with him.

"No, Ms. Aris, no." He insists. "A trick. He made a trick so if you did get out, he would have more time to catch you. He knew you'd stop to check. All empty. I swear it."

Jason really did think this out because even though I trust

Pyl implicitly, it takes real effort to turn and follow him down the hall and not go check each cell for myself.

With a groan of frustration I turn away from the cells and follow Pyl.

We're just turning the corner of the hall when the door at the end whirs to open. The defensive rumble in Pyl's chest tells me this was not part of his plan. The hallway itself isn't very long, maybe 50 feet. So when the door opens and two men walk through, I don't hesitate. I push past Pyl and send my spear into the first man. The force of my throw penetrates his weak body armor, Kevlar by the look of it, and sends him flying back into the door, slamming it shut. His buddy is just reaching for his radio when I close the remaining distance. I run up the wall a couple steps to give me better leverage as I pull out a second spear and send it into his neck.

They're both dead before my feet hit the ground.

I dart forward and pull my spears out of the dead men, careful not to damage the tips of them. Around the neck of one of the men is a key card. Giddy with my kills and my good luck, I lean down and pull the key card free, turning to wave it triumphantly at Pyl.

"That is helpful!" He crows, running forward to give me a high five.

I can't help but laugh, wild and almost free, as I slap my palm against his. While Pyl moves the body of the man I slammed against the door, I turn to the other man and grab his weapon. While I love my spears, I need to be efficient in my kills and guns help me do that. I scold myself for not thinking to grab one of the conclaves when I first left.

A gentle beep tells me Pyl has opened the door, grinning like a kid in a candy shop as he holds up the key card.

"C'mon," I tell him, smiling. "Let's do this."

"Let's *do* this, Ms. Aris!" Pyl whispers in excitement, following me out the door.

We meet resistance almost immediately. The hallway we have opened up to is more heavily guarded than my own hallway, wider too. Some of the rooms have windows. It looks like labs for experiments occupy some of them. We make it maybe a dozen feet before cries of "she's out!" fill the corridor.

I have one heavy advantage other the men I aim my gun at. They are clearly under orders not to hurt me and I have no such dispositions. Snarling, I do not aim to take prisoners as I mow through man after man.

I keep Pyl in my peripheral, these men have no qualms about killing him and make that fact well known. It slows me down some, having to turn back to protect Pyl again and again but over my literal dead body will I leave him behind. Not ever and not especially after what he's done for me.

"Pyl!" I yell, raising my gun.

Thank Athena he understands. Pyl picks up the man he's fighting by the throat and slams him into the ground before bending over him. Opening my line of sight to the guards behind him.

I can see people running around in panic in the windows, rushing to protect whatever they deem necessary. I send a spray of bullets into the windows along one of the walls. Screams and shattering glass fill the room. All kinds of alarms are blaring, including from one of the rooms that looks like it may have been pressurized.

It doesn't take long for Pyl and I to clear the room, other than the scientists who don't count as they don't carry weapons.

"Pyl," I call to him, popping out my hip that the key card dangles from. I stand a few feet back from the door, gun raised and ready.

"Oh, yes, yes," Pyl answers, clopping forward to do as instructed. After scanning the door, he counts down from three and then wrenches the door open.

As expected a garrison of guards waits on the other end. I don't know why they're so surprised by the animalistic attack that greets them. But they are. Cries of 'stop' and 'please' and 'have mercy' mingle with my gunshots.

They want mercy, huh? Where was their mercy for me, when I was held captive for a month? For my mother, when she was slaughtered in front of her daughter? I have no mercy for these beasts.

I leap over the dead bodies into a large and open room. A chow hall, I think. It's surprisingly empty. But it hasn't been empty for long. The long tables are filled with half eaten trays, books cast aside and more than a few broken cups on the ground that were thrown away in haste. My steps are wary as we make our way through the room. I'm coiled tight as a wire, my heels rarely touch the ground as I creep forward.

"Very quiet," Pyl remarks, reaching out to graze my elbow, reassuring both of us that we're both still here and together.

"Mm," I murmur, "too quiet. Do you know where we are?"

"Yes," Pyl murmurs back, following my lead. "Very close to barracks and his quarters. Barracks that way and his quarters that way."

Pyl points to a door along the far left of the chow hall first, then another, tucked in the corner by the front of the room. My blood sings in anticipation as my eyes lock onto my target.

"Which way to get out of here?" I ask, pausing for a moment.

"Same way, Ms. Aris. His quarters right by front door."

"Excellent," I murmur, stalking forward again.

When we get to the door, I hold up my hand to stop Pyl and press my ear to the door, listening hard. I'm not surprised when the sound of muffled orders and shuffling bodies greets me. Of course he would call all of his guards to protect his ass like this.

I step back, a crease between my eyebrows forming as I think.

"Is this the only way to his quarters?" I stand on my tiptoes to breathe into Pyl's ear, my hand clutching his forearm. "And to outside?" He follows my lead again and bends his head down to mine. His breath fans my hair around my face as he answers me.

"Yes, Ms. Aris. Only way. For security." I mouth a swear word as I pull back and take in the scene in front of me. My face lights up as I notice the old flag post a couple of feet above the door. Vaguely, I wonder if this used to be a school or something.

I motion for Pyl to follow me and point to the flag post, miming him boosting me up. Pyl gives an excited dance as he understands what I'm saying and locks his hands together for me to step in to. As he boosts me up, I reach up and grab a hold of the post and pull my legs up so they're wrapped around it.

With one hand, I keep the butt of my gun pressed into my shoulder, with the other I hold myself up and out of the way of the door. I give us both a second to get settled and ready. Finally, I lock eyes with Pyl. His bright yellow eyes are leveled at me, waiting for his signal.

"One, two, three," I mouth to him. When I nod he pulls the door open, tucking himself behind it.

Athena hear me, I think as I let go of my hold and swing forward, twisting to face my enemies. Their surprised and fearful cries sound like music to my ears as my gun tears through their flesh.

In the silence that follows I drop back down to the ground, landing on silent feet and standing over my massacre.

Pyl moves to stand at my shoulder. "Ms. Aris kills her enemies," he whispers in awe.

"Yes, I did." I respond, grimly. "And I'm not done yet."

Pyl gives a growl of enthusiasm at this declaration. I begin to pick my way through the bodies, my gun held at the ready, fully anticipating one of them to be playing dead. Waiting for a cold hand to latch onto my ankle.

But the dead stay dead and I can't help the shiver of relief that ripples through me as I step free of the bodies.

The corridor remains empty as we make our way through it. Just as I'm thinking that the remainder of Jason's guards are the ones who I met at the first door, Pyl cries out from behind me.

I whip around, raising my gun. Three guards are swinging at Pyl with cattle prods, the blue electricity dancing between the prongs.

"No!" I yell. "Pyl!" I squeeze the trigger of my gun but roar in frustration when I feel the locked trigger, telling I now have an empty magazine. "Shit!"

Throwing the gun to the ground I snap off a bracelet, the golden bronze tip of it shining in the darkness. Just as I'm about to charge in, the crackle of a cattle prod sounds off dangerously close to me.

I swing my spear to the right, knocking the cattle prod out of the guards hand and bury my spear in his neck before he

307

can process what's happening.

But he wasn't alone and soon four, five, six of his buddies are between me and Pyl, pushing me back.

"Pyl!" I scream hysterically, as I watch him try to defend himself against the onslaught he's enduring. "Pyl! I'm coming, Pyl!"

But I'm not. I'm just managing to keep the guards at bay and keep myself out of the reach of their blue lights. Pyl knows this.

"No! You go!" He bellows to me, tossing one of the men into the wall. "Ms. Aris will go! I will find you!"

Even though I know he's right, I don't want him to be. I don't want to leave him. I don't want to lose him. Both as a protector and as a friend.

"GO!" He roars when he realizes I'm still there.

"Shit!" I yell as I turn quickly. I put my head down and I run. I hear the guards give chase but they won't catch me. I'm too fast and they're weighed down by their armor and weapons.

As I approach the end of the hallway I see two doors, one dark oak with a golden sign on it, the other worn metal with a 6x6 inch window for speaking to those who might come knocking. And then... I see him. He's exiting his quarters with an overnight bag over his shoulder. He freezes when he sees me bearing down on him. For the first time, pure terror floods his eyes and stays there.

And like the coward he is, he runs. He throws the heavy metal door open and bolts out of it. Like a rabbit that has heard the baying of the hound that's caught its trail.

And I don't lose the trail once I've caught it.

I leave the guards in the dust, as I sprint out the door. He didn't even bother to slam it in his wake. But I do. Sacrificing one of my spear I barricade it, and pray to Deimos to protect Pyl.

V

Part Five

30

Chapter 30

The sea breeze on my face almost brings me to my knees. Fresh air and the warmth of the sun. My breath quickens for no reason other than to suck down as much of the fresh air as I can, terrified it will be taken away again.

My pulse thrums in my neck as I begin scanning around, looking for where he's gone. About two hundred yards to my right is a large, metal garage. Like the kind that farmers use to store tractors and stuff. I can hear the sound of keys rattling, his panicked breathing and him swearing under his breath.

I run over, slowing to a hunters creep as I approach. Jason doesn't see me. His back is to me as he turns over dozens of key rings in his hands, trying to figure out which ones go to the SUV in front of him.

Something alerts him to my approach, he throws the keys to the side and pulls a sword out of his waist. Bronze, inscribed with something in Ancient Greek.

"Pretty," I note, as I stalk towards him. "Where'd you get that?"

His hands shake as he holds the sword out to me. "Don't

worry about that, whore. Just- just-" he licks his lips, "get back to your room, now!"

I throw back my head, cackling. I twirl my spear my body, putting on a show, around before leveling it at him.

"I am not your dog to order about. I am not the princess you've got locked away in the tower. *I* am the spear of Athena. The greatest warrior to come out of our conclave. And you... you stupid bitch, have made me your enemy. I swore to my mother I would kill you. And I intend to keep that promise."

"You just couldn't accept your fate! Couldn't accept that we were meant to be together!" He raves, his eyes wide and crazy.

"Weird how people react when you murder their family and lock them in a cell." I seethe back. "I don't care what gods and spirits you've curried favor from. What quests you've completed. I have more. I *am* more. You are *nothing* compared to the might of Athena's spear. May my goddess hear my words now and wrap her mighty aegis around my shoulders. May she stand aside me as I strike down our enemies. As I water the earth with their blood. With *your* blood."

His hands tremble and I can see the sweat the covers his upper lip. He knows he's at his end here and he's terrified. Whatever deal he made to capture me... he's not ready to pay that due yet.

"I will eat your heart raw in front of your mother," I vow to him. His eyes widen as he registers the promise beneath my words.

With a shriek he flies at me, sword raised.

I raise my spear to block his blow before retaliating with one of my own. His anguished cry is my reward as I slice the inside of his thigh. I expected more. I expected him to have blessings over him, spirits fighting with him, the same way that Desma did. I keep waiting for it, keep stalling the fight, afraid of ending it and triggering some kind of catalyst for something I can't understand.

And finally it happens.

I noticed he had been muttering to himself under his breath, but honestly thought he was just talking to himself like the crazy man he is. Until he throws his arms out to the side and tilts his head back to the heavens, crying out in Ancient Greek.

Use me, Lord! Let me be your weapon!

My eyes widen as something fills his body. Black and wispy smoke. Like a demon possession from some television show. When his head snaps up again, his eyes are flat black, a cruel smile fills his face.

I push my shock down and bare my teeth at him. With a yell, I attack.

His movements are clumsy but strong. He doesn't make contact with me often but when he does, he sends me flying across the lawn. My poor ribs have taken quite the beating lately, and I find myself hoping that my blessing doesn't get sick of cleaning up my messes and stops working.

"Son of a—" I cry out as he lands another blow, sending me flying back into the side of the metal building. The heat of it from the afternoon sun still lingers on the metal and burns my bare skin.

I begin to chip away at him, slashes and stabs wherever I can get them in. Unlike Desma, Jason doesn't have the blessing of a god to interfere with whatever is possessing him. But like Desma, Jason can only withstand the presence of an ancient spirit inside of him for so long before his mortal body begins to break down. Desma knew the risk she was taking when she allowed the possession for her, but something tells me Jason doesn't.

He's surprised by the pain of it, he looks down at his chest, gasping as it begins. As his molecules begin to burn him alive from the inside out. My spear spared Desma the worst of the pain and although I want this coward dead by my hand, for a moment I consider standing by while he burns alive. Jason makes the decision for me.

"*THIS IS ALL YOUR FAULT!*" He roars. "I was supposed to go down in history! I was supposed to be one of the greats!" Insanity fills his eyes as he raises his sword again.

I don't let him get that far.

I give my mightiest war cry as I lunge for him. With one smooth movement I've disarmed him. Because no matter how much strength he has, he has no training. No skill. No defense. His sword clatters to the rocks below us.

"*No!*" He screeches as I swipe his feet out from under him. He lands flat on his back, his arms flying up to protect his face. "*Avenge your servant!*"

With a grunt, I bury the head of my spear into the screaming face of my once captor. Silencing him for good.

I plant my foot on his forehead as I pull out my spear. For a moment, I just stand there. Sucking in deep breaths. Allowing myself to revel in the peace, the security, that this kill has brought. My sisters are safe. My Lady is safe. *I* am safe. Well as safe as can be, my ribs ache— again. There's a nasty gash across the top of my bicep and another one, I can't see how bad it is, that follows the length of my spine. My feet are aching and bloody from fighting barefoot on the rocks of the drive way. I'm breathless and exhausted and aching for home. But even still. I'm safe.

I should've known that feeling couldn't last.

"I really wish you hadn't done that." I don't turn right away. Just close my eyes in horror as I stand, feeling the blood of my enemy drip onto my bare feet.

Slowly, so slowly, I turn to face Deimos.

And there he stands, gorgeous and deadly. And grim. Covered in ink black battle armor, he looks formidable. Though his black eyes are filled with unfathomable sadness.

"What're you doing here?" I ask him, knowing the answer.

He heaves a sigh as a spear materializes in his hands. "Avenging my servant."

I nod slowly as I look down at the corpse at my feet.

"You knew..." I begin. "You knew he was going to do all of this... and you said *nothing* to me. You let me share your bed, knowing the *beast* that was listening at the door would do this to me."

"No," Deimos tells me adamantly, raising a finger. "I didn't know exactly what was going to happen."

"You knew enough." I shoot back, my eyes accusing.

"What did you expect from me, Aris?" He demands, throwing up his hands in frustration. "I'm bound by the oldest of laws!"

"That's bullshit, Dei." I tell him. "There are ways around those laws, to some extent. You could've given me some kind of warning, but you said *nothing*."

"I-" Deimos fumes, then gathers himself. "Please, Aris. Let me fulfill the calling of my servant and be done with this."

The calling of the servant. The crying breath of a dying man is a weighty thing. Vows and curses are strongest off the lips of someone who knows there is no hope for them. Never did I think think might be a possibility. The law that allows for this is ancient, brought to power by an all but nameless god. I had all but forgotten about its existence. No respectable devotee would subject their patron to such a humiliating act. If Jason had curried enough favor with Deimos, which he obviously has, he could call Deimos in to finish his fight for him. It's a cowardly and low-life thing to do. Just the type of thing for Jason. He might have even done it to spite me, to spite us. Knowing if I managed to kill him, Deimos would be forced to fight me. It's just the type of thing his sadistic mind would drool over.

I regard Deimos as I think this over. There are different levels of oaths. Deimos wouldn't kill me, not willingly. So if he's calling for me to let this be over quickly, I imagine he just has to disarm me, or maybe knock me unconscious. He's right. I could give him a half-assed effort of a duel, let him do what is being required of him so we can move past this and I can get home.

But all I can think of his how he comforted me as I sobbed over having to kill one of my sisters. How he said nothing when he saw me running full throttle towards the unforeseen danger that was waiting just up ahead for me.

I shake my head at him, my eyes steady and locked onto him.

He roars in frustration, spiking his spear into the ground. He strides forward, his handing clamping down onto my biceps.

"This is ridiculous! Aristomache! Look at yourself! Look at how bloody and broken and tired you are. Let me strike you down and then my obligation is complete and this nonsense can end."

"This nonsense will never end!" I retort. "Because you will not give me justice. You did not punish him— *no* don't you dare lie to me and tell me that you tried. Because you did not. *I* had to punish him. *I* had to end his life. And what guarantee do I have of the punishment he will face in the Underworld? Do you know what the three judges will rule for him? Because I don't! So he's dead, yes. But I was denied my justice." I break free of Deimos's grip and move back several paces.

"You let him stay on as your servant despite him being a threat to the woman who shared your bed! The woman you claimed to love! Was that not grounds enough to dismiss him? He murdered my mother, he wanted to murder my sisters and he threatened my Lady Medusa with his moronic plan in his quest to abduct me. Worse yet, you knew he was behind this and said nothing to me. I shared your bed and gave you my love and companionship and yet you said *nothing* to me."

"I *couldn't*! I'm bound by our laws, Aris!" He thunders, his fists clenching as he steps towards me, again. He catches himself and throws them to the sky instead. "I tried to warn you! Protecting you has always been my number one priority! I begged you to take godhood as my wife—"

"I DO NOT WANT YOUR GODHOOD! I WANT MY MOTHER!" My rages fills my body with red hot anger. My voice booms, filling the space that separates us. "I never wanted the palace in the sky and the underworld parties and fear and automatic respect that comes from hanging on the arm of a god. All I have ever wanted, for my entire life, was my mother's pride, my sisters admiration and the respect of my comrades."

"So you despise the idea of being my immortal wife so much that you will raise your spear to me, knowing you will not survive this battle?" Sorrow fills his voice and I know he is not trying to trick me. The idea of causing me pain, real pain, battling me for real, breaks his immortal heart. "Knowing that you are broken and bleeding and exhausted and that I will have no choice but to strike you down?"

I can't help but give an exhausted, helpless laugh, covering my face with my hands for a moment before planting them on my hips. "You're right. I am broken and bleeding. I am so tired I do not remember what it is to not be tired anymore. I am so full of grief and sorrow it sometimes feels as though I am *choking* on it." I take a deep breath and grip my spear with my trembling arm. I square my shoulders and my raise my chin.

"But, unfortunately for you, that is not all that I am. I am also one of Athena's chosen. A member of a conclave so ancient it rivals the ichor that courses through your body. I am my Lady Medusa's Protector until the day the Fates cut my string and call me to the Underworld. I am not your wife, or anyone else's, nor will I ever be. I am not even the woman who warms your bed at night. Not anymore. I am Aristomache Kallis, daughter of Atalanta Kallis, granddaughter of Lydia Kallis. I will raise my spear to you, Lord Deimos. And I will die. But I swear to you here and now: I will paint this ground golden with your blood before you take my life."

"Why do you always have to make things so difficult?" Deimos seethes, his lip curled over his perfect teeth. "Why do you insist on challenging me?!"

"What can I say," I manage a smirk and I can feel the dried blood on my lips as it cracks with the movement. "I was born to fight gods."

And then I charge.

Deimos is not Desma. He is not Jason. He is not even Dolos. He is the god of fear and terror. Son of Ares, the god of war. He is a formidable opponent.

I wish I could describe our battle better. I wish I could detail the strikes and parries and wounds. But to battle against someone who was once your lover... I think a part of me shut down. Blocked it out. I did not want these memories tainting so many pleasant ones.

I did not want to think of Deimos's arm wrapping around my neck, the pressure robbing me of my breath. Not when those same arms used to hold me so lovingly. So tenderly.

I did not want to think about the knife in my hand coming down, aiming for his chest, aiming to maim and draw blood. I did not want to think about succeeding in that and watching as his black shirt becomes stained with gold. Not when that's where I used to rest my head to sleep.

I tried not to think about those things anyway. I tried to think logically. Moves and countermoves. Strikes and parries. Feints and attacks.

I wish it worked half as well as I wanted it to.

With a roar, Deimos throws me up against the SUV. I hit it, shoulder first and slide slowly to the ground, grimacing in pain. Every part of me aches. More so than any other fight I have ever had.

"Why are you making me do this?" Deimos roars, fighting back tears. Golden blood drips from his fingertips, from his thigh, from his chest. I have painted the ground gold in his blood. I have lost quite a bit of my own red, mortal blood, thanks to a particularly nasty cut across my shoulders. "*Yield!* My love, *please*!"

Shaking my head, I stand on shaky legs. I stand as tall as I can, as tall as my body will allow me to and meet Deimos's tear-filled eyes.

"I will not," I tell him breathlessly. "Yield."

His lips tremble as I approach again, leveling my spear. "*Please.* αγαπητή please don't make me do this."

I don't answer him as I wield my spear. With a cry, I attack, piercing his foot before unsheathing my knife and stabbing it into his thigh.

His roar echoes through my chest and it happens so fast. His millennia old instincts kick in. You can tell it's an unconscious movement. He uses his other foot to break off my spear as he rips my knife out of his thigh. He easily blocks my exhausted efforts to fight back and within seconds, buries my knife into my stomach. My gasp causes the snarl on his lips to slide off, replaced by a horrified grimace.

Our eyes widen at the same time as he realizes what he's done. My hands tremble as they come up to cover his that still holds the handle of the knife.

My breath comes in shuddering gasps as my knees give out.

"No, no, no!" Deimos cries, catching and cradling me against his chest. "NO!"

I whimper as Deimos lowers us to the ground. His roar of grief echos in the very marrow of my bones. My body shakes with both his grief and mine. I hold my hand as tightly as I can to my wound. My hand fumbles around, reaching for the handle to pull it out. Deimos grabs my wrist to stop me.

"No, my love," he sobs, pressing his forehead to mine. "No, leave it in. You must leave it in."

Some part of me is still aware enough to recognize that what he's saying is right because I stop trying to fight him.

"My mama," I beg. "Don't leave her here. Let her go home."

Deimos's hand, painted red in my blood, comes up to stroke my face, his tears falling fast and frequent onto my face. I wish he wouldn't. I feel so cold already and the wetness of his tears drying on my face only amplifies this feeling.

"I'll take her home. I promise. She won't rot here, I swear it."

"Good," I breath. "Thank you."

"I'm so sorry," he whimpers to me again and again. "I'm so sorry. I'm so sorry. Please forgive me."

I want to answer him. Tell him it's not his fault. That I was the one who raised my spear first. But none of these things happen. My vision swims in front of me and I'm so nauseous I'm afraid if I open my mouth I'll vomit.

A loud crash brings my attention back to the compound, as Pyl manages to break down the door I had barricaded. I feel my heart shatter as I realize he must be able to see Deimos and I on the ground, knowing this will break his heart.

"Ms. Aris!" He cries out, at first in joy, as he runs up. "You have Ms. Aris!" He doesn't register I'm hurt at first. Maybe he thinks I'm just relieved or exhausted or all of the above and that's why we lay on the ground in such a way. He's smiling and holding his arms out as he runs up, but he stops short when he sees the tears staining Deimos's face. When he sees his shredded clothes and the ichor that stains the ground. I watch as he tries to deny what has happened. He doesn't want to connect the dots of what is being displayed in front of him.

His eyes quickly become wide with horror as he sees me cradled in Deimos's arms, whimpering and grimacing in pain, silent tears streaking down my bloodless face as I cradle the knife in my stomach. Sees the guilt and pain clearly etched onto Deimos's face.

With a pain-filled roar, Pyl drops to his knees. His hands flutter around me, wanting to help but afraid of hurting me or making it worse.

"What you do?!" He demands. "WHAT YOU DO?!"

Deimos shakes his head, rocking back and forth as he crushes me to him. "I didn't have a choice Pyl! She refused to yield and he called for the servants vengeance!"

"Oh Ms. Aris." Pyl sobs, stroking my hair with his fingertips. "Poor, poor Ms. Aris."

"You have to get her home, Pyl." Deimos says desperately. His one hand reaches out to grip Pyl's forearm. "I can't. I'm not allowed. You have to take her home. Maybe- maybe they can save her."

I can't be saved. Deimos must know that. The skill of my healers are almost godly they are so great, but even they are bound by the laws of nature. I am past saving. I can feel it in the thready and weak beating of my heart.

"I take her?" Pyl asks, doubtfully. At first I think that maybe he's just scared he'll accidentally hurt me more. But then he adds, "She will not make it."

"No she will!" Deimos insists. "She will! You take her. You take my car, it's very fast and you'll get there in time and they'll be able to save her! The best healers, short of Apollo himself, are at the conclave!"

He truly thinks I can be saved. He's in so much denial he refuses to acknowledge the blood that covers the bottom half of my abdomen. Refuses to see how pale and clammy my skin has become.

The only sound for a while is the shuddering and rasping of my breath.

"I will take her." Pyl agrees finally. He lifts me as gently as he can but still, I can't help but cry out hoarsely as this new position agitates the knife. "Sorry, Ms. Aris. So sorry."

"S'okay." I manage to gasp out, my teeth chattering.

"S'okay, Pyl."

As soon as Deimos has made sure I'm okay in Pyl's arms he goes tearing off, disappearing and reappearing in his car mere seconds later. I always did like his car, a 2024 Koenigsegg Jesko Absolut. I'm glad I get to ride in it one last time. Though, I am sorry I'll get bloodstains on the seat.

"Here, here," Deimos says frantically as he runs up to take me out of Pyl's arms again. A bout of nauseous hits me as he runs with me to the passenger side and I barely manage to turn my head to the side fast enough to avoid puking down the front of both of our shirts. Deimos is unphased, without a second thought he uses the bottom of his shirt to wipe my vomit off my face.

Pyl should not be able to fit in this car, but of course it's not a normal car. It is the chariot of a god, made to look like a car. So he slides in with ease and comfort as Deimos eases me into the passenger seat. I grit my teeth but can't help but cry out in pain as I'm jostled around. Deimos keeps up a steady stream of "so sorry's" as he buckles me in.

When I'm finally buckled and settled, Deimos holds my face between his hands, his thumbs stroking my cheeks. "I'll retrieve your mother and have her sent home." I don't even have time to thank him for this before he places a soft kiss to my lips and retreats, closing the car door firmly.

"Get her home, Pyl!" He orders, pounding on the hood of the car. Pyl responds by revving the engine and peeling out of the drive.

31

Chapter 31

Breathing is becoming harder and harder by the second and soon my breaths are short, painful gasps.

"Where- where are we?" I force out, biting back a groan as Pyl hits a particularly large bump in the road.

"San Diego." Pyl answers tensely, eyes focused on his fast paced driving. I close my eyes in exhaustion and in defeat, because yes, some part of me hoped that I was wrong and my healers would be able to save me. But San Diego is nine, almost ten, hours from the conclave. I'll be lucky to make half of this journey.

"Too far," I murmur.

"Not too far," Pyl insists, punching down the gas pedal. "Not in god car."

Pyl had a point that Deimos's car would get us to the conclave much faster, but it would still take at least a couple of hours and by that time I'll be mostly dead. Beyond saving. I don't say that though. No sense in breaking Pyl's heart ahead of time.

As I sit there, gasping and whimpering all I can truly think is *'this is how my mother felt as she died'.* Of course she died a lot faster than I am but her wound was a bit different, a little higher, the knife a little longer. If I had to guess I'd say one of her lungs had been perforated whereas mine was not. Although, one of my organs definitely took a beating. Again, if I had to guess I'd say probably my liver. Maybe a level 3 laceration. But I'm not a medic, so it's a guess, although I feel fairly confident that it's an accurate guess.

Now I really look like my mother, I think suddenly. It's true, I've always looked identical to my mother and now even in death we look the same. Blood-covered stomachs, with clammy skin and a look on our pale faces that shouts of our anger at the world. I can only hope Alena doesn't follow suit.

I let out a sob as I think of my baby sister. This will break her heart. Both her mother and sister gone, claimed by Hades. Killed in the same manner, within hours of each other. This will forever change the trajectory of her life. I hope in a good way. She'll be so excited when the car pulls up. Her sister is home. Her hero. Maybe she brought back a gift or some new stories. I hope Tessa has the sense to keep her away. She must know that if I show up without calling that something is wrong... that the unthinkable has happened. Or will she too, be so blinded by excitement and pride she won't think about such things?

I wonder if I'll still be alive when we get there to find out.

My teeth chatter as I watch the world blur past us. We're definitely making good time, perhaps if my wound had not been so severe I might have made it home in time to survive this.

"Pyl," I croak out. I clear my throat and try again. "You can't- you can't drive up to the compound. You'll have to stop just short and carry me on foot."

"Faster to drive, Ms. Aris!" Pyl insists desperately.

I nod, licking my lips. "I know... but if you drive this car, especially this fast... up to the compound... they'll blow it up..."

It's becoming harder and harder to find the energy to speak. My entire stomach is coated in my blood— I don't even want to think about how much I've lost. I grope one hand up to my neck to feel for my pulse and even that simple action leaves me breathless and light headed. Too fast. My pulse is too fast and too weak.

'Too fast and too weak!' A medic barks out, their fingers on the pulse of a woman. 'Aris! More pressure damn it!'

'I'm trying!' I grunt out. I'm straddling the woman, both of my hands cover a wound on her thigh. I'm shocked by how hot and slippery her blood is. It's my first time seeing this much. I had been out on a run with one of my Instructors. They wanted me running the steep, rocky paths that surrounds our conclave with the idea that it will improve my speed and stamina. It was working, too. I was thirteen and going toe to toe with much older girls. At least it was working until my sprints had been cut short by the sound of squealing tires, the desperate cry of a woman and then metal crunching and glass shattering.

My Instructor, April, and I had ran over. I was breathless and sweaty and overheating but the sight of the maimed woman on the ground gave me a chill to my bone. I didn't know what to do, I was a warrior not a healer.

'Move, Aris!' April snapped, kicking up dirt as she made her way to the woman. I followed closely behind, eyes wide and hands shaking. 'Here,' April ordered. 'Put your hands here.' When I hesitated she moved them herself, putting them on the wound of the woman's leg.

We stayed with her until the ambulance came, my hands kept pressure on that wound the entire time. It was so long, I could feel my shoulders shaking from the effort of it. I found out later that our efforts saved that woman's life. And I was glad for that. But as April and I had walked back towards our car to head back to the conclave, all I could do was stare at my blood covered hands. Stare at them and stare at them, until we got back to the car and April stopped me from getting in.

She grabbed my shoulder with one hand and the back of my neck with the other and forced me to meet her eyes.

'You are a spear of Athena, Aristomache.' She told me gravely. I nodded. I knew this already. She shook her head at me, tightening her grip. 'There are going to be a lot of times in your life where your hands are going to be covered in blood. But there are going to be much fewer times where they are covered because you were saving a life. So if you have the opportunity to save a life, you do it. Do you understand?'

And I did. In that moment, I did. I thought I knew, in my adolescent arrogance, what it meant, to be a member of the conclave. To be a spear of Athena. But I didn't... not really. Not until then because, as April leveled this words at me, I read between the lines and those words stuck with me, playing in my head every time I wielded my spear.

There are going to be much fewer times where they are covered because you were saving a life.... that played in my head like a broken record every time I watched someone's life end. End by my hand.

So, I always knew I would die with blood coating my hands... I guess I just was always too arrogant to think it would be mine.

"MS. ARIS!" Pyl cries out, shaking my knee. "Open your

eyes!" The desperation in his voice makes me think that he had been calling for me for a while.

With a gasp, I force my eyes to open. My head has lolled to the side and I can feel when I open my eyes that they had been rolled back into my head.

"Open," I mumble, reaching out to pat Pyl's hand. I can't tell if I quite manage it or not. "They're... open..."

"Keep them open!" Pyl insists desperately. I think I manage to nod. Now that I have this mission to keep my eyes open I realize how hard it is to do it. They fight me every step of the way. I can feel them fighting to roll back into my head. Fighting to plunge me into unconsciousness, to let me escape this pain and suffering. But Pyl is right to tell me to keep them open.

I don't know what will happen if I let them close again. They might not ever open again. And I need to tell my sister goodbye myself.

I can't help but wonder what will happen to me after I die. How aware are you of your body when your soul is no longer in it? Will I feel it when they burn my body on the pyre? Will I hear their cries as they beg Lord Hades to grant me entry and allow me peace? I've wondered these things before but much more idly than I am now. Of course, it's a much closer reality right now than it was previously.

How long with Deimos mourn me? I have no doubt he will for a time... but time and emotions are so much more different for gods than humans. I mean when you measure time in millennia, it tends to change the game a bit. Will he mourn a day? A week? Maybe a month? What about Pyl? How long will he mourn me, with his surprisingly gentle soul?

So many thoughts one has while waiting for Death to come.

Will I be escorted? Or close my eyes as though I'm going to bed and wake up with Charon staring down at me, asking to see my coins?

And what of Athena? Has she been watching this unfold from her throne on Olympus? Does she know one of her spears is about to greet Death? Does she care? Will she mourn my loss?

This line of thought is interrupted by a coughing fit, one that shakes my bones and leaves blood coating my lips. I choke on it, leaving me coughing even more. I feel Pyl's hand hovering over my back, his instinct to pat on it to help me clear whatever is obstructing my airway, but undoubtedly afraid of causing me more harm. I feel a rush of affection for him, for this Underworldly creature who has only ever shown me kindness and respect, though he, at first, had no reason to.

My coughing fit ends but my breaths wheeze, echoing in the confined space. They burn my chest with the effort it takes to produce them. It's even harder to keep my eyes open now. They roll wildly, almost keeping pace with how my heartbeat races in my chest. I want to ask Pyl how much longer until I am home. It feel as though we've been driving forever, though admittedly, I am a poor historian at the moment.

Maybe I manage to wheeze out my question or maybe Pyl is more talking to himself than me but suddenly he breaks the almost-silence. "So close, Ms. Aris. Just few more minutes."

Just few more minutes. Almost home. I'm almost home.

And just like that I give up the fight. I stop trying to keep my eyes open, stop trying to keep my breathing even.

I'm dimly aware of the car squealing to a stop. The force of it jerks me forward before my seat belt locks but I'm so far gone I don't even register the pain that the movement undoubtedly

331

caused.

I feel the thick, hot air of my beloved forest as my door is ripped open.

Home, I think as Pyl mutters nonstop under his breath. *I get to die at home.*

I'm lifted up in Pyl's arms but am unable to lift my head up, leaving me to hang limply in his arms. I hear the roar of voices, the clicking of weapons being loaded. The soft *whooshing* of air as spears are summoned. I hear the words but can't register their meaning.

"PUT HER DOWN"

"STOP! STOP RIGHT THERE!"

"On your knees! ON YOUR KNEES!"

"Oh Athena please! Is she dead?!"

Deimos must have prepared Pyl for this, or maybe Pyl just took a desperate guess and guessed right. But he drops to his knees and holds me out away from his body, as though in offering.

"I beg the help of the Gray-Eyed one!" He cries out. "Heal her body and protect her spirit!"

There's half a heartbeat of silence before footsteps swarm Pyl.

"Don't move!" Someone commands him. "Don't move!"

Pyl does not move an inch, not even as spears and guns and all kinds of weapons are held on him. He bows his head and continues to hold me out.

"Aris?" Someone else asks, breathing in my face. Their breath smells like oranges. Their callused hands brush my hair from my face. "Aris, can you hear me?"

I manage to loll my head towards her and lock eyes with Hannah, our head healer and surgeon.

"She's alive!" She announces, scooping me up from Pyl's arms. "Tell the team to prep NOW!"

So much is happening around me. One second Hannah is cradling me to her chest, the next I'm transferred onto a field gurney and I sway and jostle with the movement of four running bodies as I'm rushed towards the infirmary.

All of a sudden a primal sort of fear grips a hold of me. I'm about to die. I know I'm about to die but I don't want to! I don't want to die! I have so much I want to do with my life still! I want to watch my sister grow older! I want to help her grow into the amazing woman I know she will be!

I begin to whimper and reach out blindly. Someone catches my seeking hand, they hold it tightly with both of theirs, chaffing it slightly as though they hope to warm it. I manage to roll my head towards whoever it is, desperately seeking any type of comfort as I hurdle towards my death. My lips press together. I can feel the blood that coats them and the fear that fills my eyes.

Kore's black eyes are filled with terror, though her voice is steady and her hand that holds mine is strong. Her face, more than anyone else's, brings me the most comfort I could get in this time. She will not fill my ears with hollow lies of how I will be okay, nor will she weep when it is my turn to. She will be strong for me, if that is what I need from her.

How many times, in the past fifteen years, have I looked over and seen her black eyes staring back at me? Right before we would raise our spears and charge towards our enemies together. How many times have we stood back to back, protecting each other from danger? I'm equal parts relieved and devastated that she hadn't been with me when I was dealt this last blow.

"You look like hell, Initiate." She can't quite manage the smile she's going for though and her bottom lip wobbles with uncertainty. She chafes my hand again as I drink in the sight of her. Out of all of my sisters, Kore was always the one I felt closest too, my second in command, I wonder how many battles have we fought side by side? I feel my own lips try to smile, but I doubt I actually manage it.

"Ah well, you know me," my breath is ragged and wet with my blood. "Always the drama queen."

Kore shakes my hand lightly. "Always so damn dramatic. Couldn't even take a bath before you came home."

My eyes roll back into my head for a moment before I can form a response. "Sorry," I murmur almost silently. "It's been a long week."

Kore's free hand comes up to stroke my sweaty, dirty hair back from my forehead. "Well you're home and safe now. Rest. We'll protect you."

A feeling of comfort comes over me. Despite everything my eyes finally slide shut and I plunge into memories.

32

Chapter 32

I stand at the foot of a bed, looking down at the gasping memory of my mother. She's kneeling on a bed, her hand braced on the wall in front of her. One of her hands clutches my grandmothers.

"Breathe," Grammy intones, rubbing a knot on my mothers shoulder. "Breathe, Atalanta."

My mother lets out a groaning breath as another contraction hits her. "Ohhh, this fucking sucks!"

The older women, the ones who have bore children of their own, give chuckles to that as they mill about. The midwife who kneels beside the bed, checking my mothers progress, gives a laugh too.

"I know darling, but believe it or not, you're doing fantastic."

"Aghh! All due respect," she grunts. "Fuck off."

The midwife pats the side of my mother's thigh. "Don't worry, I don't take it personal."

My mother opens her mouth, probably to say something like 'you should' but yet another contraction comes over her and she bears down on her pushing. "I feel it!" She gasps, her eyes wide and wild. "I feel the head!"

Quicker movements around her, fresh towels, more water.

"I want to lay down," she tells Grammy. "I want to lay down."

"Okay love," Grammy tells her, smoothing her hair back. "Okay love, here we go."

Grammy and another midwife help my mother turn to lay so she's on her back, propped up against the headboard of the bed.

"Better," she pants out. "Better." Her next breath is a long, teeth-clenching groan. She clutches Grammy's hand so tightly her knuckles are white. Suddenly, I remember Grammy telling me that my mother had broken her hand while she was in labor. Judging by the look of distant pain on Grammy's face, this is the moment when it happened.

Soon the room is filled with cries of "push!" and "yes!" and "almost there!" and within minutes a bloody, wriggling mass is pushed out into the world, screaming her displeasure at the sudden cold.

"It's a girl, Atalanta!" The midwife announces happily. My mother sobs and reaches out.

"Give her to me. Give me my daughter."

They hasten to obey and soon the babe is placed on my mothers chest. The midwives begin to wipe off the baby while she lays there, revealing a thick head of black hair and rich brown eyes.

Even before the baby is completely cleaned off my mother is nuzzling and kissing her. She looks so young here. Younger than I am now.

"Do you have a name picked out, love?" Grammy asks

gently, smiling and cooing down at her granddaughter.

"Aristomache," my mother answer, smiling down lovingly at me.

"Aristomache." Grammy repeats. "In her honor."

"In her honor," my mother coos back., stroking my infant face.

* * *

"Come back here, Aris!" Someone calls for me, stroking my face. All of sudden I have a feeling as though I'm rushing down a tunnel and find myself drawn back into reality.

"She's going to throw up," someone else announces, hurriedly. Whoever they are, they're right. A set of hands helps me turn my head as I begin to vomit and then wipes my mouth with a washcloth when I've finished.

I can't make sense of the scene in front of me, my vision swims and dips around me. One woman sits beside me, her arm extended out.

"In Her honor, sister." She tells me gravely, reaching out to squeeze my hand. My eyes follow the needle in her arm to the needle in mine. I want to tell them to stop. There's no point in her wasting her blood if I'm going to die anyway.

Two women stand on either side of the bed I'm on, working on the wound on my stomach. They wear tight looks of concentration, their eyebrows knit together. If their faces weren't covered by surgical masks I imagine their lips would be pursed together as well. Beside both of their elbows stands their surgical assistants, healers in training. I know before I look that one of them will be Elpis. Sure enough, there she stands, on the left side of Healer Hannah who works on the

337

left side of me. She feels my eyes on her and meets my gaze. She pulls down her mask so I can see her face.

You keep fighting, bitch. She mouths to me. I try to smirk but don't know if I quite manage it.

My eyes roll back in my head again, seeking unconsciousness but a hand taps my face again, demanding they stay open. I look around, trying to see who demands this of me and find flat blue eyes staring me down.

"Keep your eyes open." Tessa commands, her voice gravely in her grief.

Slowly, I shake my head back and forth at her. Her eyes tighten in anger.

"I'm not asking, Initiate!" She insists, her voice cracking at the end. The hand that clutches at mine shakes with her grief.

"My..." my voice is a soundless rasp that she has to lean in to hear. "Mother..."

"She's here, child." She whispers, stroking my hair. "Lord Deimos kept his word."

I try to say "good" but nothing comes out except for a feeble whimper. Just saying those two words sapped all of my energy. Some part of me wonders how much blood I've lost to be this disoriented.

"Shh," Tessa murmurs. "Shh, it's okay. We're gonna fix you up." But they're not. They can't. I can feel the blood I'm still losing pouring over my sides. I can feel my mental capacities dwindling and the fevered, clamminess of my exposed skin.

Tessa meets my eyes and sees this acceptance in them. Tears fill hers as she lays her head next to mine. Her gasping sobs fill my ears. I can feel the wetness of her tears on my neck. "I'm so sorry, child. I'm so sorry."

I want to answer her, I want to tell her that none of this is her fault. I know she must be blaming herself. She is the one who insisted I take the mission, despite my vocal insistence that I didn't think I should take it. But Jason had one thing right: you can't fight Fate. The Fate's decreed my string was up and they acted accordingly. There is nothing that I or Tessa or even my Lady Athena could have done to stop this from happening.

But I don't say any of that. I don't have the strength. I don't have the desire. Tessa knows all of those things, it's just at this particular moment her grief is blinding her to such logic. So I don't bother with empty reassurances.

Instead all I can manage is a breathless murmur, voicing my last request.

"*Alena.*"

* * *

"You understand what this means for you?" My mother asks me as I walk. I'm pacing around the arena room, my bare feet cut through the sand of the arena as I drag and kick them along. My mother stands just off to the side, her arms folded as she watches me. I roll my eyes when my my back is turned to her, not bothering to answer at first. I don't want to be having this conversation with her. It hurts too much and brings out too many emotions that I don't want to deal with.

I'm eleven and full of so much attitude it seeps out of my pores. My eyebrows raise in disdain as I look at my mother out of the corner of my eye. An annoyed look comes across her face. She can't help but give a small roll of her eyes as she sees the look on my face.

"Aristomache."

"No."

My mother forces a deep breath, undoubtedly trying to keep her cool. I watch her take another slow, deep breath, her eyes locked on the ceiling, and all I can think is *why are you leaving me*? But I don't say that. I just keep up my path around the arena, watching my footsteps cut a pattern in the sand.

"It means your role in this conclave and in our family is about to change." She tells me, her voice heavy with the implications of her words.

"I don't see how you being knocked up has anything to do with me." I respond back casually, kicking up the sand around my feet.

"Aristomache," my mother grinds out through gritted teeth.

"What?" I demand, still not looking at her. "I haven't done anything! I'm not pregnant! Why does anything have to change for me? What if it's a boy? Then I won't ever even meet him."

If a member gives birth to a boy, the conclave pays for the member to have a house or apartment off of conclave grounds but nearby they are able to help if something happens. Boys are not permitted to enter the conclave. Because of this, if a woman has a boy she either retires to raise him or gives him to retired family members to raise and visits when she can.

I don't need to ask which one my mother would choose and so this unborn, theoretical brother is a threat to me and my relationship with my mother.

"You could," my mother tells me, stung by this. I wave this away.

"And when would I have the time to go visit you two

wherever the conclave puts you up at? I'll get to see you even less than I do now and I won't ever see my sibling. You're the one who tells me all the time that this here is my job and my life. Telling me how much of a commitment it is to be a member of the conclave. I'm *two years* away from taking my vow and being inducted." I shrug. "This baby is none of my concern." My words stung my mother, I could tell. But in my adolescence selfishness, I didn't care.

I didn't keep that attitude, though. Supporting each other is one of the pillars of the conclave. No matter what you might think of the woman. So I stepped up, helped my mother through her pregnancy and learned what to do in an emergency. And when my mother went into labor six months later, I was right beside her, holding her hand. Grammy was on her other side, holding her other hand.

I distractedly comfort my mother. I was too eager, waiting for the midwife to call for me. Finally, *finally,* it happens.

"Aristomache," the midwife waves me over. I let go of my mothers hand and skip down next to the midwife. I eagerly grab the towel she hands me and pay as much attention as I can as she shows me how to support the baby's head as they come out. "Right here, now just support. Don't squeeze or pull."

"Okay," I whisper excitedly, my eyes as big as the moon. "I got it!"

And so I was the one who caught my new brother or sister.

"It's a girl!" I announce immediately. Cheers fill the room and I see my mother collapse in relief and exhaustion.

I wrap her in the blanket gently and smile down at her beautiful brown eyes as I cradle her in my arms.

"What shall we name her?" My mother asks, smiling at me.

My eyes grow wide and my mouth falls open. "I get to name her?" My mother nods, smiling wide. "Seriously?" She and Grammy laugh at the look on my face.

"What will it be, darling?" Grammy asks me, her arm tight around my shoulders.

As I hold my new baby sister, the dawning light streams in through the large, open windows, lighting her face in a heavenly glow.

"Alena." I announce, my voice firm and proud. "Alena Kallis. In her honor."

"In her honor!" They all echo as I hand Alena over to my mother. She smiles adoringly at both of us. One of her arms cradles Alena to her, the other reaches up to stroke my cheek.

"Aristomache and Alena," she croons. "My pride and my joy."

* * *

A cold hand presses against my cheek, calling me back to my body again.

"You have to hold on, Sissy." Alena whispers tearfully.

My eyes begrudgingly open again to find my eleven year old self, staring back at me. But it's not eleven year old me, of course. It's my sister. My heart shatters knowing she will now have this memory burned into her forever.

May it make her stronger, I find myself praying.

Her hand, always so cold, comes up to cup my cheek. Tears wet her face but she doesn't bother to wipe them away. She looks around fervently and then bends low over me. Her breath tickles my ear as she blows my hair around it.

"Please try to wait for Mama," she begs, startling me with

the intensity of her pleadings. This is not what I was expecting her to say and I struggle to make sense of it at first.

"Wait for Mama to get there first." *Oh.*

Vaguely I smell smoke on Alena's clothes. With a slight start I realize she must have just come from Mama's funeral. From burning her on the pyre. I lock eyes with my sister and see the grief and heartbreak that fills them... but also the acceptance. She has seen my wounds. Maybe even heard how I got them. She knows I cannot be saved. She knows I will die.

"Wait for mama," she repeats, laying her head on mine, stroking my face so gently.

Wait for mama. Unlike the women who work on my body so fruitlessly, my sister has no doubts about my mortality. All she wants is for our mother to be the first one to greet me. Fresh tears begin streaking down my face. Not in pain. but in relief.

This will make her stronger.

I close my eyes and fervently thank Athena for giving me this last blessing.

Wait for mama.

I'm going to do just that. I will wait for my mother.

33

Chapter 33

Just as I've decided to hold on as long as I can, to give my mother time to cross and prepare, I feel my breath stop in my lungs and then begin to hitch and gasp. I feel my heartbeat pounding away in my chest, fighting to replace the blood I am losing so quickly.

"Shit!" Someone cries. "Shit, we're losing her!" Vaguely I wonder if they're right, if this is it for me. But it's hard to think clearly as I start to get less and less oxygen to my brain.

The last thing I'm aware of with any semblance of clarity is being fiercely relieved as I see Tessa carry a sobbing Alena out of the room. No matter how strong she is, she doesn't need to see this.

I begin to gasp and choke on my breaths. I can feel my back arch off the bed as my body fights to bring oxygen into it.

"Damn it!" Someone yells. "Damn it, damn it, damn it, get me more sponges!"

"I need another clamp here!" Someone else screams out.

Someone tries to shove something into my mouth, to clear my airway probably. I fight them, my head rolling back and forth. Hard hands grab my face, forcing me to stop. My breathing becomes more shallow by the second and the edges of my vision turn black. I lay there, watching as the blackness grows and grows and grows until it is all I can see.

A warm, callused hand touches mine.

"I think you should come with me."

My eyes flutter and when I open them I find I'm breathing again and my pain is gone. I sit up carefully and notice the scene of chaos is no longer happening around me. I blink and look behind me and see an empty bed glaring back at me.

"Aristomache." A stern voice calls for my attention. I look back over and gasp, jumping to the ground and sinking to my knees.

"My Lady Athena!" I gasp out, my forehead touching the ground.

"Rise, child." She tells me, after a moment. I stand slowly, not believing my eyes finally lift my head. And find myself standing eye to eye with the goddess Athena. She stands regally. Tall with long chestnut brown hair, in a stunning gray chiton. Her helmet covers her head but no spear fills her hands. Her gray eyes stare down at me, clever and assessing. Assessing what, I couldn't tell. I just hoped she liked whatever it was she was reading from me.

"Take a walk with me," she orders and before I can respond, turns briskly on her heels and strides out into the hallway.

I hasten to follow her. As soon as I step over the threshold the room changes. I'm no longer in the conclave. We're in some long, hallway with rich walnut floors and hundreds of matching doors down both sides. Each one has different things written on them and deep red and gold wallpaper cover the walls. I think I've seen this in a movie before.

"Am I dead, then?" I find myself asking as I look around.

"Mm." Athena says noncommittally. "Not yet, but soon enough." I nod in response, the only real feeling I have about that is surprise that I've held out this long.

"You have lived," Athena begins. "Quite a life, haven't you, child?"

"My Lady?" I ask, confused as to where this is going.

With a wave of her hand, dozens of doors open for us as we make our way down the hallway.

I stop to peek in one. It's the day I was Inducted as an official member of the conclave, a week after I turned thirteen.

I wander to the next door and see fifteen year old me, yielding a spear in training with such force and accuracy the level 7 I was dueling yields. I watch the sinuous fashion I twirl the spear around, as though it is a part of me. Maybe it is. Or... was.

The next door is me with my friends. Music is blasting in our room from a speaker as we dance and jump on our beds, singing at the tops of our lungs. The song changes and Rose and I reach for each others hands squealing in excitement. We begin to twirl around the room in a pretzel dance. They others boo and loudly proclaim their hatred of country music. Rose and I laugh and ignore them.

Another: me helping Alena learning how to walk. Letting her chubby baby hands clutch at my fingers. My back aching from bending over as she insists on walking around and around. She hated to be still, but then so did I.

Another: Horseback riding through the canyons with my mother. She's beating me, her long, black hair whips around her face as she looks back at me, gloating.

Another: Laying, naked, in bed with Deimos. We lay facing

each other, still tangled together. His warm hand strokes my hair, my back, my hip. My own hand curls around the sharp edge of his jaw. He ruins the silence and asks me to be his wife. I tell him that I can't. That I won't. A fight ensues.

Memory after memory. Personal memories, conclave memories, memories from quests and missions I've fulfilled. Good and bad and everything in between. I am made of memories it seems.

Finally the doors disappear as we reach the end of the hallway. A large, ornate, wooden door stands in front of us. Lady Athena pushes it open and steps through without pausing. I follow her through. After my eyes adjust to the blinding light I realize we're standing on a stone veranda and judging by the trees and ocean around us, we're in Greece.

Lady Athena stands at the parapet, looking down at the scene below. I join her silently, the stone parapet is hot under my hands as I brace on it to lean over and look below.

It's Initiates I realize. I look over at Lady Athena, startled.

Her lips quirk up in a smirk. "The first generation."

"Wow!" I breathe, greedily drinking in the scene in front of me. Dozens of women, dueling and learning. They bear the same marks on their face as me, plus some I have never seen before. I watch a pair dueling with knives. They are vicious and lightning quick in their attacks on each other. Filled with the blessing of Athena and their own pride at having been chosen their movements are sure and deadly. Inside the house of the parapet we stood on... I thought I could hear the quiet hissing of a snakes. Lady Athena draws my attention back to the dueling pair.

"There is your ancestor," Lady Athena points out. "Aglaia Kallis."

I look to where she is pointing and see one of the women, the faster of the two but not the stronger, with rich brown hair and, even from here I can see the, stunning brown eyes she has. She looks just like me, with small differences.

She is cunning too, as I watch she outsmarts her bigger opponent and, with one quick move, has her down on the ground, a knife pressed to her throat, a vicious grin on her face.

"So I say again," Lady Athena says casually, eyeing the rapt look on my face as I continue watching the scene below me. "You have had quite a life. You became the greatest Initiate your lineage has ever seen. You took a god as your lover. You became the greatest spear in my name that this conclave has ever seen."

I curl my lip in distaste as she lists these things off.

"And I was bested by a man." I say bitterly.

"No." Lady Athena answers sharply. "You were tricked by a man who was under the guidance of several gods and even then you beat him in the end. Do not think so little of one of my greatest spears."

I stare out at the ocean as I think on that. Strangely, I find myself focusing on the last thing she said more than the rest. A spear. Is that all I really was? Yes, I was a daughter and sister and friend and lover but... in the end, was I just a weapon for a goddess? And did I care if I was?

I didn't know.

Lady Athena sighs heavily beside me. "You have endured much in my name."

I shake my head, my eyebrows knit together. "It was my greatest honor to serve you, My Lady."

As I tell her this, I realize I mean it. In that moment, I decided

I don't care if all I was in my life was a weapon. Because I know in my heart that that wasn't all I was... all of those memories...

"Oh..." I say out loud. "Oh you are *good*, My Lady." Lady Athena gives a small chuckle as she realizes I've connected the dots.

"Do not think so little of your life." Lady Athena says simply. "You were much more than just a spear of Athena. Although, you should never forget that you were that as well. No... you were a good daughter, a loving and devoted sister, a kind friend, a strong and trusted leader. Your loss will be felt in the conclave for generations."

I can't help the pride that swells my chest at these words, especially as I hear them from a goddess. Nor can I help the tears that well in my eyes.

"That's why I would like to make you my Lieutenant."

"What?" I gasp, snapping my head over to look at my goddess. Lady Athena turns her head to meet my gaze, her eyes sharp.

"I would like you to become my Lieutenant and to serve by my side so that I may have a faithful servant and confidant by my side for all of time. Should you want it." My jaw drops open.

"You're offering me immortality." I don't believe it. "As your Lieutenant."

"Yes, that's what I said." Lady Athena responds.

I give a disbelieving laugh. I wish I could remember how to close my damn mouth.

"My Lady you..." I give another laugh and shake my head. "You honor me more than I deserve."

"I honor you exactly as you deserve." When I don't respond and keep my gaze on the sea, she presses on. "You could take

349

Deimos as a husband, if you chose. I won't require you to take the vows of Maidenhood if you don't desire it. You could watch over the conclave as much as you desire, help them on quests, help keep the base safe."

I force a very deep breath into my lungs. "You honor me." I repeat. I release my shaky breath. "What of my sister? Will she be offered immortality, when she is older? Or any of my friends?"

"No, child." Lady Athena seems confused by my line of questioning, her head cocks to the side as she regards me curiously. "No, you will be the only Initiate to receive this offer for several millennia. But I would allow you to watch over your friends and sister until their passing."

"But I wouldn't," I hesitate and bite my lip. I remember my conversations and arguments with Deimos. "I wouldn't love them the same... right?"

"No..." she answers slowly. "No it's hard for an immortal to love a mortal, it's almost like they're two different species."

I nod slowly and take another shaky breath. It's a long moment before I think of another question.

"Am I allowed to know what my fate would be in the Underworld?" I ask.

"No, child." Athena answers gently. "The Fates forbid it. And so do I, for that matter. Not everything is meant to be known."

Silent tears streak down my face as I nod.

"This is quite the decision then..." I murmur, mostly to myself I think. A heavy hand rests on my shoulder.

"Sit out here as long as you'd like. When you've made your decision, simply speak it to the wind. They will take you where you want to go."

I nod again, swiping at more of those pesky tears. I close my eyes as I hear the shift in the air. In a burst of light, showing her true form, Lady Athena has gone and left me to my decision.

With a tearful sigh I sink to the ground and sit with my back to the stone parapet. I draw my knees to my chest and wrap my arms around them. I mash my lips into my knees as I stare at nothing.

Somewhere, my body lays, dying. My family and friends gather around it, begging for me to hang on. For me to stay with them. And now I can. Now I have a way I can stay with them always.

I remember one night, laying in Deimos's bed. I had sat at the foot of it, naked except for the sheet I had twisted around my waist.

What's it like for you? I had asked him. He lay lounging at the head of the bed, one arm behind his head, the other holding a wine glass.

What's what like, love?

To be with a human?

You're not human, had been his first automatic response.

You know what I mean.

He had stared at me for one, long moment, swirling his wine around.

It's different, he admitted, finally. *Knowing I cannot keep you in my bed always. Knowing there will be a day when we do not walk this Earth together. It makes it hard to fully devote yourself to someone... knowing that. You tend to keep them at arm's length more naturally.*

I nodded to that, it made sense.

Do you love me? I had asked, curiously. My head tilting to the side. He stared at me again, his black eyes closed off, before motioning for me to go to him. I humored him and crawled back up to the top of the bed. He tucked me against his chest, his arm tight around my shoulders, his thumb stroking my skin. He downed the rest of his wine before answering me. His voice sounded sad and faraway when he finally answered.

As much as I am capable of. His grip tightened on me, as he said this. I think a part of him was afraid I would take offense to his answer and try to leave. But, I understood what he was saying. Of course there is only so much you can love someone when you must live with the knowledge that one day their life will end and yours will keep going.

Was that what I wanted? To love my sister and my friends as much as I am capable of? To spend my days knowing that one day they will die and most likely be together in Elysium and I will never be there with them? I would not even be allowed to visit them there. Hades' realm will be off limits to me as a god.

And what of Deimos? I could have him. All of him. For all of eternity. Did I love him that much? Did I love him at all? Or did I just love the attention of a god?

I think back to my last day with him... not the day we dueled but dinner at the diner. Of how I had been unable to cry until I was with him...

Yes... I loved him. No matter how angry I was at him for the situation with Jason, I would have gone back to him had I not found myself here. Our fates were as bound as mine was to the conclave. Meant to be. Meant to never be.

But was I willing to give up my love for my sister to be with him?

With a sigh, I tilt my head back, feeling the hard stone

beneath it. The hot sun rays beat down on my face and the calls of the Initiates below me fill my ears like magic.

My instinct is to pray to Athena for guidance but something tells me she might be a bit biased in this situation.

I unwrap my arms from my knees so I can mash the heels of my hands into my eyes as I think.

And think.

And think.

34

Chapter 34

Pain.

Everything hurts. Even as I stay separate from my body I can feel the ghost of the pain as it rushes through my ruined body.

The surgeons have finally given up trying to save me. Healer Hannah stands off to the side, her one blood covered hand braces against the windowsill while the other covers her eyes. My family gathers around me, saying their final goodbyes.

Alena lays with me, curled against my side, her arms wrapped around my neck as my hair soaks up her tears. But even in her grief she shows compassion and wisdom beyond her years.

"It's okay, sissy." She murmurs in my ear. "You can let go. I'll be okay."

Zoe sits beside her, her hand firm on my sisters shoulder. She doesn't say anything to me. She just allows her tears to fall while she stares intently at my battered face as tears fall silently down her face.

Elpis stands at my feet, her palms pressed to the soles of

them. Her body is racked by her silent sobs as she too, studies my face. The guilt and anguish she feels is carved onto her face. Tessa moves to stand beside her. I watch as she wraps an arm around her shoulders and presses a kiss to her temple.

"It's not your fault, girl." She mutters to her. "The Fates simply called her home. There's nothing more that anyone of us could have done to stop this from happening." Elpis squeezes her eyes shut as another sob shakes her. She shakes her head, whether in denial or in grief, I can't tell. Tessa continues to mutter reassurances to her.

Kore and Rose take turns leaning over me to press lingering kisses to my forehead. Their tears also fall freely, splashing down onto my face.

"Rest easy, sister." Kore instructs, her voice muted in her grief. Poor Kore, the only person who will be more affected by my death than her is Alena. "You have served both yourself and your goddess with honor and dignity. Go with grace and peace." She retreats, sniffling and wiping at her nose. Rose takes her place, her eyes roving over my face. As though she's trying to see past my wounds to the face she's lived along side for almost a decade now.

"My greatest honor was calling you my friend," Rose whispers, sniffling tearfully. "May you find the peace you deserve. You have fought so hard, so valiantly... you have earned this rest."

My heart warms, despite the pain, as I'm reminded of just how loved I was in this life. What is it that lowlife said? *You have never known real love.* Fuck that, I think, as I watch those who mourn my mortality. I have known real love from the moment I drew breath. Despite everything, despite the pain and the arguments and the high expectations, I have never

355

not known what it is to love and be loved. My Instructors and leaders all gather in my room, wiping tears and murmuring prayers for easy passage to the next part of my life.

They will feel your loss for generations. That's what Athena told me and I admit I hadn't believed her. People die all the time. But seeing all those who have gathered... who wear their grief so clearly on their face. They will feel my loss for generations.

I turn to look behind me and see the door. Am I ready to leave them forever? I don't know. But I have been taught to push past fear and do what needs done. So with a deep breath, and one last glance at my family, I walk out the door.

* * *

I open the door to Deimos's bedroom. A grand thing, it still bears the resemblance that I asked Deimos to give it. When we first started seeing each other, it was black with no natural lighting. All doom and gloom and trying to act tough.

At my insistence, the room shifted. Deimos had acted annoyed by it, but Pyl told me once that Deimos keeps the bedroom reflecting my preference even when I'm not there. Even now it seems frozen as I had picked it, a shrine to the mortal who had won over the god of fear. Now, thanks to me, a whole wall is dedicated to floor to ceiling windows, that almost always sit open. The bed, once black as night, with a blood red head board, now has soft white linen sheets on it and a rich mahogany headboard.

Deimos stands at the window, his beautiful face expressionless. He stands still as a statue, in a way that only an immortal can. He does not flinch as Pyl comes running in, breathless. Pyl rocks back and forth awkwardly for a moment. He holds the keys to Deimos's car in his hand and he's clearly torn between returning them and pacing the room. Finally he throws them onto the bed.

"Has she passed yet?" He asks Deimos, wringing his hands anxiously. Deimos doesn't take his gaze off the window. He just shakes his head minutely in answer to Pyl's question.

Behind Pyl, peeking in the door, I can see some of the other staff members of the house. The cook that always indulged my midnight snacking, the maid who loved to help me pick out my outfits when Dei and I would go out clubbing. They hold each others hands, their faces impassive, ignoring the tears that fall down them. They say nothing to no one, not even each other, as they watch their god mourn the loss of a mortal.

Pyl shifts from foot to foot for a few moments, glancing behind him at the other workers, before asking: "do you think she will choose to stay with us?"

So they know then. The offer being given to me. I wonder if this offer is the reason Deimos offered me his hand in marriage in the first place. Knowing I would not accept it as a mortal, but that I might as a goddess.

Deimos defrosts just enough to sigh and furrow his brows.

"That's one of the things I love most about Aris," he murmurs. "I never know what she's going to do next."

Pyl frowns unhappily at this and sits at the foot of Deimos's bed with a huff. It creaks under his weight, but neither him nor Deimos react to the noise. Pyl looks over to the nightstand that sits beside the bed, on the side where Deimos sleeps. On it is an ornate gold frame with a photo of me inside. I've never seen it before and it makes me wonder how long Deimos has

357

had it.

"Oh Ms. Aris," Pyl mutters, tears flooding his eyes as he stares at the photo. "So brave, so strong."

With his back still to Pyl, Deimos sheds his own tears. He doesn't acknowledge them as they fall down his face and onto his shirt.

I reach out to stroke the back of Deimos's arm. He shivers slightly but does not turn. I turn and glide back out the door.

* * *

I enter the first hallway again. But it's not full of doors and memories now. To my right, I see the faint glow of Olympus. I can feel it calling for me. I see a figure, blurry and shadowy, waiting just on the other side. It looks as though they are pacing.

Deimos? I think faintly. Somehow I know this figure is him. Waiting impatiently for me to make my decision. He never was any good at waiting. My heart and soul both warm at the thought of him waiting so desperately for me.

I start to follow that pull towards Olympus, towards Deimos and my Lady Athena. I could do it, I think. I could give up the love I have for my sister and my family for immortality. It would help them, in the long run. Lady Athena already said she would allow me to be guardian to the conclave. I could protect and guide them, maybe more directly than Athena is allowed to.

Aristomache, they whisper.

I stop in my tracks and look to the other side of the hallway. A gray mist fills the space, shadows wisp around inside of it. Just as I knew the pacing figure was Deimos, I know these whispering voices to be my ancestors, the women who came before me. And now they are calling for me to join them in the Underworld.

Come home, daughter. They beg me. Their voices are all the good memories I have of my life, they are love and strength and support. *Come home to us.* Their wispy hands reach out of the gray for me, calling me home.

Aristomache, the other side whispers. I turn back to Olympus. Hands reach out for me from that side too. *Come home to us, child.*

I drift back to the middle of the room, my head swiveling from side to side as the hands from both sides continue to reach for me. I think of the women who wait for me in the gray. Who wait to welcome me with open arms. Who are the memories that have guided me for my entire mortal life.

Then I think of the immortals who call for me to join them. What an honor to be considered worthy of godhood. They are not the memories of my past but they could be the memories of my eternity. They show me glimpses of the future. I see Alena, an Instructor at the conclave, with a beautiful baby girl on her hip. She bounces the child while correcting a young girls fighting stance with her spear. She calls the child Aristomache.

My ancestors call for me, they show me my past. They show me their shadowy figures and how they have stood behind me for my entire life. They wait to embrace me, to celebrate with me. They beg me to join them.

The shadows call for me, reaching for me to join them in power and immortality.

My ancestors whisper to me, begging for me to come home to them.

I close my eyes. No matter what I choose, someone will be

left brokenhearted. But I cannot think about that. I must think about what I desire. For the first time in my life, I must truly think about what it is I want. Every step of my life has been for others, for the pride of my mother, the honor of my goddess, the safety of my sisters. But now... this... it's about me. After all I'm the one who has to live with my decision. For forever.

Tears fall from my eyes. Tears of regret, of joy, of sadness. I suck in a deep breath, filling my lungs to the brim. As I exhale I feel every muscle, joint, ligament and tendon release all at once. For probably the first time in my entire life, I am totally relaxed. Even the stiffness in my neck is gone, I realize with some surprise.

The hands on either side continue to reach for me.

With a feeling of serenity, I open my eyes and reach back. Hands clamp down on my hand, my arm, my waist, my shoulders. With joyous cry they pull me towards them. Towards my new beginning.

Towards forever.

Made in the USA
Columbia, SC
11 May 2024

35580429R00200